THE LADY OF ARLINGTON

HARNETT T. KANE

THE LADY
OF ARLINGTON

*A NOVEL BASED ON THE LIFE
OF MRS. ROBERT E. LEE*

DOUBLEDAY & COMPANY, INC.
Garden City, New York

PART I

"I am a wanderer on the face of the earth . . ."

MARY CUSTIS LEE, TO A FRIEND SOON AFTER HER MARRIAGE

Chapter 1

"You're ready, Mary, all ready?"

The high-pitched voice came from the cool dimness of the hall. A moment later there appeared in the doorway the round, worried face of Mrs. Custis. The skin, slightly wrinkled, grew still more so when she saw that her daughter sat before the easel at the window rather than at the dressing table.

"Mary Custis." The small head with its cluster of tight, graying curls shook in annoyance, and the voice rose yet higher. "With our guest due right soon . . ." Mrs. Custis' plump form moved forward with short, purposeful steps, and then, as she peered over the girl's back, her tone softened: "Well, it's a nice view of Washington City over the river. It's from the left side downstairs, isn't it?"

Mary Custis nodded and pointed with a musing smile to the heavy, almost monumental pillars of Arlington House on the brow of its hill, with the terraced lawn dropping to the Potomac, and the gray-green spread of the town in the distance. Before the girl could answer, "Miss Mollie" talked on, as if in a race with the minute hand of the clock. "You've put children on the portico again. Why, I don't quite understand . . ." Miss Mollie did not finish; after indicating what she thought, Mrs. Custis frequently considered the sentence complete enough for anyone's purposes.

"Oh, I put children there because I like them. That's all." Mary Custis shrugged, and her smile disappeared. She was remembering the times she had stood at the window in earlier years, staring below, conjuring up playmates on the green. One girl on

7

an estate with a handful of white adults—mainly her father, mother, and the overseer—and a working force of seventy-five . . . But since then it had seldom been as cheerless as that, and she could hardly pretend so, even in a rare moment of gloom.

Mary's silk robe hung loosely about her shoulders, their rounded curves shining as she bent forward. A sliver of sun caught the tip of her nose, more firm-tipped and more pronounced than some considered ideal, and the line of her wide lips. Out of the silence the crystal prisms of the chandelier tinkled lightly in the breeze.

Miss Mollie touched her daughter's arm. "Mary, you'll hurry now, and you'll—well . . . ?" As she waited, Mrs. Custis thrust at the lock of hair that her energetic movements sent regularly over her forehead.

"Oh yes." Her daughter made a last brush stroke against one of the gray pillars, and rose with a glance of wry humor. "I won't shame you; I won't be—what do you call it?—impulsive."

Miss Mollie's sharp nose lifted, and her stare had a hint of dismay: "That isn't enough, Mary; please make an effort. Sam Houston's just thirty-five, and he's already been a governor. He may even get to be President. It's something to think about, child."

When her mother paused, Mary gave a shrug. "If he's so fine, should *I* do the proposing?" For weeks she had been hearing about the qualities of Sam Houston, and she was tired of the subject.

Miss Mollie's light eyes had a hurt look. "Your father and I are only thinking of your own good."

"I know." Instantly regretful, Mary pressed her lips against her mother's cheek. To herself, however, she thought in amusement, People always said that when they wanted you to do something unappetizing. As she took her place at the dressing table, she saw that Mrs. Custis was scratching new notes on a paper taken from her pocket—her "chore list," revised endlessly each day.

After a moment Miss Mollie ran an experimental finger along the back of a chair, hunting her enemy, dust. Like most of Arlington's furnishings, the chair came from Mount Vernon, the some-

8

what dimmed relic of George Washington. Mary's father was Martha Washington's grandson by her first marriage; the first President had adopted him at the death of the boy's own father. Mary looked affectionately around her, recalling the way occasional callers stared with awe.

What was it one had asked? "Don't you feel you shouldn't even touch that chair?" She smiled again. Still, she told herself sometimes that the past lay over Arlington, to be touched and seen and savored, like a perceptible thing, always beside them . . . By now Mrs. Custis, starting for the door, halted before the canvas. She squinted at the last figure her daughter had sketched against a column, that of a uniformed young man. Miss Mollie's gray eyes darted toward Mary with a searching question. She was about to speak, but she tightened her mouth and slipped out.

In the room behind her Mary Custis' cheeks burned and she felt an impulse to call out that it *was* the young soldier that Miss Mollie suspected, and why shouldn't she put him there if she wanted?

A grunt sounded from the landing, and the timbers of the upper floor shook under the pounding of a towering figure, the aproned Salina Gray, the great, tall assistant housekeeper who had been at Arlington ever since Mary remembered. Salina swept in, her starched skirts crisp about her heavy brown legs. Nearly six feet tall, Salina appeared solid rather than plump; though generally silent, when she spoke it was with sharp authority and in a booming quasi-baritone voice. Two maids waited in a room nearby, but Salina had come to "see after things" for herself.

"Hm. You do real po' with yo' hair." Salina's glinting eyes made an inspection that missed no detail of Mary's lightly waved brown hair, wrapped in a casual knot at the back of her head. Absently Mary nodded and Salina's hands, deft despite their size, made a swift rearrangement.

Drawing away, Salina crossed her wrists before her in a way that, Mary realized, represented her attitude—respectful yet eminently relaxed. "I manages in my own way," Salina had said on some long-past occasion, and the girl had not forgotten. Salina did everything required of her, and more; nevertheless she main-

9

tained her own firm individuality. Now her head moved, and Mary caught a flash of tiny jet earrings.

"Now, miss." The housekeeper caught up the soft crepe from the high plateau of the four-poster bed, surmounted by the brocaded canopy. As the girl, standing, dropped her robe and raised her bare arms, the filmy skirts went up, then down over her. In the long mirror against the wall Mary saw the bright brown color against her skin. Yes, Miss Mollie had chosen well, finding almost a match for her eyes. She herself would not have been so clever.

Briefly she continued her self-appraisal, noting the hollow at the base of her long throat; the low full bust, and the waist that she need not lace so tightly that, like one of her many cousins, she could speak only in wheezes. While the crepe maze sank around her, with its hint of the sachet in which it had been stored, Mary heard Salina's querulous rumble:

"You ain' excited like the res', about this General Houston?"

The deep voice ended abruptly, and Salina stared down at Mary with the calm confidence of the house servant who knew a great deal and made shrewd guesses at the rest.

"Why should I get excited?" Pressing at the lace that lined the deep circle of the neck, Mary kept her head turned. "He's just a caller, like anybody else." That, she reflected at once, was not quite true. She and the gruff Houston had met at several Washington City parties, again at President Andrew Jackson's reception; then, somewhat ceremoniously, General Houston had asked Mr. Custis' permission to call. And Mary wished he had not.

Salina had no intention of quitting the subject. The gleaming black eyes probed further, and the voice became almost a bass. "Whole lot o' man, though. *Nearly* as big as he act'." When the unexpected laugh broke from deep inside the powerful frame, Salina let Mary understand she was inviting discussion.

Face lowered, Mary smiled; the last words represented roughly her own opinion. Then swiftly Salina shifted her approach: "Still, Miss Mary, you goin' on twenty-one, and a husban's a husban'. Good or bad, you got 'im!"

Mary's cheeks flamed. Though the words were different, that was precisely what her mother had been throwing at her head;

and she liked the thought less than ever. Salina, like others of the staff, came of a Mount Vernon slave family that had moved here with her father. Nevertheless, Mary assured herself angrily, Salina talked too much.

The color spreading from her widely separated cheekbones to her throat, she shook out her skirts. "I'll finish for myself." With a long look Salina stalked out.

At the mirror the girl considered Salina's bleak words. She was not a belle; she had never deceived herself. She studied the strong nose, the mouth that was too full, the high forehead that she usually declined to cover as Miss Mollie urged.

Then, furiously, she told herself that in any case she had won her share of glances; and there had been several proposals. Each time it was a boy of whom the family approved, a "nice" boy, but that was all. Each time Mary said no, and nobody's feelings were hurt, except perhaps her mother's.

Mrs. Custis had spoken earnestly. "You should smile more; it changes your whole face." For the better, Miss Mollie obviously meant; and still, Mary asked, could she go around grinning all the time? Nevertheless, certain of the young men, tiring of vapid prettiness, often returned to her. . . . She could have a good time nearly anywhere, she decided. She liked the mellow conversations over which her father presided. Yet hadn't George Washington Parke Custis himself sighed the other day and said that in this modern day conversation had become a last, if not quite lost, art?

She had a thoroughly pleasant life at Arlington—guests who filled the extra beds, long visits to relatives in the country, the summer springs. It was a sunny, wind-swept spot, this flower-bordered crest of the highest hill for miles. Today, from the profusion of Arlington's gardens there came a scent—of rose, of honeysuckle—that had hung there since the rain of last night. Whenever she arrived after an absence, the garden's welcome assured her that home awaited her . . . Her head rose. As for the danger of being an old maid, she had plans of her own, or at least hopes.

"Mary? They say somebody's riding up the hill." Ready for their guest, Mrs. Custis stood nervously in the doorway. "I don't know where your father is. As usual." Miss Mollie's tone was regretful but also resigned. For her life often seemed a battle between her own industry and her husband's more leisurely habits; though she seldom won for long, she accepted small victories with thanks and confidence that others would follow in time. Meanwhile she peered past the box hedge at the side toward the less precise vegetable plots in the distance, and murmured; "Somebody ought to be down there to meet . . ."

As the worried voice diminished, Mary squeezed her mother's arm. "Let's greet the general ourselves."

"Oh." The round face tightened. "He certainly wouldn't expect to find *us* waiting."

"Then let's surprise him!" The girl's brown eyes darkened in amusement. She started forward with a long stride, to be stopped by Mrs. Custis, no longer irresolute: "Remember, Mary, not so fast. A lady——"

" 'A lady should look leisurely, even when she's in a hurry.' " Mary chuckled; her swift movement had always pained her mother. Slowing, she linked hands with Miss Mollie and continued along the hall toward the rear stairs. This passageway, bigger than most rooms, served in summer as a favorite family chamber. Skirting the two long rosewood sofas, with their carvings of birds and wheat, they paused before the window at the end.

Several years ago Mr. Custis had planned it as a door to a balcony at the back. Then, as often happened, "the Major" turned to something else—the glassed greenhouse now attached at the rear. Casual in most matters, he could be unshakable when he made up his mind; the extra balcony remained a closed subject.

A roll of wheels on gravel drew Mary's eyes to the court below, with servants' quarters and kitchens flanking it, and a circular drive leading to the paneled door. Not one but two carriages halted, several men and women stepped out, and Mary made a clicking noise with her tongue: "Strangers again."

She was not entirely surprised; callers appeared at all times at this show place, including some like the man with a family of ten who had arrived the previous week at eight o'clock in the evening. Today a pair of dark helpers walked forward from the temple-like entrance of the brick stables, its columns much like those of the house; almost simultaneously a short rumpled figure rode up on horseback, and the most imposing of the newcomers strode over to him:

"My good fellow, could you show us around?" From above, Mary saw the coin glint in the outstretched hand.

The plump man touched careless fingers to his open throat, then gave a good-natured shrug. "Glad to assist." The thin, reedy voice had a friendly note. "I'm Washington Custis, the owner." To confused apologies the group started off; Mrs. Custis sighed and Mary looked fondly after her father. It was not the first time the Major had been taken for one of his staff.

For a few minutes Mary's eyes followed him. One of the last to continue wearing old-style knee breeches, he cared as little about appearances as any person she knew. The Major's light blue eyes looked out genially from a sun-browned face of a pleasing irregularity. The long nose reached far down toward a large, somewhat indecisive mouth, which smiled a great deal.

As he disappeared from view, Washington Custis was talking on in his thin voice, rubbing his hand ruminatively over his scalp with its light, fast-thinning hair. His manner had an open kindness, and also, Mary reflected, an acceptance of things. Suddenly she asked herself, Had she ever seen anyone more truly contented? He liked people, all kinds of people. At her last protest against a talkative visitor, he had chided her: "Child, living in a place like this gives you a sort of obligation." His placid eyes had appealed to her, and she nodded. It was hard to differ for long with the Major.

Going downstairs, Mary and her mother made last inspections of the parlors to the left and right, with their arches opening into adjoining rooms in the wings. From the beaming young maid, Cassie, they took armfuls of roses for tables and mantels, and they were still working over them when Washington Custis' voice reached them again. By now the Major had taken the sight-seers quickly past the fields below the house, the pastures and apple orchard, gravel pit, river landing, and auxiliary buildings. Standing before the great pillars outside, he spoke proudly:

"I picked out the best spot in this river land that I inherited, and had the building made from the exact measurements of a Greek temple." From the voice Mary realized he was smiling. "But I had to do things bit by bit. First the two wings back in 1802; then the war with England came, and also bad times, and it took fifteen whole years to finish. They called it 'Custis' Folly,' but they don't any more." His satisfaction had a quality that was almost childlike.

"You know"—one of the women on the portico had turned excitedly to him—"it looks as if they laid out Washington City just to be seen from up here!" Mary exchanged glances with her mother; that was what she herself had once said at a family party in her teens, to the amusement of the guests. And then she remembered how the house would appear at this hour from over the river, its columns gleaming in the late afternoon against the background of long-armed oaks and chestnuts—a dimming curtain that would disappear in the evening.

It was her favorite hour at Arlington, a time of special serenity in this place that meant, above all to her, rest and repose. Life was ordered here, by task and by season. Wherever she went in future years, she wanted to return to this spot.

Footsteps in the hall drew her attention. Washington Custis had taken a place before one of the tall oil paintings: "General Washington, of course—Peale's portrait as a Virginia colonel; and my grandmother, Martha, when she was Mrs. Custis." He led the strangers toward the steps: "Upstairs there's Washington's four-poster bed and . . ."

In his singsong voice Washington Custis filled in the story Mary had heard so often: the death of his father, who had been the general's aide at Yorktown; his own early days at Mount Vernon, his stay in New York with the President, before the capital was transferred to the new Potomac city named for Washington; and the final years at Mount Vernon. From the general and others Washington Custis inherited several estates with 15,000 acres and two hundred and fifty slaves. The shadow of George Washington lay over everything here. The sleepy town of Alexandria, with its old docks and neat red brick houses, had been Washington's town; at Arlington the dead general sometimes seemed almost another resident.

Mary turned toward the pictures on the walls, with their eyes that followed you across the room, watching through day and night. . . . As a child, Mary, hearing the older servants talk of those people in the frames, had feared them. Now she looked on them as friends.

From the stair came a murmur. ". . . and one young lady will inherit everything." They must have been discussing her, and Mary was glad she had missed the beginning. Head lowered, her mother went to the window, Mary staring after her. There had been three other children, two before her, one after Mary. All died early, the last a few days after his first birthday; from her childhood Mary remembered her mother's gaunt face whenever the subject was mentioned. In the silent room Mary wondered: What *would* it have been like to have brothers and sisters around her?

At a pounding from outside, Mary gave a start. The thumps were so purposeful that it could only be Sam Houston. Not one but three servants raced separately to the door, and Mr. Custis and his party of sight-seers reached there simultaneously, all talking at once. General Houston entered, to stand puzzled at the confusion and handshakings, until Mrs. Custis stepped forward and led him into the drawing room.

Later Mary recalled mainly her astonishment at the sight of Sam Houston in calling costume. He reminded her of the first rainbow she ever beheld. The general's wide, flushed face beamed above a ruffled shirt, green trousers, reddish coat, and stock so ornately patterned that not even the most flamboyant of Virginia youths would have sported it. Before this peacock Mary felt like an inferior hen. Now, with a sweeping gesture, Sam Houston took her hand.

"Miss Custis, the fair young lady at fair Arlington!"

Her lips quivered in amusement. She could be grateful for a compliment, but not one so inflated as that. Miss Mollie's eyes grew round in surprise, and nervously Washington Custis drew their guest's attention to the thick china bowl, newly filled with a spiced wine punch.

"General Washington's favorite . . . You see the ship painted inside? For parties he insisted the bowl be filled to the height of the mast and emptied to the bottom!"

Sam Houston stared, and Mary sensed his slight disappointment; the bowl had been only partly filled. An awkward pause followed; for the moment Mary could think of nothing to say. Taking their guest to a chair, Mr. Custis served him, and a moment later the general almost shouted his approval.

"The best I've had"—he nodded to Miss Mollie—"since last year in Nashville with some cousins of mine. It was so strong that one of the men got into a fight, a real fight with his neighbor."

"A fight?" Miss Mollie's voice was thin.

"With knives, too. He practically cut the other fellow apart." At once, catching the astonishment in her face, Sam Houston explained: "Very sad, and of course that kind of thing doesn't happen often."

As the words went on, Mary saw her mother's hand go anxiously to her chin, and the girl managed to bring the conversation to safer ground, Arlington itself. Her thoughts were racing: Mr. Houston came of a well-placed family, and surely he should know that such matters were not conversation for the parlor.

By now Sam Houston was commenting to her father. "Your lands must keep you busy. Still, you have a lot of overseers to make sure you get every bit of work out of your slaves, don't you?"

Washington Custis' shaggy eyebrows lifted up his forehead, and his words had an unexpected firmness. "Just a few. Some of my friends say I should operate my properties without thinking of the slaves themselves. But I've never allowed families to be separated or people pushed too hard." Mary felt that her father might have added that he had denied every overseer's request for permission to whip field workers or to order other harsh disciplines.

She paid even closer heed when the Major resumed. "Quite a few of us around here belong to the Colonization Society, the one that was formed a long time ago to free slaves and help them get a start in Africa." Washington Custis' eyes had a gleam of interest that reflected his wife's and daughter's; to the family the subject was an important one. "Are you in the colonization movement?" The Major asked the question casually of his guest.

"Why, no." Sam Houston blinked as he turned from Mary to her father. "Where I'm from people are bothered more about getting hold of slaves than getting rid of them!"

Mary smiled; it was a direct answer, and honest, unlike some of the weasling ones by visitors who did not altogether agree. But General Houston nodded slowly as Washington Custis went on. "Slavery's been the thing that's held the South back; free labor is good labor, willing labor. George Washington himself wanted slavery to end; Mary's uncle, Mr. Fitzhugh, freed all his people. I've let some of mine go when they've shown they're able, and in my will I'm freeing every one of mine."

Washington Custis' sunburned face showed all of his earnestness, and Mary felt a surge of pride. Careless though he might be in some things, he would not let himself be shaken on matters in which he believed. After a moment, his interest evident in his heavy features, Sam Houston bent forward. "If you think like that, you ought to run for office!"

Automatically Mary answered, "No. Father makes lots of talks, though, and writes articles on subjects like that and—and the way George Washington felt about them. He speaks to agricultural meetings on ways to save our soil and run farms economically; you know he was the first to breed American sheep——"

Out of breath, Mary was annoyed at herself for so ardent a defense. If Sam Houston thought the Major—well, visionary, as some did, let him go on thinking it. More quietly she added, "Father's given a lot of his time to writing down his recollections of Washington, and has painted dozens of scenes from his life."

Mary indicated a large canvas of the President. General Houston got up for an inspection, and finally murmured: "Er—interesting." The flat word carried its own meaning.

Washington Custis shrugged and Mary felt a bristling anger. Her father was no professional, and yet more than one visitor had thought his work had value. Then Houston spied a blanketed red man at the edge of the picture. "A *real* Indian!" His astonishment over his liking for the figure had a naïvely engaging note, and Mary's resentment disappeared.

"I'm the adopted son of a Cherokee chief." Their guest addressed them all. "When I was a lad I spent a year with them, sitting around the fire with the long pipe, sleeping under trees, wrestling, stalking bear . . ." Sam Houston's eyes had a fresh fire, and Mary's interest livened.

"I took some of their religion, and there's a lot that's fine about it—spirits and gods and devils that drive people." As she watched, Mary saw that her mother's lips had become a white line. Sleeping with Indians, and "devils that drive people." Those were hardly things recommended by the Protestant Episcopal Church, and Miss Mollie followed a rigid orthodoxy. "Sir"—the general faced her father in eager inquiry—"have you ever been in a Cherokee green-corn dance?"

At the suggestion of the plump Major in a green-corn dance Mary intercepted her mother's bright, indignant glance. And now that their caller had begun to flounder so obviously, she felt a touch of pity for the great fellow, so anxious to please and not yet aware how he had failed. Somehow the embarrassed Major led Sam Houston from corn dances to governmental affairs.

"I've just been to West Point," General Houston started again. "I'm in charge of the Congressional visiting board, and I've never seen a finer body of boys."

West Point . . . Mary lost the rest of their visitor's remarks. Among the upperclassmen inspected by General Sam Houston there must have been Robert Lee. West Point was the last place the general should have mentioned today. For, like several others who had come here to see Mary, Sam Houston had an insurmountable handicap: He was not Robert Lee, the tall figure she had painted on the canvas in her room.

As she sat, nodding faintly, Mary's mind went to a ruddy face with a long chin and black hair that grew in new sideburns down to the jaw line, and warm brown eyes with an open look, and lights that appeared suddenly when the scene amused him. Robert would have been amused today.

Opposite Mary, Sam Houston wondered why Miss Custis had become so preoccupied, so distant. And suddenly he knew he had traveled to Arlington for nothing.

After the carriage rocked off, Mr. Custis returned slowly to the room in which Mary remained alone. Hearing a sigh, she went toward her father, and then stopped.

Washington Custis looked up with a small smile. "All right, child; you don't have to say it." Arms folded over his chest, he grew solemn. "But that doesn't mean I'll agree with you about young Lee."

At his first words her heart had pounded happily; now, with a sick sensation, she let her hand fall to her side, and she demanded:

"What do you have against him? Nothing." Her voice shook in a way that she could not control.

"Enough." Though Washington Custis' temper was increasing, he tried to be reasonable. "He's a good enough boy, but, Mary, what future has he? None, and you know it. A fine family—and no prospects at all. Robert will never be what the other Lees were." The Major was about to say more when Mary broke in. "He's only twenty-three now, and he'll soon be out of the academy, and everybody says he's done well there. Very well." She frowned, watching the effect of her pleading words.

"Child, just consider . . ." The care with which her father chose his words made her suddenly furious. He went on. "Robert inherited nothing, nothing at all from his father. Why, he's had so little that he mightn't even have had any training—law, medicine, or any other profession—unless there had been a West Point. No property, nothing to draw on . . ."

"Well, wait and you'll see how well he does in spite of that!" Even to Mary herself this sounded vague, uncertain, and her spirits sank.

"I'm willing to wait." This was the closest to sarcasm that the usually benign Major would ever go. Another flash of anger swept her, but before she could answer, Washington Custis asked quietly, "Has the young man said he wants to marry you?"

Momentarily Mary could not speak; the blow was a well-aimed one. When her voice came it had a strained note. "No. But I'm sure it's for some of the reasons you've used." To herself she asked, Was that true? If she could be certain, she would feel a great deal better now.

"Then Robert has good sense." Washington Custis nodded

quietly and started off. Her pulse thumping, Mary called after him:

"We'll see about that, too! It's going to be Robert or nobody."

If her father heard her, he gave no sign. She remained in the center of the room, biting her lip, until she became slowly aware that Salina Gray stood in the arched doorway. "Miss Mollie say to tell you sixteen people comin' to supper soon, and you're to fix up for 'em?"

Salina's gemlike black eyes had lost their disapproval of an hour or so earlier; the gaunt face had taken a look of deep compassion and understanding. Suddenly Mary sank against the heavy shoulder and cried.

"Thas' all right." Salina stroked her head. "It's going to come out the right way. You wait, an' jus' give Mist' Robert his chance." The brown hand caressed more gently than ever. "But min' you, don't keep *on* waitin'. Not too long . . ." Mary cried harder than ever.

Chapter 2

At the end of the lower hall, working at the desk in her mother's room, Mary started a note to a Richmond friend: "I hope to visit you, though my plans are indefinite." Lowering the pen, she mused ironically: Yes, her plans were indefinite—because they depended on a young second lieutenant. For the third time that day she asked herself: When would she see Robert Lee again?

He had finished West Point with honors and would soon be taking his first assignment, and in Virginia, she hoped. Several times during the months since Sam Houston's visit they had met at friends' homes; but whenever Robert appeared, Mr. Custis seemed accidentally to hover nearby. Once or twice, catching Robert's eye, Mary had smiled at the transparency of her father's purpose. Yet, transparent or not, it worked, she told herself sadly.

Today Mary heard snatches of conversation from the adjoining room where her father and mother sat with Aunt Nellie Lewis, the family beauty, who had danced and chatted her way through those earlier days at Mount Vernon. Her father's sister had retained much of her loveliness, with her chiseled nose and full-blown figure. She had made a great match, marrying Mr. Lewis, George Washington's nephew.

Mary's head went up suddenly. Had her father invited Aunt Nellie for a reason, as a good example? The girl shrugged. Nellie Custis had made her choice, and she would make her own.

Her father's voice rose. "Sister," he was addressing Nellie, "did you see this article in the *Intelligencer?* Man in the service five years, and still a lieutenant."

From the other room Mary heard only the sound of the women sewing. Furiously she shoved her letter to one side. Everybody had to start somewhere, as a second lieutenant or something else. . . . Her father left, and she jumped at a soft movement beside her. Into the room on padded feet walked four cats in a row, all yellow, all demanding her attention.

Stroking them, she began again to argue the matter with herself. She and Robert were distant cousins; the families had known each other for generations, and she had practically grown up with him. She could hardly recall her first meeting with him and his brothers and sisters, after they moved to their small brick place in Alexandria from the Lee mansion, Stratford Hall, in Westmoreland County.

Stratford, the once magnificent property of the Lees, with its great double towers and spreading outside staircase . . . Mary saw it once as a young child on a trip with her favorite Aunt Maria Fitzhugh; for years afterward she could describe the details of its fortresslike proportions, its vistas of passageways and brocaded red hangings. Yet even then, somehow, she had understood there was trouble for the Lees.

When she had touched one of the draperies, she found it stiff with dust, and she detected an emptiness about the place—rooms with one divan and nothing else, corridors closed off, a musty wing. And Mary Custis had read, too, the saddened, haunted look of Robert's mother. With her children around her Ann Lee inquired kindly about the Custises, and tragedy had stared out of her shadowed eyes.

Many times Mary had seen family pictures of Robert's father, one of the most celebrated of the line and, she knew now, one of the most unfortunate. "Light Horse Harry" Lee, Revolutionary cavalry general, had been a close friend of Washington, who considered him a superb military man. After the war Light Horse Harry had gone on to become governor, and some mentioned him for the Presidency itself.

Mary remembered the way others talked, their eyes warm as they pictured Harry Lee—a man who stormed through life, full-blooded, generous, a great orator, a great fighter, and also, un-happily, a great money waster. How had her wise Aunt Maria put it: "The best of hearts and the worst of judgments"? He made poor investments, he threw away money in speculations; Stratford Hall grew grayer, shabbier, and the Lees moved into a few rooms because they could not keep up the rest.

Aunt Maria Fitzhugh, repository of family gossip, had told her how, as the bills piled high, the sheriff would call, "but Light Horse Harry just sat there, ignoring him, and hung chains across the big doors to make sure he didn't break in." In time, however, even chains could not keep off the law, and Robert's father went to debtors' jail for two years.

Before Mary there passed a recollection of Robert's face on the day he described the incident to her. "They took him from us, Mary. He was a fine man, though. Restless, yes, and sometimes he did run to excess. But he was brave and—and good. Most of the stories people tell are lies, just lies!" The young Robert had flushed in fury. It was then that she realized Robert Lee had a capacity for anger that few strangers saw.

After that, quieting, he explained how Light Horse Harry even-tually left jail, making one effort after another to re-establish him-self. "He might have managed things even then, Mary, until the last trouble—and that wasn't his fault. It was something to his credit!"

Others would agree with Robert's words. An editor in George-town had taken a political position resented by many people; a mob rose against the man, who fired back and was jailed; but the crowd got at him and his friends, among them Harry Lee. The things they did to Father . . ." Robert winced at the bloody se-quel.

"Those people killed some of the men with Father, and tossed the wounded into a heap to die. He was beaten badly and thrown down in the street, and even then they pounded him with clubs and poured hot candle grease into his eyes. And one"—Mary shiv-ered at the details—"one took a penknife and started to cut off Father's nose, but Father crawled away. He never really recovered from that."

In time Robert's mother had gathered her small funds and

moved with her children to the town of Alexandria. The broken Harry Lee, trying to regain his health, went on a long voyage and died on the way. Mary closed her eyes; she could not forget young Robert's stricken look as he told her about it.

"I always thought he'd come back, Mary." In her friend's eyes she read his pride in the father he considered a great man, and also his hurt that fortune so mistreated Harry Lee . . . Afterward the widow maintained her family by strenuous economies; the older boys went off to school and Robert took on chores around the house.

Mrs. Lee, long ailing, became an invalid. When Mary and Mrs. Custis called, they often found Robert bringing his mother's medicines, or setting out to do the marketing. The widow had ownership or part ownership in several slaves, hired out to others, and also the service of the decrepit old Nat, the house servant.

Now and then, on Mary's visits, Robert slipped away with her to the small garden. While they talked his warm laugh would ring out. He could joke about himself, his "great big beak," as he called his strong nose, and the way he forgot orders at the store. Mary soon recognized his way of laughing slowly, almost by degrees; a slight lift at the corners of his mouth, a wrinkling of the edges of the eyes, and finally a deep rumble.

When had she first known how she felt about Robert? It had been a gradual realization, an interest that increased little by little as they saw each other at friends' homes or on the Alexandria streets. Then, about four years ago, Robert began at West Point and for months she had heard only irregularly of him.

At the end of his first term, arriving unexpectedly at the Fitzhugh place, she saw from the back a trim figure in military blue, and asked Aunt Maria who the newcomer was. "You've forgotten?" Mrs. Fitzhugh asked, her head on one side. The young man turned, and Mary saw Robert, a much-changed Robert.

He had grown heavier, taller, with more self-command. His long, smooth face brightened, and she thought of those days in the Lee garden. Lifting his hand, Robert approached with a walk that had more than a suggestion of the military; and Mary Custis told herself that he looked as if he had been created for that uniform.

She made a quick appraisal of the flushed skin, the thin lips and firm, heavily cut nose; and for the first time she understood how handsome a man Robert Lee was. A moment later she forgot everything else as she recognized his stare of admiration. "It's been a long time, Mary, a long time!"

"Oh, a school year—eight months, wasn't it?" She tried to sound casual.

"That's more than long enough." He took both her hands, and Mrs. Fitzhugh disappeared into the background. Robert's touch was warm; his brown eyes had a searching light, and they talked seriously about each other, about his brother Smith Lee, now of the Navy, and other Lees and Custises.

As if she watched a new person, Mary noticed that one of his dark eyebrows went higher than the other; it gave an irregularity that made the symmetrical face more appealing—that, and also the way his hair, no matter how recently combed, hung about his ears. Then she smiled; when Robert laughed at one of her remarks, she saw that he still did it by stages: the lips, the eyes, the low rumble.

As he took a place beside her that day, Mary realized, too, that Robert had a certain—she searched for the word—candor that revealed itself at once. "Oh yes, I'm glad to be at West Point, for more than one reason," he said with a direct look. "I like it, and also I'm no longer a burden on anybody." He added, "And I'll be following my father, though I'll never be the soldier *he* was." Robert ended with an outward thrust of his chin, as if defying her or anyone else to disparage his beloved Light Horse Harry.

Then, however, as on other occasions, Mary had caught an undertone of sadness. She wanted to draw him to her, to comfort and reassure him, and with that she understood what had happened to her.

Today, finishing the letter to Richmond, she fixed the seal, and began to listen to her mother and aunt in the room beyond. Nellie Custis Lewis chattered: "I've seen the town grow from nothing more than pigs' pens and mudholes, to what it is. Mind you, though, Washington City still has so little . . ." This was a common theme, and Mary's attention wandered until a name made her start.

"Yes, Robert's half brother, *Black* Horse Harry Lee. His wife's back with him again, and I hear they're getting along well enough. But if ever a woman had to take . . ." Aunt Nellie lowered her voice, and Mary sensed that she would miss the most interesting part. Black Horse Harry—it was the bitter name given by others to the son of General Lee's first marriage. Mary paused, remembering the strange, elegant man, twenty years Robert's senior, and as different from Robert as he could have been.

Tall and well formed, this older man had features of an odd irregularity, making him ugly and handsome at the same time. He had also a sweeping composure, a "manner" that had a bit too *much* manner, and a reputation for unconventional ways. For Mary there had been a certain mystery about the half brother. When his father and the younger Lees left Stratford, he took it over; by his mother's will it passed to him. Black Horse Harry married well and lived in the mansion for several years, then lost it under some kind of financial trouble.

It had been months since she thought of the man, and she wondered: Why shouldn't she know the full story? Jumping up, she went to the other room. As Mary entered, Aunt Nellie's hand, moving in a bright gesture, fell, and she halted in midsentence. "Mary," she said, smiling serenely, "we were talking about the funny thing that happened at your mother's class for the servants, when she was teaching the alphabet to Cassie and . . ."

Mary tightened her fingers in helpless resentment. They still treated her like a child, and she could do nothing about it. And there must certainly be something odd in the matter of Robert's half brother! Mrs. Custis lowered her gaze to her sewing, and Aunt Nellie dropped her airy meanderings. Then Nellie turned to Mary with a serious look.

"Child, they brought a message just now from Maria Fitzhugh's. Robert Lee's mother is there, and right ill, they say."

As Mary stared she felt her mother's quick scrutiny, kind yet curious. But she did not care; she was thinking of the sick woman and of the son who had been closer to her than anyone else in her tragic life. For Robert this would be a bad blow.

"Oh, Miss Mary." Cassie, the dark young maid, spoke from the doorway. "Your comp'ny, that you been expectin' all mornin', comin' up the road now." Cassie giggled. "I sure like to hear that funny Miss Claudia!"

Nodding, Mary turned and went out into the hall. She wished she could agree with Cassie about Claudia McBride, her remote relative, several years her senior, with the perpetual smile and gentle phrases tipped in acid.

At the door a rich, liquid voice greeted her. "Well, Mary, it's certainly nice to see you alone, for once." A quick kiss ended in a searching look. "Nobody else going to be here this time, my dear?"

Miss McBride could make a simple question sound somehow like an accusation; now her lips parted in the blandest of smiles, disclosing what seemed to be several too many teeth. Lean and pale, Claudia had ash-blond hair, plaited about the narrow face like a tight cap. She appeared more angular than ever in a gray coat and dress that had only slightly less color than her complexion. Mary remembered the remark of a male observer: "Miss Claudia has a lot of—personality." Today she was exercising it.

Throwing off her coat, Claudia gave her a sidelong glance. The eloquent voice began again. "One of your friends is near here. Got in last night—Robert Lee. To be with his mother; they say she's sick, but I suppose it's no worse than usual. For heaven's sake, Mary, don't look guilty just because I use the name of Lee. You'd make a stranger think Robert's a lot more than a distant connection. He isn't, or is he?"

Quivering with annoyance, Mary remained silent, but her guest continued. "Robert's not like his father, though that might be to his credit, I say!" To this she added with a yet sharper stare. "And not like his Black Horse brother, either. You've heard the latest?"

Before Mary could frame an answer the avid Claudia, sitting down, warmed to her subject. "Harry inherited all his father's wildness and more, you know; whatever he does, he starts trouble without even trying."

Understanding Claudia as she did, Mary had an impulse to silence her; but now at least she would be getting the answers to

27

some of the questions she had asked, and she listened in growing fascination.

"Anyway, Harry's bride brought him a fine property, and didn't *he* know what to do with it! For a while they had a gay life at Stratford, with parties, dances, and fox hunts—a merry-go-round, twenty-four hours a day."

Pausing, Claudia ran her tongue over her lips, as if she indeed enjoyed her own words, and the rich voice resumed. "Then Harry's wife got sick. She had brought her pretty young sister to the house, and the girl stayed there. Well, with his wife ailing, and the girl thrown so much with Harry . . . He took advantage of his sister-in-law."

Claudia stressed each syllable, getting full value out of her story. Perceiving Mary's astonishment, she continued relentlessly. "Why, he's admitted it. He'd gotten to be his sister-in-law's legal guardian, and her people went to court to make him account for her property. Then President Jackson gave him a position abroad, but the Senate heard the whole story and voted him down."

Mary got up. Now at last she could understand her mother's manner. Then she forgot everything else as she thought of Robert Lee. After his father's difficulties, how the disgrace must hurt. To know that people were talking behind their backs again, and to guess at what they snickered . . .

As Mary stood there, head averted, Claudia shrugged. "I shouldn't have expected you to understand much about such things. The way you've been brought up, so protected and—dependent." Claudia patted her arm with an abundant smile. "Still, it's nice here, isn't it?"

Mary's flesh crawled. She had heard such words before—Miss Heiress, and the like. And yet she really had little chance to *be* anything except protected at Arlington.

Before Claudia spoke again, Mrs. Custis and Aunt Nellie came out into the hall. In the greetings that followed Mary escaped a further quizzing. As the others moved toward the sitting room, she felt a pair of insistent eyes trained upon her from one of the archways. The statuesque Salina, wrists crossed before her in her usual pose, hovered in the distance; when Mary's eyes questioned her, Salina made a slight gesture toward the back of the house.

The girl needed no further explanation. Murmuring a word to the others, she left.

Heart thumping, she heard Salina's low words. "Mist' Robert say he got only a few minutes, and please can he talk to you."

Something had gone wrong, or Robert would not have arrived in this way, and with such a message. Approaching the back door, Mary thought momentarily of her appearance, and Aunt Nellie's rule: "Present yourself only at your best, child." But she wanted to see Robert Lee at once; she had no time for mirrors. Her fingers touched the part in her waving hair; she moistened her lips and went down the back steps.

He was standing at the edge of the garden, hat in hand, profile toward the river. Mary searched the smooth-shaven face; the late sun picked out lights in his dark hair, and the slight knobs of his cheekbones left shadows across the ruddy face. Even in repose the angular chin had a suggestion of firmness; but in every other line Mary read a deep dejection.

"Robert?"

In his concentration he had not heard her until she approached within a few feet. He looked up and his high color deepened; his hands took hers, and tightened in a grip that momentarily pained her. There was suffering in his eyes; at first he could not speak, and then the words, slow and broken, began.

"It's my mother, Mary. A few hours ago. I was able to get to her for a while before—before it happened."

As he continued, Mary's eyes clouded. Ann Lee had meant more to Robert than a mother to most sons; he had been at her side during most of her days, ministering to her, helping her with her small funds and many obligations. He was thinking now of the unhappy woman who had left her secure existence at Shirley estate as the bride of the heroic yet difficult Harry Lee. But Mary knew that for Ann Lee her success with her children must have made up for a great deal. And though the other two sons might achieve more than her young Robert, and be longer remembered, he had always been her favorite.

Mary spoke softly. "Did she suffer much?"

"No, thank God. I'd expected this to happen, and so had she. That didn't make it easier, though . . ." His voice thickened.

Mary searched for words. "You've all turned out well, and that must have meant a lot to her."

"Well . . . my sisters have married happily, and both my brothers are starting nicely enough." She saw his depression return.

"But you yourself," she cried out to him, "you've been right at the top of your class. And didn't Aunt Nellie tell me they asked you to be an instructor?"

The brown eyes met hers, and looked away. "That doesn't mean a lot, Mary. They need instructors badly." In this self depreciation there was a flicker of amusement, and then his face sobered again. "But it *has* helped me—ten dollars more every month."

Mary blinked, as she realized that ten dollars obviously meant a great deal to Robert Lee. She thought of her father's remarks about lieutenants, and began to reflect: The Custises had never been extravagant at Arlington, and yet a mere ten dollars a month . . . Robert had maintained an even more frugal life than she realized.

After a pause he added quietly, "I decided I had to let you know . . ."

His look told her more than his words. So he had come to her first of all, after the blow had fallen. She lifted her face and her eyes widened.

Behind them Mary sensed that Salina Gray was watching, and she knew the housekeeper was sympathetic. She moved closer to Robert, and he drew her quickly against him. His lips pressed against her cheek, and then hungrily against her mouth.

The breeze blew wisps of her hair against his face, and she could feel her heart pounding. Long afterward she connected the bliss of that moment with the fragrance of Miss Mollie's roses and lilies in the garden beside them.

They might have gone on standing there indefinitely if a sound of warning had not reached them from the back door. The faithful Salina, who had turned her back on the couple now called to them in dismay, "Miss Mollie's startin' down the hall."

Mary drew away and faced the house. Robert stood beside her, his hand touching her; the moment of enchantment had gone.

"Will you be in Virginia for a while?" She asked it as calmly as she could.

His low-pitched answer was filled with regret. "Not for long. I've got to leave, and soon, for my first engineer's assignment—somewhere out of the state."

Mary lowered her eyes. He would be farther away than ever, and when he did come back to Virginia . . . She remembered her father's sardonic remarks about second lieutenants, and there was a sick feeling in her throat.

Young Cassie, her eyes ovals of alert interest, came out to ring the plantation bell behind the house. From the door her father and mother were looking toward Robert in surprise. In the distance Mary heard the cries of the men as they headed in from several directions for the noontime meal. The clang of the bell came like an insistent reminder: Arlington and its people stood between her and Robert. They were thoroughly outnumbered.

Chapter 3

The tiny Mrs. Maria Fitzhugh, Mary's Aunt Maria, asserted her *grande dame's* privilege and waved away the chair set out for her at the edge of the porch. "I prefer this one." She nodded her dark head with its pert, inquisitive nose, as if informing herself of her decision. Smaller even than she seemed, Aunt Maria held herself so erect that some thought she needed only a jeweled crown to complete her queenly attire.

Now, with an elaborately casual glance, Mrs. Fitzhugh looked back into the hallway toward the last couple at the buffet table. Her niece had arrived yesterday on a visit to Chatham, the Fitzhugh place on the Rappahannock River; and it was, as Maria announced brightly, a "complete accident" that Robert Lee rode up today on his return from his first year's service on the Florida-Georgia coast.

Kissing the lieutenant, Aunt Maria had taken him from one group to another and ended, accidentally again, by leaving him at Mary's side. A gong sounded, and Maria Fitzhugh went to work to shepherd the forty guests, plates in hands, to points about the house and lawn, with its gradual slope toward the stream. For a few minutes servants sped back and forth to the ovens at the rear, bringing out platters of steaming meats, baskets of napkin-covered biscuits, pitchers of cream, and decanters of wine. Accepting their dishes, guests picked places at will.

As Aunt Maria watched through the door, Robert and Mary approached. From the side appeared Claudia McBride, who had also been watching.

"Mary . . . Robert!" Claudia's rich voice rose like a trumpet over the conversational hum. "What a fine pair you make, and I'm sure you know it. Let's sit down here and have a long talk, the three of us!" The head with its light, braided ropes nodded, and with iron determination, she led them toward a table.

"Oh no, miss." Stepping forward with a speed that Mary had not thought possible, Aunt Maria inserted herself between Claudia and the young couple and headed the interloper in a new direction. Her jeweled hand gestured. "My girl, I've been wanting a chat with you. Mary, the tree over there is ready for you and Robert." The dowager's alert eyes made certain they went to the spot indicated, and then she turned majestically to the spluttering Claudia.

As soon as they were alone Mary exchanged a smile with Robert; Mrs. Fitzhugh's maneuverings made her feel like a fellow conspirator, and Robert clearly enjoyed sharing the experience. At her first glimpse of him today she had noticed that more than ever he fitted the uniform and the uniform fitted him. Gone, she saw, was the cloud that had hung over him at their last meeting.

They sat on the river side of the oak, out of earshot of the others, the only sounds a whirring of birds in distant reaches of the tree and the faint click of forks and fragments of remarks from the other groups. For the past few minutes she had been rehearsing what she would say; now the words did not come.

"We've all thought about you and the work you're doing," she ventured, fretting at the lameness of her words.

"And I thought a great deal deal about all of you, and especially you, Mary." Robert said it simply, with none of the smirking, self-conscious gallantry that she found difficult in some of the young men she knew.

Then, while she watched him, Robert's expression slowly altered. About to speak, he tightened his lips, and she asked herself, Was he worrying about his position in relation to hers? The poorly paid lieutenant and the landowner's daughter—or so Claudia would put it. Mary searched for a safe subject.

"Robert, what was the country like, out there on the coast?"

He rubbed his hand against his long chin. "All right, I suppose, though nothing of the sort you've ever seen, Mary. Flat land,

34

mainly salt marsh, and one waste after another under a sun that bakes like an oven over you." Frowning, he shook his head. "Easier to talk about than to live in, especially with the mosquitoes and bugs."

She put her plate aside as he explained how he directed the building of fortifications in gluelike soil, and watched fever-laden fogs that seeped along the semitropic swamps. A feeling of apprehension went through her: "I didn't understand things were as bad as that. You could have died before any of us knew you'd gotten sick!"

Robert's manner grew wry. "We Lees can stand a lot. And the service wouldn't suffer much with one less second lieutenant." Quickly his face brightened again. "It wasn't all work, you understand; we were able to get into Savannah from time to time, and made some good friends. Especially the Mackay family and their daughters. The girls lightened our evenings, very nicely."

At his easy humor Mary felt a pinch of annoyance and also, she realized, of fear. It was simple jealousy, she knew, but that made it no less hard to bear. Suppose Robert had come back with one of those Mackays for a wife?

From the nearest bench there rose a rippling laugh. A vivid brunette from New Orleans passed within a yard of them, the wind outlining her figure under its embroidered skirt and waist. Robert's gaze lifted, and Mary read an unmistakable appreciation. Miss DeVille looked back, obviously grateful for the lieutenant's interest.

Mary picked up her plate, then put it down again. She could hardly expect him not to show his natural reaction; nevertheless she did not enjoy seeing it so close at hand! She was about to make an excuse to leave, when Robert spoke.

"Mary, a man may admire a girl like that, but generally he doesn't marry her." His tone was gentle, and she realized that he had been studying her more carefully than she knew. He had never talked to her in this vein, and she waited, hoping that he would follow it up. When he remained silent she became exasperated, remembering Aunt Maria's careful instruction of an hour earlier: "Today it's up to you. It's my guess, Mary, that Robert

35

mainly needs a little encouraging." Miserably she wondered how she could manage that.

"How's Nat now?" she asked after a while, recalling that Robert had taken with him the family servant, who had wanted to be as close as possible to him.

"I kept him in a cottage on the mainland for a few months." Robert's face had contracted. "He really couldn't do anything; he'd gotten very feeble, but he insisted on coming. Otherwise he'd have felt—well, put aside, I suppose." Robert looked past her. "I could see him whenever our work let up, but finally he died, Mary. Anyway, I think he went happily."

She was moved. "It was a fine, generous thing," she whispered, and impulsively she touched his arm. His hand pressed hers and remained upon it. Another long pause followed, and Mary looked down the bank to the cool river flowing imperceptibly below, and across to the roof tops and church spires of the little town of Fredericksburg.

A breeze ruffled the water, as if a finger had flicked at it from the side, and then swept past them with a dry rustle of leaves. This was a spot as placid as it was lovely, thought Mary, momentarily aware of the scents of early summer rising from the fields, and the drone of insects in the branches just above their heads. Or was it simply that Robert Lee rested beside her here?

He stirred and, with brow slightly furrowed, told her his own immediate plans. "They're about to give me a new assignment, I hear. Old Point Comfort, on the coast."

Mary straightened up. At least, she told herself automatically, he'd be away from those Mackays and their daughters! She realized too that the transfer would bring Robert back to Virginia—some distance from Arlington and Washington City, yet nearer to them than before.

Robert scarcely noticed her reaction. His gaze was fixed on the opposite side of the river. "Sometimes I've wondered about trying to make a start in planting. Tobacco, corn, or anything else. A lot of Lees have worked the soil, and it's a good life, Mary: a place with crops around you and water nearby, and hills to watch in the evening. And none of the bickering and meanness and the pushing that's everywhere else . . ."

His half-musing voice continued, and he had a look almost of pain as he said, "But I couldn't hope for anything like that, of course." Mary realized that in these days of poor agricultural conditions and declining yields in Virginia a man without inherited property had scant chance as a farmer.

Then her thoughts took a new turn. If she and Robert were married, he would have Arlington or one of the other Custis properties—White House plantation, Romancoke, or some other. Together they could prove that, in spite of his father's spendthrift ways, his son could manage a successful career.

"Robert——"

She stopped. How could she even hint her meaning? In any case she knew that he would say no to any suggestion that he live off the Custises; and that was how he would interpret her idea.

He waited for her to continue, and when she did not he said with a frown, "Outside of farming, Mary, I'd like most to be what my father was, a good soldier. If I could only do part of what he did . . ." Robert's words trailed off, and in his face was a doubt and uncertainty that puzzled her.

She replied instantly, and without thinking, "Of course you could do it. You can be whatever you put your mind to, Robert!"

Mary's eyes were full of confidence. His hand tensed over hers, and in his face there was gratitude, and also a growing tenderness.

"Mary, the way things have been going with me, so far, anyway . . . there isn't much left to support somebody else. Especially somebody who's used to a great many things. But—"

Though these were not quite the words for which she had been hoping, he had started well enough. Mary's fingers tightened on his arm and she spoke huskily. "Robert, stop fretting whether you can or can't do things. You can!"

Certainly he needed no more than that. They rose together, napkins falling to the grass, and then, from a few feet away, a voice rang out: "Well, you two, I'd give more than a penny for your thoughts!"

Claudia McBride, having finally eluded Aunt Maria, was bearing down upon them. Mary saw that Robert's face had whitened with anger, and a vein stood out in his temple. Her own resentment went quickly away. She had accomplished a lot today; not

37

everything, yet a great deal, and all because of Maria Fitzhugh. The old belle emeritus had known all the essential steps in the campaign.

In the wide hall at Arlington the master, mistress, and daughter took their places several weeks later beside a flustered young officer. A pair of the Major's dogs came over to welcome Robert, and to receive a friendly cuffing and stroking; shortly afterward three of the master's cats arrived, one to pre-empt a space on the lieutenant's lap, the others to assume ceremonial posts at his feet.

Washington Custis ignored Robert's approval by the animal portion of the household. He sat in a chilly posture, arms folded over his stomach, eyes raised, as if he were making a minute study of the Mt. Vernon lantern that hung near them.

Following the direction of the Major's scrutiny, Robert tried a remark. "The old lamp has seen a lot of things happen around it, hasn't it?" To this Washington Custis muttered a vague agreement, picked up one of his cats as if rescuing it from Robert's reach, and settled back in a barbed silence.

With a thoughtful stare Mrs. Custis gathered her sewing and went to work. Between darts of her needle she glanced up for brief surveys, then dropped her gaze, and her round, wrinkled face for once was mystified rather than worried. During the past few weeks Miss Mollie had turned away repeatedly from any direct discussion of Robert Lee; when Mary led up to the subject, her mother nodded slowly, and that was all.

Miss Mollie looked up. "Mary, stop it." With a shrug the girl complied; she had been tapping her fingers against the vase on the table beside her—a mannerism of which Mrs. Custis did not approve. Mary nodded, and quiet settled again; and once more Mary tried to think what Aunt Maria would have done in the situation. Her eye went to the easel at which she had been painting that morning, and stopped at another of those figures of uniformed young men who bore a remarkable resemblance to Robert Lee. Edgily she covered the canvas.

Meanwhile Robert crossed his legs, clasped his hands, and unclasped them. Both he and Mary gave a start when Mrs. Custis spoke.

"Mr. Custis?" Miss Mollie smoothed the garment in her hands. "Isn't it time . . . ?" Since her husband caught her meaning, she saw no need to finish the sentence.

"Time for my nap? No. I'm wide awake." Washington Custis passed his hand over the shining crown of his head, and seemed ready to prove the statement. He shifted in his chair: "Robert, you once told me about your classmates at West Point. Have you heard from any of them since you left?" Listening closely, Mary decided that her father had planned the question with care.

"Well, mainly 'the Colonel,' Joe Johnston. You've met him, sir; we're both Virginians and we were thrown together a lot. Everybody says old Joe's going to amount to something." Robert smiled, but nervously, Mary thought.

"Indeed. What's 'Colonel' Johnston's rank now?" The high voice went higher than usual.

"Second lieutenant, like mine." Although Robert spoke calmly, his last words had an edge, and Mary watched the two men with a growing concern.

Mr. Custis persisted: "How long will it take before 'the Colonel' is a real colonel?"

"I couldn't guess that, sir. So many things would have an influence." As Robert continued he threw back his head in an unconscious gesture, and Mary recognized the sign that his temper had risen. She made a short prayer: Please, they mustn't quarrel, they mustn't say things that would mean trouble. As her lips moved she felt the perspiration on her forehead. Touching her handkerchief to her face, she saw herself in one of the carved mirrors; she looked tense and unhappy.

The sight made Mary more angry than ever, and she stared at her father, a retort on her tongue. It wasn't Robert's fault that he had no inheritance to draw upon, as had Washington Custis; and at least he was striking out for himself, and not leaning on family position! And even if the Major disinherited her, keeping Arlington and everything else, he still couldn't keep her from going to Robert whenever he asked her. The words would hurt her father, as they hurt her to think them. Nevertheless . . .

Mary swallowed, remembering the story of a Custis woman of several generations past who had done much the same thing.

She had never been allowed into the house again and, according to Aunt Nellie's version, the father did not mention the girl's name until he lay on his deathbed. To be turned away from Arlington . . . Her hands tightened. Only now did she realize exactly what Robert meant to her.

How much of this she would have said to her father, under the spur of the situation, she would never know. As Mary's lips moved Mrs. Custis leaned forward, speaking in time to halt her daughter.

"Robert, one of Mr. Scott's books arrived the other day. Wouldn't you like to read a few pages to Mary and me?"

Robert reached out for the leather-bound volume, his relief evident. He read slowly:

> "There was a soft and pensive grace,
> A cast of thought upon her face,
> That suited well the forehead high,
> The eyelash dark, and downcast eye;
> The mild expression spoke a mind
> In duty firm, composed, resign'd . . ."

Despite her tension Mary was suddenly amused. Robert could not know it, but he had picked a passage describing a lady who rejected Walter Scott himself in favor of a man of greater wealth. Mary sniffed to herself: "Mild expression," "duty firm," "resign'd," indeed. The woman could hardly have cared much about Scott!

"Hm." Almost peremptorily her father intruded. Robert read on in a flat, droning tone, as if heedless of the meanings. Mary's nostrils widened in an increasing anger; would Washington Custis have his way after all?

At that moment Mrs. Custis intervened again. Clearing her throat, she remembered her favorite panacea, food. Whatever the problem, Miss Mollie said, a good meal would help it. "You sound tired, Robert." Her head inclined toward him, and her smile demanded his agreement with her words. "Now they didn't give you anything to eat on your way here, did they?"

"Why——" As a matter of fact, Mary knew that he had dined before arriving at Arlington. When Robert hesitated Mrs. Custis nodded confidently. "I thought not. Mary, will you . . . ?"

Mary heard Salina moving in the next room, and young Cassie was murmuring to the ancient nurse. For a moment the surprised Major appeared about to point out these facts. Mary rose at once, and Robert more slowly.

"Go on." Mrs. Custis gave a brisk wave of her hand. "Both of you."

At her last words Mr. Custis swung around, as if to get up with the younger couple. Hastily Miss Mollie handed him the book. "My dear, do you like it as well as Mr. Scott's last one?"

The Major, at least at this moment, had no opinion whatever as to the relative merits of Mr. Scott's productions. He mumbled a reply, but by then Mary and Robert had gone across the hall.

In the dining room, walking past the long central table, Mary approached the old oak cupboard with its spiced scents that seemed never to leave it. Opening the upper door, she groped within.

Inside the dark cupboard Mary touched the remains of a plump fruitcake, and, picking it up, turned toward him. Robert took the plate to set it on the table; the cake tilted and dropped to the floor, but neither noticed.

"Robert, I think——"

Whatever she thought, she did not tell him. He bent down and kissed her, tentatively at first, then eagerly and possessively. Through her thin silk dress she caught the beat of his heart; she closed her eyes and was conscious of the pressure of his palms, of his chest against her, and then of nothing except his lips. This was what she had been waiting for all of her life.

Her hand went up to his dark hair; she smoothed it, and her fingers remained there. From the next room came a sound and they drew apart.

Through the silence Mary heard her mother, speaking without letup, and she felt a rush of gratitude; Miss Mollie was working hard for them. As if he understood, Robert snatched up Mary's hands.

"I'd planned it differently, Mary, and I thought of the way I'd start, and explain how things should be with us. My work and assignments, I mean. But now——" His words rushed out. "You'll marry me, Mary?"

In her delight she saw that his eyes had darkened with feeling, until they were almost black.

"Of course I'll marry you. Of course."

Robert took her in his arms again, more swiftly than before, and she caught him tightly in return. His voice reached her as from a distance. "Mary, you'll have to be with me at Fort Monroe, and live the way the others do. And it won't be altogether easy for you."

He spoke with an earnestness that could not be mistaken. She drew back. "Why, yes. I'd expect that."

The frown between his eyes did not relax. "You'll have to live off my salary, and nothing else at all."

A faint anger stirred her. Of course she would stay within his income; why shouldn't she? The quick retort died on her lips and she nodded, smiling at him.

A fleeting thought, a thought that had been inside her mind for days, suggested itself. Suppose, after all, Robert eventually decided to go into planting; might he come here to Arlington, and the whole family would be together? It was the thing that she wanted most in life—next to Robert himself.

He was watching her, one eyebrow raised above the other. "What are you thinking about?" His eyes had a humorous light.

Some instinct warned her: No, wait. To suggest it now would be an error.

They heard a stir of movement, and in the doorway stood Washington Custis, hands limp at his sides, staring at them with a look that was part chagrin, part anger. Robert's arm went behind Mary, to hold her against him, and they faced her father. The older man opened his lips, and then his hand rose and fell.

By now the Major's presence hardly mattered; and his eyes indicated that he fully realized the fact. Into the room behind him walked Mrs. Custis, her steps more purposeful than ever. Her time of indecision had ended; she was her old, firm self. Her smile, when it came a moment later, was an enveloping one, but also, Mary realized at once, a placating one.

"Things are going to be right nice," Miss Mollie remarked to all of them, and Mary saw that her mother had already begun to plan the ceremony. The girl turned, and now she could let Miss Mollie see the fullness of her gratitude.

By midmorning on a day at the end of June 1831, Arlington stirred with successive flurries from portico to henhouse, arbor to Potomac landing to back gates—changes in accommodations, word of imminent arrivals along the road, calls for additional helpers from upstairs bedrooms that had become dressing chambers.

"Did Lieutenant Tilghman's shoes get polished yet?"

"We got another carriage that los' its axle!"

"They say the cream give out in the kitchen, already. . . ."

Under the dimming gray sky, vehicles lined the road, and late-comers ordered coachmen to find places on the lawn beyond. Older women, murmuring composedly, allowed themselves to be led from room to room, accepting compliments and cups of wine and finally taking places of vantage. Someone found a cluster of cats on a sofa, and the giggling Cassie picked them up and put them in Nurse's room at the back. Upstairs the six male attendants were working at the collars and neck gear of their full-dress military attire, rubbing cloth over brass buttons and epaulets.

On the main floor Washington Custis ended another harried tour past the archways with distant relatives who must be shown the Mount Vernon relics; he bowed to several more whom he did not recognize, and took the hands of Robert's brothers, the bland-faced Smith Lee, and the smiling Carter Lee, who stood there calmly, exchanging pleasantries. Aunt Nellie Custis swept by, throwing out bits of light gossip, making her usual stir as a celebrity; the smaller Aunt Maria Fitzhugh, dark and self-contained, kept a covey of eight- and ten-year olds under control.

Finally Mary's father took his position at the steps, and his hand passed steadily over his bald pate and his gleaming cheeks. The Reverend Mr. Keith was late and already—Mr. Custis' nervous eyes surveyed the clouds—a drizzle had begun.

"Like a minister not to be on time," the Major muttered.

"That's all right, Mr. Custis." Though she herself felt concerned, his wife tried to soothe him. "You're usually late yourself." She glided away to supervise five or six different matters.

All that Mr. Custis had to do was follow the directions she had given him, she told herself.

In her room, with three servants around her, Mary made a detailed inspection at the long mirror. Summoned from downstairs, Cassie pushed a curl into position, and continued to chatter until Salina hissed her into silence. Nurse worked silently at the hem of the cream-white skirt, thrust out by well-starched petticoats, and the towering Salina nodded as she straightened the filmy veil.

Mary moistened her lips and rubbed dutifully but without enthusiasm at her cheeks. She was trying to remember her mother's emphatic directions: "Walk slowly, slowly. For once be stately." Yet could she ever be stately, no matter how she worked at it?

The rain began to make slanting streaks against the window-panes, and the trees, whipped by the rising wind, swayed against the side of the house. Still no signal had come from below. Over Salina's protests Mary stepped to the door, skirts billowing, to peer through the crack. For a moment she heard only a general hum of voices, and then from a few feet away a familiar sound, the acidulous confidences of Claudia McBride.

"It's very nice, and I hope it will work out well. Still, neither one's a child. He's twenty-four, and she's a good twenty-three."

Mary gave a rueful smile. Always Claudia! About to go back, she caught another of her friend's observations:

"Of course, Robert's the lucky one. Those Lees usually marry well. Look at his father and that half brother of his, Black Horse Harry, the wild one. You notice nobody talks about *him.* . . ."

There was more, but Mary recalled mainly the remark about Lees, who "marry well." Miss Heiress again, and others would whisper it. Closing the door, she remembered one of Claudia's earlier jibes: Mary had been oversheltered. And suddenly she was more afraid than she had been in years.

She *had* been dependent; she could not deny it. Her hands trembled, and the servants watched her curiously. In Salina's face she read compassion, as if her old attendant understood everything. Salina went to her, ostensibly to straighten the veil; but the dark hand on Mary's shoulder patted her encouragingly.

"Thank you," she whispered, and her head went up. Robert's

beloved face came before her, and she could hear his reassuring voice. With that she saw Aunt Maria at the door, making a final appraisal. The dowager squeezed her arm. "Mary, I suspected it before, but just to look at you now, I know it. You were born to be a wife, and a good one."

Brushing Mary's cheeks with her lips, Mrs. Fitzhugh left. The hands that held the bridal bouquet tightened. Born to be a wife . . . Whether or not she had thought it before, she did now.

A knock sounded. Across the hall she heard rumbling voices, and a bridesmaid swept in. "Poor Mr. Keith's just arrived. Rode here on his horse and got all wet. None of the younger men have anything but their uniforms. So Mr. Keith's wearing your father's britches, and they reach only to the middle of his legs."

Mary tried to smile. Downstairs the music began and the bridesmaids took places. Her father waited, as proudly as if the wedding had been his thought from the beginning. At the piano Aunt Nellie craned her neck and beamed a greeting. Below, under the great arch, until now forgotten, stood Robert Lee.

Opposite Mary late that evening Robert sat with two of the bridesmaids, sipping the last cup of coffee. The candles burned steadily, flames lifting and falling with each opening of the doors; over everything lay a fragrance of flowers, of wine, the women's mixed perfumes and the scent of wet earth. Drops of water fell from the vines and leaves outlined against the sky; and a wind, sweeping across the Potomac, carried a hint of swampy places below the hill.

In the next room toasts were being exchanged between her father and his friends around the big punch bowl with the ship painted inside. It had been filled and refilled, and an oblique memory struck Mary of Sam Houston on the afternoon Mr. Custis showed it to him. Momentarily she wondered where General Houston was tonight.

For hours she had heard speeches, jokes, and more speeches; her face hurt from her efforts to keep smiling. Now the carriages were rolling away; the rain had stopped, and the stars hung close to Arlington. Mary and Robert went to the door to wave good-bys.

Now they were alone except for Mary's family and the other members of the bridal party. For several days most of the attendants would stay at Arlington for rides about the country, dancing, and picnics, and finally she and Robert were to make a series of visits to relatives before going to the fort.

It had been a happy wedding. Through it all Mary saw Robert's face near hers, with its high color at the cheeks, and the tenderness that came whenever their gaze met.

He rose now, eyes shining. With a gesture he lifted his cup. "To Mary. Mary Lee."

With a clatter the others got up. Mary lowered her head, lifted it with an effort, and looked to them and back to him. Mary Lee. This was the first time she had heard the new name, and it had a good sound. A hush fell over the room. Her husband put down the cup, and went slowly to her. In silence she took his arm, and he led her to the stairs.

Chapter 4

A man's shout came through the night, echoing over the water beyond Fort Monroe. Waking slowly from a restless dream, Mary pushed herself up and frowned at the dim gray wall beside her. For a moment she thought she was at Arlington, until the outlines of the narrow room brought her back to the present. She shivered. Though it was only August, two months since their marriage, the air along the Virginia coast already had a chill. The shouting started again, and Mary reached a hand out in the dark. "Robert, something's happening!"

She stopped; of course he was not there. Hours before—the previous morning, in fact—a stranger had galloped to the fort with stories of trouble on plantations near Norfolk. Regular Army artillery had been rushed out and the engineer officers, assigned here for construction work, had been summoned to the commander's office. Since then rumors had spread: a slave uprising, ambushes, killings . . . Robert, where could he be now, and what had happened? Preparing to leave, he had assured her there was nothing to worry about. Soon afterward he said something that made it certain she would worry: As a precaution she should lock the downstairs door. Once more Mary shuddered.

From somewhere below the slit of their bedroom window there came several more calls, the last a snarling one; and then she heard only silence, in which the wind whined across the bleak waters. After a while the twenty or thirty dogs that roamed the post began to bark. In the court outside tubs rattled dismally in the wind; and all at once she heard a scraping noise, close at hand. Her blood chilling, she jumped to her feet.

"Oh, Miss Mary!" She sank back in relief; it was the plump Cassie, using her key downstairs. The girl, brought over from Arlington, occupied a room some distance off. She must have run the whole way. When Cassie stumbled upstairs Mary realized the girl was even more frightened than she was.

"Miss Mary, they gon' kill all the colored. Nobody safe!" Her maid fell to her knees and Mary, drawing on her robe, went to her. Nothing must happen to Cassie. During these recent weeks Mary had come to be very close to the girl who was awkward, half trained, yet anxious to learn.

"You're all right here." She patted Cassie's arm. "Now just get the fire going." Yet in spite of her efforts to be calm, Mary felt a growing alarm. Was Robert safe? She remembered the old people's stories of slave rebellions, spears driven into the backs of fleeing men and women, children burned to death while mobs screamed outside; and afterward, lines of black bodies, hanging from the trees . . .

Trying not to think such thoughts, Mary managed to light the oil lamp. At the tiny grate, which was only half the size of those in the servants' cabins at Arlington, Cassie worked without much success. The smoking fireplace sent fumes through the room. Mary stared at the roughly plastered ceiling, and the poorly fashioned chairs and table against the wall. The faded cloth rug covered only part of the floor; with Cassie's help she had put up a dozen pictures and flowered curtains. Robert had complimented her, as had his superior, the easygoing bachelor, Captain Andrew Talcott, who lived downstairs. Nevertheless she knew that their two rooms remained grim and cramped. Tonight the sudden sight of them made her want to cry.

From below, without warning, came another sound—the irregular footsteps of several men. "Ah, God, God . . ." Cassie caught at Mary, her hands like ice. As both stood rigid the door opened downstairs and Mary had an impulse to retreat, which gave way suddenly to furious anger at her own cowardice. If those people tried to get Cassie, they'd first have to cope with *her!*

Snatching Robert's sword from the mantel, she took several

steps forward, swung open the door, and saw a man in the dim light below.

"Stop there, damn you!" Her voice, strong and defiant, surprised her.

"My dear, what's the matter?"

It was Robert. As he ran up the stairs she made out the familiar dark hair and the strong nose. The sword clattered at her feet and when Robert drew her to him, she cried half hysterically. He whispered a message to Cassie, who scurried past him, and then, murmuring to Mary, Robert carried her across the room.

Sinking into the rocking chair with her in his arms, he told her, "It's all right, *all* right, Mim." Soon after the wedding he had called her that; it represented a special name, shared with nobody else. "The slave trouble's over, or at least in hand." Still speaking softly, he smoothed her long hair back from her cheeks.

Mary's eyes, washed clear by her tears, opened and she settled against her husband, her self-possession slowly returning. With his hands warm upon her, she reminded herself that these had been good weeks. Robert was understanding, gentle; she had only to see the lift of his eyes, the flush that further colored his cheeks when he rejoined her after an absence, to know that he loved her. As for her own feeling, she still trembled to recall the recent hours; had Robert been killed or hurt . . . It was impossible to think of going on without him.

Her curiosity reasserted itself. "What happened?"

He spoke hesitantly. "The engineers waited on call, but only the Regular Army men went there, Mim." His look became troubled. "There were people killed on both sides, attacks and ambushes—it must have been terrible for a while. I'm sorry; you're not used to things like this, and these surroundings."

Impatiently Mary shook her head. "None of it was your fault. I'll get accustomed to everything. I wish, though, that you'd told me a little more before you left; I'm not a child."

Bending over to comfort her again, Robert kissed her cheek and then her lips and throat. As she lay in his arms she felt that in many ways she must have seemed like a child to Robert. Back came the memory of a dozen irritations and upsets—her trouble in keeping inside Robert's careful budget, her purchases of food that went bad overnight, and "bargains" that cost twice the usual price. One day he had asked her in embarrassment, if she would not hunt "bargains" for at least another month.

Now he reached down and took her hands. "Your bad habit." He had found she had an unconscious trick of rubbing one hand inside the other in time of strain. She looked down at her hands and smiled.

"Do you really like it at the fort?" His eyes watched her closely.

"Why, yes. At least when you're not away." She spoke the truth simply, using the first words that occurred to her.

After a moment she added, "I'll get used to it; you'll see." She looked away; she could never tell him of her dismay when she first stared at the cheerless expanse of these weatherworn houses, uneven brick walks, and the stretches of mud and water.

She had thought then, as she did now, of the vista at Arlington, the swerve of the river and the high hilltop clothed in green the year round. She saw few greens here and no flowers. On that day of her arrival Robert had murmured, "The officers and their wives generally aren't at the fort for long, and they have to shift so often from one house to another. . . ."

Mary had nodded, but the same week she and Cassie went to work on the narrow plot of earth beside their quarters. By the government boat which came down the river from Washington— the trip was longer than the map indicated—her mother sent cuttings from the Arlington gardens; Robert and the good-natured Captain Talcott helped in the planting. Nothing grew, however; perhaps it was her inexperience, or the exposed location. The blank spaces still reproached her.

When Robert released her hands, her thoughts came back to the present and she realized that it was getting light outside.

"I think you'd better get dressed, Mim. I haven't had time to tell you, but we have a visitor downstairs. He's with Andrew Talcott, and I've asked Cassie to start the coffee."

"Of course." Swinging her feet to the floor, Mary asked with sudden interest, "Who is it?"

"Somebody you've heard me talk about. Joe Johnston. He's just been assigned here with the new artillery." His face had brightened, and she smiled back; the young "Colonel," Robert's special

50

West Point friend, was somebody about whom she was more than curious. She reminded herself again how much her husband liked people, enjoyed small parties and good conversation. And people liked Robert in return. Sometimes she was surprised to hear how much they told him about themselves, frankly, confidently. In that respect, at least, he reminded her of her father.

She soaped her face at the washstand while Robert, shirt off, shaved with swift and accurate strokes. In the wavy mirror she watched for a moment the play of the muscles in his upper arm and the movement of his heavily proportioned chest; and then, powdering her face, she stared critically but happily at the image before her.

This marriage had improved her looks; she needed nobody to tell her that. Her mind went back to Robert's question of a few minutes earlier. She wanted nothing more than to be with him; and yet, did it have to be in this place? . . . Frowning, she drew on her stays, two petticoats and a red woolen dress, buttoned and trimmed in a darker red. As usual Robert was ready before she was and he waited for her at the top of the stairs.

"Mary, this is Lieutenant Johnston." Beside the towering Andrew Talcott was a short and quite dapper young man with a shining forehead, a narrow mustache and a look of quick intelligence.

When she greeted him, Lieutenant Joseph E. Johnston made a bow, hands stiffly at his sides, almost as if he stood before a commanding officer on inspection. Here was a little rooster! At once she regretted the ungenerous thought.

Did he sense the impression he made, or was it only a natural defensiveness? In any case the newcomer regarded her briefly with an air of suspicion. Suddenly, however, the flesh around the small dark eyes crinkled, with a smile that approached a grin, and a voice, surprisingly deep, told her, "Robert has done well for himself." Joe Johnston wanted to be friends, wanted to be liked, and Mary responded immediately.

Setting to work to put their guest at ease, she led him into Captain Talcott's small dining room. As she settled herself at the end of the table, she smiled at the heavy Talcott. "That's right, take the big chair; you're the largest one here."

Opposite her, to her amazement, Lieutenant Johnston flushed a deep red. Obviously this was a sensitive individual! It seemed a good time to excuse herself for a conference with Cassie over breakfast plans; when she returned the tension had gone. Rising to his feet, Joe Johnston gave her another friendly look, and she heard the end of his remark to Captain Talcott.

". . . West Point never turned out a better officer than Robert."

The new arrival's gaze was warmly admiring, with none of his previous restraint; her husband appeared embarrassed, but Mary did not hide her own delight. Clearly the man had a rare judgment of people! She was still smiling when Cassie brought in the coffee urn, a mound of biscuits, and slivers of curling red-brown ham from the Arlington smokehouse. Robert said grace, and all at once he was making motions to her.

"Why, what?" Stammering, Mary looked down; she and Cassie had forgotten a detail, the plates.

The girl brought in the missing dishes and the three men made hasty efforts to introduce new topics of conversation. Somehow the moment passed. Mary listened as Robert, buttering a biscuit, turned toward Joe Johnston.

"What's happened to Jefferson Davis—you remember him from the academy, Davis from Mississippi?"

"Oh, he's in the Army, somewhere in the West." As Lieutenant Johnston spoke Mary caught an expression that told her he did not greatly admire Mr. Jefferson Davis. She must remember that their friend was a man of firm opinions.

For a moment Mary thought that Joe Johnston would make a barbed remark about Mr. Davis. But Robert intervened with a quiet word, as he often did, that steered the conversation to a safer subject. As the two men went on, Mary continued to study the interesting newcomer.

After a pause Captain Talcott, with a serious look in his eyes, addressed the man beside him.

"Lieutenant, do you understand the situation at the fort? The Regular Army's in command, of course, but we engineers are unwelcome guests, highly unwelcome."

"Indeed?" Lieutenant Johnston's air, suddenly noncommittal, let Mary know he had heard of the matter, and also that he would have nothing to say about it. She stared from one to the other; neither Robert nor Andrew Talcott had mentioned any of this to her.

Captain Talcott went steadily on. "Yes, the regulars would like to handle the construction themselves, and kick us off. Every time our backs turn, we hear of schemes to get us out." Across the table Robert showed his surprise at his superior's words; and still Joe Johnston sat silent. By now they had finished their food, and Mary got up.

At the door Lieutenant Johnston bowed, exchanged several pleasant remarks with the others, and left. On the way upstairs Mary asked herself what she thought of him. Several things, some contradictory. A man who could charm those around him, then bristle angrily in a second's time—he would certainly not be the easiest of people to get along with. Then she remembered his manner as Captain Talcott spoke, interested yet wary. From a half-forgotten incident came her father's comment on a French army officer who visited them: "A gentleman with an eye on the future." Perhaps she was unfair; she would see.

When they returned to their room she tried to find out more about the conflict which Captain Talcott had mentioned. "Robert, this fight with the Regular Army, why didn't you tell me about it?"

He hesitated. "I didn't want to disturb you."

"I want to be disturbed," Mary broke in, and all her accumulated annoyances rose inside her. "I know I'm awkward, and late with things and careless about money. But to hear outsiders told about affairs that concern me . . ." Close to tears, she stopped.

"Mim, I'm sorry." Robert's arms went around her. "From now on you *will* know." As he continued, she found she could not speak. He meant what he was telling her; she had no doubt of that, and she felt the beginning of a deeper bond between them. For that, at least, she could thank this crowded morning.

"I ought to be going now."

She saw a pulse move in his throat, a sign of fatigue that she had come to recognize. Even before the slave trouble he had been

53

working steadily and without full sleep; only recently had she realized how he drove himself.

"Couldn't they do without you for a few hours?"

He shook his head. "They might, but my responsibility's out there. We've got an outside wall to finish this week."

She should have understood; for Robert life meant, above all, duty, conscience, discipline. No matter what else happened, he would do what lay ahead of him. As she nodded he remembered something and pulled a paper from his pocket.

"Mim, I didn't want to set up your hopes until I got word from Washington City." Tired as he was, his face looked happy. "We'll be able to get back to Arlington for Christmas. I suppose you'd like it?" Robert's smile was a joking one.

In her delight she kissed him again. She would be home once more, if only for a short time. To her, of course, Arlington would always be home. And Christmas was a ceremonial occasion, carried out in the old style by her father. In a flurry of activity she summoned Cassie to the day's routine, airing, scouring of the rooms, wiping of windows. As she arranged the books on Robert's table she heard the girl behind her. "Miss Mary, you ain' feelin' stomach-sick?"

"No." She took up her sewing. "Why?"

"I just wonder' if you pregner yet." Cassie's expression was both shy and curious.

"That's something we have to leave with God," Mary answered. But she also had been wondering; she wanted a baby, a number of them—boys with firm bodies and strong faces like Robert's, and a few girls, a nice minority of them. She remembered her own early years as the only child on the estate; yes, she hoped for more than one child.

A light knock brought her to her feet, and Cassie admitted the bustling Mrs. Jensen. The older woman, plump, pink-blond, tossed off her plaid coat and puffed. "I'm going to town for two days, and thought you'd like me to get you something."

Mary returned the smile of her motherly neighbor, thus far her closest friend at Fort Monroe, and her gaze went to the worn chairs and sofa. "Why, yes. Six or seven yards of damask, a good shade of red—something to cover our furniture."

Mrs. Jensen's eyes widened and her look became a protective one. "I can understand what you mean. But, child, so much material, at today's prices?" All Army wives knew how much the husbands earned. "Why don't you give me a little money and see what I can get with it?"

Guiltily Mary nodded. And she promised herself that she would learn about economy! Her mood deflated again and she stood at the window, dejection in every line. Mrs. Jensen took her arm.

"Mrs. Lee, may an old Army woman say something? The way you're feeling—it's the same with most of us at the start. Don't get impatient, and don't lose heart or hit back because it isn't the way you expected. Wait, and matters will work out. You'll see . . . Well, the carriage is downstairs, and hired by the hour." With a hug, Mrs. Jensen sped off.

Behind her Mary remained at the door, turning over the words in her mind. "Don't get impatient . . . matters will work out." She would try, of course. Then, she reminded herself: They would be going back to Arlington, and for the time nothing mattered except that she would be there again, and have Robert at her side.

When they rode together up the hill on Christmas Day, with a light snow drifting around them, Mary sat slightly forward. Although Robert put his arm around her and pulled her back, she still stared anxiously, willing to miss no detail of the Arlington scene. Behind the screen of powdery flakes the curving landscape lay partly visible, with its clumps of evergreens and the edge of the high hill overlooking the river; somewhere beyond, already lost, was the federal city.

As they approached the house—by now it stood out like a great white toy atop a frosted cake—her heart beat heavily. Then they swung into the circular road behind Arlington, and Salina and old Nurse were looking out and waving to them. The big door opened, and when Robert helped her inside they were greeted by a mixture of aromas—cedars in the corners, spiced sweets, the burning of dozens of candles, eggnog and brandy in bowls. Moving forward, Mary caught glimpses of the pictures along the hall, the doorways to the rooms beyond, and the arched openings. The house had already filled with dozens of people, and out ran the tiny figure of Aunt Maria, to take Mary and then Robert in a breathless embrace.

The group opened and Mrs. Custis stood before them, hands extended. They clung together and Miss Mollie drew Robert to her. "My children," she whispered. "We have you again." Mary was crying softly to herself.

A singsong voice asked, "Does anybody remember me?" Washington Custis' irregular features worked as he bent over Mary; he, too, had come close to tears. "You haven't changed, girl," he murmured, and appeared surprised at the fact, and also grateful to his son-in-law. They were still together when Daniel, the coachman, sidled up, a smoking brand before him. "Time for to light it, sir."

With the gesture of a patriarch Washington Custis strode to the fireplace to set the Christmas log aflame. It was a high moment of his year, and as he leaned down he spoke with fine cheer. "Now I can remember when George Washington himself began Christmas Day . . ." Mary's eyes sought Robert's, and her hand slipped inside his. Yes, she was home.

The holidays over, Mary and Robert went for a series of short calls from which she came back tired but in a happy mood. The change in routine, these meetings with families they had known for years, brought back so much of earlier times, earlier scenes. For nearly two weeks she was able to forget the shadow at the corner of her thoughts, the impending return to the fort. By mid-January, however, she had begun to stare at the calendar. They must be there in another week.

One night she had a dream so vivid that she woke from it. She had been before the columns of Arlington, and on the porch stood her father and mother. Out of the garden walked Robert, not in military uniform but in a light planter's costume; after a moment she understood that Arlington was now his home too. The joy that followed brought her to swift consciousness; she stirred against the pillow, and her hand lifted to touch her husband's face.

Mary opened her eyes to see him looking down quizzically, his dark hair hanging in a tangle over his forehead. His lips went to her cheek, to remain there, and a drowsy content settled over her. Might things work out as she had dreamed? Robert had told her of his hope someday to be a farmer; and she remembered the way Captain Talcott had protested against the frictions at Fort Monroe. Certainly Robert had yet to make a great mark for himself in the Army. . . .

Cassie knocked; they were to leave early for a last visit or two over the Potomac. In spite of her efforts to put it aside, the dream persisted through the morning. The day was gray and overcast. As they went from heated houses to the chill outdoors and back to a warm building, she found her head throbbing, her throat rasping. Robert touched her brow, and immediately ordered the carriage headed toward Arlington.

On the river boat Mary shivered under blasts that roared about them, and pressed her head against his thick coat. At the landing Robert bundled her into the coat and urged Daniel to hurry the horses. When they got back to Arlington Miss Mollie ordered hot waters and medicines. As Mary glanced sleepily at the panorama through the window, she thought of the dreary prospect at the fort. Through waves of half consciousness she heard her mother's voice:

"Couldn't both of you stay a while longer?"

"No, Mother," Robert answered emphatically. "It wouldn't be possible."

"My son, you don't know how much we've missed Mary." The voice faded, then began again. "We've never had her gone so long, and we're lonely here, Robert."

Lying there, Mary could make out only Robert's folded arm; his fingers tensed over the cloth at his elbow.

"Well, she can stay a few weeks more." When he spoke he moved into full view, and Mary's eyes let him understand her appreciation. A few minutes later she had dozed off.

As his departure time approached she sat up in bed to work at her hair. She had chosen her shawl with care, a light brown wool that brightened her eyes. She had something important to say, but at the last moment she could find no words. Frowning good-naturedly, he took her hands. "Don't cry, Mim. It won't be long."

"That's not it." She shook her head. "It's because I'm happy."

He stared, and she told him. "Robert, I'd hoped for this, but I wanted to be sure first."

"Sure of what?" He scratched at his side whiskers with a familiar gesture.

"Robert!" She had an impulse to shake him. "That I'm going to have a baby."

His dark eyes softened, and the gradual smile spread over his face. He kissed her and said something, but his words were lost. "I've been afraid I couldn't." She spoke slowly. "Cassie asked me so often that I began to worry."

Robert's hand restrained her. "We've nothing to fret about now." His last words indicated that he, too, had been worried.

The snows stopped, to be followed by long days of winds that sent slivers of ice sliding from the roof. Her chest troubles continuing, Mary rested for hours at a time, with the Custises hovering around her. They were talking of her health one day when, rubbing at his chin, Washington Custis told her shyly, "We've got to think of that new son of ours."

Mary laughed. "Suppose it's a girl?"

The Major's mild eyes blinked in surprise. "Don't think of such a thing." His wrinkled face brightened. "He has his work cut out for him. Someday he'll own Arlington, as the first-born, you know."

The news touched Mary more than she would have thought possible. She took her father's hand, and they remained in a silence broken only by the settling of the logs in the fireplace. Salina interrupted them finally by coming in to deliver a letter from Robert. There was good news from Fort Monroe.

"Andrew Talcott's getting married, at last." The bride-to-be was Harriet Hackley, a Custis connection. Mary was happy for both of them. In any case, Robert felt that with a child to look after, the Lees would need a larger house and he had already started making inquiries.

Mrs. Custis began to plan the new home. ". . . two sofas, a pair of cupboards, and those chairs in the storeroom." As they talked

58

on and on Mr. Custis laughed. "It sounds already like a twenty-room mansion, crowded in four rooms." His words went unheeded.

February arrived and then March; Robert had located a house, and preparations had started for her arrival. How soon would that be? He wrote lightly that one or two of his notes had been lost on the way, and "despairing of ever hearing from you again," he had considered cutting his throat. Soon the house was finished, and he asked again when she would return.

Now, however, Mrs. Custis became ill, and her recovery took more weeks. Mary had moments of depression; how much she wanted to be with Robert, hearing that low, strong voice, and going to his arms. Still she hated to leave Arlington. As the weeks went by Mary went to occasional parties, seeing relatives, learning again how pleasant this life could be.

Her father sent a note, asking if Robert would mind her staying a little longer. Almost at once Robert wrote her directly and in firm terms: He had several times agreed to an extension of her visit. Now she was due back at the fort, "and I cannot consent to your remaining at Arlington longer at this time."

Mary's astonishment gave way to fury. What did he mean, he could not "consent"—as if she were a chattel, a slave! Her feet tapped over the floor as she started to her desk. There, pen poised, she slowly let her hand fall. She remembered her own longing for him, and also Mrs. Jensen's words at the fort: In the Army things were never managed exactly as one wished; she must learn to wait, and matters would work out.

Quietly Mary replaced the pen. Robert had a right to send her that message. She was his wife, and she had been too long away from him. Her dream that he might somehow give up his career and that they might stay here, locked away from the world . . . It was just that, a dream and a foolish one. The time had come for her to wake up.

Late in the summer, as layers of heat pressed down upon the room, Mary turned heavily on her back. She had never known weather like this, or such wrenching pain. Poised in alarm a few feet away, Cassie touched the shoulder of Mrs. Jensen, who watched with the young Mrs. Talcott and two other women. To Mary all of them looked like strangers, hostile ones.

"Oh . . ." A paralyzing tremor went through her.

Out of the glaring light a man came to her, and she struck at the doctor's hands. In a moment her mood changed to helpless fear. Suppose the baby died, or she did? As her lips moved, she tried to form the words: If she had to give up, let the baby, let *him* live. *Him*. It mustn't be a girl . . .

When someone pressed her arm Mary stared drowsily and tried to focus her eyes on the object placed beside her. A muffled cry rang from a brown-red mouth that made up most of a face the size of her fist. She touched the chin and nose, both already strongly formed, like Robert's.

"Mr. Lee is outside, and the doctor says he can come in now."

Mary looked up. "It's a boy?"

Mrs. Jensen was laughing. "Oh yes. Nobody told you?"

Mary closed her eyes for a moment of happiness, and reopened them. "Let him in. I'm ready."

When he stood at the foot of the bed, Robert stared for a long minute from her to the baby, and she saw a tenderness and a concern that stirred her. The others had left them alone, and the scene dimmed before her as he took a place at her elbow. For the first time she understood how much he had yearned for the child.

"He'll be everything you want," she told her husband. "And so will I, from now on. With my money accounts and appointments, too, and even my bargains!" Still silent, he was kissing her hand, and she rushed on. "And I won't even think about Arlington."

At the last words Robert glanced at her in a surprise tinged with amusement. At that moment a pink hand pushed out of the blanket, rested on Robert's sleeve, and both looked down in growing wonder.

Chapter 5

Standing at the curtained windows of her new quarters, Mary motioned to the other woman that the party on horseback was approaching. Instantly she caught a tremor of excitement behind her; President Andrew Jackson, on an inspection trip of new fortifications, was no ordinary visitor. With Andrew Talcott absent Robert was showing the walls and foundations to the President; and, somewhat to her surprise, General Jackson had accepted her hesitant invitation to stop by their home.

Behind her the helpful Harriet Talcott took the year-and-a-half-old baby, Custis, out of the way. Cassie and the other Negro girl, borrowed from Mrs. Jensen, took their stand near the table of cakes and warm breads. Mary made a quick survey of her rooms. In these days she managed things better. She now followed the habit of making daily lists like her mother's—or at least, as she told herself ironically, she wrote them down.

The past eighteen months had gone well for her; the number of women who came to their home was a demonstration of the fact. She had been "accepted," and she felt much the happier for it. She had come to know practically every woman at the fort, and to like the easy camaraderie, the informality of Army ways. Now and then an act of rudeness or a coarse word startled her, but for the most part she was fitting herself to this changing scene.

As for her husband . . . She frowned. Robert worked, if possible, harder and more conscientiously than ever; but at times, walking unexpectedly into his room at night, she had found him staring glumly at his papers. Though he never referred to the matter, she thought she understood the reason. He had yet to earn his first promotion and he, like Mary, wondered why. Andrew Talcott, his superior, was his good friend, and yet no word arrived from Washington City.

President Jackson and his party were dismounting from their horses in the street below. The President's long face, corroded by time, appeared in the doorway. After him came Robert, calm, earnest, and silent, and suddenly she saw, at Andrew Jackson's elbow and speaking at a furious rate, the mustachioed Joe Johnston. Her hand clenched the handkerchief in her pocket. Why did Robert let the ambitious little fellow outtalk him? She wished her husband would learn to look after his own interests as well as Lieutenant Johnston did.

She forgot everything else as the President and his five or six companions bowed to her. "Mrs. Lee . . ." Andrew Jackson had a kindly manner. "I remember our previous meetings, and happily." He greeted each of the other women and then grinned. "Well, what's here?" Going to the blue-clad Custis, plump and solemn in his chair against the wall, the President snatched him up with a delighted cry. Surprised, the child blinked as Robert explained.

"We call him Boo. He's a long-nosed fellow, like his father, and hardly any beauty."

"Boo." Andrew Jackson cocked his head. "What do you think of this old war horse?"

With a fixed stare of his grave blue eyes Custis reached up to fit his hand neatly over the Presidential nose, and tugged at it. The President howled with delight rather than anger, and Mary remembered the tragedy of Mrs. Jackson's death. As everybody knew, the Jacksons had never had children; she sensed his yearning for them in the way Andrew Jackson hugged Boo.

When the servants brought coffee and food, the President talked quietly with the women and answered their questions. Then, turning around, he addressed Robert. "Lieutenant, I could have used a dozen men like your father in my fighting days. Our country's never produced a better officer."

Mary saw Robert warm to these words; she knew that he would not soon forget them. Andrew Jackson cleared his throat. "And of course I know your brother Harry. Brilliant, for all his misfortunes."

A slow silence settled upon them, and Robert leaned over as if to study his son's features. Mary wanted to reach out to him; only she could understand how painful the matter was.

The President changed the subject. "Lee, you're doing good work here; nobody can say you aren't getting magnificent training, too." With that, Jackson reluctantly surrendered young Custis and went toward the door.

Bowing good-by, Mary felt a glow of satisfaction, heightened as she scanned Robert's face. Such commendation was precisely what he needed, and she would remember Andrew Jackson in her prayers. . . . With varying degrees of enthusiasm the women left until only Harriet Talcott and Mrs. Jensen remained, and now Mary discovered that their reaction did not reflect hers.

"Well, Mr. Jackson meant well enough, but he doesn't realize how the engineers are being pushed around." The young Mrs. Talcott spoke solemnly. "You know what the regulars in Washington would do if they had their way . . ."

As Harriet's words went on Mary felt once again like an overprotected child, exposed suddenly to stern experience. Mrs. Jensen sighed and said little.

Her two friends left, and Mary waved affectionately to them. In the past few months her cousin Harriet had proved herself at every turn. Meeting her again after several years, Mary suffered a twinge as she studied the ripe pink lips, slightly parted, and the statuesque loveliness. She had forgotten that Harriet was such a beauty. Then she had heard Cassie's comment: "Miss Harriet behave' so nice you never think she pretty at all!" Nobody traded less on her charms, and silently Mary had agreed with her maid.

Harriet had assisted her especially in an undertaking which meant a great deal to her—the establishment of classes in religion and reading for Negroes of the fort. This reminded Mary that her students were due now. From her window she made out six or seven of the servants moving toward the house, each bearing instruction books sent over from Arlington.

Some months ago, discovering that no one had thought of religious or any other kind of training at the fort, she had asked several of the Army wives to help her launch such classes, like her mother's at home. For weeks she could get no pupils to join Cassie. One or two women said they needed their servants in their kitchens, and another announced flatly that she "wanted no truck with black education or abolition either."

Mary had tried to speak calmly. "It isn't abolition to tell them about God and help them read and write." A shrug was the only response, and Mary asked herself: Did military life isolate some people so much that they lost touch with everything except Army gossip?

Finally she had managed to enlist this group, and as they took places today she noted their neat costumes and the businesslike way in which they set to work at their chairs before her. Only a few months had been needed for this change. What could be accomplished in a few years?

"Very well. We have a long lesson today." She smiled. "Louis, you start. *Doc-tor,* that's fine. You still want to be one, don't you? You did well with your boy's arm last week. Well, we may manage something about that yet." Her smile had gone; *what* could they do? Her father had helped one of their workers to get medical training; but Mary thought she knew what Louis' owner would say to such a suggestion.

"Now, Cassie. The word is *peas-ant* . . . Oh, well, it means a kind of slave." As she answered, Mary felt certain of one thing: Those women who had sniffed at her efforts could not keep people ignorant simply to have docile servants!

"Now, where is the Mississippi River? . . ."

She was conducting her class a few weeks later when she heard a rap, and Cassie opened the door for Harriet Talcott. Her cousin stood breathless, holding a cape against her throat, and Mary, alarmed, led her into the next room.

"Well, it's happened, the way I said it would!" Close to tears, Harriet handed her a sheet and Mary read it in confusion. The Army itself announced that it had taken over construction work at the fort, and Andrew Talcott had received another assignment. "So they've won just what they wanted." Woebegone, Harriet turned to the window.

64

"Then Robert and I will have to leave too?" Mary's voice was muffled.

"For a while, at least, no. He's going to stay, under Regular Army direction." Harriet's anger broke suddenly. "It will be worse for you, in a way. You're going to be moved out of this house to make way for a Regular Army man, and sent to the 'outer edge.'"

The latter was the derisive term for an exposed and barren spot, without even water facilities. Mary stared in disbelief, and bitterly Harriet anticipated her remark: "Oh, they let people out there take water from our cisterns. By special permission!"

Mary scarcely heard her. After she and Robert had finally made something of this cottage, to have to transfer in the winter to a third place at the fort, a wind-blasted outpost . . . Hadn't a child died out there a year or so earlier? Then she thought of Robert, and the way he must now work under the victorious Regulars. For him, of course, it would be hardest of all.

Mary's eyes lifted slowly to Harriet, and for the first time she realized what it would mean to say good-by to her and to their other friends, the Jensens, the Andings, the Emersons. Sadly she told herself: This was what they had said Army life was like—making friends, losing them, creating a home, only to be shifted overnight.

After Harriet left Mary dismissed her pupils. When the door closed she shut her eyes; no matter what happened, she'd keep right on with those classes! Let them try to stop her. The lock clicked and Robert stood there. His mouth was a thin, tight line, and his skin had a gray tinge. As she went toward him she said, "We'll manage, Robert, anywhere they put us. Anywhere."

He nodded as if he barely heeded her, and lowered himself into the nearest chair. Catching her hand, he held it for a time, and told her: "We were beaten before we started, Mary. The engineers are stepchildren of the Army, ignored, starved . . ."

His words died away, and she grew more and more uneasy; she had never seen Robert so dispirited. Then from outside they heard a stumbling of feet. A man slipped and others pulled him unsteadily on.

His head in his hands, Robert continued, almost to himself. "We're seeing more and more of that. I suppose you can't expect soldiers not to drink occasionally. But there's discontent here, Mim. Is it something in Army life itself, the idleness and sluggishness, the lack of a chance to show what you can do?" A pause, and Mary heard words she had never expected from Robert:

"I've half a mind to quit, the first moment I can!"

Seated beside him, heart pounding, she drew his face to hers. At almost any other time, she would have cried happily at such a statement from her husband. Yet if he left the Army now he would be going in defeat; after several years he had received some praise, a few good words, but not a single promotion. She knew Robert well enough to understand how giving up the game now would affect him.

She heard herself crying to him, "Robert, think of the things the President said about your work—and also your father. If you stay on here, for a while anyway, you'll be finishing what the engineers began. Your own work."

While she argued on, she watched his body relax, his head rise. She had succeeded, and she thought she knew one reason why; she had mentioned Light Horse Harry. With a brightening look Robert nodded, and she got up. "Both of us need some hot coffee." As she poured the dark brew their eyes met, and she felt very close to him.

Even in that moment of apparent victory she was not sure she was altogether right in urging him to stay in the service. At intervals in the years that followed Mary was to wonder about that many times. . . .

The next few months she remembered as a period of acute discomfort, of uncertainty in Robert's work and in many of her own activities. But it was also a time of determination, hers as well as his. Aloofness developed on the part of certain members of the Army command at the fort, and she caught hints of unpleasant whispers against her husband, and also against her because of her class for the slaves. Since Robert went on, so, too, must she; and she did.

She had, however, some bleak hours. A blow fell when the once friendly major, owner of Louis, who had hoped to become a doctor, withdrew the youth from her instruction. Though Louis said little as he told her good-by, his eyes held a cold despair.

66

Afterward Mary sat alone for a long time. There was nothing that she could do, and yet it was hard to forget the episode, or Louis himself.

Late one day Robert brought completely unexpected news: He had been offered a new place as an assistant in the engineers' office in Washington City. "Oh, it will be only temporary," he warned her. "I've never wanted to be tied to a desk. That's not for a young man, you know."

She nodded her head, but her heart was singing within her. However small Robert considered the opportunity in the assignment, they would still be leaving the fort under better circumstances than had seemed likely; and, more important for her, they would be living at Arlington.

The light from the early evening lamp at Mrs. Custis' elbow threw a friendly illumination over the rug, the polished floor, and the andirons before the fireplace. Its reflection gave a glow to the ceiling. These past few months at Arlington had been good ones, and Mary was enjoying them to the fullest. Her own circle, she told herself with a luxurious sigh, was almost complete; Robert would soon be riding in from his office. Within her lay their second child, and from the day she had told Robert she had watched her husband's happiness increase. A new baby . . . By now it had become the main concern of Robert and her family.

The only sounds were the purring of the Custis cats and the click of Mary's needles; and now after a time the soft breathing of the sleepy boy, his pudgy body bunched over his toys. The Major lifted his glasses: "Every time I look at Boo, he's bigger and his clothes have gotten tighter."

Miss Mollie glanced over her own knitting. "I'm afraid his self-will is bigger too. You used to call him a dove; now he's more like a lion." Chuckling with pride, Mr. Custis returned to his records and murmured, "I'll be needing Robert's help with the orders for those fences. Last month he saved me a hundred dollars."

Mary nodded; she missed no signs of Washington Custis' increasing respect for Robert's abilities. She thought how much had happened since Robert proposed to her in the nearby room, in spite of everything her father did to stop him. Now there was a real peace here, the warmth of a family love, quiet and unspoken, yet nevertheless all around them.

Only one personal problem worried her. She had been suffering irregular, puzzling aches in her arms and legs, and she had been unable to walk as quickly as she liked. The doctor appeared mildly concerned about her condition. "Nothing definite to alarm you," he had said, pursing his lips. "Still we'll have to watch a little more carefully from now on." She tried not to think of the matter and generally she succeeded.

At the back of the house the dogs barked, and Mary recognized Robert's step. In a few moments young Custis roused himself, snatched at his father's sleeve and clung to Robert as he sank down on the sofa. "Just a quiet day," Robert told them in a low voice. "Two delegations from Congress—one less than usual, and so we could do our work with fewer interruptions. And, oh yes, letters from Joe Johnston and Andrew Talcott." He seemed dispirited, and Mary asked herself with sudden alarm how much longer he could stay, or would stay, in the engineers' office across the Potomac.

She had her answer from an unexpected source. Salina appeared at the door with a familiar figure, that of the white-haired General Charles Gratiot, head of the Army Engineers. "Ah, my friends!" The short, spry general, a Creole from St. Louis, and a family friend, had a volatile spirit, a warm gallantry, and a pair of very bright eyes. Accepting a seat, he said briskly:

"I know you're asking why I'm here, and I'll tell you. An emergency. You may have heard of the boundary dispute in the Great Lakes section, between Ohio and the new Michigan territory?" Recalling a few newspaper accounts, Mary had a quick foreboding, which increased as she listened. "Unless we settle it, there'll be shootings, riots, worse perhaps. I've asked Captain Talcott to make a full survey"—the fine old head went forward—"and I would like his friend Lieutenant Lee to join him."

As General Gratiot ended Mary saw that Robert was both upset and embarrassed. "I'm flattered," he began, "but you see, it's a matter of time. My wife . . ."

"Hm." The Frenchman had, of course, used his eyes from the beginning. "The work might be over in, say, five or six weeks."

Mary stared at her fingers, twisted in her lap, remembering the doctor's words: "There may be complications. Too early to worry, and still . . ." All at once she realized how much she wanted Robert to be with her when the time arrived for the baby; and she knew, too, how worried she had become. She lifted her head and then discovered her mother standing beside her, one hand on her shoulder.

"I think I know how Mary feels." Mrs. Custis' words were spoken more quickly than usual. "She wouldn't want to keep Robert from taking such an offer. She knows it means a great deal and . . ." Miss Mollie allowed her sentence to remain in the air. The pressure at Mary's shoulder tightened slightly, and she made herself nod her head.

The next month passed slowly. Regret in his fine eyes, General Gratiot rode up with the latest report. Andrew and Robert were doing important work, adjusting differences between the two sides in their findings; and still delays occurred, with several points in bitter contention. The Creole was contrite: "I hope, Madam Lee, it will take only a little longer."

Mary tried not to show him her alarm. General Gratiot could hope, but that would not bring Robert back. The pains in her legs and arms had become more pronounced; the ache seemed to reach to the bone. Robert wrote frequently and in detail, telling her of his work and also his concern over her health. The doctor worked to soothe her, ordering a special diet and hours of rest; he explained that it was a "rheumatic complaint" and would probably ease with the passing of time. She groaned; how much time would have to pass?

Holding young Custis, her mother hovered around her, and at times Mary gave silent thanks for their earnest attention. But that was not enough. With Robert here she would not have felt so helpless, so alone.

When General Gratiot called again she refused to see him; for the present she hated the old man. As soon as he left, she sank despondently against the pillow. The assignment was for Robert's good and she understood that. Nevertheless . . . For the first time she asked herself: Suppose something happened to the baby and it were born dead?

Closing her eyes, Mary tried to reject the thought. That night and on the following nights it returned in dreams of funerals and processions to the cemetery; and always she reached out for Robert, to find his place beside her empty. Another month crawled by, a third, and a fourth began. In her room she lay in bed, conscious of the flurry in the house and the apprehensive efforts of Salina and Nurse to ease things for her.

Then gradually the stress in her limbs lessened, and the birth itself took place with comparative ease. She looked down happily at the girl, dark and strong though smaller than her first-born. For a few days she enjoyed the delight and mystery of the meager form in her arms, basking in the joy of motherhood. Miss Mollie picked the baby's name. It would be another Mary.

General Gratiot arrived with another note from Robert; the survey had ended, and he had already started home. In her excitement she wanted to kiss the gentle fellow, and now she could enjoy the knowledge that she had tried to hold before her through these recent months. Robert's work would make a great difference to his career in the engineering corps.

But late the following week began an attack of pain worse than Mary had ever known, worse than she had ever imagined. She could no longer keep her whimpers to herself, and she heard her father and mother whispering in the hall. At Miss Mollie's insistence the Major sent Daniel for the doctor.

As they waited outside her door, the doctor made another examination. When he pressed at the joints of her hands, she bit her lips to keep from screaming. With a sigh he stood back, hands clasped behind him, rocking slightly from heel to toe.

"This time I want you to tell me everything." Mary had tired of hesitations and evasions, and she wanted the truth. In spite of her determination, however, she was not ready for his slow words:

"Well . . . I would call it primarily a serious rheumatic condition, inflammatory, the kind people get more and more in these modern times." The doctor's manner was kindly. "Chronic, I'd say. Perhaps it started as an accompaniment to childbirth, a pelvic trouble; just how it developed we'll never be sure."

Her heart turned as she listened. "Mrs. Lee, we don't understand a great deal about such cases. Yes, they're influenced somewhat by the state of mind. Those who recover best manage to stay in good spirits, and don't give in to excitements or moods. You'll have to rest steadily and keep on a strict diet—simple foods, fruits. Before long, too, a trip to the springs."

There was more, she felt sure, and now it came. "Mrs. Lee, you'll have to fight this for the rest of your life. Otherwise you may be . . . handicapped."

In her panic her words sounded muffled. "You mean crippled?"

"Not necessarily." The doctor was selecting his words with care. "It depends on you." She understood, and she had a last question: "Does it mean I won't have any more children?" In her anxiety she felt a drop of perspiration slip down the small of her back.

"Again that may depend on the care you give yourself." He would not promise, and only then did she know how fierce was her longing for more of Robert's children. In the silence she heard one of her father's cats clawing lightly at the curtain, and a dim humming from back in the quarters. "Fight . . . the rest of your life."

Alone again on a morning two weeks later, Mary raised her head to survey the road beyond her window, and went back to the task of preparing herself to greet Robert. Dizziness came and went in waves as she tried to hold herself upright. She had lost more than twenty pounds, and under her thin white robe her body seemed shriveled. Nor did she need the mirror to tell her of the purplish blur beneath her eyes and the new semicircular lines at her throat.

In the hand mirror her skin looked the shade of the ivory ribbons at her throat. She put on a layer of powder and another; they would help, but not enough. She felt strangely shy and ashamed to welcome her husband. Breathing heavily, she lifted the comb to her tangled hair. Where had Cassie gone? Her weak call echoed through the empty upper hall. In a fit of helpless anger she raked the comb upward; it snagged in the thick brown hair and she sobbed hysterically. He'd be here almost at once, and what could she do?

71

Beside her on the table Mary spied her mother's scissors. Snatching them up, she snipped at the curls, without realizing what a foolish thing she was doing. Then she started to cry again, as her father called from downstairs. "Robert's riding up the hill!" She pulled on her bedcap as Cassie came in with Custis, a restless figure in starched blue, and her mother carried the new little Mary, pink and pale and docile.

The baby beside her, Mary extended her finger, and the hot, velvetlike hand clamped over it. Already the girl had her nickname, Mee. When she whispered it, the child opened her large black eyes, and Mary felt her tears close again. She looked up and Robert was in the doorway, flushed and smiling.

Mary saw his stare go to her, to the baby, and back to her. "You're—worse, Mim?" In his low voice was all his astonishment and shock. Though she had written him of her illness, she had not prepared him fully.

"I'll be better now. You're what I've needed." She laughed a little, but the sound was hollow.

With an effort he smiled, and felt into his pocket. "Your present from the lake country, my dear." From the rectangular box Mary took out a silver comb, intricately ornamented. Her eyes lowered, her fingers touched her shorn head, and in silence she reached up to tear off her bedcap.

Chapter 6

It was her mother, working cheerfully at her side during the next sixteen months, who kept Mary at her new routine. Unexpectedly it was Robert's sister Ann who gave her the incentive to continue through some of the worst hours. But it was Robert himself who made everything bearable at this time of her testing; Robert, she told herself, who saved her.

Weeks passed before Mary could stir from her bed. Any movement brought a throbbing agony of knee or ankle or both; if she tried to lift her arm the effort ended in sweating frustration. When Robert ventured in one morning, he found her biting at her lips.

As she collapsed against him he held her in silence, then told her softly, "Mim, I'd be willing to take this on myself, if it were possible. But I can't. And you're going to get better; you've got to know that. I've written to the springs, and we'll leave in a week."

"Leave? How can we?" Her head burning, Mary almost screamed at him. "I can't even put my foot on the floor!"

"We *will* go, next Saturday." This was a different Robert, and she was infuriated by the change. Who did he think she was, one of his army workers who jumped when he rapped out orders? She had no chance to say it, for he spoke again. "And, Mim, you're going to walk a little, now."

Her head jerked up in astonishment that he appeared not to notice as he whisked down the covers, threw a shawl over her shoulders, and, his arm around her, lifted her to the floor. "There, madam . . ." His words had a playful note that took some of the sting from her resentment.

"Oh . . ." In her alarm Mary forgot everything else. Though Robert held her, her legs gave way in the torment that ran swiftly upward. "I can't do it!" Her cry broke from tensed lips, and yet somehow she was walking. Through a haze of pain she felt herself in motion. Later she realized that she must have looked like a rag doll held by the shoulders.

Nevertheless she walked. Staring at the mirror, she saw her face, drawn and yellow-white, and Robert's; in his she read a love and also a sadness that altered his features. His cheeks and forehead were wet and red with the strain; in his eyes she recognized his own fear, worse perhaps than her own. She understood what he was asking himself: Would she ever move without help again?

At that her hand, hanging limply over his back, grew rigid. She was going to make her way forward even if she went crashing to the floor. Feeling her own strength, she cried, "Let me go, let me go!"

"Mary, I'm not sure you're ready to try it," he protested. "Not yet."

She pushed him aside and made one step, another and another. Robert stayed near her, advancing as she did. The only sounds in the room were her labored breathing and her small cries as the pains went through her. Once she had to stop; the breath choked in her throat. When Robert's hand went out, she lunged ahead to avoid it. Tottering, she managed to sink into a chair. She could feel the wet strands of shorn hair at the back of her neck, and her legs were moist.

A voice reached them from the doorway. "You *can* do it." Only then did she discover that her mother had been watching for the last few minutes. Mrs. Custis bustled in and handed Mary a glass.

"Now, your medicine, miss, and see that you swallow the last drop. The part that you've been pouring into the flower box hasn't improved the lilies; they don't have rheumatism." Miss Mollie whirled around. "And, Robert, if you're really going next week, you and I have a lot of arranging to do. Beginning this minute."

Already, Mary felt sure, her mother was making up new lists

74

in her mind. Before she led her son-in-law downstairs, Mrs. Custis handed Mary a wide-mouthed jar from which rose a dim lavender scent. With a quickening interest Mary went to work, sinking her hands into the cream and rubbing it into her face and throat.

Yes, she still looked like a crone, a blotched one at that. But this time she was going to do something about it. She pressed the oily stuff into her chin, at the corners of her eyes, working so hard that she scratched one cheek. Momentarily the irritation made her forget her pains, and she laughed. It was the first time she had laughed in months.

At the springs Mary remained for days in her room or on the porch that surrounded their cottage. With Robert or her father nearby she walked steadily, forcing herself forward step by step. She had always enjoyed such places—the informality, visits from cottage to cottage, dinners in the central rooms with dancing that followed. Now she shrank at first from contact with old friends, hesitating to go to the main hall. Then, however, people were seeking her out, stopping at her porch, and in their generous interest she found an unexpected tonic. It was good to know that they felt for her, and also to hear their cheerful talk.

After a time she was able to go with Mrs. Custis to the enclosed waters, where they swam slowly around in loose gowns. On earlier visits to the tree-bordered spring she had thought little of her skill as a swimmer; now she enjoyed the sheer wonder of movement through the warm, clear water. If only it were possible to move so easily on dry ground!

As her spirits improved, she saw Robert's mood was also more cheerful. He brought word that his sister Ann, who lived in Baltimore, might join them if her health permitted. Happily Mary acquiesced; she remembered several earlier meetings with Ann Lee Marshall, whose fragility, close to emaciation, had surprised her at their introduction. She tried to recall the story. Ann had suffered an early and serious infection of the hand or arm; it had been saved only after great effort. For Ann Lee, Robert had always shown a special, protective affection, which Mary could understand.

Mary was now well enough to spend considerable time with her children. One afternoon she found little Mary sitting up, dark and intent, watching Custis as he ran in circles with a toy wagon. At the sight of his mother the boy gave a look that struck her as almost wary, and asked, "Mamma, when you goin' to get sick again?" She had an immediate shock, and then sadly she remembered a remark of Cassie's, that Custis had a far less disciplined time when Mary was in bed. With a sigh she settled beside the pair; she had a great deal to make up for.

The tiny Mee, she quickly discovered, had a growing will of her own. When Mary held out the girl's set of toy furniture, she took the pieces, turned her back, and quickly arranged them in an order that she liked. Mary bent over to help, only to receive a reprimand. "No, Mamma." This one would be no meek miss. Mary stayed beside her, working hard to reacquaint herself with her children.

Going to bed a few hours later, she found that her hours on the floor with Custis and the girl had given her a cold. The doctor had warned her in such cases; promptly she swallowed a hot mixture and extra medicines and let Robert wrap her up. In the morning, waking before Robert, she knew at once that she was in trouble. She could barely move her neck; arms and legs burned with the old pangs and new ones as well. After all her effort, that long and bitter siege, she was back where she had started.

Yawning, Robert turned to see her staring white-lipped ahead of her. "I can't stand this," she whispered. "I might as well be dead." At that moment she meant what she said. She meant it again as she murmured the words several times during the day. Robert and her mother sat near her side, and the hastily recruited doctor frowned and tried to look as if he understood something about her ailments. Later, with young Boo, Washington Custis knocked again to find her alone and in despair, her face to the wall.

"Please . . . Let me alone." At the words her anxious father led Boo away. Mary groaned; such scenes were bad for the child, but what could she do? . . . A few hours later the door reopened, and Mary heard a rustling movement. "Let me see you, my dear." The feminine voice, soft and musical, startled her, yet she remained motionless.

"You can turn, Mary, if you really want to."

With that she recognized Ann Lee Marshall. For a moment the realization that the older woman had come upon her in such a condition brought her close to tears. Then she told herself that she had to respond; her sister-in-law was one of the kindliest people she had ever met. Slowly Mary forced herself up on her side.

The small, gray-haired, gray-garbed Ann bent over to kiss her. "That's better, child." As Ann settled in her chair, Mary saw that Robert's sister appeared even more worn than at their last meeting and that her swollen hand was covered with a bandage. "Oh"— Ann Marshall's bright eyes followed hers—"a relapse of my old condition. It will be gone soon; anyway I don't want to miss the dances they've been telling me about at the springs."

With the last words Ann became less casual, and she went on, so softly that Mary had to strain to catch the words: "I've never talked with you about my—my own trouble, have I? I've been sensitive, but now I'm going to do it. A few years back, you know, I felt just as you do now."

Ann's sensitive face, lightly framed by hair drawn back in a currently unfashionable style, tightened with the memory of her pain. Her eyes looked out with a great deal of Robert's direct candor, and she resumed:

"Mary, they told me the condition of my hand had gotten so bad there was only one thing to do, amputate. The doctor had it settled in his mind: that, or the infection would spread and I'd die. They gave me a day or so to get myself ready for the operation. I wouldn't agree; I made up my mind to fight back, and I did."

Quietly Ann Marshall spoke of massages, exercise, heat applications, ointments. "The arm swelled and turned several colors" —she smiled, her gaze unwavering on Mary's face—"but I kept it. Sometimes I wasn't sure from one day to the next that I hadn't lost. But I still have my hand, and I still have to take precautions."

At the beginning of Ann's remarks Mary had listened with a dull stare; she didn't want to hear about somebody else's difficulties. Now she felt a sharp reproach. Here she lay, pitying herself, whereas Ann, faced with what might have been far worse,

77

had shown a courage that none around her could approach. Inside the small figure in gray, sitting so calmly at her side, was a will that shamed her.

Silently Mary maneuvered her body so that she could push herself up, then lower her feet to the floor. By slow degrees she started forward, and Ann held out a hand to her. "There you are, Mary. There . . ."

The effort was no less difficult than the previous one; in this case, however, Mary knew it could be done, and she knew also the limits of her strength. Again Robert stood at her side, counseling, cheering her when she needed cheering. Unending attention, diet, rest . . . It was almost a matter of mathematics, she decided; each hour of application brought so much in return. She could hardly move with her old speed, and yet she was walking. With a smile she told herself that Robert's expression was a certain barometer of her improvement; and in these days he laughed more and more often.

Ann Marshall, with two young sons in Baltimore, had to leave the springs before them. Preparing to go, she sought out Mary as she sat with the children under a low-limbed tree near their cottage. The silky grass swallowed her footsteps, and she came upon Mary, with the little Mee playing with Boo before her and Robert reading a newspaper a few feet away.

Robert's sister stopped and her gaze went from one to the other and finally to Mary, the dappled sunlight across her face, a slow, musing smile at the corners of her mouth. Slipping into the seat next to her, Ann spoke softly. "Mary, everything is all right now. Next time, if there is a next time, you'll be prepared——"

Mary looked up to thank Ann and say good-by to her. In these weeks she had come more and more to respect her sister-in-law, and she hoped someday to be with her for a much longer period. This visit to the springs had meant a great deal in Mary's life.

By the time their party returned to Arlington, the worst of her pains had gone. She had regained much of her old roundness of cheek and her color, and though lines continued at the corners of her mouth, they were faint. And a few weeks later she discovered that her instinctive fear of the previous summer had been needless. They would have their third baby, and the doctor told her:

78

"No need to worry, if you keep on caring for yourself. In fact, in some cases pregnancy brings a temporary improvement of rheumatism. Why, we're not sure. . . ."

But suppose she had to go through another black siege. Yet Robert's response to the news was so automatic and so joyous that she could not allow herself these fears. Both of them wanted the new child, and it was simply her duty to watch her health.

At home she sighed with the heightened appreciation of one back from exile. She felt still better when General Gratiot, meeting her by chance on a short trip to Washington City, whispered word for which she had been waiting a long time: Second Lieutenant Lee would now be First Lieutenant. With burning excitement she started back to Arlington, and only after a few minutes had passed did she remind herself: It had taken Robert about six years to make this small advance. How long would it be before the next?

On Connecticut Avenue her carriage ran into a maze of vehicles, stationary for several squares. At that Mary became aware of a figure in pale green waving vigorously to her from another vehicle. Claudia McBride, for the first time in several years . . . She called a greeting, and promptly regretted it. With her first words Claudia let Mary know how little she had changed. "My dear, it's been so long," she cried across the space between them. "What ever *became* of you and Robert?"

Claudia's smile revealed still more of her many teeth, and the braided ash-blond head bobbed up and down. "Let's see, by now he must be Colonel Lee, at least!"

Bristling, Mary dropped back in her seat and drew the curtain. The malicious words rankled. A few weeks later she remembered them again when, after putting the children to bed, she found Washington Custis reading a newspaper dispatch from Texas. Dropping the paper, her father faced Robert. "They're doing great things down there, my boy. A new country, with only the skies to limit it!"

Robert's look brightened. "Yes, it's a place a man could put his heart into. More chances than you'll ever get here; anybody with an eye to the future would start there now." Beneath the warmth in his voice there was an undertone of dissatisfaction. "That fellow Sam Houston—everybody's talking about him. He's had some erratic times, but nobody will ever forget *him*."

Mary turned her head. Those six or seven years ago Mr. Houston had stood over there, almost in Robert's place; had she responded to him when he called, she might be in Texas today under the new republic. As her father sat enigmatically silent, his small eyes half closed, she wondered if he thought she had made a mistake.

Well, she hadn't. She took up her knitting with trembling hands. Someday they'd see how well Robert would do, what a role he would make for himself. Sam Houston had had bad years, years of failure and even scandal; then practically overnight he had become the military personage, the statesman. Just let Robert——

"Mary." Her mother's glance probed deeply. "Don't rush so much. It exhausts me just to watch you." Mary looked up at Robert. His hands had dropped loosely to his sides, and he was frowning at the floor. At her glance he got up abruptly and went to the window. Mary followed him. "What is it, dear?"

The swiftness of her question startled him, and he hesitated. "This whole—situation, Mim. Other Army men are out doing things while I fight red tape in a cubbyhole. I've watched good assignments go to one, then another. Mary, I'm twenty-nine, and practically a clerk." After a pause he went on.

"You know how Andrew Talcott's felt about the things that have happened to him. He's quit, to start out in private engineering."

"After fifteen years!" She blinked; it was hard to believe. I can't think of Andrew as anything except an Army man."

"Nor can I. Still, Mim, big changes are happening over the country—canals, railroads, internal improvements. Andrew says new engineering companies are the real prospect ahead of us. Traveling down the lakes and rivers, extending the lines, pushing to the West . . ."

At these words Mary heard no more. Suppose Robert went dashing in every direction like that. So far they had been together or at least near one another. At her expression Robert reached out and took her hands. "We'll see, Mim. We don't have to decide right off, do we?" He smiled, but she could see the lines of unhappiness in his face.

Spring arrived with bursts of irregular brilliance about Miss Mollie's spreading gardens. The new baby was due within a month; occasionally Mary felt the old pains in her legs, yet nothing that approached the earlier spells of inflammation. As she rested on the sofa one night Mary read an increasing tension in Robert's half-turned face. Going to the window, he stared across the lawn, seeing nothing of the scene before him in the moonlight; his fingers drummed steadily at the sill.

"Please tell me what it is?"

Robert turned to face her. "Nothing. Nothing, really."

She continued to look at him in silence. One of his dark eyebrows lifted still higher than the other; he shrugged. "I don't think it's the time to talk about it."

"Look, didn't you agree once to tell me things?"

After a heavy silence the words came at last. "General Gratiot's sending an engineer to St. Louis. The Mississippi's been acting badly, building up sand bars along the shore, and the town may be shut off as a river port." Glints of light began to brighten his eyes. "Whoever goes will have a lot of authority to carry out a real project."

"And you can have it if you say yes?"

He nodded slowly. "But, Mary, there's the matter of the children, and you and your health. St. Louis is a long way off, hard travel by land and water. They say it's pretty primitive, not the place for any of you."

There was a dull hurt inside her, like the pressure of a hand against her heart. He had never gone so far away, and for so indefinite a stay; she would be sending him from her children and herself. But this time she did not need her mother at her elbow to say what had to be said.

Her voice was low and tense. "You're not going to give this up for us, Robert. Go alone, at least at the start. Please, tell the general you'll take it, before he changes his mind! Or don't you really want it?"

He spoke with difficulty, half in pain, half in relief. "I do want it, Mim."

In the rose-hung arbor of her mother's garden Mary ran again through several of Robert's letters. He had found St. Louis grimy, his work slow and hampered by a score of impediments. Nevertheless the prospect fascinated him. It was a more challenging task than he had anticipated, in a general terrain of sweeping plains and forests. He had made a long trip to explore upriver rapids, sleeping now in a log cabin, again on a shaky steamboat. She shuddered at the image of his privations, but her eyes glistened with tears when she read:

Tell the Boo I have closely inspected all the little boys on my journey, and have looked long and wistfully to see if any were like him. It was all in vain, and my feelings each time were sadder than before . . . Now that the anxiety and excitement of the journey are over, my thoughts return more forcibly and longingly to all at dear Arlington . . . I dream of you and the dear little children nearly every night, and our last romp together was a race on the hill, in which the little woman flew like a gazelle and far outran the Boo. Even I had some difficulty in keeping pace with her . . .

Had she needed any reassurance as to how much he loved them? Her eyes went to young Custis, rolling on the grass with a cousin, while the sturdy Mary, Robert's "little woman," set out in search of blossoms for a necklace. And, bending over the cradle that had been passed on from child to child, and its present occupant, the three-month-old "Rooney," she thought of the day, shortly before his departure, when Robert saw the new baby for the first time.

"Well." He had pretended to make a scientific appraisal. "Another long-nosed one, and hair as black as an Indian's. That big mouth—do you think it will ever close?" That same day they had picked a name, William Fitzhugh Lee, for Mary's uncle who had freed his slaves. She mused: Let God give the boy something of the integrity of that courageous man . . . She smiled. Within a few hours William Fitzhugh had acquired his nickname of Rooney and now nobody called him anything else.

"Oh, Miss Mary!" Cassie's voice startled her out of her dream. "Master Boo won' stop fightin'." Mary dropped the letter, rushed over to the fray, and separated Custis from his much-subdued victim. She felt a sharp pain; did she imagine it or did she suffer these twinges only when she felt disturbed? She stumbled back to her chair, and picked up Robert's letter again:

Our little boy seems to have among his friends the reputation of being hard to manage—a distinction not at all desirable, as it indicates self-will and obstinacy. Perhaps these are qualities which he really possesses, and he may have a better right to them than I am willing to acknowledge; but it is our duty, if possible, to counteract them and assist him to bring them under his control . . . You must assist me . . . and combine the mildness and forbearance of the mother with the sternness and, perhaps, unreasonableness of their father . . . I pray God to watch over and direct our efforts in guarding our dear little son, that we may bring him up in the way he should go . . . Oh, what pleasure I lose in being separated from my children.

His words about young Custis depressed her. Robert had been gentle and ironic, and yet how seriously he had considered the matter. Perhaps she and the admiring grandparents had spoiled the boy; she must try to improve her discipline. Her depression gave way to longing as she read Robert's words about their separation. He felt it as badly as she did, or worse, for he was among strangers. Her need for him was all but a physical thing. She corrected herself; it was that, too.

In these days the gentle General Gratiot came on frequent visits to Arlington, to tell her of Robert's progress and also to chat with her father. Watching the two older men as they sat together one night, talking on and on without regard to anyone else, Mary realized how similar they were. Even their ideas were alike. Each man had a rare good will toward the world, and at the same time a high degree of individuality so that, though some people criticized them for being visionaries, they did not care.

One night her breath caught when the white-haired chief of engineers informed her with a smile: "I think you may expect a certain lieutenant for a visit by Christmas. Ah, only a few weeks!" The fine wrinkles multiplied in the pink face. "Isn't that better than nothing?"

It was a great deal better than nothing, Mary told him with gratitude.

83

Through the long November days it was impossible for Mary to keep her mind on anything except Robert's impending arrival. When she greeted the continuing procession of sight-seers at Arlington, her mind would wander and, more often than not, the visitors would have to shift for themselves. But November passed and there was no further news of Robert. Arrangements began for the holidays. As December advanced her hopes declined. It appeared that Robert had still not left, and now he could hardly make it in time.

Mee contracted a deep chest cold, and doctors advised several weeks in her room and heavy dosages of medicine. With this new concern Mary remained continually with the children. Two days before the great holiday the household went early to bed, more or less resigned to Christmas without Robert. Still Mary could not convince herself that he would not be here. And when she at last fell asleep, she dreamed he was very close.

Hours later she woke with a start, aware of a disturbance below. Daniel's muffled voice reached her and at once she understood. As she approached the landing, her gown flowing behind her, Robert ran up, three steps at a time.

"Robert, I'd practically given up." It was all she could say.

"I almost did too." Then he was kissing her; she touched his cheek, his hair, and her arms tightened around him. After a time she became slowly aware of the others. Beside his smiling grandparents stood Custis: "You got any bearskins, any Indian scalps?" For the boy his father was now a symbol of Western adventure.

Young Mee, small legs apart, awaited her father's embrace. As he gave it they heard a cry from Rooney's bed and Mary led her husband forward. She took the child and Robert reached out to cup the downy head in his hands. The eyes, blinking at the light, regarded him curiously, as if asking who the peculiar stranger might be. Mary's hand caught her husband's and they looked at one another. Their faces sought the light and Mary could see that Robert's eyes were shining.

During the first days of his leave at Arlington it almost seemed to Mary that Robert was as far away as if he were still in St. Louis. He spoke of nothing else but his labors on the Mississippi:

84

"Mim, the more I see of the assignment, the happier I am that I took it. To help save St. Louis—it's the biggest thing I've ever done."

At first she shared his delight, until he added with a meaningful glance, "I was a fool even to think of leaving the service. This is my life, Mary. The Army." She nodded with less certainty. He sounded so final; he had closed, at least for some time, the chance that he might be with them in one way or another at Arlington. Yet she could not put aside her hope that eventually they would live together again in this house. As the days went by he became increasingly absorbed in the children and she felt that the life of Arlington was slowly bringing his thoughts back from the lonely wastes of the Mississippi.

Late one afternoon she looked up to find Robert entering the sitting room with a small, slim companion whom she did not immediately recognize. Then she cried, "Joe Johnston!" Her pleasure brightened her eyes. "It must be the civilian dress that confused me. I think somebody told me you'd married, but I hadn't expected quite so much of a change."

Robert's friend flushed to the top of his balding head, as if she had implied something discreditable, and she reminded herself that Joe was unusually sensitive. His reply was strained and defensive. "You see, there simply isn't much future in the Army. It took me nearly seven years to get even a first lieutenancy."

"That's all I've gotten so far." Robert gave a wry grin. "Less than a year ago, Joe, I felt exactly as you do. Now, though . . ." As he told them of his work in St. Louis Mary saw the change in Robert's face, the flush of excitement that she knew so well. Joe Johnston listened intently. "As fine as that," he shook his head, "and you're still in the service!" Did his voice have a suggestion of envy?

"What are you doing now?" Mary inquired.

"Baltimore and Ohio Railroad. My father-in-law, Louis McLane, is president, and we're connecting the Atlantic with the West." Mary nodded; it sounded like quite an enterprise, and how lucky Joe was. To be sure, that had been a most fortunate marriage to the daughter of a man who had been Andrew Jackson's Secretary of State. Promptly she checked herself; she mustn't go on thinking like a rival Army wife, or like Claudia McBride!

At that moment Custis ran into the room and stared slyly at the visitor. Johnston smiled at him and his lean face was transformed; his eyes had a tender light such as Mary had never seen there. "He's one of three," she explained. "I suppose you have some of your own, Joe."

The trim figure turned and the voice was low. "No. No children." From the tone of his voice Mary could tell that for the Johnstons there would be none. Her earlier resentment faded and in its place she felt an instant pity, a feeling which remained with her as the two men resumed their discussion of Army affairs . . . As he spoke she realized that Joe's tone was pensive, almost restless and unhappy. In spite of his civilian standing, the man yearned for the service, she was sure. There was some lingering sadness about him, as if he had a secret longing for something unattainable. The thought depressed her.

Their guest left for Washington City soon afterward. As they saw him disappearing down the path, a small, almost forlorn figure, Robert said sadly, "I hope things work out for Joe, any way he wants them."

There was a certain tension in his manner as they turned to join the Custises at dinner. Whenever he held down the corners of his mouth as he did now, Robert had something on his mind. She did not have long to wait. As soon as grace was said, he lifted his head and quietly addressed the family, with his eyes upon the older couple. "I've been thinking, and it seems to me that Mary and the children ought to go back to St. Louis with me." He took up his fork, and turned to her, his voice a whisper. "If she agrees."

Mary looked at her mother's face and saw that it was flushed. Miss Mollie's voice trembled. "Oh, Robert, it's such a journey— more than a month, and those hardships. Days and nights on steamboats and stages, for Mary, with her rheumatism, and the smallest ones . . ." Mrs. Custis' words fell away. Her husband nodded his agreement.

Robert was staring down at his plate, and now Mary's heart contracted. She recalled his stories of terrible crowding in St.

Louis and epidemics in the town that was still hardly more than a frontier settlement. She would be giving up the help of all the Arlington house servants, involved in one way or another in the care of the children; there would be no special rooms for their play, no family doctor nearby for emergency calls.

Opposite her little Mary, her eyes on her elders, was swallowing with some difficulty; and she recalled the girl's continuing weakness. Perhaps, considering everything . . .

At that Mary's back stiffened. She had grown altogether too much accustomed to the servants and the comforts of Arlington; she had to make herself less dependent again, learn to care for her own household. She turned to her father and mother. "It's going to be hard on the children, but I think I should go."

Robert's grateful look was her immediate reward. But after it came a dizzying sensation, a kind of afteremotion such as she had known when, as a child, she jumped across a deep ditch and glanced fearfully back. Having completed the act, she wondered how she had achieved it.

"What about Mee?" Hesitantly Miss Mollie faced them.

"Well . . ." Mary's heart lost a beat, and she sat silent until Robert answered, "She's nearly three." He swallowed and went on. "And since she's been sick, it mightn't be good to take her. Mother, don't you think we ought to leave her here for a while, till things are better settled?" It had required a great effort for him to say it, Mary knew, and she felt the hurt as he spoke. And he was right; there was no other course.

As she looked from one silent face to another Mary realized that she had reached a turning point in her life, that this decision was a crucial one. She felt neither triumph nor a sense of defeat, only a physical weakness.

The weeks flew by in a flurry of preparations. There was so much to be done and so little time to think that it was not until she and Robert were in the carriage, watching young Mary waving plaintively from her grandfather's arms, that the separation became real. From the porch she saw the girl's hand make a limp circle, then fall.

She burst into tears. But Robert's hands held her shoulders and his husky voice came to her. "Please, Mim, don't . . . It

87

won't help." He gave a signal, the carriage started off, and Mary, head lowered, would not let herself look back until they were out of sight of the figures on the portico.

After that she turned, and her last clear view was of the great rounded columns in the morning light. It had an element of consolation. No matter what happened Arlington's pillars would be there against storm and sun, wind and chance.

PART II

"Life is indeed gliding away, and I have nothing of good to show for mine that is past."

ROBERT E. LEE TO MARY CUSTIS LEE

Chapter 7

"Look out there, lady!"

A whip cracked through the heavy afternoon air; the wagon behind the team of sweat-lathered dray horses sank into the molasseslike brown mud of the St. Louis street, and rolled out with a sucking sound. As it did, a spray of earth splattered Mary's red velvet dress from hem to belted waist, and another splashed the face of her maid, Kitty. Cassie had been needed at Arlington, and Kitty had taken her place.

"Oh, Miss Mary . . ." she whimpered. For the past six months practically everything Kitty met in the robust, overcrowded river city left her amazed or ready to cry or both. This time Mary consoled her almost automatically. "Hush, now," and handed the girl a handkerchief while she hastily wiped her own dress. "It's just a little muddier than usual. And a bit noisier."

Five or six grimy peddlers stood on a single corner, roaring and waving tinware and cloth. Brassy music echoed from a tavern, from which an Indian wearing green trousers and two feathers in his felt hat stumbled out in a rum-soaked fog. A pair of French trappers strode by, their costumes leather-fringed, impressive pelts thrown over their shoulders. A small gentleman in a bright-checked suit leaned against a siding, his hands in his pockets and a huge cigar in his mouth. A river boat gambler, she understood.

The wheels of carts, wagons, and carriages, with a lumbering ox wagon at the end, clattered over the partly cobbled street. It was a strange town. When she had first arrived and struggled against lack of comfort, soaring prices, and the memory of her little girl and family in Virginia, she had feared and hated it as Kitty did now. But as the months passed and she had learned more and more about the place, she had found herself liking it and its spirit.

A cart swung by; several women in gingham, with flapping poke bonnets, waved their hands. Looking about, Mary realized that they were hailing her, and she returned the salute. This was an America such as she had never known, with none of the settled quality, the leisured manner of the East and South; at St. Louis the new West had burst its seams. Some of her friends would call it a brash place, but she had come to accept it.

The trip had been a series of privations, smoke-filled steamer cabins, jolting stage rides, upset stomachs for the children, and her own intermittent throbbing pains. Breaking the journey at several points, they had stayed first with Ann and William Marshall, and Mary had renewed her friendship with the soft-voiced sister-in-law and her husband, a scholarly attorney; Custis and Rooney had played with the two Marshall boys. When they left, the affectionate smaller son had wept at losing them, and Mary promised: "We'll be back." Again she reminded herself that someday they would spend a long time with the Marshalls. . . .

"Oh, Miz Lee, wait for me!" The shrill summons from across the street made her stop. Once she might have been repelled; now, recognizing the round red face and rounder red hairdress of her neighbor, Mrs. Worth, she thought instead of that first cold morning in St. Louis, when she turned in confusion from the screaming Rooney to the older Custis, sullen and ridden with a cold.

They had been lucky enough to find a large, stately brick house on First and Vine Streets which they shared with the Beaumonts. But on that day nothing had gone properly. Robert had left early for his work on the river. The fire would not start, they could locate no crockery, and a shelf crashed, spilling their single bottle of milk. Standing in the center of the room, ready to weep, Mary heard a heavy knock, and Mrs. Worth was there, beaming a welcome.

The tiny green eyes, half swallowed in plump flesh, had taken everything in at once. "You poor thing," she boomed. "I know all about it. When I got here from Tinnissee, we hunted two days before we even got a room, and I felt so bad I almost hit Mr. Worth!"

The flour merchant's wife took over at once. She dispatched Kitty for another kind of firewood, plunged her hands into the grate and made it work, called to her daughter for a substitute bottle of milk, and eased Mary and Kitty into the kitchen to help them prepare breakfast. And later the rough kindness did not diminish, and it was to Mrs. Worth that Mary owed much of the comparatively easy settlement in St. Louis. The friendship strenthened over the weeks. Today Mrs. Worth was frantically waving a newspaper and as Mary came closer she saw her face was even redder than usual.

"Child, I suppose you've heard about this. Your Bobby Lee is the man of the hour here!" She thrust the paper into Mary's hand and pointed to a long article. Mary read: "St. Louis citizens had adopted extended resolutions praising Robert Lee for vast skill, enterprise, energy . . ." The St. Louisans were insisting the government let nothing interfere with a swift prosecution of the work. She flushed.

"It's—it's certainly good news" was all she managed to bring out. "Look over there," Mrs. Worth said, "and you'll see why we're all worked up." Mary's eyes widened at a towering steamboat; its twin funnels and white filigreed woodwork were closer than she had ever seen a vessel at this point.

"*He* did it." Mrs. Worth placed her large hands on her hips. "Two years ago boats were going aground right out there, one after the other, and nobody knew when things weren't going to get still worse. I heard people say St. Louis would be left high and dry. Now he's made the river scour in there and cut away its sand bars, just as if he dug it out with his hand." Mrs. Worth added, "My husband says he's cracking his whip, and the river's jumping like he says!"

Mary looked toward Bloody Island, a wide, thickly grown impediment in the middle of the Mississippi and a smaller, similar obstruction closer to the levee. From the first island a long dike extended to the opposite, Illinois shore, turning the main current of the river toward St. Louis; at the other end of Bloody Island

93

she made out the beginning of a second dam, to help the water along in the same direction.

"You see?" Mrs. Worth was as triumphant as if she herself had conceived the scheme. "The old river's tearing out its own sand." Mary saw. Robert was showing them exactly what he could do, letting them know how good an engineer he was. It was almost worth those years of disappointment to hear this! She must hurry home to talk over the news. She was almost running as she approached the cool, whitewashed Creole building, the new Lee home. Inside she found the two boys playing on the floor, and Robert himself, coatless and bent over his desk.

"Hereafter, Miss Mary," he said as he kissed her, "you'll have to be more respectful of your husband." He held an official note, and his face had a look of boyish pride.

It was a commission that made him captain of engineers. Her hand trembled as she caught his arm. "I knew it would come; it had to."

He patted her cheek. "Leave it to you, Mim, and I'll soon be a general."

Fondly she shook her head. "Why laugh? I don't see any reason why you won't be one." But Robert's smile faded.

"We'll take that as it comes. There's more to worry about here and now. I'm not sure everything's working out with the river plans." He bit at the edge of his lip. "The Mississippi can be a treacherous enemy, Mim. Every few days something happens that we hadn't expected. It may build a new bar at a point no one ever expected, and then overnight we lose a whole month's work. It's acting badly at one end of Bloody Island now; that's why I'm here early. They're going to pick me up at three-thirty in the morning."

Mary tried to hide her disappointment; even on an occasion like this, when others might celebrate, Robert's conscience made him plunge again into work. A resentful impulse took hold of her. Why wasn't anything ever completely right?

But there was no time for such thoughts with the children clattering from the next room. "Steamboat, steamboat!" shouted Custis, now six and large for his age. With pride Mary watched her two boys clambering up the stairs.

Under Robert's firm management their behavior had already improved a great deal. Rooney was the cheerful one, eyes crinkling at the corners when she approached, his laughter ringing across the street. Custis, or Boo, had acquired a more stoic air and harder fists, which he used, alas, too often.

And little Mary? The image pained her. She did not realize that her thoughts could be read in her expression until Robert went to her, and put his arm around her.

"I know what's on your mind, Mim. I hadn't realized it would take so long to get the work in full swing. But I still hope we can get back for Christmas, if only for a little while."

As often as she could manage it, Mary stopped by the waterfront to inspect the barges from which loads of heavy rock and brush were dropped between rows of piling, to form dikes to hold the current. Seeing the broken rock sink quickly under the surface, she sometimes shuddered; how could anything they did keep this monster of a river under control?

Robert had other matters to concern him. In spite of the petitions from St. Louis, Congress failed to provide full appropriations, delayed, then held up funds. And on her husband's face, Mary saw the doubt giving way to despair. "Mary, we haven't done half of what's needed. Everything may be thrown away!"

What could she say? She put her hand in his, and they sat silently together for a long time. The situation looked hopeless. She was closer to this river work than to anything Robert had ever done, and she knew what it would mean to him to meet failure now, when he had had this first great success . . . Long after he had gone to sleep she lay awake beside him, and when she fell into a restless slumber she dreamed that she and Robert had walked proudly into a great gathering, a ballroom with flags hung from the ceilings and soldiers in gleaming costumes. General Gratiot himself lifted a glass in toast, and hundreds joined in honoring her husband. Then somehow the scene altered and she and Robert waited outside the same hall; she could make out men and women talking gaily, ignoring them. A sentry barred them at the door; Robert drew back, but she knocked at the french windows as if in a frenzy. Yet no one answered and still the crowd looked past her. When she awoke, she found she was shivering.

Late in the afternoon on the following day, as she was putting the children to bed, Robert rushed in to her. "We're moving ahead *without* Congress, starting tomorrow!" The light danced in his eyes. "The St. Louis people have gathered all the money they can lay hands on, and they want me to keep up the supervision. Mim, the fight's going right on."

There was a pause. Mary realized that Robert had something more to tell her and that he hesitated to do it. In the hall mirror she made out his anxious features.

"Mim." Suddenly she knew what he had to say. "Mim, with all the delays, the work schedule's far behind. Now, no matter how hard we push things, we can't get through in time."

"You mean we won't be able to make the trip to Arlington for Christmas." She felt a slow chill.

"No. A few weeks later, though, if things turn out well." Robert's eyes dropped, as if he were to blame.

"A few weeks won't matter," Mary whispered, squeezing his arm, and she tried to make herself believe what she said. Without speaking they went upstairs to look at the two boys in bed. In the light of the corner lamp Robert put his hand on Rooney's wide, moist forehead. She stood in the shadow. How could she tell Robert the message she received that day? Little Mary, confident of their return, was asking God in her prayers to make the holidays come sooner . . . Seven months had passed since they had left the child. Sighing, Mary left the room.

That evening she woke to an insistent knock from below. Dog-tired, Robert for once did not hear the sound. Throwing on her robe, she went to the door.

"Mrs. Lee, I'm sorry. Could I talk to the captain?" She recognized the French-accented voice of General Gratiot's brother, who lived in St. Louis. Robert, coming behind her, called out anxiously, "I'll be right with you." His words did not conceal his alarm, which quickly communicated itself to Mary. Had something happened on the river?

Returning to the bedroom, she listened through the partly opened door to a sentence or two, and sat upright on the edge of her bed. This was an entirely new matter, involving General Gratiot alone.

"It's not a lot of money, and the general says every bit of it's rightly due him, even more—commissions, allowances." Mr. Gratiot spoke in agitation. "But they brought it up suddenly, and the Treasury wouldn't accept his explanation and now the President's had him removed. Dismissed in an hour and blackened, blackened. And there'll be court charges against him, too." The Creole's composure broke.

Her heart beating heavily, Mary caught the volume of Robert's anger as he tried to defend his old friend and comfort the distraught brother. "Why, they've accepted those allowances over and over again! He may have been a bit informal in his bookkeeping. Still, a man with his years of service, his war record . . . If anybody ever gave the government more than he was paid for, it's been the general!"

Mary was close to tears. She recalled Charles Gratiot's almost paternal concern with their welfare, his acts of kindly interest. And suddenly her mind went to her own father, so like the old Frenchman, easygoing, goodhearted, in a way that some more practical men did not understand. When at last Robert rejoined her his face was white.

"Mim." His voice was flat. "I think I'd feel this less if I'd heard he was dead."

Knowing her husband, she well understood that it might be better to die than to live on with a blot on his name. Robert sat down heavily on the side of the bed. "Somebody had a grudge and built this case against him . . . No wonder a lot of decent men don't want to serve their country!"

If this could happen to the general, it might also happen to Robert Lee. Suppose an opponent found it in his interest to point the finger of accusation at Robert? She thought of Arlington and the contrast of life of the planter. One day, perhaps . . . She would never give up the hope.

It was a sad Christmas. Before a small tree they exchanged gifts, gave carefully wrapped presents to the two boys and to Kitty, paid calls on the Gratiots, the Worths, and other friends.

Mary made herself smile over the greetings, but throughout the day she told herself: At this hour at Arlington the family would be standing before the big fire; then the flaming pudding would be wheeled in; and Mee, what had she said and done when she realized they would not be with her?

That week Mrs. Custis' latest letter carried news of special interest. Cassie had been accumulating her savings, and as they knew, when a slave showed he could care for himself, the Major frequently liberated him. Now Cassie had met a free man of color who wanted to marry her and take her to New York. What did Mary and Robert think?

She passed the note to Robert. "Cassie's had her training— along with me," she smiled. "Do you remember the missing plates, the cakes that fell, and the omelettes that wouldn't rise?" Mary would always have a friendly affection for the plump and cheerful maid . . . They did not have to discuss the matter; Mary wrote a quick note of assent, and all of them, she suspected, would feel the better for it.

Taking her letter, Robert left with a tender look. "You know how much I respect the Major for things like this, don't you?" At his words, so gentle in their praise of her father, Mary was deeply touched. How fortunate she was that matters between the two men had worked out so well. They might have ended as hateful enemies, after that early difference; instead each had fitted himself to the other's ways.

Robert did not get in that night until long after she had gone to sleep, and during the two weeks that followed he labored with relentless energy, missing more meals, losing rest and weight. Mary had never seen him apply himself so doggedly. From time to time she complained: "Robert, you're overdoing things. Why, your coat hangs like a sack; you practically rattle around in it."

Though she kept her tone light, she felt a genuine fear as she traced the deep lines under his eyes and at the side of his nose. His response was a smile, a grunt, and then he left to answer an emergency call. As she stared out the window at the chill river and the file of vessels on which Robert's forces worked, she cursed the Mississippi as an enemy. She was still frowning when

Mrs. Worth entered with a hearty cry, to surprise her into an admission of her mood.

"Why, child, that poor man of yours is working against time itself." The eyes, like round green berries, held fond concern. "If you start home before the January freezes, you can make it by way of the rivers. If not, I don't see how you could ever do it on land—whole weeks longer, especially with those young ones. Could you?"

Mary understood, and now she began to study the calendar and the weather reports and also, on visits to Robert's office in a warehouse near the levee, the piles of records that showed the progress of his operations. Seven or eight days went by and late one afternoon she made another trip to his headquarters. A glance at the mounds of papers told her he had completed his main tasks, and she sat happily beside him. Intercepting her glance, he nodded his head. "Yes, they're done. But look over there."

Taking her to the uncurtained window, he pointed toward the Mississippi. Against the early dusk she made out a few irregular gray lumps, bobbing as they floated past the levee. "The freezes have started on the upper rivers, Mim." His voice had a note of sorrow. "For the boys the trip just wouldn't be possible."

When Mary tried to speak the words caught in her throat. So they must wait at least until spring. And then . . . Her eyes met Robert's, and read his thoughts. The baby was due in mid-June; how could she make any such journey, which was difficult enough under the best of circumstances?

With an effort she got up. "I'll manage it. You just couldn't keep me from taking that trip." At her solemn look he nodded, and yet she knew he doubted her words. Well, he'd find out, she assured herself; he'd find out.

Waking the next morning, Mary had a terrifying sensation in her legs; the rheumatic twinges had returned! Gingerly she shifted to the side so that she did not disturb him and, staying in bed on the pretext of a headache, succeeded in hiding the signs of her ailment. As soon as Robert had left the house she sent Kitty for the doctor who had been caring for the boys.

"Madam, these relapses do occur. Yes, I would judge it the identical trouble. This damp climate may help induce it, of course." She gave him a blank stare, and then smiled grimly. One more reason to leave St. Louis!

She took the drug he left her and limped to the next room to begin her treatment. She rested for a few hours, sent Kitty after additional items for her diet, and tried to dispel the rising hysteria that pressed upon her.

At Robert's first glance that evening Mary realized she could not hope to hide her suffering. When he approached her, deep concern in his eyes, she started to cry, but at the same time she called out, "It's nothing. It will really pass quickly, and I'm warning you—I'll still go back in the spring!" He said nothing, but tenderly helped her to the sofa. His silence seemed to her a sign that he accepted her helplessness. She would make him see he was wrong; she would make all of them see . . .

During the weeks that followed, now optimistically, now gloomily, Mary struggled against her condition; and by slow degrees she improved. For several days at a time she found herself unable to walk, and then for hours she pushed her way across the room, from chair to sofa, sofa to table. Robert's face cleared as he saw her steady gains.

By now, of course, she felt awkward for another reason. The time for the new baby approached, and she had to stay more or less indoors, studying the gray landscape, the leafless trees, the whirling of papers in blasts from the river. As the winter ice began to thaw, she sat nervously at the window, waiting, sewing, waiting. It had been nearly a year since they left Arlington; would these last weeks never end?

Another shadow passed over them. General Gratiot had been called to St. Louis to face charges in the matter of the government funds, and on a gusty March day Mary went to the Gratiot home to await his arrival. On such an occasion what could she say to any of them? After a few halting words she remained silent. Long afterward she could trace to herself the dark blue pattern of the curtains and hear the slow tick of the clock in the overheated, gaslit room.

The two, Robert and the general, arrived together. Her husband's face had a gaunt look, as if he were the accused man, while the general smiled broadly. "So you're all here to welcome the prodigal!" In another man the sentiment might have sounded bitter; the white-haired Creole gave it a suggestion of gaiety.

The general took Mary's hands. "Madame, though we've met under happier circumstances, you've never been handsomer." His eyes had the same brightness that she had seen many times at Arlington.

He himself brought up the subject that was on all their minds. "Well, my friends, they can't delay the case any longer." He opened his pink palms. "Robert's been with me to see the attorney." To this her husband added quickly and apologetically, "The whole affair will work out for the general, of course."

Charles Gratiot nodded, but now his eyes darkened and a look of deep sadness came over his face. Mary realized that, whatever the courts ruled, the damage had been done to his reputation. Uneasily she wondered what he would do.

The general answered her unspoken question. "You know, I've put in applications with several bureaus in Washington City. Oh"—he read the surprise around him—"for a clerkship." Mary saw the fresh shock and pity in the eyes of the Gratiot relatives; she had already heard that the impulsive old soldier had saved almost nothing. A clerkship for one who had held his rank . . . The time arrived for them to leave, and as the general escorted them to the door, she heard his fervent whisper to Robert. "Thank you. Thank you, *mon ami.*"

From his words, and the sudden droop of his shoulders, Mary sensed that few others had come forward in Charles Gratiot's behalf. While Robert signaled for a passing carriage she murmured, "There'll be people in Washington who won't like the way you've acted today."

Robert looked at her sharply. "I'm sure of that, Mary; and I'm going to the courthouse with him again next week." When Robert took his place beside her, she bent over to kiss his cheek; she felt prouder of her husband than if all Missouri had assembled to shout his name.

The journey to Virginia by steamer and stage lasted almost two weeks. During the long week on the water, and in the rocking ride that followed, Mary had to fight several times to keep back her cries of fright and pain. She remembered the earnest warnings behind her: A bad fall, a sudden alarm could be disastrous to her. Once, badly jostled, she feared the worst; again a twist of rheumatic pain deep in her legs sent her into an apprehensive sweat. The trip seemed endless.

At Wheeling, as they stepped upon land, Robert's grip tightened on her arm. "Mary, it's the Old Dominion, our Virginia." His eyes filled, and she realized again how much their home state meant to her husband. He too had liked the West of St. Louis and the Mississippi; yet it had not been Virginia . . . In the bland spring air the dogwood had broken into irregular ribbons of bloom, unrolling to the horizon. Until now she had never understood the simple loveliness of this western region of the state.

It was already night when the stage rattled through the capital. As they swept by in the darkness the familiar city never looked so beautiful, as if it were on display. At last they crossed the Potomac, swung slowly up the hill, and Arlington's columns rose in the pale light out of the frame of greenery. Across the moon-whitened steps moved a woman and a man, a smaller figure between them.

"Robert, help me down!" Mary cried, but before he could do so, the Custises were holding the excited girl up to her. And Mary gathered to her the child she had not seen for so long. As the girl's fingers tightened inside hers, she could only think: This separation must never happen again, with any of the children; and she promised it would not.

It was arranged that she remain with the two boys at Arlington for the arrival of the baby. As for Robert, the spring work at St. Louis must begin at once, and only a short ten days after their arrival he rode off again over the long route across the country. A month later a tiny, protesting girl cried in Mary's arms, and she named her Ann Carter Lee, for Robert's mother. When she looked up in the afternoon of that same day, she saw little Mary hovering in the doorway, and beckoned her in.

The child entered the bedroom slowly, stared at the infant in Mary's arms, and asked, "The next time you go away, you leave *her* home and take *me?*"

Chapter 8

When, long afterward, she tried to recall many of the details of the next few years, they ran together in an uncertain progression. For one season after another, moving between St. Louis and Arlington, Robert hardly knew where he would be stationed; and Mary assured herself wryly that she remembered the days mainly for two reasons: the problems that developed, and the new babies. (The two, to be sure, were not necessarily related.)

Before one of his trips to Missouri, Mary told him that their fifth child was on the way. Robert's face brightened, and he rubbed at his long chin; she saw the slow widening of his lips, the beginning of his smile. "The Lord has a bountiful hand with these blessings. Still, I wonder if this one mightn't have waited a bit longer." She, too, had worried about the additional expense. Now she shrugged away her misgivings; the Lord would help provide.

Again it was a girl, placid and composed; they picked the name of Agnes and nicknamed her "Wig." Sitting beside the child as she began to walk, Robert looked from Mary to Agnes and back again. "She'll be a handsome one, Mim, but no handsomer than her mother."

His dark eyes held a loving admiration, and Mary's glance lifted to the mirror; by this time she realized she was one of those women who would be more attractive in later years than in her youth. During this interlude her health improved a great deal, and her face softened; the fuller cheeks took emphasis from her chin and nose, and her manner was warmer, happier. Across the room Mrs. Custis and the Major smiled as if they too understood. For the Custises, Mary told herself, these years were happy ones; they had her and the children with them, and sometimes Robert as well.

Robert had done a great deal for St. Louis, and St. Louis had done a great deal for him. He had shown everybody, including himself, how he could handle a hard problem. What would be next for him? As before, they could only wait and see.

She counted the time of his frequent absences by his letters.

You do not know how much I have missed you and the children, my dear Mary. To be alone in a crowd is very solitary. In the woods I feel sympathy with the trees and birds, in whose company I take delight, but I experience no pleasure in a strange crowd . . . If I could only get a squeeze at that little fellow turning up his sweet mouth . . .

And again:

I think their visit has been of some benefit to the country, as I see now a finer class of children than formerly . . . A few evenings since, feeling . . . out of sorts, I got on a horse and took a ride . . . I saw a number of little girls all dressed up in their white frocks and pantelets, their hair plaited and tied up with ribbons, running and chasing each other . . . I counted twenty-three nearly the same size . . . I do not think the eldest exceeded seven or eight years old. It was the prettiest sight I have seen in the West, and perhaps in my life.

She put the letter away. He felt "alone in a crowd"; all his sadness and all his love for them spoke from the pages. And what of the feelings of those at home? Sitting at her knee, young Mee asked, "When's Papa going to visit us again?" The question hurt; the children should not be thinking of Robert simply as a caller in his own home. Yet how could they help but think that? His trips were now so short and so uncertain that she could hardly uproot herself and the children to follow him.

Taking Mee with her, she rejoined her two other little girls in the playroom. Since her return she had worked hard to reassure young Mary, to regain her affection; she had, she thought, succeeded. But this oldest of their daughters still surprised her with her independence, her self-reliance.

"Mamma, Mamma!" It was the two-year-old Annie, blond, lean almost to fragility and thus far the weakest. Perhaps because of the child's thinness, or perhaps because she bore the name of his mother, Robert showed Annie a special affection; whenever he came home, his eyes followed the child about the room . . . As for the youngest, the pale-eyed, quiet Agnes, Mary knew by now that Robert had been right in his prediction; Agnes would be the beauty of the family.

Drawing the younger ones close to her, she glanced around at the beloved walls with her father's oil paintings of George Washington, the faces of the President and his wife and other Custises. They were like friends, old and understanding; Arlington itself seemed a friend, ever open to her, ever receptive.

"Miss Mary, this just come."

It was Salina. The housekeeper laughed; she had recognized Robert's handwriting, and understood why Mary fairly ripped the letter apart in her eagerness.

"It's good news, Salina. Captain Lee is on his way home."

On the afternoon of Robert's arrival, seated, elbows on the window sill, Mary watched her husband and her eldest son taking a walk over the snow-covered grounds. The boy had fallen behind his father, and as he walked he seemed to be stepping very deliberately in Robert's footprints. She laughed. How like a father and son.

But when they had returned from their walk, and Custis had gone to rejoin the other children in the nursery, Robert said, "Mim, hereafter I'll have to walk very straight. That fellow's already following in my tracks." He did not smile; for Robert this was a solemn moment.

Sleeping heavily that evening, Mary heard nothing of a muffled knock and whisper shortly before five o'clock. Robert touched her shoulder. "Mim, Mim—something important." To her startled eyes, his face had the color of the dawn. "It's a note from our brother Marshall. Their younger boy—he's been crushed to death, and Ann's almost out of her mind. He'd like me to be there." Trying to regain his control, Robert looked away and reached for his clothes with trembling hands.

For a moment Mary could not believe the bitter news. To lose a child under any circumstances, but in that way . . . She remembered the bright boy and the way he had cried when they left Baltimore on their trip to the West. She had promised to bring Custis and Rooney back again.

How could this have happened to one of the most selfless of women, the one person who, ailing herself, had brought Mary back to health at the springs? It was a strange world.

After Robert's departure the household waited in an agony of fear and silence. At last he returned, gaunt and weary. He allowed Mrs. Custis to draw him to the table, but he ate little as he explained in a broken voice: "The boy had asked Ann if he could go out, and promised to keep his coat buttoned and stay on the sidewalk." Robert put aside his plate; he could not eat.

"Hardly five minutes later the bell rang, and six or seven men stood there. It was a loaded dray . . . When Ann looked down, she wouldn't have recognized the child except for the coat." Robert bent his head. "William has been afraid to leave her alone; for a while she didn't even know who I was. Now at last she's improving."

As he went on, the words came more easily. Unable to leave Ann, Mr. Marshall had asked him to take the small coffin to Ravensworth, Aunt Maria Fitzhugh's estate, to be buried beside his and Ann's mother. "This has been an unhappy week," Robert murmured. "It has stirred a great many memories." Mary took his hand, and without a word led him upstairs. The thought plagued her: How could she have taken the blow that Ann had received?

Later that week, while she worked at her easel, Robert came in with such an alert and changed air that she dropped her paintbrush. "Yes, it's news," he smiled. "First, I ran on the trail of a friend, Joe Johnston. Did you know he's gone into the Army again? Gave up railroading, and now he's fighting Indians in Florida."

Sitting beside her, he continued. "They want me to take over the reinforcement of the forts in New York harbor. The work may go on for several years." He watched for her reaction.

"A good assignment?" Any Army wife would ask the same question.

Robert's eyes were bright. "Yes, I'd think so. They're overhauling the port's defenses, and of course it would be an important place to defend if we get into another war." Before he finished Mary had dropped the cover over her easel. "How soon do they want us? Whatever it means, I'm ready."

She had reason to remember these words when they were settled at Fort Hamilton in Brooklyn, and she faced the inadequacy of the living arrangements. The house itself was little better than a hut; she had seen better shacks along the muddy stretches of the St. Louis waterfront.

"When it's painted it will be nicer." Robert's half-guilty reply to her look of despair made Mary force a smile. It was hardly his fault. It was her problem to solve and she realized she now faced a new test of her self-command. But no sooner had she arranged the tiny rooms to her satisfaction—no small task with five children underfoot—than a bulletin arrived. The Army needed the quarters, and the Lees would have to find other housing outside the fort.

She took Robert's arm in a stammering fury. "Why, why—after the way we've struggled over this hovel! Doesn't that count for anything?"

Robert reddened. "In this case, my dear, I'm afraid it counts for nothing whatever."

As Mary glared around her, each improvement she had made stood out like a reproach. Yet by now she should have accustomed herself to Army ways . . . She checked her anger. "Well, we'll simply have to find another place." It took several days before they located one—a buff-yellow wooden building with yard and barn; while not large, it had more space than the other house.

After the problems of moving a husband, children, and six roomfuls of furniture were over and the family was located almost comfortably, Mary brought up the subject of buying a small carriage, the first of their own since the marriage. "We have such distances to go, it will be cheaper than hiring a hack." Saying it,

Mary tried to convince herself that she was not extravagant. After some coaxing, Robert agreed. They rode to church in a certain grandeur after that. And although she dared not admit it to herself, Mary's spirits brightened.

But while life in Brooklyn became almost pleasant for Mary, her problems with the children grew. Custis had taken on an ever more quarrelsome manner toward the good-natured Rooney, and the others as well. Was it jealousy, because the others received more attention? She had seen the boy scowl at the younger brother and fight over his toys. But when she tried to talk with Custis on the subject he sulked. She could be certain only that he had reached a difficult stage. Often, sensing trouble among the children, Robert would leave the room to quiet them, saying with a shake of his head, "Mim, our brood has learned everything except how to obey."

But however difficult the children were, she felt pleased that she was to have another. This pregnancy was easier than the others. Her rheumatic troubles, though they flared up on occasion, were now quiescent . . . Thus far, three girls to two boys . . . She suspected that Robert hoped, as she did, for another boy. If prayers helped, it would be one.

"The prayers did it, Robert." Mary's face was luminous when the doctor let him see her on that October night of 1843. Robert peered at the small squealing shape before him and chuckled. "Just like his father, Mary—big nose, big mouth, everything but side whiskers!"

When she told him the name she had chosen, Robert Edward Lee, Jr., his eyes filled. "Thank you, Mim," he whispered. "You could have picked any number of better ones." But he had been profoundly touched.

Their life entered a placid stage; Mary met fewer of the Army wives than in other places, if only because the children required more and more of her time.

Occasionally she and Robert crossed into New York, to ride up part of the astonishing length of Broadway, to stand before the new four- and five-storied buildings and stare at the fantastic parade of people on the broad avenues. A great deal of her life, she realized, was now spent among those whom some Southerners would call "Yankees." She liked their brisk manner, their clipped speech.

Often, as they explored this strange new city, they saw large gangs of free laborers in the streets. There was something almost lighthearted in the way they worked. When she mentioned this to Robert, he looked hard at her. "A great deal of that is because they *are* free, my dear." Years later she was to remember the remark.

Returning from one of those long walks one day, they heard a shrill shriek coming from the children's room. "Miss Mary, Mister Robert, come quick!"

They found Kitty, her eyes big in fright, beside young Annie. On the floor lay a pair of scissors, and a line of blood ran from the child's eye. "I told 'er not to touch them . . ." Robert took the child in his arms, inspected her closely, and gave her to Mary. "Mim, don't let her touch the eye. I'm going for the doctor."

The door slammed, and for Mary the next few minutes were an agonized blur; in her sleep she would hear Annie's cry: "Mamma, it hurts bad," and her own answer: "Please, baby, it won't be long." The blood ran faster; to her horror the eyeball was now covered. It seemed hours before Robert returned with the doctor. They watched him work silently over the child. After nearly a half hour he turned to them, and Mary asked the question in a whisper. The doctor delayed his reply. "We can't tell yet; it's too early." Sitting at Annie's bedside that night, Mary could not check her bitterness. To have it happen to this least robust of their six children . . . At least, if it had been one of the boys, his physical appearance might not matter so much.

When the bandages were removed the damage could not be mistaken; with the other eye covered Annie made out only a haze. The doctor nodded. "Madam, I still wouldn't give up hope."

"You *wouldn't!*" Mary's voice cracked. If Annie were his child, the gentleman might not be so glib. She was about to tell him so, but she caught Robert's pained glance, and she was silent. How could she make it up to Annie for the thing that had happened?

Robert's love for the girl, too, increased. He stayed closer to

Annie in her play. On his arrival in the evening his eyes sought her first of all. Neither mentioned it, but both knew that this child would always have from them a special affection.

One evening, as they sat down to dinner, she noticed a large, official document in Robert's pocket. Following her eyes, he flushed. "They'd like me to spend a few weeks at West Point, on a commission handling examinations. No great feat, but . . ."

"But recognition?"

"Of a sort." He nodded, not without pride, and to her came a flash of memory, of the day Sam Houston called; he had gone to West Point for an official inspection, and Robert had been one of the upperclassmen who passed before him. Now her husband would go there in a similar role. The knowledge meant more to her than he could guess. He left a few days later.

Although Robert was too shy to admit it, he enjoyed this experience. "After work we had some pleasant evenings—old friends and a few new ones," he told her when he returned. He listed several names, then added, "And General Winfield Scott."

Mary stared. For a captain the commanding officer of the American Army was surely someone unusual to sit around with! Robert smiled. "What are you laughing about?" she asked.

He lifted an eyebrow. "Oh, some of the stories they told about the old general. He's certainly a—well, an *individual*. Nobody ever charged him with false modesty, either. You know, Mim, he can't stand to lose any game, including whist. They say he once came out badly at it, and solemnly said to the other player, 'Do you understand what happened? It was just because I got up to spit, and lost track!' "

Her father had spoken often of the general. Half of Washington snickered over his strutting manners, his almost naïve boastfulness. She did not like the thought of the pompous old man. Robert read her thoughts. "Yes, and I'm sure a lot of those other tales are true, Mim. Still, nobody can say he isn't a fine soldier." Mary simply shrugged her shoulders.

If she had expected any immediate change in her husband's rank to result from his meeting with the commanding general of the Army, she was disappointed; the months went slowly by and they heard nothing. Soon she forgot about a possible promotion, for she had a more personal concern. After nearly two years of waiting she found herself pregnant again. At first Robert pretended chagrin, and with a smile she read his joking note to her mother: "Upon my word, if this thing goes on so regularly, I shall in good time equal King Priam." Nevertheless she understood well that the prospect pleased him.

Then, as she sat at her window, her eyes on the softly streaked sky, her mind went to less happy matters. For weeks she had detected signs of restlessness in Robert's manner; even with their children he would often become distracted. His thoughts seemed elsewhere. One day before dusk, in the middle of a discussion of his current work at Staten Island, one which involved the duller aspects of engineering work, she put her hand gently on his shoulder.

"Do you really like this assignment?"

In the silence a coal settled suddenly in the grate; he paused, and she had her answer. "It has its value," he conceded, "but there aren't any great construction problems here, Mim. A man, though, has responsibilities to think about." Here was the closest to a complaint that she had heard him make in years, and she felt its full effect. If Robert had fewer obligations at home, might he be striking out now in a more forthright fashion? The suggestion was disconcerting.

Before she could answer there was a knock at the door. "One of my assistants, to talk about a new contract," Robert explained, and Mary left the two men alone. The walls of the Brooklyn house had not been built to muffle voices, and as she knitted, Mary caught some of the conversation. She paid scant attention until she heard: "Sir, you think we're in for a war this time?"

"Well . . ." Robert seemed to weigh the question. "We've had trouble in Texas before, without real fighting. And we've certainly been playing the bully with Mexico."

For some weeks she had been reading occasional newspaper stories and accounts of Congressional debates over Texas; after further arguments it would be part of the Union, she supposed. Why a war, then? As patiently as she could she waited for their guest to leave; by the time Robert had closed the door she was standing near him. "Tell me about it, please!"

With a deliberate gesture he tried to calm her. "Mary, there's been talk about troop movements to the border and Mexican countermeasures, but nobody actually knows. There may not be anything to worry about." For hours after she went to bed, however, she lay thinking of the men's words. If war developed, how would it involve them? As she turned restlessly in the dark, Robert's arm went out to her and finally she slept.

That week and the next Robert brought reassuring news; the flare-ups had ended. And with a lighter heart she began to make preparations for their Christmas visit to Arlington. With Kitty she took several trips into New York to buy outfits for the six children. On a sharp November day, returning from one of these trips, she was barely out of the carriage when she saw one of Robert's helpers running toward her: "Miss Lee! Now don't you worry. It's just—" Jim's forehead was beaded with perspiration— "just that Master Rooney went to the hayloft, and that straw cutter you warned him about——"

She shook the man. "For God's sake, what happened?"

The rest came slowly. "It's his left hand. All but cut off one finger below the nail, the other at the top. At the horspital the doctor sewed the tips back on . . ."

Rooney, the child who was always so good humored, so easygoing . . . Mary disappeared inside, to discover the pale Rooney sitting alone in a bleak and frightened silence. "Ma'am, he bled like fury and we had to wait a long time for the doctor. But he stood it just like his father would've done." For Jim that was praise indeed.

A harsh self-reproach seized Mary. The second such accident, and she herself was to blame. If she had been less indulgent with them . . . Suddenly she recalled her thought at the time of Annie's eye injury: Had that been one of the boys, it might not have mattered so much. Was she being punished?

For a week Robert and Mary sat nightly beside the boy's bed, to make sure he did not disturb the bandaged hand. After several weeks the ends of Rooney's fingers seemed to be growing back, but an ominous coloration at the finger tips set in, and, as the doctor concluded, there was nothing to be done but to amputate the tips.

The boy's plight made Mary think again of her tragic sister-in-law, who had suffered so much more than she had. When Rooney was well enough to move about, Robert made a short trip to Baltimore and returned to report that Ann was still ill and it would be a long time before she recovered. "Still, she has consolation in that older boy," Robert said. "He's bigger than ever, and he'll be entering West Point soon."

Mary bent her head. Her own were growing up, ever more quickly. For several years she had taught them herself, with the help of occasional tutors. Now the fourteen-year-old Custis was going to a nearby academy, and before long Rooney would join him. Time indeed had passed . . . .

It was at Arlington, once more with Robert absent, that the new baby was born, a girl whom she named Mildred. When she was able to sit up again the doctor told her she would have no more. Lying there, considering his words sadly, she heard her mother say almost in a whisper, "Mary, you've been lucky." Miss Mollie was sitting at the other end of the room, her face in a shaft of lamplight from the table beside her. Mary looked at her. The lines around Mrs. Custis' mouth, suddenly lax and tired, had a sadness that her daughter had seldom seen there; and Mary remembered that of Miss Mollie's four, only she herself had survived. Yes, she was fortunate.

For some reason, perhaps because she had recently been reading one of Joe Johnston's frequent letters, she thought suddenly of their old friend's look of yearning on the day he met the young Lees, and the way he had let her understand that he and his wife would have none. How lucky she had been! She had had this seventh one before she was thirty-nine.

It was several weeks after Mildred's birth that the dark news of a Mexican crisis reached Arlington. Her father called out from his newspaper, "There's shooting along the Rio Grande, between Zachary Taylor and the Mexicans. Down in Alexandria they say the President's sure to call for war!" The Major's face was pale.

Mary tightened her hold upon the sleeping baby. During the past weeks she had heard more talk of war, but she had shut her mind from it, clinging to her recollection of Robert's soothing comment. "There's nothing to worry about." But now she could not lock out her fears. Perhaps they would not take engineers. Yet she knew that hope was vain. Each day callers brought fresh word of feverish developments over the Potomac.

"Ten thousand volunteers, twenty . . ."

"General Taylor can handle it alone. You'll see."

"They'll need General Scott yet. It's only politics that's keeping him out . . ."

Through it all Mary remained silent, as in a dream, waiting only for Robert to come to confirm either her hopes or fears. It was almost the first question she asked him when he returned, some weeks after the declaration of war.

"Why, yes, Mim. I want them to take me, and I expect them to." He frowned. "Don't you see? The Army educated me, trained me for service, and that's where my place is now, just as my father's was."

A wave of fury swept over her. "Why, simply because one set of fools shot at one another in that foreign place, do tens of thousands of people have to risk their lives, their hopes and futures? Why do *you* have to protect *them*? You said yourself this country had acted a braggart's part in the whole affair!"

He took her hand in his. "I'm afraid we can't think about that now. We're in the war, and we have to fight it and let the history books settle the point."

From his serene face Mary realized that her husband meant exactly what he said, that he had long ago made his decision. With a sense of defeat she looked away, and he spoke in a saddened voice. "Also, Mary, you have to understand this. Any real advancement in the Army will go to the men who prove themselves in Mexico. For the rest they'll repair walls and pile up stones the rest of their days."

All the frustrations of the past year were reflected in these bitter words. She remembered the way his eyes had dulled over unending routine. Might that be the story of his life, the end of his career? Against every inclination of her own, she tried to tell herself she was willing to see him leave. And when his call to service arrived a week later, she had accepted the situation.

On the day before he was to leave Robert announced to her that he had made his will. He had given an equal share to each child, with an additional amount for the handicapped Annie. And he provided for the freedom of the last few slaves left by his mother . . . Though the time before his departure was short, Robert had been anxious to take care of this matter that had often concerned him.

On a bright day, a day of cooling winds and softly drifting clouds, she waved good-by to him from the upstairs window, then went to her room and shut the door. She stood for a long time with hands clasped around one of the bedposts, crying as she had not cried even during these last unhappy weeks.

Chapter 9

Robert wrote frequently, and from his letters, Mary could follow almost every movement of the engineers. They had dug roads across the Mexican hills, thrown bridges over the rivers and entered one village after another. Beyond San Antonio de Bexar, town of the Alamo, the Americans made pontoon crossings of the Rio Grande, to press on with little opposition past adobe huts, ornate churches, and cactus flats, with the glory of silver mountain ranges against the skies.

In June, eight months after his departure, Robert had been transferred from Zachary Taylor's army to the newly arrived forces of the commanding general, Winfield Scott. Mary's father had heard that General Scott had specifically asked for Robert's services. So, after all, Robert's chance meeting with the general at West Point had later repercussions.

But to Mary the news of Robert's transfer had an ominous note, for the *Intelligencer* just last week had reported that Taylor's army was to be shunted aside, and Scott's was to bear the main burden of the war—and the hazards. Once, strolling in the garden, Mary had overheard two of her male cousins, who had been visiting the Custises, discussing her husband.

"All that talk about Robert. I always think of him as just an engineer, and no soldier at all."

She caught an ironic chuckle. "He's never seen any real fighting. Never fired a bullet in a skirmish!"

Mary's annoyance gave way to fury. How unfair they were, and how mean. It wasn't Robert's fault that his work had not taken him to the Indian borders or that there had been no wars since he entered the service. Yet perhaps he did lack something of the soldier's spirit, the love of violence and bloody skirmishings that was demanded of the military man. Perhaps he had too much consideration for others, too much understanding. . . .

Her thoughts shocked her; she felt somehow disloyal. But, once conscious of the possibility, she could not forget it.

Later that month word came that Winfield Scott had chosen Robert as a member of his general staff, his "little cabinet," and that they were advancing toward the enemy's principal army. It was a partial answer to Robert's detractors, and still not one that would make her happy. And her messages to him, she discovered with a sick heart, frequently went astray. Mary read and reread his last one:

. . . I understand many letters have been received but as usual *not* one for me from any source. God grant that you are all well, but oh, it would be such a comfort to me to know it. How are those dear children? If I could press them all to me now, I would give up all Mexico. . . .

He had dreamed that one of the children lay beside him, but waked to find his arms empty. Her eyes blurred. He must not feel they weren't thinking of him every day and every hour; she thrust aside her sewing and her other duties to write a reassuring message. In the letters from Robert that followed there was word of old friends. Joe Johnston was with Robert at the front, and the two men managed to see one another often. Sometimes the news was sad. Joe's nephew fell in battle, and their friend had broken down at the news; the boy had been almost a son to the childless man.

There were other casualties. Captain Williams of the engineers, a nephew of Mr. Custis and one of their old friends, had been mortally wounded. Mary shook her head; Captain Williams' wife had died only three years earlier, leaving several growing children. So many deaths, so much sorrow . . . Mary wrote the young Williamses, asking them to come for a long visit at Arlington.

The Williamses came early in July—the handsome "Markie"

(for Martha), and the round-faced boy, Orton. Markie, dark-eyed and dignified beyond her years, had a certain solemnity, and her eyes went sadly from one to the other. The girl's lip trembled, and Mary saw that her hand held Orton's protectively.

Mary's arms opened, and in a moment Markie was sobbing on her shoulder. She patted the girl's head, drawing her fingers through the lightly wrapped brown hair. "Things will be all right, I promise," she whispered. She was remembering the way Markie, then in her teens, had taken over the care of her two brothers after her mother's death. Lawrence, the elder brother, had gone with other relatives. Now the girl must assume the responsibilities of the second parent. At that moment Mary decided she would do anything she could to ease the Williamses' burden.

Later in the day, when Markie assembled the three youngest girls, Mildred, Agnes, and Annie, she realized that the new arrival would be a real help to her. Markie settled them deftly in place, opened their books, and launched them into a lesson. Mary could go back to her other household chores.

A few hours after their arrival the sturdy, broad-shouldered Orton, Markie's younger brother, announced breathlessly, "I just had a ride on one of the ponies in the stable." Mary noticed that he held an apple pastry, obviously a gift of the cook. Already, she assured herself in amusement, Orton was winning his own good will. The boy had an unmistakable charm.

"Cousin Mary," Orton went on, "Papa once predicted that Captain Lee was going to be a great soldier—and we'd all be talking about him someday."

Could the boy have said anything that would have delighted her more? She was interrupted by the sound of her father's footsteps down the stairs. She followed him and as he summoned the coachman he said, "There are a lot of rumors of new battles, and I thought I'd go down to the war office and ask." Mr. Custis could not disguise his apprehensiveness.

"We'll both ask." She gathered her coat, shawl, and hat. During the journey across the river into Washington City neither spoke, but each knew the dread in the other's heart. Inside the faded brick building that housed the engineers her father spoke to the officer at the door, and she watched the man look from one to the other with an odd, knowing way. He excused himself, and her mouth went suddenly dry.

Was it what she thought? Captain Williams, Joe Johnston's nephew, and so many others . . . Dear God, let nothing happen to Robert. The colonel's door opened, and her fear increased to terror. "Mrs. Lee and Mr. Custis?" The colonel smiled. "My congratulations! We've had a victory, a real victory at Cerro Gordo, and Captain Lee's shown himself a brilliant officer. Volunteered for a dangerous assignment, risked his life; and General Scott— I've never known him to write such things about anybody!"

And she had hoped only to learn that he still lived . . . Mary sank into a chair. The colonel went on. The Americans had discovered the enemy entrenched in the mountains, practically impregnable behind heights that bristled with guns. "Captain Lee went on reconnaissance, working over the treacherous ground to locate a passage. Then he got back, after going for many hours without sleep, and guided our forces all around the enemy flanks. One slip and they'd have been butchered, every man of them."

And then he added, "We've reason to expect he'll be brevetted major."

Her heart had been pounding so hard she was unprepared for this last. She longed to be home so that she could absorb this astonishing information by herself.

More months of tension passed and Mary tried to keep her mind occupied with the children; she resumed her painting, then dropped the brushes after a series of vain efforts. Markie Williams alternated between weeks at Arlington and visits to other relatives, and Mary found the warmhearted girl a great help. But though she forced herself to keep busy, she could think only of the distant battlefields and Robert's danger. She started nervously whenever one of the children cried, and woke at night to clench her hands.

The old sensations of warmth and pain in her legs and hands returned, the most pronounced she had known in several years. She reproached herself; she must not get sick now, she must not. She saw the doctor and started a fresh system of walks, better diet, and, in his words, "a calmer attitude." If only that remedy were as easy as the prescription! Still she had to follow orders, and she did.

Toward the end of September, Robert wrote her that during a skirmish he heard a cry and found a ragged little girl. She pointed to her bugler brother, half conscious on the ground, his arm smashed. A dying soldier had collapsed on the boy, who lay trapped and helpless. Robert stopped to make sure that both victims received immediate medical care.

Her plaintive note of *"Mil gracias, señor,"* as I had the dying man lifted off the boy and had both carried to the hospital, still lingers in my ear.

She remembered his love of children; the experience must have hurt Robert, as it hurt her now.

Again the capital city rang with rumors; something important was happening, one of the decisive battles of the war. For more than a week Mary spent nights without sleeping, fighting against the throbbings of fear and of physical pain. On one of those long nights, after Mary had retired early to her room, she answered an impatient knock at the door to find her father and young Orton Williams standing in the hall. The Major could barely get the words out fast enough:

"Mary, Mary! I met the War Department's man in Alexandria, with a message. Robert's done more than ever; he scouted through a dangerous lava field and led our men for thirty-six hours through rain and dark. And—and three generals praised him for his daring, and they're brevetting him again, as a colonel!"

The tears that welled up were those of happiness, almost of exultation. Then she saw a hint of uncertainty in Orton's face, and her eyes went to her father. He had the same uncertain look, and then he told her: "Mary, he was wounded. Oh no, not seriously, not seriously."

But although she winced at the thought of Robert's wounds, a wave of joy went through her. Robert was on his way home!

Before noon of the day set for Robert's arrival the family assembled in the Arlington hallway with Markie and Orton, other Custis connections, and Alexandria friends. The war had ended; Robert had been gone twenty-two months, and it had seemed much longer. Today even the family cats and the terrier, Spec, acted as if they understood this was an occasion. Mary glanced at the sixteen-year-old Custis, tall and big-boned; the younger Rooney, almost as tall and already heavier, and the younger children down to little Rob, his hair curled, blue dress starched.

Mary sat at the rear window, her eyes alert. They had sent Daniel, the coachman, to meet him. Each time a shadow moved she was sure it was Robert. She leaped up, only to turn back in disappointment. The barking of the dog made her heart pound harder. She made out a lone horseman way out in the distance. This couldn't be her husband.

Mary kept her eyes on the advancing figure. The rider wore a uniform of some kind; his face, partly shadowed, had a heavy mustache, and yet she recognized something vaguely familiar about the man. The stranger lifted his hat, and it was Robert. She realized that she was running down the stairs, as she had not run since she was a child. By the time she reached the foot of the stairs he had tossed his reins aside, and he caught her in his arms.

As she clung to him, he seemed almost a stranger to her. Could he have changed? His arms had a greater strength, his skin a brown stain of sun and wind; and she noticed for the first time that his hair was streaked with gray. It would be a while before she could get used to the bristling, faintly ridiculous mustache. But as he held her more tightly she knew that this indeed was Robert Lee. He stroked her hair, and when the ends blew across his cheeks as they had in those earlier days at Arlington, an old joy swept through her.

He released her to go to the children, who were standing silently by, waiting for recognition. Beside young Rob was a playmate from the town, about his age and size. Bending down, Robert cried, "There's my big boy." A second later he had caught up the wrong child!

Astounded, humiliated, Rob pressed the tears back. With a sheepish smile, Robert took his son into an embrace of added warmth. And meanwhile the other children looked at Robert in confusion, as if they were meeting the mustachioed, gray-haired man for the first time. One of his first tasks would be to re-acquaint himself with his sons and daughters.

The next few weeks marked a period of almost complete happiness for Mary, marred only by the fear that Robert's new assignment might take him away again. That problem was soon happily settled; Robert was asked to superintend construction of the new Fort Carroll in Baltimore, and she and the children moved there to be with him. After the arched expanses of Arlington their rooms inevitably seemed cramped. Robert grinned. "Even my tents in Mexico were bigger." Nevertheless the narrow-fronted house on Madison Avenue had three stories, a garden, neat iron fences, and, not least important, a welcome quiet.

Robert's work at Fort Carroll went smoothly. As Colonel Lee (the title continued by brevet, and he was as yet not a full colonel), he had a higher standing; yet, as she had heard her father complain, her husband had fared far less well than some: Jefferson Davis, for instance.

The normally amiable Washington Custis had a sharp dislike for Mr. Davis, Robert's West Point schoolmate. "That one moves in and out of the Army at will," the Major had fumed. Starting in the service, Jefferson Davis had quit to become a planter and officeholder, returned for the Mexican war and resigned again for politics. It developed that by a happy accident President Zachary Taylor had been the father of Mr. Davis' first wife, and now Senator Davis had a welcome place at the White House . . . Mary could not help feeling envious, but she knew she must not let her loyalty to Robert make her unfair.

A year and a half passed quickly and quietly in Baltimore, the longest period in many years that the entire family had been together. The estrangement between Robert and the children had long since worn off. He was with them as often as he could be.

Resting in her bedroom on a warm day in late July, Mary heard Rooney ask his favorite question. "Tell us about Mexico!"

"Not unless you young ones tickle my feet. No tickling, no talking!" It was an old private game, and a chorus of laughter broke from the circle around him. Mary smiled.

"Papa, what about the dark little girl and her brother on the field?" Mildred was already an assertive, strong-willed individual. Like the absent Mee, off at school, Mildred had acquired a brisk air of management.

"And the Mexican ponies, please." It was the soft-spoken Annie, frailest of the children. Annie still saw almost nothing out of the injured eye, and, watching strangers inspect her covertly, Mary sometimes felt a pang of guilt.

"All right, first the battlefield, *then* the ponies." Robert tried to favor none of his children over the others. By this time Mary realized that the middle girls, Annie and Agnes, were the gentle spirits; the other two would dominate. Agnes, it appeared certain, would always be the handsomest, and yet also the shyest. The other three had a plainness that remained during even their most vivacious moments. A feeling of affection came over her as she thought of them. And still she had begun to worry. Four girls to be married!

Mary paused. With the boys she had something else to worry about. Of late the older one, Custis, was almost withdrawn, inclined to say little; once or twice he complained that Rooney and the others "get everything they wanted," while he took what was left. She frowned. Poor Custis had once ruled the household, of course; but with six brothers and sisters he should long ago have realized he must give way in many things.

Rooney continued gay-spirited, unconcerned with the world around him—perhaps too unconcerned. Neither boy was a good student, and both found ways to evade her rules, though she admitted this would not be difficult. On the other hand, Robert could always manage them. The boys were rather in awe of him. During his long absences he had become a kind of Olympian figure. . . . The thought disturbed her, and she got up and began hastily to dress.

In the next room Robert rose. "Time for your mother and me to get ready to go out," he said. But as he entered Mary's room Custis followed him.

"Did you ask him, Mother?" he said.

It was too late to avoid the issue. "Robert, Custis is very anxious to go to West Point."

Robert gave both of them a quizzical look. "You've hinted it enough, young man. The Army's far from easy, and you've been frittering away your time at school."

Custis blushed, and Mary saw his hands were clenched. She intervened. "He wants it badly and he promises he'll apply himself very hard. Won't you, Boo?"

"Yes, *ma'am!*" Hope lighted the boy's face. "I'll study day and night. Saturdays and Sundays, too."

"Weekdays would be enough, if you studied at all." Robert frowned, then added, after a pause, "We'll see."

At that Custis flashed a grin; they had carried the day. Nevertheless, as she watched her son disappear rapidly down the stairs, Mary wondered if West Point would be the answer to Custis' lax habits. It made her uneasy. "Mim, we're due at the Marshalls' by five." Robert looked over. "Even if we hurry, we'll be just a half hour late!"

She laughed; she was accustomed to Robert's jokes about the time it took her to dress. With her maid's help she put on a frilled blue satin with one of the new, loose waists, and adjusted her flowered headdress.

The assignment in Baltimore meant, as much as anything else, an opportunity to be with Robert's sister and brother-in-law. But she knew that Ann's condition had become more and more difficult. "Is Sister Ann better?" she asked.

Robert answered in a muted voice, "She's about the same, I suppose. William said today he'd persuaded her to walk about again."

Both fell silent. Poor Ann had never fully recovered from that black hour when her younger son was brought to her, dead and mangled. For weeks she would rally from her melancholy, and then Mary found her a rare companion; before long, however, Ann would become again a tragic, unnerved woman.

"Oh"—Robert changed the subject—"William told me General Scott's in town and said that the general would be glad to join us tonight at supper." At his announcement Mary's eyes widened. This would make Ann's role harder than ever tonight; the commanding general of the Army had the reputation of being a most cantankerous guest.

As they entered the door of the Marshalls' home they were greeted by Louis Marshall, a sturdy boy of Custis' age. "Father asked me to bring you right up; Mamma's not well at all." Usually easygoing, the boy looked grim. Tossing aside her wraps, Mary sped to the second floor, where she came upon her bespectacled, scholarly brother-in-law in the middle of the room, his eyes darkened by anxiety. He was saying, "Don't torture yourself, Ann. Please make up your mind to be with us downstairs; or simply go to bed." William Marshall's voice was weary.

"No, no! In either—either case they'll be saying I'm not a good wife." Ann's broken words carried a note of hysteria. Ann Marshall looked at Mary with an expression of mingled shame and appeal. "I've done something bad somewhere in my life, and I'm being punished!"

Mary signaled to her brother-in-law, and awkwardly Mr. Marshall withdrew.

Settling at once beside Ann, Mary pleaded and coaxed, "You know that's nonsense. You're one of the truly *good* women I know. I'll go with you to the doctor tomorrow; you know your hand is better, and your physical condition is well enough. Ann, it's only that you let matters bear down on you, worry you. Don't you see?"

Mary reached for the powder, dried her sister-in-law's red-lined eyes, and adjusted Ann's dress. She was sadly reminded of the day when Ann had appeared before her at the springs, to try to draw her out in much the same way. Could she manage as well?

A half hour later Mary glanced from the window. "The first carriages are arriving, Ann. Now you *can* carry it off; just let the rest of us do most of the talking . . . Let's go down, together."

In the long silence Ann's dulled eyes searched her face in the mirror; then she got up and descended the stairs at Mary's side. Both husbands were watching intently, and Mary felt her own pulse quicken. Could they get through the evening?

As she had expected, General Winfield Scott was late, but his name was already on several tongues. "A real stickler for form," one man chuckled. "In Mexico he went to bed early on a hot night; a staff officer wanted water and slipped into the general's room in shirt sleeves and trousers. Well, Scott jumped up and had him taken to the guardhouse—for improper dress!"

In the laughter that followed, Ann Marshall sat in strained silence, her hands trembling in her lap. Robert said, "He can be like that, I'll admit. Still, he's one of the most completely honest people I've met, and I've never known him to do a really petty thing. He even——"

The butler entered. "General Winfield Scott," and an immense, florid man stalked into the room. With his medals flashing against the brightness of his uniform, Mary felt she was looking at a hero on full parade.

"Mrs. Marshall, Mr. Marshall, ladies, gentlemen." General Scott's greetings burst like a blare of trumpets. Ann sat in a terrified silence, her face white, and Mary thought her sister-in-law would faint. Before the tension should be noticed Mary took over.

"General, allow me. I was just a girl when you first came to Arlington." Then, taking his arm, she led him about the room, introducing each awe-stricken guest.

"Washington Custis' daughter, of course, of course!" The general made the prisms of the chandelier quaver. "He introduced me once at a rally." Winfield Scott proceeded for nearly five minutes to repeat every compliment that Mary's father had paid him. Obviously the general *was* his own favorite subject of conversation.

He exhausted that subject, however, to Mary's surprise, and proceeded to talk for almost twice as long a time—intently and in detail—about Robert and his career. He seemed to know practically everything Robert had ever done in the service, and almost as well as she did. As supper was announced, he whispered in her ear: "I've told others, and I might as well tell you, madam. Robert Lee is the finest soldier in America today!"

When Mary looked at him she realized he was not joking. Throughout the meal, watching Winfield Scott from across the table, she thought over his amazing remark, struggling at the same time to keep the conversation going.

Listless at first, Ann eventually took part, and by the time dessert was served she was in control of herself. For Ann a crisis had passed. The evening was finally over and even appeared to have been a mild success.

On the way home Mary told Robert what the general had said about him. "Has he said that before, and so strongly?" With a smile Robert rubbed at his mustache. "The general can be as wrong as anybody else," he told her, and changed the subject.

Custis went to West Point that September. His letters indicated that his enthusiasm for the school had not waned. He had made friends, and liked his teachers. He seemed to be involved with school life. Yet when his grades for his first semester arrived, they were far lower than she or Robert had expected, and there were many demerits. She hadn't expected him to achieve his father's high record at West Point, but these marks! . . . Both parents sent letters of appeal and encouragement, and Custis' replies implied that the boy was taking their disappointment in him to heart.

But a month after the beginning of the second semester Mary noticed that Robert was strangely solemn, concerned about something. For the first time in years she hesitated to ask what it was, perhaps because she was certain for some reason that it had to do with Custis.

That evening, after the children had been put to bed, and they were at last alone, Robert took her hand. "Mary, I can't keep this from you any longer. One of the inspectors found liquor in Custis' room, the room he shares with several other boys. They've been arrested by the officials and they may all be"—he almost could not say the word—"dismissed."

To Robert there could be no worse disgrace. "What does Custis say?"

"That the liquor wasn't his."

She knew her boy. "Then it wasn't!" she said flatly.

"No. I don't think so either. He's never lied." Slowly Robert shook his head. "But there's nothing we can do, nothing but wait."

They heard a few days later that every member of Custis' class had signed a voluntary agreement, which had been turned in to the authorities: If the academy would ignore this case, all of them pledged themselves not to violate the liquor rule for the rest of the year. Robert explained. "It's a special West Point tradition that the men sometimes follow. It means, Mim, that they like our boy and have faith in him."

Robert's eyes were reddened. "I've written, of course, that I think Custis couldn't accept the offer, in honor, and I don't think he will."

Mary stared. This might be men's logic, but it was a logic that confused and irritated her. Yet when she saw the set of her husband's lips she realized he would never alter his position.

By week's end they heard from the superintendent at West Point. After weighing the evidence in the case the authorities had acted with leniency, and Custis and his roommates received demerits instead of dismissal.

The experience had its effect on Custis. By the new year the boy's marks rose swiftly and the penalties declined. By the year's end Custis was in the upper ten of his class; Robert was able to write, much to Mary's amusement:

You must press forward in your studies. You must "crowd that boy Howard." You must be No. 1. It is a fine number. Easily found and remembered. Simple and unique. Jump to it, fellow."

The military academy was to have a further influence on their lives. On an early June morning that same year an official letter arrived for Robert. As he read it a quizzical frown came over his face.

"Bad news? You certainly look as if it is!"

"Not exactly." Robert cleared his throat. "Mim, they've offered me the superintendency at West Point. But I'm not sure. It's not the kind of work I'm qualified for, that I've been trained to do."

"Robert." Mary's voice was sharp. "It's one of the best positions in the Army, and you know it. They wouldn't ask you to take it if they didn't think you could do it, would they? Anyway, Custis is there, and I want to see my boy!"

"Your logic, my dear, is most feminine." He laughed. And as he did, she knew that they would be going.

Chapter 10

Years later Mary recalled their time at West Point as the least clouded of their lives. She felt a dignity, a sense of quiet achievement in Robert's position. Best of all, she and her husband saw each other more often than they had in years. Though these were days of hard work for both of them, they were always within calling distance at least.

Mary liked the placid academy grounds, sweeping back from the Hudson, the solid structures that looked as if they had been standing for centuries, the forested edges of the fields, the tramp of cadets. There was a sense of long tradition about the place.

As the superintendent's wife, Mary had responsibilities of her own. Arrangements for housing and entertainment of visiting officials, Army leaders, and their wives were left to her, and often they had to be made at an hour's notice. When she told Robert, "I'm in harness as much as you," she meant it. She added, "I'm enjoying it, too," and she meant that as well.

The official residence proved to be a big stone house with a garden and stables. The younger children loved it; the older girls, Mary observed, did not fail to appreciate their new status as the superintendent's daughters. In young Mary, the independent one, she saw an even greater poise; command might be a better word. "My drum major," Robert nicknamed her.

Mary had already decided that her children were travelers by inclination; whenever possible they went from one friend's house to another. "Someday," Robert said with a shake of his head, "they're going to start out on a tour, and we'll never hear from them again."

Robert labored steadily, changing rules, adding buildings, driven on as much by his sense of thrift as his love for the school. Daily he arrived at his office before the attendants; at dark Mary occasionally sent one of the family to fetch him. "I've got so much to do," he would say frowning, "and so little to do it with." But before the first year passed it was obvious that West Point had a changed spirit, and a new shape.

To her disappointment she saw little of her cadet son Custis. The boy continued to stay in the barracks. "He has to study hard," Robert reminded her one night. "Boo's practically at the top of the class, you know." Apparently his father's arrival at West Point caused Custis to work more, not less, intensively.

"About the only time I see him myself is at drill," Robert added. "My eye picks him out and I follow him over the field, as long as I can." Mary patted his arm. It was not long before she conceived a way to bring Custis home more often—light Saturday-afternoon suppers for cadets. The quiet Custis took over responsibilities. The boys indicated they approved the project and the circle widened. The two Lee girls passed plates of food and were joined later by a young visitor, the handsome Markie Williams.

Markie was later joined by her brother who had been in New York. When Mary saw him she could barely recognize him. The plumpness had disappeared. Orton was now a tall, dark-haired youth with a decidedly Latin face and an air of casual self-possession. With his easy manners he resembled Rooney most of all.

Was this charm really an asset? Robert's favorite comment on Rooney was: "There's a lot of good in him, but it doesn't always show."

After one of their weekly suppers for the students, while they were clearing the dishes away, Rooney, who had been behaving strangely all evening, came up to Robert and said, "Father, I want to ask . . ." The heavy hands emerged from his coat pockets. "When I finish next year's classes, can't I come here to West Point?"

Mary tightened her hold on her fan. Her husband, then Custis,

132

and now a third one in the Army . . . She was relieved when Robert said, "You're too young, and anyway, in the first two months you'd certainly be dismissed for demerits."

All of Rooney's charm was summoned to his aid. Rooney coaxed and pleaded until Mary feared that Robert might give in. "No," she intervened, with as firm a manner as she could achieve. "Why don't you first go to college, and show how you can handle yourself? After that we can judge."

Rooney scowled. "All right, I'll think about Harvard." He made it sound as if it were an enormous concession. She sighed. In his father's day a chance to go to such a college would have meant a great deal. A few days later their youngest son, the snub-nosed, nine-year-old Rob suddenly revealed to them that he, too, had a military urge. He wanted them to promise to send him to the academy.

"Don't you get enough of the Army here?" Mary cried, and reached down to smooth the cowlick of Rob's brown hair that stood up at the back. More gently she added, "Haven't you missed your father often enough?"

Hurt and blushing, Rob turned to his father. "What's so wonderful about the Army I don't know, boy," Robert said.

"I still like it!" Rob began to cry. But if the matter seemed to be settled for Rob at least, the next morning after church she saw Robert install a small bunk in Rob's room and show him how to maintain it in cadet style. "I'm only humoring him," Robert explained. Nevertheless she did not like the direction the humoring had taken.

From Baltimore letters arrived from Ann Marshall. Robert's sister continued to alternate between months of illness and shorter periods of uneasy improvement. Mary wished she knew what was going to happen to poor Ann. As for her own condition, she had several returns of her rheumatic troubles; each time she went back to the doctor's prescriptions, and usually she recovered without extended pain.

It was obvious that West Point marked a new development in Robert's career. In spite of his firmness nobody could fail to notice how much the staff and cadets liked him. If only they could stay on indefinitely . . .

For Robert the days were not always serene. The work was often frustrating. "The Secretary of War's office—it's always that office. Politicians and interference!" he would mutter as yet another "influence" changed their working plans. Now a new Democratic administration was taking over, with another Mexican War soldier, Franklin Pierce, as President. One of Mr. Pierce's close friends had been Jefferson Davis, and Mr. Davis would be war secretary. She tried to check her slight envy of Davis' success and hoped the new administration augured well for West Point.

Robert began what was to be a long correspondence with Davis, and she dared not tell him of her own feelings about the man whom her father had regarded so unfavorably. Davis' letters seemed to indicate he was a man of intelligence and high principles. "At last we have a superior who knows what the Army should be—and no more pressures from this and that outsider," Robert would say. Later, however, she watched him open several notes from the Secretary and toss them aside in anger.

"Our Mr. Davis can be quite curt." At his desk he began his reply; as his lips moved she realized he was composing a direct, yet at the same time, a conciliatory message. Robert would not give way; but he could get along with almost anyone.

Though there were times when the friendship seemed at the breaking point, the warm relationship grew, and a year after the correspondence began, the Davises were invited to spend the week end at West Point. Mary had never met Mr. Davis, and as she greeted them she was surprised, almost shocked, by his appearance. He looked far older than she had expected, and tired and ill. At closer range she made out a sensitive, bearded face with a sharp nose and extremely high cheekbones.

Mrs. Davis was much younger than her husband, Mary was sure; Varina Davis had large flashing dark eyes and handsome features. "You're kind to accept us on such short notice, Mrs. Lee—though of course I know of your family's tradition of hospitality." The Deep Southern voice had friendliness and self-control, in equal parts.

Then Varina Davis added in a whisper, "Could Mr. Davis rest a little while?" At once Mary understood that this woman had to keep unending guard over her husband's health; she directed the two guests upstairs and summoned Markie to help with new arrivals.

That evening Mary gave a small supper party in honor of the Secretary of War and his wife. As the party wore on Mary noticed that Varina Davis not only joined, but, practically led the men's conversation.

Inevitably the conversation led to the Mexican War. "It's amazing," said Robert, "how everything that happened in that war seemed to have been determined by accident." Mrs. Davis shrugged her shoulders. "Well, everything in life is coincidence —a big accident or a combination of little ones. You look as if you don't agree, Mrs. Lee."

Mary flushed. "I can't. There must be a pattern, a meaning in what happens to us. If I didn't believe that . . . I couldn't think of any reason for existing!"

Could Varina Davis really believe what she said? Happily, a captain from Massachusetts changed the subject. Perhaps not so happily, for the conversation shifted to the fuming question of the day: slavery and anti-slavery agitations.

"Many of us in Virginia have always favored the colonization movement to Africa." Robert spoke gravely. "Slavery is a bad thing for the white man as well as the black. It has to go, if not at once, then certainly in time."

Mary bent her head; certainly they could all agree to that. A second later she discovered that Mr. Davis definitely did not agree. The gaunt face seemed to narrow, and his words came out rapidly in a choked, emotional voice:

"*Our* South doesn't think that way, sir." He looked directly at Robert, as if there were no one else in the room. "Once we may have been interested in colonization, but no longer. Slavery is our system, our hope! We must fight for it, or the North will crush us."

There was an embarrassed silence. The Northern captain stared openmouthed at the Mississippian. Mary anticipated a scene, and for a moment she did not care if it developed. One section crushing another, fighting for slavery . . . For the first time she realized the difference between the old Virginia view-

135

point, and that of the newer, cotton South. Fortunately dinner was announced at that moment, and the atmosphere cleared.

For the rest of the evening everyone shunned the more explosive topics, by unanimous consent. But it was clear that the hollow-eyed Mr. Davis was a man of strongly accentuated opinions, and one who would never hesitate to speak them.

Several weeks later Mary received word that Mrs. Custis was seriously ill.

It had been months since they had visited Arlington; and the last time they had seen Mrs. Custis she had been so well, so energetic. It didn't seem possible. Mary left that day.

Because of the approaching commencement Robert could not leave for Arlington with her, but he planned to join her there in a few days. The journey lasted two days—days of panic and physical pain. Her head ached, and burning sensations in her legs returned. She could sleep for only a few minutes at a time, and when she managed to do so, she dreamed that she had arrived at Arlington, but that the houses were no longer there. The jolting ride was a nightmare.

She arrived too late. Her mother had died a few hours before. Her father was sitting alone in her mother's old room and when she saw him, his mouth slack, his eyes lost in shadowed sockets, she began to cry. "Mary, what will we do? I never believed she'd go first. . . ."

His dark face was altered, as if some unseen hand had drawn it out of shape, and he clung helplessly to her. Bleakly Mary remembered the supper party at West Point, and her own words to Mrs. Davis: a pattern to everything in life. What was the pattern here? His will be done. In His infinite wisdom . . . She had believed it before; she must believe it again.

It was now up to her to handle everything. She thought of Miss Mollie's untiring hands with their "daily lists," her quiet efficiency, her tenderness. And as she looked up at the portraits of the other Custises and Parkes and Washingtons lining the walls, she felt a deeper sense of commitment.

Robert and Mary decided to stay at Arlington for part of the summer. Never had the estate appeared so empty, as she went

136

to the garden that her mother maintained through the years, to Miss Mollie's old workrooms, her favorite corners about the house.

Young Custis joined them in July. During his stay there was discussion of his hopes after graduation the following year. Robert suggested he could go into the engineers' corps.

Yet Custis was far from pleased at the prospect. "Well, no, I'm not thinking of anything else," he replied. "I just haven't decided." Did this new generation know *what* it wanted? Or was this unsettled state of mind simply the result of Custis' own personality? If only he had a touch of Rooney's humor, the ease of manner of their middle son . . .

She sighed. Custis, as the first-born, had always been Robert's favorite among their boys, as—she could not deny it—the light-hearted Rooney was hers . . . Gradually Custis came to a decision about his future. After graduation he would accept an Army Engineer post in Florida. But, although she was relieved that Custis had made up his mind about his career, his departure was still a wrench for her.

Since her mother's death Robert seemed preoccupied, and Mary interpreted it as sorrow over a loss which was almost as grave to him as it was to her. But when the time came for Annie and Agnes to be confirmed late that summer, and they journeyed to Alexandria to make arrangements with the minister, Robert closeted himself with the clergyman. Later he said quietly, "Mim, you know I've never been confirmed, and Miss Mollie used to worry about it. I think I'd like to join the girls."

Too pleased to speak, Mary was silent. Nothing more was said on the matter. This must be a personal affair; if Robert wished to tell her more of his religious feelings, in time he would.

In mid-August Robert took his place in church between the two girls for the simple Episcopal ceremony. A shaft of sun picked out the increasing strands of white in Robert's hair, and as his voice lifted in affirmation, Mary was enveloped in a sense of peace. Whatever followed for them, each would have greater inner resources on which to draw.

That fall a detachment of thirty Army men was wiped out by Indian marauders on the Wyoming frontier. Waves of indignation swept over the country. For months Jefferson Davis had been asking vainly for increases in the Army quota to protect the frontier. With public feeling at its height Congress ordered several new infantry and cavalry units sent to the West.

In the spring of 1855, Joseph E. Johnston was appointed lieutenant colonel of one of the new regiments, and Robert E. Lee of another.

The news of the new command shocked Mary. "The cavalry . . ." Her voice was muffled. "You'd be leaving the engineers, after nearly twenty-five years."

When he nodded she asked abruptly, "Do you have to take it?"

"Well"—Robert was surprised—"No. But unless a man's unfitted for an Army appointment, he should always accept."

"Robert, it's not right to send you to that wild country." And she added, "At your age."

He flushed. "I'm only forty-eight," he said, and his voice had a bitter edge. "My future may yet be ahead of me, Mary." When he used her Christian name and said it so flatly, she knew she had hurt him.

He went on. "My place is with you, Mim, if it's possible. I'd hoped I'd never have to leave any of you again. Still, I couldn't expect to stay on forever at West Point, and this appointment is a kind of advancement. Most of all, this is a matter of duty. I've been trained for the assignments my superiors choose. Of course, if I want to resign . . ."

Robert left for the frontier just a month later. After five years of close family life, this latest separation was the hardest. Packing away the furnishings they had used for so many years, Mary felt more alone than ever before.

She returned with the smaller children to Arlington, now a saddened, changed place. Washington Custis himself had altered. He dragged his feet as if he drew weights behind him; it was the first time she had realized that he was an old man. Mary was certain that something specific was troubling him; she had not long to wait to find out.

One morning her father handed her a large bill for feed. "I just don't have the money," he said. She could not believe him.

She went through a pile of papers on his desk, figured all his accounts, spent over an hour classifying his records. When she had finished, she realized that the Major was right; he had practically no cash, and a pile of bills that called for prompt payment.

The knowledge shocked her. She had known nothing of her father's finances and had always assumed there was money to spare. She had never realized how close to the margin he operated. The money had been draining out of all his properties—Arlington, White House plantation, and the others. When she called in their overseer she found him more confused than her father. If Robert were here, he would know what to do. That something had to be done was obvious. It was up to her. She would manage because she *had* to manage.

"Don't worry," She said, sliding her arm around her father. "Beginning tomorrow, we'll start a new way of handling things."

The next morning Mary wrote a half-dozen letters, asking two bank loans, deferment of scheduled payments, cancellation of orders for some supplies. At least that would mean a breathing spell. But the responsibilities grew by the hour.

"Miss Mary, those back fences 'bout to fall down."

"Why didn't you tell the Major?"

Salina's face, usually impassive, had a look of regret. "Told him three or four times, and so I come to you."

"Thank you. And let me know about anything else." Mary shook her head. She had no time to feel sorry for herself. She went to the kitchen, where she conferred about the day's meals, arranged for extra sugar for the week's jelly-making. Next she stopped at the laundry and looked in at the hospital to talk to the four servants who lay ill.

Another carriage stopped at the gate—more sight-seers. Well, the Major would do the honors. Time was pressing and she was due at the quarters. For nearly an hour she walked from one servant's cabin to the next. "Mamie, you ought to ask the doctor about that baby. I'll send him today." "How long have those windows needed fixing?" "Here, this will buy the extras until you sell more vegetables at the market."

Turning back, Mary reflected: Not until now had she understood quite how heavy a burden her mother had carried. She looked down; the "daily list" had lengthened in her hands. For a fleeting moment she remembered her first helpless days at Fort Monroe. How she herself had changed since then!

The months passed in this way and there was no time to think of herself. The best part of the long and tiring day was in late afternoon, when she returned from her daily visits to the quarters, to find a letter from Robert awaiting her. Robert had gone first to Galveston on the Gulf of Mexico; then to San Antonio de Bexar and Camp Cooper on the Brazos in Comanche territory. He described weeks of heat under a blistering sun, the air so heavy that the men could hardly breathe. There were fleas and ants and mosquitoes everywhere. The weeks were long, interrupted only by short expeditions against native bandits. The primitive surroundings seemed to emphasize his distance from home.

Robert wrote each member of the family individually, and tried to lighten his tone of loneliness and despair. To Mildred he wrote: "You must be a great personage now—sixty pounds. I wish I had you here in all your ponderosity." And to the younger boys: "I have made many acquaintances among the snakes." But sadness crept between the lines. Describing an Army officer's wife who looked forward to Southwestern travel, he wrote: "It is a beautiful thing to see the young so hopeful. It is sad to think how soon the clouds of disappointment darken the prospect." Robert, Mary felt sure, was speaking of himself. Others advanced swiftly while he remained a colonel by brevet only. Referring to young Rob's continued ambition to be a soldier, he wrote: "Tell Robert I cannot advise him to enter the Army. It is a hard life, and he can never rise to any military eminence by serving in the Army. He must rise out of it, and then come in as Major-General . . ."

She had seldom known Robert to write with such bitterness. So many men, linking politics with Army affairs, were gaining on the regulars . . . Then, too, he could not hide disappointment in his children. The lackadaisical Rooney was not doing well at Harvard; Robert told her that their second son must "think of something else besides running about amusing himself, and I wish him to do it at once." Now, home for the summer, the boy lounged about the house, doing nothing.

For weeks Mary worried over Rooney. It was Orton Williams

who gave her one explanation for the boy's poor record. "Look at poor Roon," Orton whispered with a grin. "Love's certainly changed him!"

Mary stared. His cousin, Charlotte Wickham, of course; she might have guessed. Charlotte was a handsome girl of seventeen, and the two families had long been on friendly terms. Yet there were drawbacks, serious ones.

"She's a fine young woman," Mary said when she found the courage to bring the subject up. "But a close cousin."

"That's all right. You and Father are cousins." Rooney's brow tightened, and quickly he marshaled his arguments. "Father's always saying people should marry early! I'm nearly twenty already."

Mary thought of the slim, patrician Miss Wickham and hesitated. "Both of Charlotte's parents were sickly and died early, and the girl herself is—well, delicate." It was difficult to say these things, yet she must.

"Charlotte hasn't been sick in a year. The doctor told the family there's nothing wrong with her at all."

Mary paused before answering. "Even if your father and I agreed, have you thought how you'd start earning your living?"

Rooney flushed. "Don't think I haven't thought of it. I don't have any way—so far, that is. Father didn't want me to go to West Point. Anyway, the trouble is, everybody can't be like him. We're not all that fine." It was not altogether easy for the sons of a man so dominant as Robert.

Still, here was the first of her children to show signs of a serious attachment. She pressed his arm. "We'll write your father, and I'll invite Charlotte here, and we'll see, dear."

Mary was in bed with a rheumatic attack when Charlotte arrived at Arlington. Rooney brought her in Mary's room and left them. The girl seated herself at the window. Her pale, clear skin, through which the blue veins stood out at the temple, had an unusually high color. Charlotte wore her brown hair drawn almost severely back, in a way, Mary judged, that made her appear older than she was. The girl had a long, angular, aristocratic face; yet when Charlotte smiled, as she did now, a warm beauty lighted the deep brown eyes.

"Charlotte, you're sure you're in love with him?" Mary had not planned to be so abrupt.

"Yes." Charlotte spoke softly and her face flushed. "I know we'd be happy."

"You'd be willing to wait a while, to see how things can work out?"

"Yes, for a long time if we had to."

As they spoke Mary was remembering another day in a room in this same house when she and Robert sat together with her father's eyes upon them. She had told herself since then that she would never stand in her children's way. She beckoned to the girl. "Well, child, let's find out now what we can do about some kind of work for Rooney."

That night the couple, together on the sofa near her bed, looked thoroughly happy, but Mary had begun to wonder just what she could manage. Though by now she was well used to taking positive steps of her own, this might not be easy.

Early the following week she came unexpectedly upon a solution. Her health was better and she rode over to Washington to discuss a bank loan for her father. On Connecticut Avenue she caught sight of the grandiose figure of General Winfield Scott, and halted her carriage. The old warrior was delighted to see her and demanded news of the family. Without considering whether Robert would like it or not, she told him all about Rooney.

Before she could finish the general threw out his arms in a grand gesture. "Madam, your worries are at an end." Roaring so that passers-by could hear, Winfield Scott went on. "He's been to college, and he likes the Army? Well, I've reason to think there's a lieutenant's vacancy in a Western regiment. We'd prefer West Point men, but under some conditions . . . You're welcome, madam, very welcome!"

To Mary's surprise and chagrin Rooney did not respond at once. "It would take me pretty far away from—all of you," he protested, his eyes on Charlotte. The girl swung around in her chair. "I think you ought to take it, Rooney. We can wait." Despite Rooney's protests Charlotte and Mary remained firm, and, seeing the two women united against him, Rooney gave in. It was only when the issue was settled and the acceptance sent off that

Mary realized with a shock that, by her own means, her second son had entered the Army.

On the evening of Rooney's departure Mary tried to lift her lamp, but it slipped and crashed to the floor. She stared at her hands. The pain had been so intense that she had dropped the lamp. This had never happened before, and she was badly frightened.

Perhaps the pain would leave her after a good rest. She bathed her arms in hot water and took the drugs that had often helped her. The past few weeks had been difficult ones—money worries, Robert's prolonged absence, and finally Rooney's departure. The doctors had warned that she must have rest and ease, and should not worry. Yet, how could she follow such directions? Twisting in her bed, she finally fell into an uneasy sleep.

As she awoke, she became slowly aware of what felt like a heavy weight pressing upon the left side of her body. When she tried to move her arm she was caught by a searing pain. It took several minutes before she could force herself up. With Salina's anxious help she bathed and dressed. "Don't tell the others; I don't want them to know." Somehow Mary made her way to the breakfast table.

Her condition did not escape her father's notice. "Mary, what is it?" When she said nothing, he sent for the doctor and rang for Salina to put her to bed. The doctor examined her for an hour.

"Your condition is worse than I've ever seen it, and I can't understand it. We'll do as before, with a new drug or two. Still" —with his hesitation she knew there would be worse to come— "I'm afraid there's something you should know. Unless I'm entirely mistaken, you may never be entirely free of these troubles again."

"As long as I live?" She could not keep her voice from breaking.

"Well . . . there'll be times when you'll have almost none."

"How many times?"

"That will depend on you."

For the rest of her life . . . As Mary buried her head in the

143

pillow, the doctor withdrew tactfully. She felt lost, utterly defeated. Moments later Annie, holding Agnes and Mildred by the hand, came shyly into the room. The unmasked fear in their eyes was like a cry of reproach. They depended on her, and so did the old man outside, and the scores of people in the quarters below.

"Come in," she told her daughters. She forced a smile, pushed her hand forward over the sheet; when they touched it, she could hardly keep from screaming, yet she managed to be silent. For days at a time she could not leave her room. Even when she felt better, it was an effort to get about the house. She mentioned her illness to Robert, but only briefly.

On one of her better days when she could move without too much effort from room to room, Salina came to her and said, "Mr. Custis actin' funny—real faint." She found him in bed, lying on his back with his mouth open. He had had a stroke. Mary sent one of the boys to fetch the doctor.

"You were worrying about me"—she tried to laugh, taking his limp hand in hers—"and you've been ignoring yourself all along. Now follow orders, and you'll be right up again in a couple of days."

The kindly face, with its sunken cheeks, had a look of resignation. "Child, I'm seventy-nine, and I've had a good life." The high-pitched voice cracked, then deepened. "Don't worry about me, Mary. I've just been waiting for this."

"Don't say things like that." But she knew that he was speaking the truth; the doctor only confirmed her fear. Throughout the night she watched over the old man. If he should die, she would indeed be alone. Toward morning, she fell asleep in her chair. She was awakened by the sound of a familiar and much-loved voice.

It was Aunt Maria Fitzhugh, never so welcome as now. "I got them to bring me over as soon as I heard." Mrs. Fitzhugh wasted few words. "Now you go to your room and rest." Aunt Maria fairly pushed her out the door. "Just watch yourself, and I'll watch him."

Mary slept fitfully the rest of the day, but awoke late in the afternoon to discover that her rheumatic pains had returned.

She forced herself to rise and go to her father. The Major was weaker than before, but for hours he remained conscious, talking in a low voice to her and Aunt Maria. At last he said, "Mary, will you send for my old friend?" She knew that he meant the minister. She could hear her heart pounding.

After the minister arrived and remained for a long time, Washington Custis smiled faintly at his daughter, and his head fell back on the pillows.

"Remember the way we built the house, and they called it Custis' Folly? We showed 'em it wasn't any folly!" He thought she was her mother. "We kept things going, kept them going . . ." The voice died down in a muffled groan, and Mrs. Fitzhugh went forward to draw the sheet.

Chapter 11

Robert started back as soon as he had word of the Major's death. It was her anticipation of his arrival that kept Mary going the past few weeks. The day of his return was unseasonably cold for a Virginia November. Robert was due to arrive at noon, but by nine o'clock Mary had already gone downstairs to her chair by the window. Her knitting lay untouched in her lap.

Long before the big door swung open, Mary had risen to her feet. "Robert!" Her husband ran toward her and she was in his arms.

"You're back, you're back." Clinging to him, she forgot all the things she had planned to say. When she drew away to take in the familiar features, she saw his skin was deeply tanned. Life in the open air had been good for him; yet, at the same time, Robert had an older, more settled look, and the gray hairs had turned into an uneven white that spread backward from the temples.

But Robert was clearly shocked by the change in his wife. He stared at her almost helpless hands, clasped against the top of her chair. He took her arm tenderly. "Please, Mim dear, sit down. Now. Tell me about your health."

She spoke quietly, leaving out nothing. "We'll whip this, Mim. You'll see." She almost believed him; in any case, they would try.

The reading of Major Custis' will was held that afternoon. "Mrs. Lee," the lawyer read, "receives the use, during her lifetime, of Arlington estate and its possessions, to be maintained intact. At her death Arlington will go to Custis Lee; White House plantation to Rooney Lee, Romancoke to Robert Lee, Jr. Each girl will receive a legacy of $10,000."

Mary nodded; she had expected such terms. The lawyer cleared his throat. "But Mr. Custis left more than two hundred slaves, to be freed not later than five years hence. In another section, however, he calls for their employment in *working out* the above terms, the girl's legacies and so on." The man looked from Mary to Robert. "The trouble is that, with all his lands and servants, Mr. Custis might be considered, technically, insolvent. Almost nothing is provided in cash, and debts reach $9000 or more."

Mary's heart turned over. Insolvent . . . She had never thought the situation was so bad. Then they might lose the place that her father had built and occupied for fifty years. The lawyer went on. "And just when the slaves are to be free, and how to reconcile this part of the will with the other—well, the courts may decide." Mary groaned; a law case on top of everything else!

Some would sneer at the will, considering Washington Custis a poor manager, a "theorist with his head in the clouds." But hundreds of other Virginia estates had financial troubles; only in the new, cotton South were there enormous profits. It occurred to her that she and the children would lose ultimately, and heavily, by the freeing of the slaves. It was an unpleasant thought. Nevertheless, this was a matter of principle with her as well as her father. They must abide by it.

She remembered the way some had called the Major careless, lax. Yet suppose his circumstances had been different, and he had had to strike out for his living, without land or the Washington background? His assets had been, in a sense, his handicap. Robert had had his Lee and Carter heritages, of course; but conditions had forced him to go out on his own. By contrast, her sons had had the security that Robert had never had. Lacking the prodding of necessity, they had suffered.

For all of them, things might be different from now on. To give up Arlington and their Washington possessions, to start again . . .

"Mim." Robert, returning, startled her. He spoke gravely. "I once said I might someday try farming. Well, we have a little money of our own to help along. I'm going to ask for a year's leave, and we'll do what we can to keep your father's estate together."

A full year from his Army life was a sacrifice for her and the children . . . So long a time would hurt his career. Nevertheless, though she realized this, a wave of relief swept over her and with it—guilty though it made her feel—a quick happiness. Arlington would be in better hands than hers; she would not have so great a daily burden. Then, too, she would have her husband back, at least for a while.

Robert appeared the next morning in his dark planter's suit. The costume was to mark the start of this new phase of their life. That day and for weeks afterward the two worked over the accounts in the office. "There's so much waste in the handling of garden stuff" . . . "They're giving no care to the animals" . . . "Mim, things are so—unadjustable. These people have been trained to do only one or two things each. Today four of them argued for an hour as to who should work on a back road." Yet he made progress; every day brought a new economy, a change in plans.

And more and more Robert worried about Mary's health. "I want you to try the springs again," he told her. She objected to the trip, remembering the rasping pains that accompanied any long ride. But he persisted and finally she went for a few weeks, with the efficient young Mary handling arrangements. At the springs she swam and drank the waters, and returned in somewhat better condition.

Upon her return Robert had a surprise for her, a new cold-bath "cure" for rheumatism; and Ann Marshall had found a Canadian "health liquid." Mary shivered in the chill waters and winced at the unpleasant medicine. After a while she moved about more easily, but was not sure whether it was the combination of remedies, or simply Robert's presence and his tender care.

When she and Robert were working at the records one day the mail brought her a much-creased letter from California. Custis, who would eventually inherit Arlington, wanted his father to take all of his rights, to handle the property in any way Robert wished. "I have no fear," Custis wrote, "that I shall ever regret anything he may do in the management of whatever is entrusted

149

to him . . . I will be the sole gainer." She handed the note to Robert; reading it, his eyes filled. Then he shook his head. "But I won't take it. It's his." She said nothing, but all her love for this man was in her look.

Together they went back to their work. An overseer had unexpectedly put in a claim for several years' back pay. "And these six bills arrived overnight," Robert gestured. "On top of last month's bad rains, that puts us very far behind." He groaned, and she realized he was more troubled than ever about Arlington.

That night her worries would not let her sleep; everything they owned was in jeopardy, and what could she do about it? As she lay there she discovered that the place beside her was empty, and from outside she heard a light, steady step. Robert, too, could not sleep. . . . The next day he made a trip across the Potomac and returned to tell her: "A year won't be enough, and General Scott is allowing me a six-month extension."

Mary gave his hand a grateful squeeze. How long could he continue to sacrifice his career? . . . Meanwhile no decision had been made by the courts on the contradictions in the will, including the time for the freeing of the slaves. The estate needed funds badly and he planned to hire out more of the field staff in Richmond and other places.

The new plan was not working long when several of the slaves ran away, though they were brought back readily. They were of the younger generation, and Salina frowned. "Some folks stirrin' them up, sayin' you cheat 'em." Mary was hurt. Surely the people in the Arlington quarters should know better than that.

Immediately thereafter an apologetic message arrived from Ann Marshall, enclosing two newspaper clippings; she thought they should see them. Eyes widening, Mary read several furious letters to the editors. The writers had learned that Colonel Lee was violating the Custis will; he "starved" the Arlington Negroes; when they fled, he had them recaptured and brutally beaten; after an overseer declined to follow orders with a woman slave, Robert Lee himself stripped her and flogged her.

Throwing the charges on the table, Mary gripped Robert's arm. "You're certainly going to answer these lies!" His face was red, and the veins on his forehead stood out like wounds. Then he said slowly, "Mim, people who know us will know they aren't true. For the others it doesn't matter." Going to the door, he sighed. "This slavery. What a misery it's brought us."

They spent the rest of the day in low spirits. At dusk they heard a bright voice, and Mary made out Charlotte Wickham, arriving for a promised visit. The girl stayed at Arlington for days, helping Mary with the sewing, counting supplies for the quarters, taking rides with Robert. Mary admired Charlotte more with each meeting. "Chass," Robert nicknamed her, and Mary could tell how much he, too, approved of his son's choice.

For months they had been receiving letters from Rooney. He liked the Army service, and he was doing well. Mary was relieved, not only for Rooney, but for the signs of a new sympathy toward him that Robert displayed. At the same time she traced in Rooney's notes an undercurrent of loneliness for home and for Charlotte. She was not so old that she had forgotten the long months before their own marriage while she waited for Robert.

Charlotte was grave when she showed a letter from Rooney that settled the matter. The Army had been good for him, Rooney said. But now, after fourteen or fifteen months, he thought he wanted something else. Since the White House property would eventually be his, he hoped to begin to manage it now—and with Charlotte beside him.

When Mary gave the note to Robert, he looked at her and nodded his agreement. With Charlotte's eager help arrangements were launched that night. As Mary listened to Robert's careful words and Charlotte's eager exclamations, it struck her how many more years had gone by. A new generation would soon be starting its life together. And already her youngest son, Rob, was in his teens.

Seven months later Mary, rising gingerly from her chair in the garden, put aside the latest exchange of messages between her son and husband, comparing finances, plowing methods, and fencing. Her spirits were high. Rooney was doing well as a farmer; buoyant as ever, he nevertheless had a growing seriousness of purpose, and Charlotte was working beside him on the White House property. Custis had been called to the capital for duty with the engineers, and once more the family was to be reunited.

She glanced around her. Arlington itself had a brighter look, an air of renewal. Crops had improved vastly; essential repairs were made, and the estate again showed a profit. In Robert's manner she read a reflection of her own relief. He had saved this place, and it would be here for their old age and their children's. She surveyed the house, the arbor, the line of great trees; those long months when they struggled for Arlington had given the place a greater meaning than ever.

When Mary entered the house, she saw Robert coming down the staircase, and the sight came as a shock. He had just donned his uniform; within a month or so he would be rejoining his command in Texas, and they were going together today to Washington on several official errands. When he helped her into the carriage with a smile, she could not return it. Riding beside him, she remained silent. As if he understood, Robert pressed his hand over hers.

On their way home their vehicle slowed up, and they were able to catch the heated words of several men on the street:

"Damn nigger-lovers from the North . . ."

"Takes somebody like Jeff Davis to call 'em thieves and rats, like they are!"

Robert frowned with disgust. The carriage rolled on. "You can't walk on the streets these days, Mim, without hearing somebody call somebody else a scoundrel. One side's as wild as the other." She nodded; she had tried to close her ears to the fury over new territories and the introduction of slavery into the unsettled areas. That was no longer possible.

She remembered Jefferson Davis' remarks during his West Point visit. Leaving the Cabinet, the Mississippian had taken a high Senate rank; and now she thought of a phrase from yesterday's paper. "Didn't Mr. Davis get up and call slavery a 'blessing'?"

Robert shrugged. "I heard so, though they say that was when he lost his temper. A lot of people call him a moderate, compared with some senators."

Mary let out a slow breath; she hoped that not too many Americans considered such words "moderate." The subdued mood remained as they returned home. She had just settled on the wide sofa when she heard a staccato knock downstairs. Past her door strode a young man, and there was a murmur of words with Robert. After a short time her husband came in to her.

"The Secretary of War has sent for me." His voice raced on. "There's some trouble at Harper's Ferry; telegrams claim it's a slave uprising. I'm to take charge of Marines and troops from Fort Monroe and the Maryland Militia." With a hurried kiss he left. Only as she watched the carriage disappear did she wake to the grimness of the episode. An uprising, with guns!

For days she stayed in her room, waiting for news. From one of General Scott's aides she heard more: "The insurrectionists caught a bunch of hostages and locked themselves with them in an engine house, and now Colonel Lee's going to send a charge against it." She picked up a paper—five to six hundred men were involved; the leader was John Brown, an abolitionist from the bloody Kansas Territory.

Mary crumpled the paper; and they still said she should not worry! One anxious hour after another she sat rigidly at her window, watching the slowly moving treetops and the capital city gleaming in the distance. She relived her hours of waiting during the uprising when they first went to Fort Monroe, and the stories of deaths and maimings that accompanied it. Feeling a burning sensation in her leg, she ignored it; she had become reconciled to pain.

With dawn a tired messenger brought a note that she tore apart. General Scott wished her to know that Robert was safe and the whole unhappy episode over. Though men had been shot to death on both sides, Colonel Lee had subdued the insurrectionists with calm and great skill.

Only after Robert rode off to the West again did Mary learn the implications of the incident. Robert himself had shaken his head over John Brown. "A poor madman, I've thought; there was never any danger that many blacks would follow him." She could hardly believe the flames of passion that arose after Brown was hanged.

The reactions of the New England journals were violent: John Brown had been a martyr, victim of bloody oppression. A Georgia newspaper, on the other hand, was equally inflammatory: The abolitionists had launched a gigantic plot to support Brown, turning the South into "another San Domingo," killing all whites in their way. "Yankee octopus, bloodsuckers, traitors . . ." Mary closed her eyes; was the nation going crazy?

"Mother!" She looked up into a familiar face—her son Custis, back from his Washington City service. She put out her arms to the bronzed youth. She sensed that Custis had changed very little. She saw the same dour look, the hint of uncertainty in the dark eyes.

If only he would interest himself in one of the girls who were always visiting here, for instance . . . But it was her son's decision to make; and she recalled the shrewd words of Aunt Maria: "The surest way to keep two young people apart is to try to throw them together."

She thought of her own daughters. None of them yet showed signs of interest in any particular boy, and she had begun to worry. Although Robert had sometimes joked with Custis about marriage, he never seemed to consider the problem of their girls. Well, *she* didn't intend to have old maids. Four in a row . . . Agnes was still the beauty of the family and still even she gave no indication that she was thinking about the subject. The outlook was mildly alarming.

From another direction arrived pleasant news. Her daughter-in-law was soon to have a baby. Remembering Charlotte's delicate constitution, Mary had worried over the prospect; and now, when an invitation came to visit Rooney and his wife, she accepted promptly. Making the trip in slow stages with two of her daughters, she suffered less than she had feared.

For months she remained at the simple residence near the slow-flowing Pamunkey River. For Mary Lee the White House estate had many a family association; it was here that George Washington had gone after his marriage to the Widow Custis. The land, level at the river, rose to distant hills, and there was peace over all the countryside. Rooney and Charlotte were managing well; the girl had a softened beauty, and her son's happiness gave a glow to his big round face, with the hair tumbling loosely over his forehead.

The birth followed without difficulty, but as Mary took the plump, squalling boy in her arms, she was sorry that Robert could not share the moment, might not even see their first grandchild for years . . . Smiling shyly, Charlotte told her: "We know what name we want—Robert Edward Lee."

At once Mary wrote her husband, and his reply told them how much he had been moved. But he added pensively, "I wish I could offer him a more worthy name and a better example," and he suggested another.

"It's going to stay Robert," said Rooney, and it did.

For almost a month Mary lingered at White House, which now had a special meaning for her. But household affairs demanded her return to Arlington, and reluctantly she left. When she got home Custis seemed greatly upset. He had just learned something that made him groan. "It's Joe Johnston. He's had a windfall at Father's expense, and other people's too. He's been smelling around for promotions, and the new Secretary of War is a cousin of his." Custis' eyes darkened. "Now he's got a fine promotion that's astonished everybody. They say General Scott submitted four names, including Father's, and Johnston's cousin took *him*, and passed over others who outrank him."

Mary frowned as Custis held out Robert's letter. ". . . It never was the intention of Congress to advance him to that position . . . advanced beyond anyone in the Army . . . thrown more discredit than ever on the system of favoritism . . ." Silently Mary folded the note. Robert's words were unusually sharp; he must have been badly provoked. So, of course, was she. Joe's career had been similar to Robert's at many points; but now, after slipping in and out of the Army while Robert remained on year after year, Joe had forged ahead.

Custis fumed. "If only Father would pull a few strings."

"If he did, he wouldn't be your father," Mary told him with more asperity than she intended. In the following months she detected an increasing discouragement in Robert's notes. He wrote her of his "long desire to see you again. I know it is useless to indulge these feelings, yet they arise unbidden, and will not stay repressed. They steal on me in the business hours of the day and the waking hours of the night, and seem to hover over me, working or sleeping."

The letter fell from Mary's hand, and she remained in the dark for a long time. . . . A note from Ann Marshall disquieted her further. The Marshalls were increasingly concerned over clashes between Northern and Southern politicians. As the elections of 1860 approached, Ann saw particular hazard in the cries of Southern extremists. A firm Unionist, Ann grew ever more fretful, and she asked, Did the Lees think the nation would break apart?

At the question, put so directly, Mary started. It couldn't happen like that; those men over in Washington's city wouldn't be so mad! Nevertheless, as she watched the trend of events, Ann's words came back to her. Markie Williams, with them for another long stay, became steadily more concerned. Her brother Orton, finishing West Point like his father and older brother, was with them more often; about to take a post in Washington headquarters, he brought frequent word of developments, and one day he bounded in, his handsome face set in grave lines.

"Those Republicans nominated the fellow from Illinois, the one they call Lincoln! Nobody thinks much of *him*." Mary felt puzzled; the name had an unfamiliar ring. Within a few days she heard people say that Abe Lincoln was an "ape," an "illiterate fool," and his election would mean one thing—secession.

Later, with a sick feeling, she learned of a split among the Democrats, with two different candidates for President. Alone on the portico, she overheard Orton's deep-voiced comment: "The cotton people say Virginia's a 'border state,' and has to choose between the South and the North."

Mary straightened up abruptly. "We have to choose, do we? Suppose we want nothing to do with either of them!" The two were silent, and her gloom deepened . . . Then on a November day, riding with Agnes along Alexandria's streets, she heard the result of the election: "They picked Lincoln, that damned Lincoln!" "That settles it, settles it *right now!*"

Mary ordered the carriage back, and on the way she spoke fiercely. "I'd like to hang them higher than Haman, all the traitors on both sides."

"Me, too, Mamma," said the usually quiet Agnes, and despite herself Mary laughed. Soon afterward South Carolina chose delegates to a secession convention, and the shouts rose for a new Southern nation, and with them, to her bewilderment, talk of reopening the long-outlawed slave trade to Africa. Robert wrote again; he felt the "aggressions of the North," but . . .

I am not pleased with the course of the "Cotton States," as they term themselves. In addition to their selfish, dictatorial bearing, the threats they throw out against the "Border States," as they call them, if they will not join them, argue little for the benefit of peace of Virginia should she determine to coalesce with them. While I wish to do what is right, I am unwilling to do what is wrong, either at the bidding of the South or the North . . .

Deeply stirred, she waited anxiously for his next letters. He wrote that he had been reading a new life of George Washington.

How his spirit would be grieved could he see the wreck of his mighty labors . . . I would defend any State if her rights were invaded. But I can anticipate no greater calamity for the country than a dissolution of the Union . . . Secession is nothing but revolution. The framers of our Constitution never exhausted so much labor, wisdom and forbearance in its formation, and surrounded it with so many guards and securities, if it was intended to be broken by every member of the confederacy at will.

He went on:

Still, a Union that can only be maintained by swords and bayonets, and in which strife and civil war are to take the place of brotherly love and kindness, has no charm for me . . . If the Union is dissolved and the Government disrupted, I shall return to my native state and share the miseries of my people, and save in defense will draw my sword on none.

So he wanted no dealings with the hotheads, the screamers; and again and again, through his letters, he let her know that he still hoped for a readjustment of the differences. Mary was grateful. Some of the leading Virginians were trying to bring a compromise, holding innumerable meetings; if others who felt as Robert did held firm . . . Yet Jefferson Davis' state of Mississippi followed South Carolina out of the Union, and then Florida, Alabama, Georgia. With each announcement her heart sank.

Louisiana and Texas seceded, and a new Confederate States of America was formed at Montgomery, with Jefferson Davis as President. At that name Mary felt a chill, and she saw again the gaunt, earnest man. Mr. Davis would not be one to adjust or compromise! And meanwhile Southern volunteers drilled, and many Southern officers were resigning from the Army. Orton reported: "Now it's Beauregard of Louisiana, and Albert Sidney Johnston," and he named a half dozen more.

"But Virginia's still staying out," Mary argued, "and look at the other officers who won't leave the Union." She thought of ten or twelve and added, "Especially General Scott." The doughty commanding general had shown himself a strong Union man, and was doing everything he could to hold fellow Virginians and other military officers to the Union. From the other side of the room Custis said, "Scott says he's as good a Southerner as anybody, but he won't quit his country."

There was a pause, while each remained with his own thoughts. Mary watched her son, wondering what he was thinking, sensing his confusion. In Orton's face she read more uncertainty. Orton's family was also a Virginia one, and he, too, wondered about his course of action. . . . Salina entered with a letter for her son, and a moment later Custis faced her. "They've called Father back, to report to General Scott."

Mary's joy was mixed with foreboding. For Robert this would be a time of bitter testing.

A stern man, cold-faced, his hair grayer than before, reached out his hand to her on that March day of 1861. After a moment Robert's look softened. "It's seemed so long, Mary, so very long."

When they sat with the children, Robert appeared enveloped by the darkness of the hour; in his eyes Mary saw a brooding sadness. He had little to say on general matters; he talked only of of the family, the household happenings. One thing she could tell him, news that brought his prompt attention: "The Virginia convention is meeting now, and it's against the hotheads and secession."

His eyes widened, and she realized that he was pleased. Soon, however, his air of depression returned, and Mary motioned to the children. "Your father's very tired." In silence he helped her upstairs and to bed. All that night he tossed restlessly beside her and at last fell into a heavy sleep. For hours she stayed awake, thinking what she might say to him. Yet the decision must be his, and she knew it.

The next day Robert rode over to General Scott's office. She knew that the general was using every argument with Robert, every persuasion. At the thought of their old friend she softened; not many people had been so genuinely interested in their welfare, and she was warmly grateful. Mary clenched her hands in sudden pain. During these days of excitement and uncertainty, her rheumatic troubles had become gradually more insistent, and she knew they might be worse again. Angrily she struggled against real fear. She must think only of her husband and his dilemma; and she almost succeeded.

When Robert returned he looked troubled. He told her: "I was with him for several hours, and he said a great deal." Some of the general's words had moved her husband deeply. He added, "There's a vacancy, a full colonel's rank in the cavalry and they're commissioning me." Robert showed a wistful irony, which she quickly understood. It was the advance for which he had hoped for a long time, and which at last came only at a time of dark and ominous changes. In the dusk Mary and Robert Lee stood together staring across the dimming lawn. . . .

During these hours of trial the Lees remained largely to themselves, as friends brought accounts of events across the river. While one side shouted and the other watched in angry silence, Abraham Lincoln took office. No guns had yet gone off, and Virginia kept apart from the Confederacy; there was still hope, Mary told herself, as if she had memorized the words.

As the orators hurled abuse at Washington City, at Atlanta and New Orleans and Savannah, United States forces awaited reinforcements at Fort Sumter in Charleston, where Beauregard commanded Confederate soldiers. For a few days Mary tried to reject the unhappy present, until Robert brought her back to it with a start. He had the overcast look that had now become chronic with him. "Mim, the Confederate Secretary of War is offering me a commission . . . as a general in the new army."

Her eyes searched his. Overnight a still higher rank than the Union side had offered! She thought of the long barren years when no advancement had come to him. A half-forgotten memory flickered in her mind. Long ago hadn't she told him he would someday reach a general's rank?

Rooney rode in from White House plantation, and he and Custis retired for a long talk with their father. From the next room Mary could hear Custis' voice. "Anything, almost anything's better than breaking up the Union." And the excitable Rooney called out, "These people behave like lunatics." Listening, Mary thought of Ann Marshall's letter. Hadn't they agreed that, in spite of Northern excesses, the Southern secessionists were wrong? They could only wait and hope. . . .

In mid-April she made out Orton's horse pounding up the road. The lieutenant stood at the doorway trying to regain his breath. "It's Fort Sumter! The United States started to send supplies, and Beauregard gave the order. Now they're shooting!"

Her breath caught. Robert, his face white, went out without a word to ride into Alexandria for further information. Hours later he came back. "Sumter's surrendered." So force had been used, and now it would be met with more force. Her husband spoke again: "The Virginia convention's calling a meeting, Mim." When Mary touched his hand, it was icy. Now Virginia would have to make its choice, and so would her husband.

Harsh news drifted over the river. Abraham Lincoln had asked for more than 80,000 soldiers to suppress the rebellion. In the meantime, both Francis Blair, Sr., the journalist, and General Scott asked to see Robert. He left at once, and Mary spent a lonely, nervous day by herself.

Toward dusk she heard the familiar sound of his footsteps. Standing at the door, his hands loose at his sides, Robert told her. "Mim, it's—hard to believe, but they offered me command of the Union Army."

She could not speak. A post that even she had not hoped he could reach, a place to which his beloved father had not approached . . . She remembered General Scott's words to her, years earlier in Baltimore; to him Robert was America's best soldier. Today the general had proved he meant what he said.

Robert's words broke in. "The Virginia convention's in session in Richmond"—his voice quivered—"I'm going to Alexandria to see what I can find out." Mary remained for hours in her sitting room, in bleak uncertainty. When Salina or Markie or her daughters approached, she answered them in monosyllables. When Robert returned he held out a newspaper. Two words jumped before her: "VIRGINIA. SECESSION." He seemed to struggle for breath, and quietly he went upstairs.

In the dark a curtain stirred, and one of the cats rubbed against her; she did not move. Above her Robert walked back and forth across the chamber. She heard a thump, and realized that he had dropped to his knees beside the bed that had been George Washington's. A chair moved; he had gone to the desk.

After a long silence Robert came downstairs, his step quicker, firmer. As he handed her two letters, he had a calm that Mary had not seen in him in weeks. She knew what he had written.

The first note told General Scott that Robert was resigning from the American Army, to which, he said, he had given most of his life; but he would carry to his death a grateful recollection of Winfield Scott's kindnesses. The second letter went to Robert's sister Ann. Virginia, he wrote, had at last been drawn into "a state of revolution." He saw no necessity for this state of affairs; he would have "foreborne and pleaded to the end for a redress of grievances." And yet he had to meet the question whether he would join others against Virginia.

With all my devotion to the Union and the feeling of loyalty and duty of an American citizen, I have not been able to make up my mind to raise my hand against my relatives, my children, my home . . . Save in defense of my native state, with the sincere hope that my poor services may never be needed, I hope I may never be called on to draw my sword. I know you will blame me; but you must think as kindly of me as you can . . .

Robert on one side, his sister on the other. Other Lees, other Custises would take the Union view; and how many more families would be broken apart? Mary cursed the agitators on both sides, the howlers and the madmen who had made this happen. Let God damn them all.

She began to cry, and Robert drew her against him. In the dim room they clung together in a world that was falling to pieces.

PART III

"If you knew all, you would not think so hardly of me."

MARY CUSTIS LEE TO GENERAL WINFIELD SCOTT

Chapter 12

Over Arlington lay a silence, as if, like Mary herself, the house waited for what the next few weeks would bring. On the day after he resigned from the Army of the United States, Robert received an invitation to call on Virginia's governor in Richmond. "I believe I'd better start in the morning, Mim," he told her. He said little more, and she did not press him, though a dozen questions came to her. Would he be returning? And would there be a need for her to leave Arlington?

Yet he must have been asking some of the same things that she did. As he gave her a good-by kiss, his manner became urgent. "Promise you'll be careful, and not do anything impulsive. Nobody knows what will happen, and I'll have to leave a lot to you."

Robert's last words, evidence of his confidence in her, made her spirits lift. "I'll manage," she assured him. Then his eyes moved over her as if he thought he might not see her for a long time. He did not trust himself to speak again. Instead he turned and went to his horse. A last wave, and he had gone. Custis silently helped her into the house.

"Thank you," Mary told her son, and watched him as he left. For days this oldest boy had wandered about, his anxiety in his face. He spoke of the unwisdom of secession, and still he had not made up his mind. At that Mary thought anxiously of the Marshalls in Baltimore. Ann's son, Louis, had joined the Northern army. Suppose Custis sided against his father? With a wince of pain she turned to the letters on her desk.

Out of the first envelope fell a letter from a Washington friend, an editor who enclosed newspaper clippings. She picked up the first: The South was a "nation of whip-carrying tyrants," "murder in their minds." Her anger stirred; so many people said those things today, and believed them. The next item declared with approval that fifteen more Southern sympathizers had been arrested in Washington City, while another great Northern army gathered, and factories poured out millions of arms for a force such as the country had never known.

Newspapers silenced, men and women seized for their thoughts . . . and those people were preparing to invade the South. She got up with an effort. *Those people*. In her mind she had drawn a line between "them" and "us," the good and the bad.

Even now, Mary reminded herself, in spite of Fort Sumter, there had still been no actual battle. Each side awaited the other's next move . . . In her room, lifting her spoon to the medicine bottle, she suddenly looked around in wonder. What gave the house so different an atmosphere? After a moment she understood. Overnight Arlington had taken on an isolated air. They had few guests, now, either sight-seers or friends.

But one friend, at least, continued to call. Orton Williams let them know without saying so that he would come and go just as he had always done. At the thought of Orton she felt better. Slightly cocky and oversure of himself though he undoubtedly was, the boy had definitely superior qualities, which gained as he grew older.

"Well, Mother, don't you want to see me?"

Mary had missed the approach of a familiar figure. In the doorway stood Rooney, fatigued, his tension cutting deep lines along his nose and mouth. His heavy frame bent over hers and he spoke swiftly. "I rode over from White House the moment I settled things. I'm going to follow Father."

While she tried to absorb the news, Rooney sank to the floor and dropped his head against her knee. "I haven't wanted to do it; I thought the way you did, that they'd settle the differences somehow. Now . . ." Mary felt a stifling sensation; so she was giving up a second loved one.

She remembered the weeks she had spent at White House with

Rooney, Charlotte, and their baby. Her happiness had reflected theirs; and now, having found the kind of life for which he was best fitted, Rooney was leaving it and his new family at White House. She stroked his thick, loose hair, and the moment brought them closer than they had been in a long time.

"I've got to go." Tired though he was, Rooney would not stay.

Her son's departure was still in her mind when she received a note with the big, awkward handwriting of young Rob, now at the University of Virginia. Rob had joined the student military corps, but now he wanted to do more, enlist in the Army!

Mary's fingers twisted; the boy was only seventeen, and when she saw him she still smoothed down the awkward cowlick. Before her came his impudent nose and serene light eyes. He was so young. . . .

Robert himself settled that matter. In his next note his first words made her feel better: "I wrote to Rob that I could not consent to take boys from their schools and . . . put them in the ranks at the beginning of the war when they are not needed." Then her eyes widened. "The war may last ten years."

Ten years, when others spoke confidently of nine or ten months! Already Robert had told her how woefully unprepared the South was, lacking in metals and other materials, outnumbered and as yet poorly organized. With mixed emotions she went to the garden, always a retreat from stress; and there, in the shadows of the arbor, she almost collided with a figure on the bench.

"Hello, there." Orton Williams gave one of his usual easy greetings. Beside him, smiling shyly, sat her daughter Agnes. The boy had an engaging grin, and his heavy brows went up and down in a manner that once annoyed Mary. It no longer did; she had concluded it was entirely unconscious. Even if it were not, wouldn't most people give Orton the benefit of any doubt?

As the youth spoke, Mary grew aware that Agnes was watching him steadily. Under her mother's glance the girl's eyes dropped; but when Mary looked again Agnes was staring once more with eager interest. Mary realized that here finally was one of their daughters with at least a romantic inclination. Yet she knew that with this diffident girl it would be unwise to bring up the matter. Nonetheless, from now on she intended to leave these two together whenever she could.

Then she saw that Orton had something to say, and suddenly he told them: "They gave me a commission today—first lieutenant, U.S.A." Mary saw his simple delight; he had won his promotion very soon after leaving West Point. But even as he spoke, Mary realized that her young kinsman felt drawn toward the Southern side. And now Orton paused again with an embarrassed air.

"What is it, boy?" she demanded.

"Well, I haven't wanted to show you this. You're bound to hear of it, though." She accepted the newspaper clipping that he drew from his pocket. At her first glance she was about to hand it angrily back; nevertheless she made herself read on:

Among the lists of ingrates and traitors . . . stand [s] out . . . Robert E. Lee. Lee once professed to greatly venerate the memory and example of the great Washington. He even married the daughter of George Washington Parke Custis . . . who . . . never tired of writing and eloquently portraying the virtues and eminent deeds of the Father of his Country . . . If Custis . . . could have lived until now, he would have good cause to be bowed down in grief and sorrow to behold his son-in-law following in the footsteps of Benedict Arnold.

Mary's face went taut with shame and fury. To say that about Robert, to drag in her dead father as well! More followed: the writer pointed a finger at Arlington, "R. E. Lee's house," and asked, Would that vantage spot for a surprise attack on Washington, now a nest of traitors, be allowed to stay in the hands of enemies of the country?

She cried out in astonishment, "An attack from here—who ever heard of such a thing!"

"Well." Orton lowered his eyes. "Some people are claiming the Confederates will fortify Arlington Heights. With good cannon they *could* bombard the city from here."

Mary winced at the prospect of any use of her property for such a purpose. Slowly she asked: Still, might it happen eventually? Or perhaps the North would take it, as the article hinted. In either case the thought of Arlington in military hands was a frightening possibility. Trembling, she went to her room. There the outrageous newspaper words repeated themselves in her mind. She remembered the editor friend who had written her, and suddenly she wanted to let him know how she felt. She began:

I do not know, my dear sir, what your feeling may be *now* towards the South, and this unhappy difference which has destroyed our glorious Union forever . . . I have lived seven of the happiest years of my life in the North and have admired its institutions, its energy, its progress, have never denied the great advantages they possess over us in their free labor, or attributed to the people the mad ravings of a few fanatics. I had no sympathy with the hasty course of South Carolina and prayed and hoped for the Union "till the course of the Administration left us no alternative but to retire and defend our lives, our fortune and our sacred honour," and I assure you there is *but one voice* now in the South.

More slowly she went on:

The idea of coercing a free people into *Union* is perfectly absurd, and there is a spirit here that will not be coerced. There is a perfect military despotism now at Washington . . . I pray daily to God to avert civil war, yet cannot conceive why Lincoln has assembled such an army if it is not his intention to *attempt* to *crush* the South . . . I have one great consolation now, that my dear parents are both laid low in their graves, where but for my children I would most gladly lay beside them.

Rereading her last words, Mary sought anxiously for some comfort in the situation, and she could find none. She wondered more and more about Robert. What was he doing now? . . . She received her answer from a newspaper account telling that he had been named major general in command of Virginia's state forces. Her heart quickened; so Robert would be a general after all. She thrilled as she read of ceremonies in which speakers paid tribute to her husband, to his father, and cited Washington and other Virginians who had preceded Robert Lee.

When he wrote again, he passed over the ceremonies and spoke directly of family matters. Their oldest son had asked which side to follow, and now Mary read: "Tell Custis he must consult his own judgment, reason and conscience as to the course he may take. I do not wish him to be guided by my wishes or example. If I have done wrong, let him do better." At these words a great tenderness enveloped her; even for his own son Robert would not try to decide.

She continued to read: "I am very anxious about you. You have to move and make arrangements to go to some point of safety, which you must select . . . War is inevitable, and there is no telling when it will burst around you."

There it was, the subject she had been trying to avoid. To have to leave Arlington; for Richmond, perhaps? . . . Robert made it clear that she could not plan to be with him even there. While he would have been pleased to have her and the girls with him, he explained, he expected to be in the field and wanted them in some safe place.

Still she argued with herself: They were not sure that either side would try to take the Arlington section. If the Union did . . . She thought of their friend General Scott; might he protect her home from damage? When Orton arrived again, she brought up the matter.

The boy hesitated. "Well, certain people in the office there are strong against General Lee, and would like to seize the place, just to show him!" Mary was startled. So they wanted to strike at him by taking property that was hers and not his own . . . Orton continued, "Oh, General Scott isn't that way. He is against the Confederacy, but he speaks kindly of General Lee. He even tried to get reports telling of Lee's honors in Richmond."

This was warming news; Winfield Scott had not closed the door on their friendship. With that, however, Orton flushed. "You know, ma'am, General Scott blames Southern women more than the men. He says General Lee never would have——" Orton halted abruptly.

Mary smiled briefly; though the words hurt, she could bear up under such an opinion. Later that day the wife of the commander of Virginia's forces did an unusual thing. She addressed a letter to the head of the hostile Union military machine:

My dear General: Hearing that you desire to see the account of my husband's reception in Richmond, I have sent it to you. No honors can reconcile us to this fratricidal war which we would have laid down our lives freely to avert. Whatever may happen, I feel that I may expect from your kindness all the protection you can in honor afford . . .

Then she was caught by a wave of regret:

If you knew all, you would not think so hardly of me. Were it not that I would not add one feather to his load of care, nothing would induce me to abandon my home. Oh, that you could command peace to our distracted country!

Who could do that now? Before sending the letter off she looked out of her window; Agnes and Orton were walking along the brow of the hill. As often as possible in these days she saw that they were undisturbed as they rode along the Arlington roads or strolled the gardens. After a time her daughter had understood what Mary was doing, and her appreciative glances let Mary know it.

That week she learned by accident that old General Scott had fallen under the scorching disapproval of his fellow Virginians. From the university Rob sent an excited message telling how their friend had been burned in effigy. Aunt Maria passed on the story that Winfield Scott's nephew had ripped his picture from the wall and chopped it to bits. And a Confederate paper called Scott a "driveling old fop" who used "a pencil of infamy" to write "traitor" on his own brow. Mary shuddered; a few miles away other men used the same words about her husband.

One morning Mary was suddenly aware that there was a commotion outside. Orton appeared in the doorway, his face sweat-streaked and pale.

"It's important, ma'am. I can't say who told me, but"—the boy gulped—"orders came from higher up. They're getting ready to send soldiers here and very soon."

Mary's hands went cold, and she grasped at the curtain. At the door Agnes showed her despair. Orton was saying something else: "I've got to go; some people in the office wouldn't want me here at all." As he stepped forward to take her hand in an oddly formal way, Mary thought of the boy's position, more dangerous than she had realized. Had she been wise . . . But now this would be good-by, perhaps for a long time.

She kissed Orton, and he went out with Agnes following him

into the hall. Alone, Mary slowly told herself: We must leave Arlington. If she stayed and dared the invaders to remove her from this inherited property, it might hurt them all, and it would do no good to Robert.

With a harsh effort she pushed herself up. A throbbing agony dug into her legs; though her face twisted, she made herself go forward. She could not indulge herself; she had more important things to do. Momentarily her rage broke. The white-livered scoundrels, to do this because they connected Robert's name with Arlington. For revenge they would bear down on a place that had the possessions of George Washington . . . She stopped; those were the things she must remember now, those treasures!

As she started from room to room she called, "Salina, I'll need you right by me." "Jim, will you bring Nurse and anybody else you can find?" She paused before the big Washington portrait, with the pink face shining out of the smoky background, and glanced at the other pictures that seemed to belong there.

At that she became aware that Agnes had returned, and she went to the girl. Her daughter's voice was low. "Will anything happen to Orton?" In Agnes' face she read an unmasked love and fear. Suddenly moved, Mary put her arm around the girl's waist. "Child, this trouble won't last forever. Things will be the same again. I promise it!"

Agnes lowered her head, then turned with a happier look. "Can't I help you get the Mount Vernon silver into boxes?" Mary nodded; the question prodded her into action. She moved toward the famous lantern, and noted the punch bowl with its painted ship. Upstairs were the tall Washington bed, and the revolutionary tent wrapped in its thick bundle . . . Each object had its story, and now she could almost hear her father's words:

"That was the day the President took my hand and told me . . . I was standing before the tent." Washington Custis had expected these relics to be undisturbed as long as the house itself remained here. How could she tear them down?

Nevertheless it must be done. Ladders were brought in, with wrapping cloths, boxes, and boards. A few minutes later Custis joined them without comment, in a burst of energy. "I can find carts, and we could send some of the smaller stuff to friends in Richmond."

An unexpected visitor joined them in the plump and determined person of Maria Fitzhugh. "Don't waste time telling me! It's an outrage, but I have more practical things to say." The several chins below the pink mouth shook with determination. The dark little dowager barely paused for the kiss and went on to Mary. "I'll be glad to take anything you want to store with me, and you and the girls too."

Mary looked away, almost overcome. In these days, when much of the world moved from them, she found any help a cause for tears. Facing the others, she reached an interim decision. "You girls will go with Aunt Maria. Custis and I will do all we can here and—well, we'll decide later."

"We can't be here much longer." Custis' voice had a glum note, and they went to work again. A dish crashed, the fragments sliding across the polished floor; the leg of a chair cracked, but it could not be helped. The hall and several rooms took on a naked look. From the bare rooms rose long-accumulated dust; through curtainless windows the sun threw slanting rays over walls with faded squares where pictures had hung.

"Oh . . ." With a groan Mary stared through the arched openings. They could hope to move only a fraction of their possessions. "We'll have to put some of the china, and the President's books, in the cellar, and the engravings in the attic. Who's out there?" She almost jumped; all unexpected arrivals now affected her in that way.

It was Markie, and her manner gave them forewarning of bad news. Sinking to a sofa, the girl began in a monotone: "It's Orton. Yesterday he made up his mind, and told them he was going to join the South. He tried to get in to General Scott and couldn't. Well——" The tears were streaking Markie's face. "The others in his office called him a traitor, and he's been arrested."

"Arrested?" Mary echoed the word, and Agnes came forward. "For what?"

Markie's eyes were brooding. "They claim that, since Orton worked in that office, he knew all the Union's military plans, and brought secrets to General Lee and you, and—betrayed the North."

Agnes cried out. Mary sank down beside Markie and pressed the girl's head against her shoulder. Her first reaction had been one of fury; Robert Lee would not receive information sneaked over in such a way! Then she thought of their young kinsman, and wondered if she were not partly to blame for his situation. Shouldn't she have realized what might happen?

Mary sensed that Markie had something more to tell them. Drawing back, the girl groaned: "My other brother Lawrence— he's staying with the North. Against us, all of us!" As Markie's voice broke Mary closed her eyes. Another family with members lined against one another; as in Robert's case, brother against sister. . . .

Custis cleared his throat. "We can't delay any longer. As soon as we've packed all we can, I'll take you, Mother, with some of the things to Aunt Maria's." He paused for a long moment, and added, "I'll go on to Richmond from there. To volunteer."

They could do no more. Daniel brought down Mary's trunk and carpetbag, and four of the cats padded after him. One of them, Tom, gave a cry and jumped to the table. While Mary rubbed his fur, the others purred on the floor. "Salina," she asked, "see that nothing happens to them, will you?"

The housekeeper nodded. When Custis led Mary to the door the cats watched, almost, she thought, as if they understood something of the circumstances. Nurse had a stricken look. "Ma'am, how we goin' to do without you?" Beside her, Daniel spoke in sudden anxiety. "They say the soldiers mean to people. Takes chickens and eggs and everything."

Mary's voice caught. "I don't think anybody will hurt you. Just—just watch that you don't get into trouble. Keep up your vegetable gardens, and that will give you money for tea and sugar and things." Her hand reached to her bag. "I wish I could leave you more, but we have so little of our own." These bills must pay her way and the girls' for some time to come. Although her tears were close, her effort to concentrate on the details helped, and she went on:

"Salina, make sure the summer grass doesn't swallow the walks." She was remembering her mother's endless care of the garden, her painstaking transfer of plants from one spot to another; hastily she tried to think of other things. Leaning on Custis' arm, she made her way with difficulty toward the carriage, and the servants crowded around.

"Good-by."

"God proteck you." It was Salina's deep-throated blessing.

At the carriage step Mary turned to stare at Arlington's graying walls and the windswept portico. Between the central pillars the cats sat on their haunches. The day had a subdued radiance that gave a burnished look to the bushes, a sharpened whiteness to the flowering vines. Everywhere was a stillness like that of death, she told herself.

"I'm coming, Custis," she whispered to her son, and her eyes went to the triangular roof line against the drift of the clouds. Then she remembered how the leaves lay often across the portico, and Salina's grumbling over the trouble they caused, and the swampy smell from the lowlands.

From the hill she looked over the river to the distant blue flatness of Washington City, with the partially erected monument in memory of the President, and the unfinished dome of the Capitol. Unfinished—was there something symbolic in that? The city itself, named for the man who had been part of her daily life from her earliest memory . . . It was strange to consider it headquarters of enemy forces; and among the enemies would be many men whom she and Robert had known for years, men who had visited at Arlington.

No matter what happened, she would be back here; she swore it. She let her son signal to Daniel, and they rode swiftly down the hill.

Chapter 13

Years earlier she had written a friend that she felt like "a wanderer on the face of the earth." Now, over a period of fifteen months, as she moved at irregular intervals from place to place in Virginia, she learned what the words really implied. For Mary the warm months of 1861 would mean the murmurs of women as they spoke of battle, and glimpses of soldiers in straggling lines. Waking daily, she would ask herself meanwhile what was happening at Arlington, and now and then she would get disturbing bits of information.

At Ravensworth, Mrs. Fitzhugh's place, she heard that the Federal troops had swept across the Potomac to take Alexandria and Arlington itself. Her property was one of the first to be occupied in Virginia, and Mary winced as friends told her it had become a well-guarded camp, with men in tents over the grounds, trenches and cannons on the heights. "And," Aunt Maria said gently, "they're cutting down the trees. You mustn't expect it to look the same."

Mary checked her bitter words. When she went back she would restore Arlington to its old state; that was the thing to remember. Mrs. Fitzhugh patted her arm, and settled down without further word. Mary was relieved; at such a time simple silence meant more than a dozen vague reassurances . . . Her thoughts shifted with the arrival of a note carrying a well-loved signature, Markie's, from Georgetown. Her heart missed a beat at the first name, Orton's.

He was safe—not merely safe but inside Southern lines, and

fighting on the Confederate side! With growing excitement she discovered that after his arrest by the Union officers the boy had been taken to New York. After a month in custody he had been released, his captors saying that by this time any information he might have given the South would be outdated. And then, Markie announced, Orton had slipped into Confederate territory. Mary smiled; for Orton, of course, always the romantic, had carried out this act in dramatic style.

She faced around. "Agnes, Agnes!" She handed the letter to her daughter, who read it while she watched. The girl got up with an uncertain smile; though her eyes retained their heightened gleam, Agnes murmured, "He'll be in the shooting now, won't he?"

Less happily she resumed Markie's note, and quickly her interest sharpened. Their cousin had wondered how the family possessions were faring under the Federal occupation and had gone over to Arlington. The sentry detained her until Salina explained her identity. At Salina's name Mary felt better. Trust Salina to "manage," even with interlopers; it was good to know that the old housekeeper stayed on, keeping the Lees' interests at heart. Markie's note went on:

I was blinded by tears . . . as I tried to gaze on scenes once so familiar, now so strangely distorted . . . The poor house looked so desolate. I went to my room and when the door was shut, gave way to the most bitter lamentations. I thought so much of you and of what your sorrow would be, to see things as they are.

Had Markie planned it, she could not have chosen words that would tear so deeply at Mary. The letter continued: Markie had heard mewing on the upper floor, and when she opened the door, Tom, the cat, crept forward. "He looked so pitiful there in his lonely garret home, but I suppose his instincts teach him not to leave it." Then Markie had stopped at Mrs. Custis' garden, to find the roses and white jasmines blooming on despite occupation and fortifications. Unable to read further, Mary put the note aside.

At her elbow Aunt Maria called out cheerily, "Isn't it wonderful that the Confederate government's moving to Richmond from way down in that Montgomery place. That should help everything." Head averted, Mary reflected ironically: Aunt Maria spoke like a true Virginian! Nevertheless, she remembered Robert's words; the choice of Richmond might well be a major mistake. Located so close to Washington City, it was extremely vulnerable, and its defense would put a heavy strain on Southern forces.

Mrs. Fitzhugh's mood was confident. "Some people talk about long enlistments. Hm! One real battle and we'll have those Yankees taking to the hills." Once again Mary sat silent. Robert worked day and night, trying to fill gaps in Virginia's fortifications, to create defenses where there were none. They had so little; they needed ammunition, supplies, ships, food—and also time. And when even an intelligent plantation woman spoke as Aunt Maria did, it was no wonder Robert worried about overconfidence.

But Mary enjoyed it here; Mrs. Fitzhugh had been a rare friend, warm and understanding. Then, however, Robert sent urgent instructions: Aunt Maria's place lay too close to the Northern forces, and the enemy might make her suffer for "harboring" his wife. Mary stared at the word with a tightened brow, and her humor returned. She had better get used to the fact that in some eyes she was a dangerous individual! Very well, she would move on.

Soon afterward the girls received invitations, Agnes and Annie from one family, Mildred and Mary from another. After further thought she agreed to their going, and then she heard Mildred and young Mary:

"Will we be near any fighting?"

"I'll bet we see lots of soldiers!"

Mary had a feeling of regret; they seemed actually to be enjoying the war. Still, she reminded herself, for the young these times had novelty and excitement. Reluctantly she told them good-by and set out on her own travels. With her relatives, the Randolphs at Eastern View, she enjoyed a short respite. Her rheumatic pains had increased once more, and now she could concentrate briefly on her health.

After a few weeks there came vague stories of changes in Virginia's military organization. With the state's mobilization finished, Robert was transferred to the larger Confederate Army.

What did that mean? She could learn only that her husband would be in some capacity under President Davis, who was also commander in chief, and that he expected before long to go into the field.

At the same time they all heard more and more about two figures: Pierre G. T. Beauregard, the handsome Frenchman who became the hero of Fort Sumter, and Joe Johnston, who had been made a major general of Virginia and had then gone directly into the Confederate forces as a brigadier general. Each had taken a command in the Virginia area. She thought of Johnston's coup of a few years earlier; somehow Joe always came out on top of those around him. Since her husband was not here to check her, she would go right on indulging her opinions of the man!

Then, as she sat in the Randolph parlor, she caught an undertone of anxiety. After she asked several questions Colonel Randolph explained: "There's talk of a battle, the first real one of the war, and not far off—Manassas. They claim Johnston and Beauregard are both near here. . . . No, General Lee's in Richmond. Haven't heard anything about him lately."

Mary bent over the canvas. Not many people were hearing about Robert . . . She saw the expression on Mrs. Randolph's face and remembered. "Your boys, where are they now?"

"Out there, both of them." It was Colonel Randolph who answered, and his wife walked slowly into the hall. With a stricken sensation Mary asked herself what she could say to her.

It was that afternoon that Mary first heard that vague thudding sound in the distance. The Randolphs tried to ignore it, but it grew steadily through evening and into early night. The next day was a Sunday, and as they met for breakfast the colonel spoke quickly. "We'll be ready for church in town, whenever you are."

Mary nodded; trying to eat, she found she could not. How soon would the cannons boom again? In this hour of trial she longed to be inside the small church. They said little on the way, nor again when they went to their pew. So many around them must be in the same position, their nerves taut as they waited.

Within the ivied walls the music drifted away and the minister began. Mary followed his words until there came a muffled boom off in the distance. A woman rose with a half cry, and Mary's knuckles went to her mouth. In the cold silence the congregation sat rigid for the next blast.

"And the Lord saith, to those of little faith . . ."

A comfort settled upon them, like a hand placed gently on their shoulders. A low rumble sounded, and a heavy boom, much closer; beside Mary, Mrs. Randolph sat, lips moving. Each time Mary heard the blast she thought of her husband and her two boys and Orton, wherever they might be. She could almost feel the urgency of the prayers which were offered by those around her, and she prayed herself: Please, keep them safe, keep them safe.

The service finished, and the long, tense Sunday went on. Hours later, in the descending coolness of the July night, she stared across the road, dimly lighted from the house. The slow silence alarmed her more than the roars. Looking down, she saw that her tightened knuckles stood out like ridges.

At the same moment she and Mrs. Randolph caught the creak of an advancing wagon. They went down the steps, Mary clinging painfully to her cousin's arm, and as the vehicle crept into the light she gasped. Five or six bloodied men were stretched across the boards; one lay back, supported by a friend. His arm hung crazily, the jagged bluish end of bone sticking out of the flesh; one cheek and most of the nose had been shot away, as if a scoop had passed over his face.

But others were shouting, "We won!" "Got the God-damned Yankees runnin' home, tails between their legs!" Colonel Randolph came up at a run. "They're going to push on to Washington and stop the war right now!"

Elation broke around them, but the broken bodies were still being spewed out of Manassas. Only gradually could Mary absorb the joyful news. If it were true, Robert and their boys would be safe and they could go home away from this miserable hate and fear. Through the night she waited for further word.

Before noon the next day the wild predictions about an onslaught on Washington City died down. The war would continue, and from the Federal city word arrived of vast preparations. Her heart sank. "Well, we've had victory enough for a while," Colonel Randolph cried, like others around them. "And nobody can match our officers, Johnston and Beauregard. They're practically *all* we need!" The Confederacy had its two great heroes.

Mary applied herself to her sewing. She was happy, of course, that things had gone so well; yet only a few months earlier the whole state had been honoring Robert Lee. . . . When his next letter came from Richmond, he told her that while he had wanted to take part in the fighting, ". . . the President thought it more important I should be here." He praised Beauregard and Johnston: "I could not have done as well as has been done, but I could have helped and taken part in the struggle."

In his words Mary read his disappointment at the recent turn of events. The letter continued: "I leave tomorrow for the Northwest Army." She had a new sensation of emptiness, of sudden loss; he was moving still farther from her, and into the exposed front in Western Virginia, where things were going badly for the South.

That same day she had a burning sensation in her arm; a dull ache which centered there for most of the day, gradually growing worse. Mary recognized the signal; she must try the springs, accept one or another of the recent invitations. That summer she moved several times before she reached the hot springs in Bath County, which gave her some relief. And meanwhile, through late summer and fall, she snatched up every report from Western Virginia.

For weeks she tried to discount rumors of new troubles, hints of increasing setbacks. She realized later that her friends made efforts to prepare her: "That part of Virginia isn't like this, you understand. Very few slaves." Already she knew that Union elements had declared this region a separate state. Worst of all was the last explanation: "We started wrong out there from the first, with politicians for officers, snapping at one another. Sometimes they even refuse to accept orders!"

From Robert's letters Mary learned more. It had begun to rain, day after day after day, turning roads into bogs; carts halted, wagons lay trapped in the syrupy mud: "I have on my winter clothes and am writing in my overcoat" . . . "There has not been sunshine enough since my arrival to dry my clothes" . . . "We are without tents, and for two nights I have lain buttoned up in my overcoat. Today my tent came up, yet I fear I shall not sleep for thinking of my poor men."

Reading on, she winced. A third of Robert's men lay ill with measles, typhoid, and other diseases. It became impossible to get information about the enemy, while the mountain people told the Unionists of every Confederate maneuver. Sadly she thrust the note into her pocket, to find the other guests in the living room of the resort gazing curiously at her. One of the men, holding a newspaper, pushed it casually, too casually, behind him. She bent forward, extending her hand, and he spoke in a nervous rush. "Mrs. Lee, papers do get things mixed." Then he gave her the journal.

Despite her preparation the words had an almost physical effect on her: *"General Withdrawal in Western Virginia. Failure of Plans."* The writer pointed his finger at Robert Lee. The general, he said, had demonstrated complete incapacity, and should be retired to pursuits in which he could do less harm. The public demanded it. . . . Aware of the stares, Mary excused herself, to sit alone with hands clenched before her. It hadn't been Robert's fault; the assignment was an impossible one. Yet nobody could deny that in less than a year's time her husband's career had fallen to its lowest point.

"Mrs. Lee?" A younger woman stood in the door, and her look was compassionate. "We thought you'd want to hear this. They tell us Mr. Davis has called General Lee to Richmond."

Mary's anger blotted out every other emotion. Before her appeared the narrow face of Jefferson Davis, and she hated it. Let Mr. Davis call Robert to Richmond, discard him, or do anything he wanted! Then she and her husband could go off quietly to a farm and be free once and for all.

"Mrs. Lee, you don't understand. Mr. Davis has let people know he doesn't agree with the criticisms of General Lee, and he's going to give him another command."

She got slowly to her feet. So Robert would have his chance again; and for this she must always remember Jefferson Davis. And now she wanted suddenly to be with Robert, and she thought of her relatives, the Carters of Shirley on the James River. They had been asking her to go there whenever she wished. Shirley lay only twelve miles outside Richmond and nothing could keep her away.

From almost the hour of her arrival at Shirley, Mary expected Robert to join her. He sent word that he would be with them at the first opportunity, within the next few days. It sounded odd to hear one of her relatives remark, "I ran into Robert yesterday, on Franklin Street. He's lost weight, but he looked well." Although only a short distance separated them, how far off he seemed.

Several days passed, and on a Sunday morning Mary went to breakfast with the certainty that he would arrive that day. She made an effort to apply herself to the well-aged ham, the soft yellow spoon bread, and coffee; but the food stuck in her throat. Mrs. Carter smiled encouragement. "Mary, don't be so excited. It can't be much longer."

But it *was* much longer. Breakfast ended, and early afternoon passed; for the midafternoon meal she could touch nothing, and steadily she watched the clock. At last the Carters moved to the parlor before the crackling fire. For hours she gazed into the flames, and then made her way upstairs. The eyes that followed her were pitying.

The next day Mary sat again near the clock, through the morning and afternoon. Toward dark a knock sounded, and a man handed in a note from Robert. Everything had worked against him these past few days, he explained. Once he planned to come by boat, only to find none that would make the trip when he could leave. The following day he had started out on horseback, but had missed the road in the dark and had been forced to return. Then yesterday Mr. Davis had said he could not go. But Robert expected to be with her before another week ended.

Surely the course of war would permit a man to visit his wife for a few hours. Mary put down the sheet. What right had Jefferson Davis to act so dictatorially with her husband?

Colonel Randolph returned from Richmond that evening with a worried look on his face. "Mary, I just heard about—this. The fact is . . . Yesterday, just after he wrote that letter, they sent Robert off. Unexpectedly, to South Carolina, to handle the coast defenses."

"I see." The emptiness was worse than she had ever felt. And then she knew that she must stop this visiting, that she had to be with her immediate family again. Her "second home," White House on the Pamunkey, awaited her whenever she wished to go there. Within the day she began her packing.

At the gate of the simple white establishment near the river-bank, with the hills in the distance, her daughter-in-law waited, the dark hair blowing about her lean, reddened cheeks, and holding Rooney's boy by the hand. Charlotte's pretty face brightened, and she led Mary to her room, settled her on a long sofa, and had a meal brought on a tray.

In the well-warmed room, under the cheerful lamplight, Mary sat back to answer Charlotte's questions about Robert, Rooney, the four girls, and the war. Over Mary's voice and Charlotte's the strengthening wind combed the treetops. If only there could be such serenity everywhere, and they could reassemble the family again. . . .

The youngest Robert Lee, now two, sat cross-legged beside her; his eyes, dark as his mother's and the size of walnuts, were fixed on his grandmother. Holding him, she felt the angularity of his frame. "I'll have to fatten you up, child." The young Robert laughed in glee, as if she had made a fine joke, and Mary's glance went to his mother. "You, too, Miss Charlotte." At her daughter-in-law's troubled smile she asked, "You're worried about Rooney?"

"Every day I worry more. In his last skirmish he didn't tell me his horse was shot from under him. Somebody else did." The fine eyes had a touch of terror. Reaching into the big bag that she had brought, Mary handed a ball of wool and needles to Char-lotte. "Let's knit while we talk. They can use all the socks we send."

Already Mary had begun to turn out a stream of knitted gar-ments. Under her scrutiny the girl went to work; as the older woman encouraged her, Charlotte's fingers moved more steadily. After a short silence she asked, "What did you think of that fuss General Johnston made?" When Mary lifted her eyebrows in sur-prise, Charlotte reached for a journal with a long public letter signed by Joseph E. Johnston.

It took Mary minutes to comprehend the raging words: The Confederacy had created five full generals, headed by two elderly figures, with Robert E. Lee third, Joseph E. Johnston and P. G. T. Beauregard after him. She might have understood that this would cut Joe deeply; but she was astonished at his response.

He himself, said Joe Johnston, should have ranked as "first general in the armies." By the order Jefferson Davis had tried to "tarnish my fair fame as a soldier and a man"; he, Johnston, had been "degraded" though he had "borne a prominent part in the only great event" of the war, Manassas, "for the benefit of persons neither of whom has yet struck a blow for this confederacy." One of the persons at whom he pointed his finger was Robert Lee.

Mary's own anger snapped. The self-importance of the man—his fair fame tarnished! Indeed. The little peacock . . . Although she knew she would come back to the matter, she dropped it for a moment; her daughter-in-law was speaking again, and Mary caught words that made her flesh crawl:

"They say things you left behind just disappear from Arlington. Friends have recognized some of the pictures in pawnshops; a junk dealer had a fine candlestick. And some things have been sent to a government museum—the Lafayette china, General Washington's clothes, with a sign, "Captured at Arlington." Oh, Mother, I'm sorry!"

The sight of her chalky face halted Charlotte. Mary was struggling for calm. Her family treasures, stolen like that . . . Charlotte continued to apologize for telling her, but Mary shook her head. "I'll be all right; I had to hear about it sometime."

In the following months Mary felt that she barely existed between Robert's letters from Charleston and Savannah. He was struggling with unending problems in protecting a vulnerable coast, trying to close off rivers, protect railroads, prevent new victories by Northern sea forces. Yet when he had his men use picks and shovels to dig trenches, she heard that the Carolinians protested.

"Look," she said to Charlotte after they had finished another pair of socks. "They say it's not gentlemanly to use shovels!" She recalled the previous day's newspaper; the editor had joined the cry, calling Robert a desk general, a weak man. "Grandma Lee" and "King of Spades" . . . Not many Southerners seemed to hold Robert Lee in high regard. She read his own words: "It is so hard to get anything done . . . It is difficult to get our people to realize their position . . . The volunteers dislike work."

Charlotte was just as angry as Mary. "Too many Southerners resist the very thought of work. That's our trouble."

But meanwhile Mary had begun to wonder. Robert, the tactful, generous man, who seldom forgot the feelings of others—might he lack the brute force, the driving quality demanded at the moment? In a war, perhaps, it was the violent type of soldier who won out. Yet she reminded herself that people had said something like that before the Mexican War and Robert had proved how wrong they were. He had proved it fifteen years ago, but fifteen years could be a long time.

She had been holding her grandson; at the unconscious tightening of her fingers the child raised his face. "Don't mind me," she soothed him. "I'm thinking, just thinking."

When she gazed at the boy her expression softened. With little Robert she was reliving her days as a young wife, her first-born at her side. But had Custis ever been so tiny and so pale? She looked into the luminous face; he seemed all eyes.

"Charlotte, no matter what I've done, he hasn't gained a pound," she fretted. "Nor have you." With an effort to be matter-of-fact Charlotte shrugged. "There are so many extra responsibilities now. Anyway, the first news of victory will bring me around." Each knew what the other was saying to herself, that she might have to wait a long time.

For months Mary had wondered about her youngest son Rob, and now he wrote from the university in a way that made her smile. "I really believe I am getting to be a young man . . . I am five feet ten, strikingly handsome, with a strong tendency to moustache and whiskers." Her affection warmed as she thought of his pert, sprightly face.

Their daughters still traveled, and she had trouble in keeping up with their movements. Robert sent a gently chiding note: The girls wrote him of "projected visits about the state . . . 'pleasant times,' as if enjoyment was the order of the day . . . God knows what is to become of the dear children. They seem to prefer going about to settling down quietly." Mary sighed; how long would it be before they could all be together once more?

There was one pleasant thought she kept before her. On her arrival Charlotte had confided that she was to have a second baby. On grim days Mary reminded herself of that future happiness, soon to be theirs. These months at White House were, as a matter of fact, the most peaceful that she had known since the war began. More than ever the place had become her "second home." At that her mind went painfully to Arlington, but she pushed the memory aside.

The time arrived when she could no longer avoid the clear meaning of the military tidings. In Tennessee the strategic Forts Henry and Donelson were lost and fifteen thousand men surrendered. She groaned to herself; and they needed soldiers so badly . . . A large portion of Kentucky collapsed; in North Carolina, Roanoke Island fell, with frightening repercussions. As Sunday, February 22, 1862, approached, Jefferson Davis asked the South to observe a day of prayer, and early that morning Mary forced herself to her knees with Charlotte and the wondering boy beside her.

They had just arisen when an unexpected caller knocked. Their neighbor, Dr. Macon, remained standing, his face puckered in lines of alarm, and he spoke like a man who had a great deal to say: "You know General Johnston's been guarding the approach from Washington City, and now he's drawing back from McClellan, little by little. Well, it 'pears as if the Federals were headed right this way. Johnston says it's tactics—letting the enemy extend himself while we pull back. Just the same, a lot of us are worried."

Mary looked at Charlotte, uncertain of Dr. Macon's meaning. "Don't you see?" the doctor said, gesturing. "Your place is right on McClellan's way, a strategic point—good communication lines, a railroad right by, command of the river." In the bright morning Mary felt a chill. The worried Dr. Macon added, "Oh, we hear General Lee's been called again to Richmond. For duty under Mr. Davis."

Was that good or bad? Hastily Mary scanned Robert's next note, confirming the news about his assignment. "I do not see either advantage or pleasure in my duties. But I will not complain . . . No one can foresee what will happen . . . The enemy is pushing us back in all directions." And then, to her dismay, Robert agreed with Dr. Macon: they had best leave White House.

At least they had a little time left. The next day, however, a new burden fell upon her. Young Rob had promised to finish his school term without pressing them further about his hope to enter the Army. The term had ended, and now Robert wrote that their son had arrived in Richmond and enlisted as a private. At the news Mary had a feeling of faintness, but she read on: her husband had argued, explaining that the government wished young men to finish their studies; Rob simply shook his head. And so Robert Lee had gone with his boy to help him get overcoat, blanket, and supplies.

"As I have done all in the matter that seems proper and right . . . I hope our son will do his duty and make a good soldier." When Charlotte took the letter from her numb fingers, Mary sat with tightened mouth. They could have spared her this third boy. That night, she gave up her efforts to sleep, and crept to the window, to gaze for hours in the direction from which the Federal forces were approaching.

On a dripping morning they received word that four generals had been killed in Arkansas. At Shiloh General Albert Sidney Johnston had died. Hardly two weeks later New Orleans, greatest of Confederate ports, collapsed, and with it a vast area up the Mississippi. Could the South survive all this?

As she made her way upstairs, Charlotte rode in from a trip to the depot. She shoved open the door and cried, "Joe Johnston's retreating faster than ever. He's even had to leave wounded men behind!" At that moment a noise made them look toward the road. A long file of wagons was creaking along, high with furniture; already men and women had begun to quit the vicinity.

Before Mary could reply, their friend Dr. Macon hurried in. "I think you ought to come over to my place, very soon. The telegrams are mighty frightening."

Mary faced them. "I'm not leaving."

"Mother." Charlotte spoke with earnest care. "As General Lee's wife, you're not—just another person. Some hotheads might cause real trouble here."

Suppose she made things harder for Robert if she stayed. . . . Something tugged at her skirt, and her grandson peered up with a tentative smile. "Granma, you thinkin' like before?"

The child's innocence, and his helplessness settled her mind. "Well, I'll go. But the minute things get better I'll be back, and so will you, Charlotte!" The thought gave her a certain consolation. . . . For hours she and Charlotte piled their belongings on wagons and carts, while the Federal machine rolled closer and closer. Nervously Dr. Macon waited nearby; horsemen were now dashing along the road, and with dark a dull glow on the horizon told them the Union camp had been set up a short way off.

As the two women struggled on, selecting, eliminating, there came a clatter of gunfire, and Mary heard a man shout from the riverbank, then ride away. Dr. Macon was ready to take them over to his place and Charlotte turned appealing eyes. "Mother, we *have* to go." Mary groaned, and a last angry impulse seized her. From the window sill she snatched a stray sheet of paper and wrote in big letters:

Northern soldiers who profess to reverence Washington, forbear to desecrate the home of his first married life, the property of his wife, now owned by her descendants.

A GRANDDAUGHTER OF MRS. WASHINGTON.

She nailed the paper to the door, and Dr. Macon helped her to the carriage. Dully she saw that the road had thickened with wagons, and people were trudging steadily in one direction. "Look at that." Charlotte touched her arm; vessels in the river were being filled with mud and sunk to keep them from Northern hands. And so many miles of this rich country had been given up. . . .

The next weeks were a haze. McClellan reached White House, converted it into a hospital, and friends brought her his assurance that, because of the property's associations, it would not be harmed. "He's even set up guards to protect the building," Dr. Macon told Mary, and she had a measure of relief. Then the

Union Army marched nearer again, and she woke to find several men in blue uniforms standing before the Macon residence.

Dr. Macon's words were placating. "They were sent for your protection."

"They won't 'protect' me!" Mary fumed. Later that day, when friends who lived a short way off, the Ruffins, offered her refuge, she accepted promptly. But Charlotte shook her head. "I don't want to get too far away, Mother, and it's best for little Robert to stay in one place. I think I'll go to some of my people here." Mary, hugging the boy, agreed. He looked more tired than ever; the tensions and irregularities of their last few months had taken their tolls, and he had been sick for days. The parting was hard. The bond between Mary and her daughter-in-law had strengthened during their recent companionship.

"We'll be together soon. We will," she assured Charlotte and kissed the boy again.

At the Ruffin place she caught daily echoes of the Federal battle cry—"On to Richmond!" The Union Army swept heavily forward and Joe Johnston pulled back steadily toward the alarmed city. Mary, prepared as she was, could hardly believe Mr. Ruffin's story that the Confederate government was moving some of its records to other points. Richmond, by now, was the heart and soul of the Confederacy. Robert, like others, had doubted the wisdom of its selection as capital. Nevertheless, if it went now, the war might well be over. She asked herself: And what was her husband doing while Johnston retreated?

Overnight she heard worse news. "General Johnston and Mr. Davis are snapping at one another," Mr. Ruffin explained. "They've never really gotten along since that fight over Johnston's rank. Well, they hardly speak now unless they have to. Mr. Davis wants him to stop drawing back, and Johnston says he can't. Still, the way it looks, the general might even retreat through Richmond itself!"

She thought of Jefferson Davis, then Joe Johnston; she could visualize neither man giving way to the other. From the window she surveyed the familiar signs—fleeing wagons, women riding past in tears; and again several guards in blue stood outside for her protection. But Ruffin had more to tell.

"General Johnston was shot in the fighting outside Richmond, badly enough to remove him from command. And the President has put someone else in his place."

"Yes?" She asked it in a flat voice.

"It's General Lee." In the long silence the words reverberated around her.

As her friend watched she tried to analyze her mixed feelings. After everything that had happened, after the world seemed to have turned against Robert, he would have his chance. When Mr. Ruffin spoke again, he seemed to be echoing her own reservations. "Anyone taking over now will have a terrible time, and . . ."

Mary did not hear the rest. So many people regarded Robert as incompetent, a failure. Now, when his opportunity arrived at last, was it too late—another forlorn hope like Western Virginia? Suddenly she yearned to see Robert again, if only for a few minutes. Getting to her feet, she spoke with renewed energy. "I'm going to write a message, and I want you to send it through the lines, right now."

Somehow the next few days passed, while commissions of the North and South exchanged letters and made arrangements. When they finally told her that she would be permitted to go to Richmond, Mary cried in relief. Robert was to meet her somewhere outside the capital.

For hours she rode in an ancient carriage, past sentries, past lines of men in sweating summer heat. They moved quickly along the road that cut through a deep wood, the sun slanting across the windows. Evening rains had been heavy; from the earth rose a pleasant warmth of leaf and grass and meadow flower. At last a gray house stood a short distance before her, and two officers were talking to an older man with a white beard that almost covered his face.

The bearded one turned, his hat came off, and she recognized Robert Lee.

"Mary!" His voice had the same ring, but he looked so much older, and so different with the beard. For a moment she felt a shyness, as if this were indeed a stranger. Then the brown eyes were on her, warm and understanding, and he kissed her. Yes, this was the Robert she had always known.

As he held her, she remembered that in all those fifteen months away from him, there had not been a day when she waked without longing to be at his side, to see the beloved face and touch it as she was doing now. "Even with the beard," she whispered, "you haven't changed."

They could be together here for only a little while; he had to return to his duties. The Federal Army was pressing steadily nearer, and suddenly she thought of the wagonloads of broken men that she had watched after Manassas. A cannon boomed; the earth quivered beneath and around them, so that he took both her hands in one of his.

"Mim, it's all right. It's all right."

She realized that he was looking at her much as he had when he left Arlington the last time, as if he might not see her for a long time, perhaps never again.

Chapter 14

In the scalding July heat Mary looked from her hotel quarters into a Richmond street filled with dust and movement and the pervasive smell of melting tar. During these two uncertain weeks she had stayed close to her room. With Annie, first of the traveling daughters to rejoin her, she rode along Franklin Street, past narrow brick houses ornamented by white porches and scrolled ironwork, to the square with the old church at the corner, the statehouse across the green; and she had seen it all in a turmoil of anxiety, longing to be back at the hotel, awaiting whatever was to happen.

Church bells rang, and she trembled. The previous day Annie had whispered a frightening fact: The Union forces lay so close that they could see the tallest church spire; now the enemy, too, was hearing those bells. And over them, from emplacements which seemed hardly a few squares away, went the rumble of great guns; so unrelenting was the boom that they noticed mainly when it stopped. Disaster was reaching toward them.

Below, a carriage rocked along, and after it walked several men bearing chairs and boxes of possessions—another of the many families retreating from the beleaguered capital. A cart slowed up, and Mary made out a group of uniformed men, heads hanging wearily between their shoulders. But not all suffered or took flight. Out of a nearby door there issued a volley of laughter, and into the street staggered a drunken man, who regained his balance with difficulty. From three places in a single block Mary heard the roll of dice, and gaudily dressed women rode carelessly about the streets.

Turning, she caught a muffled conversation from the hall outside: "Trouble is, we never put the right man in the right place."

"And of all people, that damned ninny, Lee. What's *he* ever done?"

The contemptuous voices died away, and Mary avoided her daughter's glance. She must not let herself think of the jarring words. "Isn't there some message from the Wickhams?" She asked Annie for the second time, to receive only a headshake.

Mary had become steadily more disturbed at letters from Charlotte's family. Little Robert had taken ill again. As she feared, the excitements of their recent movements had had their effect. "And he's always been a weak child," she sighed to Annie. Since the week's beginning there had been no word, and she could not decide whether that was an encouraging sign, or the opposite.

A knock, and Annie took the letter. Seeing the Wickhams' address, Mary tried to open it, and handed it back. "Child, I can't." If the boy were very sick, could they get to him? She was not ready for the blunt words: Charlotte's son had died the previous morning.

For a moment Mary could not accept it. Her first grandchild, so gentle and so responsive . . . Then she remembered how Robert had stood before her the day they left the White House, to ask her as she worried: "Granma, you thinkin' like before?" Her hands lifted to her face, and she cried convulsively.

After a few minutes Mary lifted her head. Charlotte—how she must be suffering, and with the second child due in a few months . . . "Oh, Annie, I wish I could be with her now."

Before Annie could answer they were both aware that something was happening outside. The artillery throbbed in a very heavy crescendo, and men shouted wildly on the street.

With Annie she made her way to the window. A quivering dandy gestured to a woman in a lace dress, who lifted her skirts and ran with him. An old man, stumbling down the street, upset another, who shook his fists and disappeared. The issue was being decided now.

In spite of the pains in her legs, Mary sank to her knees, and

Annie followed. Let their men be protected; let Robert live. After today's news about her grandson, she could not stand another loss . . . For several minutes she and her daughter remained there, and she heard Annie's hard breathing and her own whispered appeals.

"Mother, Mother!" Annie was pulling at her sleeve. Noises broke again from below, but they had changed, with a louder, less agitated sound. In the hallway Mary made out a rumble of voices.

"Yanks broke down. Pullin' back from Lee right now!"

"I knew they couldn't do it!"

She felt her pulses race, and, without understanding what she was doing she got up and went to the window again. In tight groups at the corner men were crying out, thumping one another's backs, and she listened in astonishment.

"Well, it took Lee to shove 'em back."

"Ol' Lee, Robert E. Lee!" The speaker waved his arms and did a kind of dance.

There could be no doubt of it, and a warm, sweet joy lifted inside her. Robert had saved them, saved them all, doing what none of them thought he could do. She flushed with elation.

Someone had begun to knock, and Mary's hand touched her cheeks. They were wet; she could see nobody now. By degrees her excitement slipped away, and then solemnly she gave her thanks to God. . . . After a moment she realized that, with the Federals in retreat, the area along the Pamunkey River would be in Confederate hands again. She and Charlotte could return to the White House property, and Robert and the boys might join them on their leaves. She would go there at the first possible moment.

In those days of triumph in the capital Mary and her daughters stayed a little apart. She made a few visits to President and Mrs. Davis, a handful of family friends, and no more; her health would permit nothing else, she explained; in any case she did not feel equal to the feverish gaiety she beheld around her. Strangers called, however, or stopped her on the street. "Mrs. Lee, I knew

197

your mother . . ." "If we could only let the general see how grateful we are."

Others might accept such remarks with cynicism; Mary did not. Passing their hotel, she saw elderly men halt at Robert's name, and one woman had tears in her eyes. Her husband had received an acclaim greater than that given any figure of the war. But when he came quietly to see her, neither of them talked of those things, or of the war itself.

They were to have a few days together, after so long a separation, and Mary searched his face for marks of change. He looked very tired, and yet there was a serenity there, a suggestion of fulfillment: he had done the work for which he was chosen. But most important of all for her was the fact that she had her husband again.

With some reluctance she accepted the invitation to attend President Davis' reception at the residence on East Clay Street. Her rheumatism required her to take a seat at the window; nevertheless she quickly brightened at the scene before her, as she watched the crowds about her husband, Mr. Davis and the President's wife, her brunette beauty resplendent that evening.

For once Mr. Davis' narrow face was set in relaxed lines, and Mary did not miss his look of admiration for her husband. Suppose Mr. Davis had wavered in his faith in Robert's ability, and listened to his detractors? This was not a night for such meditations. . . . Through the high-ceilinged rooms, with their white marble mantels and jars of greens, men and women passed slowly to the porch and garden; the air held the scent of candles and the perfumes of the bare-shouldered girls.

Across the room she recognized a small dark head, with short hair carelessly combed, and she felt again the tenderness that came over her whenever she saw Rob. Though taller, he had the same slight figure, the same trim waist, and the same private's uniform. It still came as a shock to realize that her youngest boy had taken a fighting role, under the celebrated T. J. (Stonewall) Jackson. And now Mary suffered another shock; Rob was bending over a miss in pink, intent on every gesture. Mary felt a flash of jealousy; what did the blond interloper mean?

The boy turned, and gave his mother a wide grin. Mary smiled;

with Rob she had never been able to stay angry for long. By this time she knew that the boy would have no difficulty with girls; at eighteen he had a way of his own. . . . She discovered just then that Custis, her eldest son, now on Mr. Davis' staff, had just entered. He had his usual dour air, but tonight she sensed a certain additional tension.

Custis crossed the room and stood behind his father. At his first chance the youth leaned forward; Mary saw her husband's eyes, suddenly grave, search for her. Robert murmured to President Davis, and soon he approached her. Something was wrong; his manner made that clear.

"Isn't it time to go, Mim?" Her blood chilled; she wanted to cry out: Tell me now, whatever it is! Instead she made her good-bys as calmly as possible, and then on the sidewalk before the tall gray-white building she faced him. In the semidarkness Robert's eyes had a luminous look, eyes that showed a compassion that was unmistakable. "Mary," he began, "you know the Union men made the White House property a big supply base. Before they left they wrecked the equipment and threw——"

"For God's sake, what are you trying to say?"

This time Robert did not choose his words. "Somebody set fire to the house—without orders, they say." When she gave a choking cry he added, "It's gone."

She felt lost, broken. The place that had meant so much when she was there with Rooney and Charlotte and their son. . . . And the promises to protect it for its associations with the Washingtons had meant nothing at all.

Robert led her to the carriage. In a dulled voice she asked, "You'll be starting out again before long, won't you?"

"I'm afraid so." He assisted her into the carriage, and there she leaned against his shoulder, surrendering herself to the helplessness of her mood. . . . The next day her rheumatic troubles were intensified, and she had difficulty in walking at all. Sadly Robert took a chair beside her. "It's time for you to go to the mineral springs again. If one won't help, try another, and especially the North Carolina ones. At least those are out of the fighting."

Mary's hand fell. So it would be; with Robert away one place would do as well as another. . . . On the final morning, near the hotel entrance she spied a short, trim figure in gray. While it had been a long time since their last meeting, she immediately recognized Joe Johnston. Under the circumstances might it be best to pass unobserved?

She noticed that his shoulders had a slight bow; as he waited there not a person addressed the man who until recently had been one of the Confederacy's heroes. Joe had just gotten up after weeks in bed; it could not be a happy hour for him, and she went to his side.

"General Johnston."

The intent face flushed and Mary thought she saw a look of hurt in the small bright eyes. But by the time he had swept off his hat he had regained his control, and he smiled. "Mrs. Lee and Miss Lee. I remember you," he assured Annie, "though I'm sure you won't remember me."

At once Joe Johnston brought the subject to Robert. "I've always considered him a very fine soldier, Mrs. Lee. Nobody could have done more for us under the circumstances."

She nodded happily; it did her good to hear such words from their friend of other years. Then she wondered: Was Joe trying to let her understand that his bitterness toward President Davis would not influence his opinion of Robert?

After a few minutes they parted, and Mary watched him start jauntily up the street, as if aware that her eyes followed. Her reactions were mixed. Poor Joe; he had been under a strain today; and he had never been a really happy man. But the following day her illusions were again shattered when a friend told her: "I just talked to General Johnston, and now he's saying that if he'd had half Robert's luck he'd be at the top right now. And because Mr. Davis disliked him he didn't get support and armies; but once Robert took over, the President poured in every kind of help!"

A cold anger grew within Mary. Joe Johnston had always been a complex individual, one moment a man of generous impulse, the next a chill opportunist. When Robert returned a few days later, she told him the whole story with considerable anger.

"Please, Mim," her husband interrupted. "You yourself didn't hear him say that. Even if you did"— Robert smiled wryly— "he may well be right. Perhaps I've been luckier than he was."

She should have known Robert would take a generous view.

Their house among the trees at the Warren County springs of North Carolina might have been on another continent, and Mary, with Agnes and Annie, devoted hours of each day to rest and the waters. Gradually her health improved, at least to a degree. By now she accepted the fact that she would not ever be entirely free from pain.

In these calmer days she could think of other matters, and Orton Williams was one of them. When the mail brought fewer and fewer letters to Agnes, Mary watched her daughter's spirit decline. After a while there were none at all. "He doesn't write his family either," the girl told her solemnly. "Markie says she hasn't heard from him in months." Mary shook her head; surely the young man, no matter how busy he might be, could scrawl a few lines. She was divided between exasperation toward the boy and pity for her daughter.

The war moved closer again, and Robert's Army of Northern Virginia reorganized. Opposite him stood a new commander, John Pope, succeeding the unsuccessful McClellan, and she quickly learned that Robert had little respect for Pope, considering him as unskilled as he was boastful.

And now from Maryland arrived a short, touching note from Ann Marshall. Her son Louis had done well, and received a promotion to General Pope's staff. The letter shook in Mary's hand. So it had come to this; her husband's army was fighting an army in which his nephew had a high rank. God guard them both, and keep them apart!

A few weeks later she managed a rueful laugh at Robert's message. A Lee family connection, conferring on an errand of truce with Federal officers, recognized Louis Marshall, who "asked kindly after his old uncle and said his mother was well." Robert added, "I am sorry Louis is in such bad company, but I suppose he could not help it . . . I could forgive his fighting against us, but not for joining Pope." Mary's smile went quickly; to her this was not a matter for amusement.

Not long after that the dashing Jeb Stuart made a surprise raid on Pope's headquarters, snatching up military papers, capturing the quartermaster. Among those who escaped by a hair's breadth was Louis Marshall.

With Annie beside her Mary bent over delayed reports of Second Manassas, brought by the manager of the springs. "Ma'am," he volunteered, "they say the two sides blasted each other till some, with their ammunition gone, grabbed stones and smashed and brained the men before 'em." Wincing, she turned to an account of the Battle of Antietam, at Sharpsburg, where thousands died on a bloody, slippery field. The war had reached a new, more brutal stage.

Antietam ended with neither side winning a decisive victory. Although Robert withdrew his forces, their morale remained good. "We're holding our own, at least," the manager informed her, and she tried to believe his words.

In late September Mary and Annie were still at the Springs; much of their time spent knitting for the Army. Pausing on the porch, Mary scanned the day's newspaper, and stopped at a paragraph. *Emancipation*, it began, and she read hastily on. Abraham Lincoln had announced that on January 1, 1863, freedom would be granted slaves in all sections of the Confederacy still unconquered. She reread the lines; what a whirlwind this would reap!

She thought of her uncle, her father and others who believed in freedom for their slaves. Robert had liberated his and would carry out her father's will as best he could. Still, to wipe out slavery overnight . . . In Confederate territory the proclamation would have no weight; and yet, with all it implied and held out, its effect would be vast. How swiftly the times were changing.

"Annie." She stared at the girl, and the listlessness of her daughter's expression made her go to her. Annie's brow was throbbing.

"Come with me." She almost carried the girl to bed, then called to Agnes. Waiting for the doctor, Mary began to blame herself. She had heard vaguely of typhoid fever in the section, and, like others, had taken no special precautions. She was applying wet cloths when the doctor arrived.

"Mm. The fever, yes. You should have sent for me earlier." Frowning, he gave hurried directions. "A lot of new cases today."

Mary sat beside Annie's bed and coaxed her to swallow one of the medicines. As Agnes joined her she shook her head. "No, I'm not going to rest, no matter what you say."

That day and the next Mary stayed rigid in her chair. Her legs became cramped; the pain spread to her hands, but she declined again when Agnes approached. "I just couldn't, child." Annie's breathing grew harder, quicker; her flush deepened. As the girl stared into the lamplight, cruelly exposing the defect in her eye, Mary relived the terrible hour of the accident with the scissors.

"Mamma, are we ever going home again?" Annie's question about Arlington, suddenly out of the silence, made Mary start. They were all thinking of the place and their days there, far more than they allowed one another to know. The patient's breathing became more labored; the fever had climbed.

Mary sent anxiously for the doctor and heard his noncommital words: "It's too early to say, madam." Her feeling of desperation increased; he was hiding the truth. At his departure she worked frantically again. . . . Annie complained of stomach pains, of trouble in hearing, and Mary realized that her daughter had become very deaf.

With that Mary's lips moved in prayer. This was the weakling, the one who had always needed her most. Let Annie live. . . . If Robert were only here, with his calming strength, she would feel less terrified.

Annie's breathing came more hoarsely than ever, and her pains were worse. The doctor had prescribed morphine; that helped only a little. The day was Sunday and the girl murmured weakly, "Give me the Bible, Mamma." Receiving the book, Annie could scarcely hold it; she leafed through the pages, her hand raised to a passage, and she let it fall.

As Mary removed the book, her eyes went to the words: "Perfect and true are all His ways . . ." Then she looked again at the tired figure on the bed, Annie was staring sightlessly at a point high on the ceiling. Agnes began to cry, and Mary Lee collapsed upon the bed.

The townspeople were kind, and, as Mary stood by the mound with the flowers thick upon it, she felt somewhat less alone. Back in her room, however, she looked bleakly through the window at the fall landscape, the brown leaves whirling before her. Was God punishing her for self-pride or some other sin; how had she offended?

Soon afterward Agnes approached with a different smile. "Mother, it will do you good to hear this. Charlotte's had her baby—a girl, and the Wickhams say they're both doing well." Mary's eyes filled. The Lord took, the Lord gave. In the letter the Wickhams asked: Couldn't she come to stay with them? Charlotte wanted her and the Lee girls too. Mary's affection for their daughter-in-law swept over her, and she decided to accept.

In early winter, as a light snowfall passed over Hickory Hill, the Wickham property in Hanover County, she and her daughters reached the roomy Wickham house. As she crossed the threshold and entered the well-lighted rooms, Mary felt better immediately. Charlotte greeted her from the pillows of a big sofa, and Mary leaned down and swept her into her arms.

"Child, you're what I've needed, both of you!" Mary looked down at the baby, to find her oddly listless, awake yet lackluster. Then, the stir of the welcome over, Charlotte settled back with a tired sigh, and Mary became uneasy. In the lamplight her daughter-in-law's face had a wan appearance and deep, hollow shadows beneath the cheekbones.

At supper she watched the girl reject nearly everything, and pull the shawl tightly around her shoulders. Touching Charlotte, she discovered that her flesh was cold. "Oh, I'm all right, Mother," her daughter-in-law told her as she drew away. When Mary reached for the baby, Charlotte tightened her grasp upon the little figure. "Please. . . She needs me."

Mary felt a growing uneasiness, and after some effort she persuaded the girl to go upstairs. Facing the Wickhams, she read a reflection of her own disturbance. "Both of them did well for a time," Charlotte's cousin explained. "But lately they've gotten worse. The doctor comes every day. The way she holds the baby, as if she's afraid to give her up . . . We don't know what to do."

The next day and for all of that week Mary hovered near her daughter-in-law, urging her to sleep, pressing nourishment to her lips and meanwhile keeping the child warm. By slow degrees

Charlotte improved, but Mary's alarm over the baby steadily increased. The little one seemed so silent, so dull-eyed.

She prepared herself, bit by bit, for the words she knew must come from the doctor. After her talk with him, it was Mary who took the news to Charlotte; and, though the girl, too, must have expected the message, she fought hysterically against it. "No, let *me* die, let me!" Only after a time did she allow Mary to take the unprotesting little form; and she held the child in her arms while it sank into its final sleep.

In the days that followed Mary was too concerned over her daughter-in-law to brood much over the loss of her second grandchild. With Rooney's letters and Robert's in her hands, she went repeatedly to the girl, reading to her, drawing her to her feet when Charlotte wept that she wanted only to be alone. "I can't face people. I can't do it!" Occasionally Charlotte's temper gave way and she snapped out words for which she later apologized. "I'm sorry. Everything's gone so wrong for us, for all of us."

Mary shook her head. "Let's not admit it." Gradually she recognized a lessening of tension in the girl's face. For even the badly bereaved, the world would go on. Rooney's war record meant more and more to the girl; he was winning successive honors, promotions, citations for bravery.

Once more the war itself intruded. A massive new Federal drive began against Richmond, and Robert's men met and smashed the enemy in the holocaust at Fredericksburg. While she read how the luckless townspeople ran to the woods, she reflected that, for her and Robert, Fredericksburg had a special meaning. It was many years ago, when they had sat under the tree across the river from the town, and Robert first spoke of his feeling for her. Fredericksburg had looked so serene then; and now it was a bloody battleground. . . .

One day, sitting near the fire with Charlotte, Mary saw that Agnes was pressing her face against the icy window.

"It's Orton."

Agnes had already started for the door. For the first time in weeks Mary's eyes brightened. She was happy for Agnes; and all of them needed someone like Orton to enliven their days.

As she had expected, Orton's bearing was debonair, expansive;

though thinner, with a hint of circles under his eyes, he looked healthy. Then, however, as he bent over her, Mary realized that the fine dark eyes had an overbright glitter, his stand a certain unsteadiness. He had been drinking, and not lightly.

Her anger boiled up. She could not expect young soldiers to act like saints; but did Orton think he could descend upon them as if the house were a crossroads tavern? Sharp words rose to her lips, and Agnes came nervously forward.

"Mother, Orton's going to spend his leave here. Isn't that fine?" The girl's face was flushed and as Agnes talked on, Mary read her surprise and hurt; at the same time Agnes was asking her mother to be forbearing, to withhold judgment. Mary hesitated. Across the room her daughter-in-law voiced her support:

"Orton, don't you want to change your clothes?"

With a bemused smile the boy glanced at the snow, melting along his sleeve, and nodded. At the door Charlotte whispered an order, and Mary saw a servant scurry upstairs with a coffeepot.

When Orton rejoined them he seemed refreshed and quite sober, and soon he was speaking easily of his experiences. "You know, not many people have served as I've done, as military aide to a bishop!" He told of his duties with Leonidas Polk, the Episcopal churchman who had taken high Confederate rank; and Mary reminded herself that the boy, after all, had distinguished himself in battle.

Orton outdid himself now, as if he understood the need to win back her favor. Slowly Mary's disapproval slipped away; she realized precisely what he was doing, and still she could not resist his charm.

"Where are you on duty now?" she asked him.

"I resigned my last commission, but I'll soon have a new one." The youth's manner changed swiftly; his eyes tightened as if a disturbing memory prodded him. "Well, the weather's better, and it's time for a ride." He jumped up. "Can't you come, Agnes?"

The girl glanced inquiringly toward Mary, who nodded, and the couple bundled themselves into heavy coats and hurried out. After a silence Charlotte spoke. "I suppose you haven't heard about Orton getting into some—trouble in the Army?"

"Trouble?"

"That is"—her daughter-in-law paused—"it was a dispute with a private, a sentry, who wouldn't salute him or was insubordinate; nobody knows the details. Anyway, they had an awful quarrel and Orton—shot him to death." Before Mary could voice her astonishment, Charlotte added, "Orton's superiors have always liked him. After what happened, though, the men turned against him, and matters got very unpleasant. That's why he resigned."

Mary's eyes fell, then returned to Charlotte's. It was a strange story, and Orton's act implied something more than instability. She wondered what Robert would say, and then she remembered that her husband believed above anything else in firm self-control. Nevertheless, since none of them had heard the full story, could they judge?

For the next few days Agnes and Orton were often together. The boy appeared more serious than on his arrival, but also, Mary decided, much more tense. "Why, you're never more than five minutes in one spot," she told him, and stared in astonishment when he frowned and left the room in annoyance.

Agnes, too, acted strangely. Returning from another horseback ride with Orton, she ran to her room and stayed there for hours. Orton did not enter the house after her, and when Mary inquired, the maid had a hesitant answer: "Mister Orton's still in the stable, I *think*." The dark girl glanced toward the back of the building, and closed her lips. Mary found it difficult to pursue the matter, and let the girl go.

Just before dark she was knitting with Charlotte when she heard a scraping noise at the outer door. The butler went there; she caught a murmur of voices, and then the servant was assisting—more properly, carrying—a slim figure through the hall.

"Is Orton hurt?" Involuntarily she got to her feet. When her daughter-in-law gave her a knowing look, Mary blushed at her own naïveté. An hour later Agnes, coming to her with reddened eyes, begged, "Don't scold Orton, or talk about the way he acts. He's worried, and unhappy. And he has a new military scheme he thinks may be important. He's sure we'll all hear of it someday, but he can't tell us about it."

Mary frowned. Robert himself had a great many more things

to worry him, including military schemes, than Mr. Orton Williams, and nevertheless he didn't go around like that! Still, for Agnes' sake she would subside.

Mary knew from Robert's letters after the victory at Fredericksburg that he had not done what he wished, what he had hoped for. Because he lacked the soldiers, he had been unable to send his army after the Union forces. They would have to fight again; the war would go on in the same fashion. And surely they should know, Mary reminded herself, that the North had a vast reservoir of men and machines, while theirs fell lower with each month.

On Christmas morning the household arose to a scene of subdued festivity—the giving of small presents and a meal for which the Wickhams' dwindling supplies had been taxed. Mary suffered sharper pains than usual, but tried not to let them hamper her. She had a special purpose today; she had made up her mind to stay close to Charlotte. For her daughter-in-law the memory of those two children, on this day which was meant for children, would be profoundly upsetting. Mary thrust away her own thoughts of Annie, under the mound in North Carolina.

When the gifts were opened her mood improved. She saw that Orton's presents for Agnes, a pair of gauntlets and riding whip, made the girl's face shine; and following dinner the couple went off together. Temporarily alone in the late afternoon, Mary dozed in her chair, to wake at the sound of words from the next room. The folding doors, usually apart, had been shut, and after a moment she realized that the voices were Agnes' and Orton's, the boy's muted, sullen, the girl's lifted in anger.

She asked herself if she should intervene, or go to her room. Before she could get to her feet the door was yanked open and the boy marched out, his lips set in a hard line.

"Agnes!" As Mary called out, her daughter appeared in the doorway and came running to her; with her head buried against Mary's shoulder, she sobbed, "If only he'd change, if—if he'd be a little different. . . like the Orton we used to know."

She comforted Agnes, stroking her hair, murmuring softly. Yet even as she did, Mary wondered: Could her daughter or anyone else really change another human being? Whatever was the matter with Orton, she was afraid, lay beyond Agnes' reach. After a time the girl slipped away, and that night a much-subdued Orton made his farewells. Taking his hand, Mary checked an impulse to ask him where he was going.

Within the week, as the new year of 1863 began, she looked curiously at the latest letter from Robert, with a legal document enclosed. The time approached, he wrote, to free the Custis slaves under her father's will; whatever uncertainties had developed in the court cases over the subject, the five-year-period had ended. For months Robert had been working over the involved documents, sending out letters, making arrangements.

Mary skimmed over the papers. It had been no simple matter to prepare them. Many of the servants remained in Federal lines at Arlington, or on the White House estate or elsewhere; a few had been hired out in Richmond before the war; others were scattered. Mary's lips moved. Another man might have delayed the whole affair, doing nothing in the uncertainties of war. Robert had considered it his simple duty to act promptly.

Mary's eyes filled; she had never been prouder of him.

Chapter 15

Summer had arrived, the crowded summer of 1863 in sweltering Richmond, and Mary settled back for a ride through the streets. The war pressures against the Confederate capital had lessened for the time being, and when Charlotte's health improved Mary and her daughters left the Wickham home to visit friends, the Caskies, in a pleasant house on Clay Street.

As the bursting greens of the overhanging trees threw irregular pools of shadow over the carriage, she looked out quietly at the rows of stores and houses. The city had a growing shabbiness, an increasingly drab air. There were fewer soldiers on the streets, fewer military wagons; and yet under the surface Mary read signs of a continuing tension.

Robert had won President Davis' approval of a bold new maneuver, a plunge into Pennsylvania that sent panic through Union ranks. Mary remembered the words of her son Custis: "If only we beat 'em there and push on! Then they'll know they can't beat Father and his army; there's a strong party in the North, and with one big victory for us . . ."

Custis' face had flushed. Whenever her glum son became excited, there was a reason, she told herself. Overnight, optimism reigned in Virginia, and today, despite the nervous uncertainty, Richmond echoed with reports of new concentrations of men. Might this be the thrust that finished the war? She had a still greater interest in whatever related to Robert's army, for young Rob had joined it as an aide to his brother Rooney. Although

Robert himself had not favored the transfer, the boy had begged for the assignment, and she felt better when it took place.

As they approached their friends' house, Mary saw that Agnes was waiting for her. From Agnes' drawn face she knew there must be bad news.

"It's Rooney." The girl blurted out her message. "He's been shot—a deep hip wound."

Mary's fingers grasped Agnes' arm. "Where is he now?" She had to know that first.

"With the Wickhams at Hickory Hill." Her daughter, she saw, was about to break down. "They let Rob take him there from the fighting."

"How can we get there?"

"They say we can use this carriage." Agnes had anticipated this question. "But we'll need time to pack."

Frantically Mary shook her head. "Throw together anything of mine you find."

Only when the carriage reached the outskirts of Richmond did Mary remember to ask:

"Agnes, what did you hear about the fighting?"

"Oh, our men forced them back, for a while at least."

"Yes?" Mary's voice dulled; her main concern had become her son and his wife. A leafy branch scraped at the side of the carriage, and as she looked out she saw suddenly how bright the day was, with a glitter of sun on the bushes, and a deep blue sky above. A bird in the thicket began a series of lovely trills, as if this were the most joyous world imaginable.

Rooney shifted his big frame on the bed and achieved a whiskery grin. "You shouldn't have come all this way," he told her in a tired voice, but his eyes shone with pleasure. As Mary bent to kiss him, he took her wrist between his heavy thumb and forefinger and pressed it weakly. Charlotte's long face showed a more acute agony than Mary had ever seen, and her lips trembled continually.

Charlotte explained: "His wound developed an infection, and he's lost a lot of blood." Nodding, Mary took her daughter-in-law to a window seat and persuaded her to lie back against the cushions. There was a sound at the door, and young Rob entered, accompanied by the younger Wickhams, to kiss Mary and hug her enthusiastically.

"My boy!" Breathless, she pushed him away. "Let me look hard at you." She studied the deep eyes, the round, flushed cheeks and the hair with the cowlick that would probably never disappear. Neither war nor stress would alter this youngest of her sons. Then Rob announced as if he had memorized instructions: "The doctor wants nobody to disturb Rooney."

Mary waved her hand. "Very well, stop disturbing him. Out with all of you, except Charlotte and me." Settling down, she drew covers around the patient and reached for the girl's nervous hands.

But Charlotte insisted first on showing her a note which somehow Robert had managed to write Rooney in the midst of a battle:

I wish I could see you, but I cannot. Take care of yourself, and make haste and get well and return. Though I scarcely ever saw you, it was a great comfort to know you were near and with me. I could think of you and hope to see you. May we yet meet in peace and happiness.

At the thought of her husband, so near to their boys yet separated from them, Mary had a choking feeling in her throat. As for his prayer that they would gather again in peace, how long would it be before that happened? . . . Rooney's wound began slowly to heal, but Charlotte's face lost little of its set look. Before long Mary was devoting as much attention to the girl as to her son.

To assure quiet, she had Rooney moved to the plantation office in the yard; about him the household centered. After a few days he had regained most of his appetite and his good cheer, smiling and accepting everything around him. Whenever she could, Mary allowed him and Charlotte to be alone. That, she realized, was the best remedy for her daughter-in-law's low spirits.

Despite the conditions under which she had come to Hickory Hill, Mary could relax a little. The junior Mary and then the talkative Mildred joined them. She now had five of her six children; it had been a long time since so many of them had been together. She wanted nothing to interfere with this interlude. Even

Agnes grew livelier, though the thought of Orton continued to trouble her.

Early one morning Mary made her way to Rooney's quarters with a large glass of milk, biscuits, and eggs. Her son gave her a penetrating look. "You're sure you have enough for this?"

"Of course we have," Mary lied. She and two of her daughters had gone without milk, and those were the last eggs on hand; in these times even the country people felt shortages. Obviously Rooney suspected something of the truth; he ate in silence for a minute or two, then put his fork down. All at once she was asking him things she had never asked before:

"*Can* we win the war, Son?"

Rooney's brow wrinkled at the direct question. About to shrug it away, he gave her an earnest look.

"Well . . . sometimes, when you see what's happening, you don't believe so. Half the governors of the states seem to be at war with Richmond instead of the Union. They're so jealous of their rights that they'd rather lose the war than grant an inch to Richmond!"

Mary listened in dismay. The plump, bearded face darkened. "Still, Mr. Davis isn't the easiest man in the world to get along with. Even Father hasn't been able to smooth over his latest trouble with General Johnston."

At this news Mary blinked in surprise, and her son added, "Johnston's back with a command in the West, and he and Mr. Davis are quarreling about strategy. Father says Johnston's had bad luck in the war, and he's trying to get the President to agree with him." As she listened Mary looked away; how strange it was that Robert would now be arguing in defense of Joe Johnston.

Sighing, she went back to the rest of the family, who had gathered on the main porch. A few minutes later there came a crackling sound in the distance, and Mary was startled. Mrs. Wickham said, "Somebody must be shooting at our squirrels. Rob, will you tell them to stop?"

Mary watched affectionately when her son started on a diagonal line toward the hickory grove at the front. Before he had gone more than a few yards she thrust herself to her feet, a hoarse cry dying in her throat. Toward them, at a gallop, rode five or

214

six Union cavalrymen. Rob was out of their line of vision, but he must have glimpsed the horsemen through the foliage. Abruptly she saw that he changed direction, to race toward the office building and his brother.

Mary stared in growing terror as the men in blue trotted toward the main house. Two, she saw, had pistols out. Silent, frozen in place, she waited with the others. Rob had disappeared inside the smaller building, and her fears veered from one son to the other. Those people wouldn't hurt a wounded man; yet suppose Rob resisted them . . .

The first officer shouted, "Where's General Lee?"

The question infuriated her. "With the Army of Northern Virginia. Where you've never been able to get to him!"

Her reply left him astonished and furious. "I don't mean the old one."

Mary reminded herself; Rooney had won a general's rank, too. But how did the Federal officers know her son was there? Even as she asked it she understood; they had received a tip, and were making a raid simply to capture her injured boy. A pulse pounded in her temple. Then, as she clutched at the railing before her, she saw, out of the corner of her eye, a slim figure leave the office porch and move off into the bushes.

Thank God Rob had decided to slip away from the raiders. But if any of the family itself glanced involuntarily in that direction, he would be trapped. Before she realized what she was doing, Mary took a step forward, talking hurriedly.

"You can search inside here. Mr. Wickham will help you, but you won't find him." Gesturing to the main house behind her, she let her words pour on, and meanwhile she kept her eyes directly on the Federal officers, not daring to look in any other direction.

The commander rapped out orders, and the soldiers searched the house. She could now risk a quick look to the side. She saw only the empty lawn, and she knew that Rob had reached the bushes. Beside her Charlotte slumped against the gallery post. From the road came the sound of the tramp of another, larger raiding party; its size made Mary's blood chill.

Two of the men went cursorily up to the office. Clinging to

the railing, Mary felt a sensation like a hand at her throat. A clatter broke out in the office, and one of the officers stuck out his head. "Colonel, Colonel, we got the bastard here!"

Mary and Mr. Wickham started toward the office, to be halted by a soldier with a bayonet. At that moment Charlotte cracked under the strain. "My God, don't let them hurt him. Don't let them!" The girl collapsed against Mary, who held her tightly. Soon a junior officer walked up to them. He had a thoughtful face, and his manner let them know he was ashamed of what he had to do.

"Could you let us have something to carry him on to the landing?"

Mary cried out. A wounded man, who might suffer in any transfer—why did they have to take him? But she knew why: he was Robert Lee's son! In fear and bitterness she kept silent; whatever she said now might hurt the boy.

Mr. Wickham spoke in a low voice. "Take my carriage, if you have to have him. But please, be easy with him." While two soldiers went for the carriage, three others backed out of the office, carrying between them a gray object, the mattress on which lay her son, his hands holding to the edges.

If the jolting broke his half-healed wounds . . . Charlotte screamed, and involuntarily Mary moved toward the invaders, until the soldier with the bayonet grabbed her shoulder and pushed her back: "No, you don't, ma'am."

Weak as he was, Rooney lifted his head and shook it at them. They must be careful, he was telling them, and cause no more trouble. Young Rob still hid somewhere nearby; as yet the Federal party knew nothing of the younger son's presence. Straining, the soldiers managed to swing the mattress awkardly inside the vehicle. Behind Mary came a thumping sound; Charlotte had dropped to the porch. They took her to a chair, and Mary wiped the girl's face; when she looked up, the carriage was rolling toward the road. .

"Please, don't go so fast!" she screamed to the Yankee holding the reins. After a moment her pent-up rage broke over her. "They must be afraid our men will get them!" For another hour the last of the soldiers continued on guard, and eventually they too rode off.

Promptly a dusty, disheveled Rob slipped out of the bushes. "Rooney made me go—said I'd make it worse if I stayed with him." The boy murmured bitterly, and his eyes tightened as they went to the sobbing Charlotte. "I wished I'd shot it out." That, at least, had been spared them; and now that the danger had passed Mary, too, could cry. Through her tears she felt an ever-growing hate. To plan a raid of that sort, using so many soldiers, simply to take a sick man . . .

That night Agnes led her to a carriage in which she beheld a sight that made her shudder. One of the other Wickhams, white-haired, feeble, had tried to halt the raiders at his small home, and they had beaten him badly. He lay on his side, bloody and spent, his broken cane and eyeglasses on the floor. The war had taken on a senseless cruelty.

The next day was an uneasy one. Rob left for a wary reconnaissance of the neighborhood. In the evening the Lee girls retired early, and as Mary sat sadly with Charlotte and the Wickhams her son approached, staring from one to the other. Rob's lean face had a distraught look; he appeared very young and much disturbed, as if uncertain what to do in a new situation.

Trying to quiet her own alarm, Mary took him into the hall and turned. "Tell me what it is, boy."

Rob stared, as if he wished he could be somewhere else. "It's something we'll have to break to Agnes."

"To *Agnes?*"

Now Rob's words began. "It's Orton. You know he was talking about a sort of new assignment? Well, he and one of his cousins went on a mission into Federal lines in Tennessee." At the horror in his mother's face Rob stopped, then rushed on:

"The Union men got them and gave them a drumhead trial— and hanged them in the morning."

Her cry was one of shock and astonishment. A moment later she remembered Agnes, upstairs and asleep; depressed as her daughter had been in the past few months, Agnes had still hoped that Orton would return. Now . . .

A low groan reached her from the next room, and she realized that Rob's words had carried to Charlotte. Her daughter-in-law was hiding her face in her hands. "They'll do it to Rooney, the same thing. I knew it when they took him!" Slowly Mary went back to Charlotte; she called for ammonia and water, and after a time she succeeded in quieting her.

After that, sitting by herself, she thought of Orton, once so promising, started so well on his Army career, and now killed so wretchedly. Rob whispered, "Nobody knows much about the mission he made, but some claim he had the idea and went without full authority, or even any authority at all." Mary bit her lips. How bold a thing, and yet not unlike poor Orton. Had matters developed only a little differently . . . Suppose she and the rest had been more forbearing, and had made an effort to understand him better. Perhaps Orton would have been less wild, and also alive today.

And still none of that would help. Mary had to see Agnes, and she would have preferred to do anything else in the world. With an effort she got to her feet. In the hallway, after a moment of silent prayer, she made herself go to Agnes' door.

Agnes proved herself better able to accept the tragedy and its implications than did the much-weakened Charlotte. The younger girl stayed largely to herself, taking long rides or sitting upstairs, working steadily at her knitting. By contrast Charlotte lay day after day in bed, staring at the ceiling. "I can't do anything," she said, when Mary tried to draw her out. "I've got to hear about Rooney. Don't keep anything from me."

Mary made an effort to hide her own fears. If only they knew something . . . Then word arrived that her boy had been taken to old Fort Monroe. It was, of course, the place at which she and Robert had spent the first year after their marriage; and today their son lay there in a cell. Again fate seemed to be poking fun at them.

Before long Robert wrote, "I had not expected that he would have been taken from his bed. We must, however, resign ourselves as best we can," he added. But indirectly from others around him Mary learned of her husband's bitter contempt for

Rooney's captors, and of the long hours he spent worrying about Rooney.

As for Orton, Robert told her: "If he did go into Franklin [Tennessee] as it is stated, his life was forfeited under the laws of war, and yet even under those circumstances I see no necessity for his death except to gratify the evil passions of those whom he offended by leaving General Scott."

Mary received a letter that the boy had been allowed to send his family before he died. Orton wrote that he wanted to meet his end as his father would have done; and he recalled Colonel Williams' words to his children as he collapsed in Mexico: "Tell them I died at the head of my column." For the last time, she told herself, the gesture was altogether Orton's.

She remembered Markie, Orton's sister, who had considered herself responsible for her brothers, and had sacrificed her own fulfillment for them. Markie had still to marry, and Mary wondered if she ever would. A moment later she thought of that elder brother, Lawrence, who had entered the Union Army. His fellow officers had killed Orton. Whose suffering could be worse than his?

Two mornings after she received Orton's letter Mary was on her way downstairs to breakfast. In the past few weeks she had felt a steady increase of her old pains. Her legs throbbed. As she reached for the banister, her foot slipped under her, and she fell violently forward.

After a time she woke from a gray monotone of unconsciousness, to find the family around her. "I've got to get up," she groaned. Despite their efforts she rose, and would have collapsed again had Mr. Wickham not supported her.

When the doctor arrived, he appeared very grave. During his examination she clenched her hands to keep back her involuntary cries. Finishing, the doctor mentioned two drugs and added, "But they just aren't available, you understand. With our hospitals requiring so much, and the blockade tighter every day . . ." Mary knew already that all medicines were scarce. She shrugged. "Still, I can do the other things—eat fresh fruit and vegetables, and go to the springs."

The doctor gave her a direct look. "Mrs. Lee, you'll have to know this. For a time, anyway, you'll require help whenever you move. I mean crutches or a wheel chair."

The blunt words stunned her. Crutches, an invalid's chair, a cripple . . . Years ago, to be sure, the other doctors had hinted about such a possibility. Yet to be told it so suddenly . . . But she had never surrendered to the disease, and she wouldn't do it now. "One of the men in the quarters can make crutches for me." She managed to smile. "Light ones—I don't weigh much." Slowly her smile went; late that night she lay awake, trying to make herself accept the change that had finally come for her.

Hot Springs, Allegheny County, in North Carolina, afterward another health resort, and then another, and still there had been no great improvement for Mary or her daughter-in-law. In a cottage with wide, shaded porches, haycocks along a brook, and mountains in the distance they received further word of Rooney. He stayed in a hospital at Fort Monroe, and wished them to know he was much better. Charlotte lifted herself on her elbow, then sank back. Hobbling along, wincing with every abrupt move, Mary took a chair near her on the porch. Charlotte needed one thing to make her recover—the company of her husband. Only now had Mary realized fully the extent of the girl's successive shocks.

"Oh, ma'am!" The proprietor of the springs followed them out on the porch. "We thought you'd like to hear this. Up in Pennsylvania, General Lee and the Yankees have squared off, at a place they call Gettysburg. Thousands of men are in it, and it looks like we're winning!"

Sitting beside her, Agnes took Mary's hand in a tight grip. From Robert's letters they knew better than this man exactly what the battle meant, how much their futures depended on the result. For hours, as insects buzzed around them, Mary and her daughter stayed together, waiting for the news from Pennsylvania. Even the meager bulletins told them of the savage slaughter at Gettysburg. Uncounted thousands were being churned into the war machine. Though both sides were suffering terrible casualties, the Southerners seemed to be gaining the victory.

Hours went by and the telegraph wires brought nothing. Over most of the South and the North as well women tried to hide their fears as they waited. At last Charlotte's head lifted, for the proprietor was approaching. This time he did not hurry.

"Our side had to withdraw." He had no more to say, and he slipped back into the darkness. In the room behind them Mary could hear a woman weeping.

A few days later, as they rested in the sunlight, Mary learned of a second blow. For months they had been reading of the Federal siege of Vicksburg on the Mississippi, with some of the beleaguered townsmen eating rats and tainted food and anything else they found to keep alive. Now she heard that the great bastion of Vicksburg had fallen before Ulysses S. Grant, and the South was cut in two.

Mary gazed helplessly around her; the sorrow and fear that hung over them had become still heavier. The springs stirred with reports: Robert E. Lee, blaming only himself for the loss at Gettysburg, had offered his resignation, and President Davis refused to accept it. From Robert came a brief note. They had done their best; the issue rested in balance for three unbroken days of terrible effort, and God had settled the result. And still again the war would go on.

That same afternoon, from the faces of the people around her and the remarks of one stranger after another, Mary realized that Robert's standing in the South had not suffered. "We see the odds he's against," their friend the proprietor told her. "His men have just too little of everything, except hungry stomachs." She nodded gratefully; she could not speak.

A second visitor had more to say. "The men under him practically worship him; they say he's the greatest soldier they'll ever know. It's more than that, though. He's *for* them, looking after things that most officers never bother about. His men will tell you that when people send him special food, he won't eat it. Sends it over to the hospitals." Mary thanked her caller; it was good to hear such things from those who had watched Robert in action.

All the news from the war front wasn't tragic. Robert wrote that just that day he'd had a message that one of his soldiers wanted to talk to him. He glanced at the begrimed boy and said, "My man, what can I do for you?"

The youth asked, "General, don't you know me?"

It was his son Rob.

Robert went on to explain that he was always running into their youngest boy. Once he discovered him without an overcoat or blanket. Half seriously he added, "I wish Miss Norvell would marry him and take care of him." Mary smiled; by now she accepted with ease her son's growing interest in several girls.

In another letter Robert asked if she could send pictures of their daughters; it was so long since he had seen them. And again he wrote: "If God spares me to the end of the war, I trust to be with you all, at least for the few remnant years of my life."

Mary's hand went to her mouth. Surely they would have a longer time together once things came back to normal. When would that be, though, and what would "normal" ever be for them? . . .

Soon afterward, rereading a paper, she frowned on finding an item she had missed. Another pair of Confederate officers, taken in Union lines as spies, had been executed; furiously Southern officials decided to retaliate, and in Richmond the prison authorities chose two Federal men by lot for the same treatment. "Northern repercussions are expected." She wondered about the last words.

Sitting by the spring that same day, her crutches beside her, she learned their meaning. She heard the voice of a recent arrival: "Mrs. Lee, all of us feel badly about this new trouble for your son."

Mary's head went up, and the girl withdrew in confusion. "Oh, I thought you knew . . ."

Hobbling to the office, Mary sought out the proprietor. He hesitated. "That fool shouldn't have said anything. It's not definite." Then reluctantly he admitted: "The Federals are saying that if the South does kill those two hostages at Richmond, *they'll* hang two Southerners. And one will be Rooney Lee."

Mary had trouble in getting to her feet; helping her, the man tried to give her reassurance. "Ma'am, it hasn't happened, and I don't think General Butler would really do that."

Mary was shocked still more. So Ben Butler, "The Beast," whose acts of mistreatment in New Orleans had brought international incidents, was in charge at the fort. Back to her came the memory of Orton's death. Her son might soon be hanging from a rope. And Charlotte—this would be hideous news for her.

Her voice was a whisper. "Please help me to the cottage. . . ."

During the weeks that followed Mary told herself that only her fears for her daughter-in-law kept her going. Charlotte reacted violently to the news. "He's dead already; they've murdered him!" Reasoning with the girl, giving her occasional sedatives, Mary stayed hour by hour at Charlotte's side, and crept exhausted to bed. She herself sometimes woke suddenly, sure that someone was knocking with a telegram to tell her her son had been executed. At times she went to the window on her crutches, to make certain no one was there.

She found herself thinking of Rooney as a boy, of his easy humor and good will, of that day she came home to see him suffering stoically after the accident to his fingers. She remembered his troubles at school and then his rewarding experience in managing White House, his happiness with Charlotte. Could this terrible thing really be happening?

After one such wretched night she wrote to Robert: Couldn't he intervene for their boy? Sadly he replied that he would not ask for Rooney something he could not ask for others. In any case he pointed out that whatever appeal he made might hurt and not help Rooney. As October approached, a telegram did arrive, and she tore it in several pieces in opening it. Her eyes ran over the words. The immediate risk had ended; reprisals between the two sides had halted, and the executions would not take place.

Mary and Charlotte cried together. "But he's still a prisoner," Charlotte sighed; and the girl did not have to add that there remained the danger of more incidents and more retaliations. . . . By now Robert had returned to Virginia, with his camp near the capital, and Mary wanted again to be near him. When she wrote, friends explained that Richmond quarters were scarcer than ever; the only thing they could find for her was tiny, high-priced —entirely unsatisfactory, they feared. She reread the note; whatever it was or was not, she would take it.

The rooms on Leigh Street proved gaunt and ugly; the iron beds, narrow as they were, took up nearly half the space; a dresser and chairs left so little room that they would have trouble moving about. At least, however, they were her own, and now she was near Robert and also to Custis, still in service in the capital. There, with Charlotte in a chamber nearby, they awaited Robert's next visit to the capital. On her first drive through the city, she rode past the brick mass of the Confederates' Libby Prison, and thought of Rooney, buried in another such place. She made up her mind never to pass the prison again.

Now, finally, Robert was due. On an overcast day, long before the time for his arrival, Mary rested in a chair by the window. Missing nothing below her, she saw that ten or twelve men had gathered at the corner, with several women, and now they were looking intently at someone on horseback. Immediately Mary recognized the beloved figure, strong and erect, his face in shadow beneath his military cap.

Robert lifted his cap, and a cheer rose from the crowd. At the warmth of their admiration her heart leaped. As she saw him more distinctly, she had a feeling of dismay. Robert had aged a great deal, with new lines dug deeply at his mouth and throat, a puffiness below the eyes; and she made out a certain nervousness of his hands.

Then he stood before her. "Mary, Mary . . ." Robert went to his knees beside her chair and put his arms around her. "I thought it would never happen again." The low voice was heavy with emotion, yet he seemed exhausted, more worn than she had ever expected to find him.

Now, gently, Robert drew back, and as dark eyes went over her she understood that he had not been fully prepared for the alterations he saw in her, the crutches, the toll of the past months. When he tried to speak the words did not come, and he lowered his head against her throat.

After a time Mary told him: "I'll be better, Robert; you'll

see." He nodded, and they talked about Rooney and his imprisonment, Charlotte and the news from Ann in Baltimore. She forced him to sip the tea she brewed, but he first refused, since it came from Richmond's meager civilian supplies. Finally she became aware from his hesitant manner that he was trying to find a way to tell her something more.

"Yes? It's about. . ."

"Arlington," he began, his eyes searching hers in anxiety. "The Congress in Washington City passed a tax against real estate in sections held by the North. When they fixed a figure for Arlington, about ninety dollars, I wrote to Cousin Phillip to present the money on my behalf." With increasing tension Mary listened as Robert named a family connection in the Union capital. "The Yankees wouldn't accept it from him. They said I would have to go there myself and claim it as the owner." Robert paused. "Now they're selling the place for taxes."

Her home, built by her father, to be passed on to her son . . . They couldn't take it away like that! For a moment a fury swept over her. The thieves, the scheming corruptionists, to set impossible conditions, so that they could steal that rich property, with its hundreds of Washington family associations, on a claim of less than a hundred dollars . . . A new determination made her head rise. Damn them all, she would not accept this loss. She would find a way to retrieve Arlington; she promised it to herself.

Mary and Robert might have gone on talking far into the night, that first evening of their reunion, but Charlotte's condition grew suddenly worse and they were summoned to her bedside. Looking at Robert, the doctor shook his head. "I'm afraid she's in delirium, and she really doesn't know what she's saying." Nevertheless the words continued. "They're killing him, they're going to hang him, no matter what they tell me . . . Make them let me see him . . ."

Mary caught Robert's arm; she could not stay to hear more of the anguished words. Outside Custis waited for them. His face looked grim and he spoke swiftly. "Look, let me tell the Union people I'm willing to take Rooney's place, as a hostage, if they'll just let him be here with her. For forty-eight hours, or any time they'll grant."

Mary saw her husband hesitate. "Custis, I don't think they'd agree." The girl's voice came weakly again through the closed door, and Robert nodded. "All right, my boy. Write out the request, and I'll try to get it through." Eyes lowered, he left them.

Before the week's end Robert brought Mary the answer. Union officials had turned down the petition. Her lips tightened in pain. Robert talked on about precedents, rules, barriers; as she listened Mary cursed the Yankees for what they were doing. After a few days Charlotte improved slightly and Mary whispered to her, "We haven't given up hope that he'll be exchanged."

Mary went on to speak of the fast-approaching Christmas, and Charlotte smiled weakly. Mary worked hastily to assemble a meager chicken, bread, a few yams, a coffee substitute. But just before Christmas Robert told her quietly:

"Mim, I'll have to be at camp. Oh, it's no new battle, or anything of the sort. It's just that—I ought to be there. I've been saying to the men that nothing's more important than our responsibilities, that the Army has to stay together. I'll be with them, spending the day as they do. Don't you see?"

Yes, she saw, and to tell him so, she kissed him gently.

On the night after Christmas of 1863, alone in his quarters, Robert Lee looked up as a courier saluted. The young man withdrew and Robert's hand hesitated, then opened the letter. His daughter-in-law had died that day . . . He reached for another sheet, tried to read it, and put it aside. Drawing back the first message, he stared for a long time, and let his head sink to the table.

Chapter 16

"They'll be passing right soon" . . . "I can hear 'em!"

From the crowd, awaiting the marching men, the cries broke out from time to time. A spring breeze from the Richmond outskirts lifted the fringe of Mary's shawl as she rested in her wheel chair on the stoop of their new home on East Franklin Street. At first, though the doctor urged it for safety, the abandonment of the crutches had been a hard decision; now she found that the wheel chair gave her greater freedom. Someday she might do without either, but not for many a month. She shrugged; considering the things that happened daily around them, she had no reason to feel sorry for herself.

The last few months had been, she could thank God, a somewhat calmer period. Robert labored on at the repair of his war machine, while General Grant gathered his powerful forces on the approaches to Richmond. The women, too, had worked; as Mary waited here, her hands moved endlessly at her knitting.

Another, thicker hand moved near hers, tightening its hold on the knob of her chair, and she glanced up at Rooney. His eyes had regained their serenity, despite his long imprisonment and the events that accompanied it. For some time she had feared he would never recover; even after Charlotte's death Rooney had stayed two and a half months in Federal custody. And then, after an exchange of prisoners, Rooney had walked slowly up these stairs, his face more forbidding than she had thought possible of this son. The old brightness, the effervescence, was gone; in its place she read gloom and defeat.

As she clung to him on that first day, Mary had groped for words. What could she say? His son and daughter, then his wife had died, to say nothing of his capture and imprisonment. "Still, there's the life ahead of you, boy," Mary had reasoned. "And they'll need you more than ever in the war."

With his recovery, however, she would lose him and her oldest son as well. Today Custis was standing at her other side, his dark face somewhat less grim than usual. After many petitions on his part, Custis was being sent from Richmond to the field. "That's hardly the best news for me," Mary told him wistfully.

Several months earlier she had moved with the girls to this tall brick house with the classic porch and simple white cornice. Custis had once used it with fellow officers; for a time at least she would have adequate space and a partial retreat from the excitements of the hour. Robert came into Richmond for conferences, and occasionally he stayed overnight. Yet less often of late; the war, she knew, slowly approached another climax.

Before the Franklin Street house a child cried, "The men's coming!" Toward them trudged an irregular file of gray-clad soldiers, and though she had known what to expect, Mary felt a shock. They were so grim and so threadbare. Elbows stuck out of broken sleeves; collars had long ago been worn away and shoes broken, so that feet flapped awkwardly through the dust. She stared harder at the tired brown faces. These were not the fresh youths she had seen in earlier years; most of them appeared in their forties or fifties.

Where were the younger men? She had the answer: In their graves, or rotting in forgotten spots in the woods, or in hospitals with their arms and legs shot off. The war had taken most of their young. But then, as she watched, Mary saw another extreme, a small, skinny lad, who looked hardly fifteen, and another with a slight fuzz on his cheek, and a third. Beside them her Rob seemed almost a veteran. She understood better what one woman had told her: The South was grinding up its seed corn. Those too old, and those too young—of necessity it took them all, and still it did not have enough.

The horses clattered along, and Mary saw their bony sides, their mouths with tongues hanging far out, and she could hear

Robert's words of the previous week. Lacking feed, his army had sent its horses away for winter forage; but now they were so hungry again that they gnawed at the bark of trees, and he thought his forces would lose a large portion of these animals. In Richmond she herself had watched women with blue-lipped babies, their bony jaws shining in the daylight, and street mobs had once more rioted for food.

Today, for a few minutes, the crowd looked on in apparent indifference. On came the tattered marchers, steadily, doggedly. Then an elderly woman in gingham called to them, "We're proud 'o yer!" A man echoed her. "Give 'em hell. Give it to 'em!" In another minute hundreds were shouting to the weary soldiers; before them gray heads lifted and dulled eyes brightened. They were stamping, swinging along, almost like twenty-year-olds! Mary found her own voice breaking in a cry of encouragement.

Two young women ran forward with plates of corn bread. They pushed them toward several of the men, who grabbed chunks, grinned and shoved the bread into their mouths. Mary recognized the girls from down the street; they had as little as any on the square, and they must have taken the last food in their kitchen.

"Look there!" Custis was motioning. A child, held by his mother, had handed a ham bone to an eager private; nearby a white-haired man passed pieces of bread. The friendly actions of the crowd spread like a contagion; from other houses emerged women with clothing—a pair of men's shoes, aged and dusty and still in better condition than the soldiers' cracked footgear; and shirts and vests and, in one case, a formal coat.

"That's welcome too." The man who got the long black coat guffawed, flourishing it on his bayonet. Others did the same thing, carrying their gifts like banners. Mary saw that Agnes and Mildred had gone out with a platter of beef and rolls from the dining room. They would have no supper that night, and they would not mind.

"Mary, this house is like an industrial school," a friend remarked. As usual Mary's parlor was filled with materials, boxes, and girls. Smiling at the friend's comment, Mary continued to click her needles as others made bandages. Although they produced items by the hundreds, the demand still came in for more.

Mary glanced briefly at the scene around her. Like the costumes of almost any other group in the capital in this early summer of 1864, the dresses had a conglomerate appearance, with one lady dressed in silk, the only such garment she had left, another in a costume part taffeta, part cotton. Mary herself wore bits of inherited lace at the throat of a twice-patched gingham. Today she and her helpers worked with urgency; a great battle had started at a point described to them as the Wilderness.

One of the women lifted her head. "They say General Lee was at the front and exposing himself to fire the other day. When the men realized he was going to join the charge, every soldier cried to him: 'Lee to the rear! General Lee to the rear!' They wouldn't go on till he withdrew; he had to do it."

There was a pause, and the needles began again. Mary did not try to speak; she was thinking of another incident of the past few weeks. When Robert arrived in Richmond on his first visit in months, he went to St. Paul's Church. (Because of her condition, she worshiped at home.) The service over, he started down the aisle, to discover that no one had stirred from the pews. Silently, without prearrangement, they stood there in tribute; women and children with their love and their awe in their eyes. . . .

Today a rumbling sound reached them, and Agnes went out, to return with a look of alarm. "It's Jeb Stuart. They're bringing him to the city, and he's dying." Stuart, golden figure of the war, gallant of a hundred exploits . . . Several of the workers were crying. For this loss there could be no replacement. And each woman was thinking of her own man at the battle fronts.

That night and the next day and the next Mary heard in horror of scenes at the Wilderness; ten thousand or more Federal men, dead and wounded, their bodies carpeting fields and slopes, so that the whole area appeared to creep and crawl with those who moaned and died slowly in the fetid air. For days the fighting had gone on, while Grant refused to ask a truce to pick up his injured and bury the bloated, blackened victims rotting under the sun.

Then at last Grant moved to another front, and Robert had to shift and prepare doggedly for their next meeting. From the North there arose shocked protest over the losses: Grant was a butcher, ready to sacrifice ten or twelve men to one Confederate loss. Sitting with the girls, Mary spoke bitterly. "He can afford it, and he'll keep on shoving soldiers against us and reach out with his other hand for more of them!" And, as if to herself, she added, "They have so many to fill up the gaps. But where will ours come from?"

Overnight the Wilderness took on another meaning for Mary Lee. In Richmond talk spread of the cartloads of dead that rolled back toward Washington City. Twenty thousand or more had to be placed somewhere, and nearly every burial ground was filled. A new spot was found—Arlington estate.

"Oh no, no!" At first Mary did not believe it as she stared at the bulletin. Her house would remain, but the property around it would be a national cemetery. Already, without previous announcement, many corpses had been placed among the trees. "They couldn't do a thing like that. . . ." Her voice died in her throat; it was like one of her nightmares about the place. Even when the Federal Government itself had bought in her place at a "tax sale," for only twenty-seven thousand dollars, she had held to the hope that the family might yet get back, somehow, to Arlington. But now, a cemetery.

As the warm months advanced, Robert and his men occupied positions near Petersburg, about twenty miles from Richmond. Several times she had visited the neat, clean-swept town, with its many families known to the Lees and Custises. In these days, however, she thought of Petersburg in a new, frightening connection. On a hurried visit Custis told her bluntly: "If Petersburg ever goes, so does Richmond." Then her eldest son went back to help defend it. Ready to hold to the end, the old town dug in for a siege; and more and more clearly Mary understood that all their futures might be decided there. From Petersburg Robert wrote her on June thirtieth, their wedding anniversary:

Do you recollect what a happy day thirty-three years ago this was? How many hopes and pleasures it gave birth to! God has been very merciful and kind to us, and how thankless and sinful I have been. I pray that he may continue his mercies and blessings to us, and give us a little peace and rest together in this world . . .

Mary lowered her head. A third of a century, and how much they had lived through together, how much lost and also gained. "A little peace and rest"—would they ever have it again? Handing the note to Mildred and young Mary, she pushed her wheel chair to her room; she wanted mainly to be alone on this day.

Their food supplies ran lower, prices higher, and at Robert's urging they went for visits to country friends. Month after month the Federal forces pounded at little Petersburg. Mary shuddered when she heard the stories of civilian suffering—wrecked homes, disrupted families, hunger, as the defending soldiers kept guard against an unending threat of a break-through. Still the Army held.

The Confederate skies grew yet blacker. In Georgia, Joe Johnston, facing General Sherman, was drawing back near Atlanta, and Mary's friends brought word such as she had heard before: "President Davis and Johnston are snapping at each other worse than ever. Johnston says he has to pull away and keep his army together; the President wants a battle for Atlanta and no more delay."

Soon afterward a startling report was circulated: Jefferson Davis had replaced Joe Johnston with the more impetuous Hood. Mary could hardly say how she felt in the matter. True, Robert had succeeded Joe at Richmond, but under far different circumstances. For Joe Johnston this new blow must have been the war's worst—and might it not also have been a mistaken step? She remembered Robert's defense of Johnston, and his lack of admiration for Hood.

August and September seemed to fly past, and soon the news arrived that Atlanta had fallen. November saw Sherman marching on to the Atlantic coast. If he reached there almost all the rest of the South would be separated from Virginia; it was a terrifying prospect.

One day she made up her mind to go back to Richmond, and never leave it again as long as the war lasted. That was her place, near Robert. Again on East Franklin Street, they resumed their life in a city that grew steadily more apprehensive. She sat alone on a morning that brought her a brief, troubled note from her brother-in-law in Baltimore. Ann Marshall's years of pain had ended; Robert's sister had died quietly, with the family around her.

So another hope was over, another dream of reunion. After the war Mary had hoped they could come together. She had so much to say to Ann. She thought of Robert's letter to his sister, asking her understanding of his position in the war. But Ann had gone without the opportunity of a final word with them. The quiet morning seemed cold and barren.

In the depth of winter Mary read ominous dispatches that told how Sherman had reached Savannah, and later moved on through the Carolinas and up the coast. And now heavy reinforcements were being dispatched to Ulysses S. Grant, to build up the monster of an army that dug in against Robert's men.

South of Richmond at Petersburg the people and the soldiers continued to huddle under the shrieking blasts of wind and the guns of the enemy. Robert stayed close to the battle lines; between the Army and the town, she knew, there had developed a bond of fellowship in suffering and deprivation. Scurvy broke out because the men lacked basic foods, and consumption had become ever more common. Nevertheless they held.

One day in February of the new year a Richmond widow brought Mary a report that must already have swept through the capital. "What do you think of the plan to elevate General Lee?"

From the questioner's tone Mary sensed that the words had been well pondered. "What plan?" she asked.

"Don't you know—to have Mr. Davis step down and let General Lee take his place as President and continue as commander?"

Mary's heart trembled, and she tried to evaluate the astonishing information. To have her husband as the leader of the Confederacy, with power to direct all its affairs, might unite the people as they had never been united under Jefferson Davis. Nevertheless she frowned. "I've heard nothing about it," she told her informant cautiously.

For the rest of the day the matter remained steadily on her mind. She remembered the mutterings of people on the street, the whispers that she had ignored: "Davis is hopeless—just not the man for the job" . . . "*He's* always right and everybody else is wrong!" She asked herself if Mr. Davis could withstand such criticism indefinitely. She suspected that the plan to make Robert President was no politicians' scheme, but was the spontaneous idea of the people themselves. For hours, avoiding her daughters' questions, she waited to hear what Robert would say about it.

When he came to pay them a brief visit later that evening, Mary received him alone.

"Is it to be General Lee or Mr. President?" she asked, her cheeks flushed with excitement.

"Mim, I'd hoped you wouldn't hear that." He shook his head. "I'm a soldier; you know I've never been anything else, except for those few months I managed Arlington. Civil affairs and Army life—they're altogether different." He spoke with emphasis. "If any offer is made, I shan't accept it."

She had anticipated his reaction but not the finality of his decision. Her mind told her that he was right, but in her heart she wanted to see him President of the Confederacy.

"Robert," she asked, "how can Mr. Davis continue in office with all the people against him?"

Her husband's smile was a sad one. "If that is so, it may well be because we're losing, Mary, and a good many people want a scapegoat." From his tone she realized that for him the subject was closed.

Yet, regardless of Robert's stand, Mary did not hear the end of the business for several days. Although she took care not to mention the matter again, the talk went on. Then overnight Mr. Davis compromised, informing the Confederate Congress that he would choose a general in chief, something his government had never done. He named Robert E. Lee.

General in chief . . . an office he might have had in the Federal armies at the beginning of the war. Seated at the window in her wheel chair, Mary felt a glow of pride, for she knew that Robert could get along with anybody, including the sensitive Mr. Davis.

His tact and understanding would help keep Mr. Davis in office and the South together. With a sigh, however, she realized that she would see even less of him.

In addition to his new duties, Robert retained command of the Army of Northern Virginia. He rode repeatedly between Petersburg and Richmond, his mind busy with plans for all Confederate forces. One of the first appointments he made as general in chief was that of Joseph E. Johnston to command the Confederacy's Western Army, restoring him to the post from which Mr. Davis had removed him.

Mary wondered if there would be repercussions, but when he came to the house again Robert reassured her. "No, Mim, Mr. Davis made no objection." He spoke earnestly. "Joe's the best man for the place." Mary smiled to herself, thinking how curiously the relationships of these three men had altered through the years.

In the weeks that followed Robert spent most of his time consulting with President Davis or on meetings with Congressmen. On his return from one session with the legislators he said wearily, "Mim, if our people only knew how badly things are going with the Army. Hundreds of men don't even have shoes. The animals are dying every day, and there aren't any replacements; our transportation is breaking down." His voice dropped. "The men, too—they're beginning to slip away. The wives write that their children are hungry. I've had to issue orders to shoot deserters, no matter what excuses they offer.

"Worst of all, the Congress just sits there, chewing tobacco and eating peanuts, while our men starve."

She took his hand, and when he spoke again the bitterness was gone. "Mim, there is one last chance and we've got to try it. We must use the Negroes. If we give them their freedom gradually, we can bring them into the Army! I'm going to put it up to Congress."

Mary thought she was prepared for the storm which would follow Robert's proposal, but as the days went by and the reverberations continued, she realized that she had underestimated it. From her window, early one morning, she heard two people talking on the street:

"Lee ought to keep his nose out of other people's business. He wants to free the slaves, huh?" The speaker made a disagreeable sound. "What the hell are we fighting this war for?"

"I always heard he favored the abolitionists and now he's proved it!"

Eventually a bill was passed to use Negroes in the Army, but there was no provision for freedom. As Robert showed her the transcript of it, his mouth was a long, grim line. "It won't help at all. It doesn't give them anything except the right to die." He had spent another harsh day with the Congressmen. "I begged for more soldiers and more supplies, and I got words and nothing else."

More quietly he asked, "Mary, suppose we have to give up Petersburg. Where will you go?"

In the past few months she had already decided that matter. "All through the war, Robert, I ran from place to place. Now I'll stay here." Though he argued she fixed her lips and did not give way. They remained side by side in the wintry room, the wind rattling the windows, the carefully laid fire slowly dying in the grate.

The next day Robert had regained his spirits, at least to a degree, and with his usual cheerful air he left for the front at Petersburg. At the sight of his strong shoulders, disappearing up the street, Mary wondered: How long can he endure these terrible burdens?

The reports which came through that week and the next were generally unfavorable. There were rumors of new battle. April began in Richmond and on Sunday Agnes, Mildred, and the young Mary went as usual to St. Paul's Church while Mary, gathering the servants, proceeded to read from her prayer book.

Through open windows the morning winds played at the curtains and chimes rang distantly over Richmond. From Franklin Street Mary heard the sound of carriages. Could church possibly be out so early? The front door opened and her daughters came bursting into the room, their faces showing both fear and excitement.

236

"A messenger walked up to Mr. Davis' pew and called him away!" Agnes almost shouted. "Everybody rushed home."

Close to tears, Mildred found it difficult to state the bare facts. "They say Father's battle lines gave way, and he's drawing back from Petersburg, and now they say the North can take Richmond."

More calmly than she would have thought possible Mary said quietly, "We'll have to see." By now the sidewalks echoed with running footsteps, and from the streets came the rattle of many wagons and carriages. Within the half hour, as Mary and the girls waited tensely at the window, their friend Mr. Caskie came with even worse news: "They're evacuating Richmond—Mr. Davis and the rest of the Cabinet. They've said they'll set the government up somewhere else, but . . ."

So this was the beginning of the end, thought Mary, realizing that she was not really surprised. She started to thank Mr. Caskie for coming, but he interrupted her. "Now, Mrs. Lee, you mustn't get too disturbed, but another report just came in about—your son."

Which son? She gripped the arms of her wheel chair.

"Since yesterday's fighting Custis has been missing. Now, please don't—"

Mary heard no more. Missing . . . That meant in a ditch, bleeding to death, or hiding somewhere. Custis, her first-born . . .

She controlled herself. Tears would do no good; they had had enough of them, and there was only one thing to do, hope and also pray. She picked up her knitting, and after the needles had clicked for a time Mr. Caskie ventured again. "You won't stay here, in your condition, and with the girls?"

"I won't leave, and I don't think they will." Mary's tone was not defiant, not sad, but a simple statement. She would be here when Robert returned, and when her boys came back, including Custis. He might be alive; she would make herself believe it.

Through the terrible anxiety of that afternoon she heard the noises from outside increase with each hour. Their servant slipped in to tell Mary: "People's fightin' at the railroad station, punchin' at one another to get on the cars. They yellin' and goin' on like crazy. Some's even cursin' the Confed'rates as they goes by, spittin' at 'em."

"Shopwindows smash' in too, and they takes everythin' they can set hands on." The maid from next door, who had run over with more news, nodded. Mary frowned; looting, murder, cowardice . . . Her face sharpened in her contempt.

Friends called and left, and several told her they would also stay in their homes. After dark the trembling girls helped Mary to bed, and she sat up against the pillows, white cap on her head; she could not sleep, and she would not try. The name of Custis remained on her lips, and they moved in prayer.

Hours later a shattering blast rattled the windows of their house. Shouts and screams rose from outside, and Agnes went downstairs, to return with the explanation: "They've blown up the ordnance works, to keep the Union from getting it. They claim the fire's spreading to stores and tobacco warehouses."

Their maid crept in, her face wet; she must have run for blocks. When she managed to speak she had terror in her voice. "All the waterfront burnin' in this direction. Las' Confed'rate soldiers jus' burn' down the bridges so the North won' come over. What we do?"

Acrid smoke swirled through the streets, and Mary forced herself up. "Somebody opened the penitentiary," Agnes whispered, "and the men are running through the town." Would the defenseless city tear itself apart? At the window Mary looked down; people were carrying boxes of food, screaming at one another. Somewhere in the shadows a child wept as if he were lost.

Panic spread inside Mary for a moment, and then she quieted it. None of this was as important to her as her husband or her boys. Let God spare them. . . . Assisting her to dress, the girls started silently to pack their belongings. She saw that the flames were closer; sparks came floating through the air, and people in the next square were standing about with buckets of water to protect their homes if they could. Mary turned. "I'll leave if the fire reaches this block. Otherwise I'm not going."

They were still standing at the window when dawn broke over the city, a dawn loud with cries and the crackle of flames. In the midst of the clamor Mary heard a knocking, and Agnes answered.

Mr. Caskie stood there, his face furrowed with lack of sleep. Then his eyes brightened.

"I just found it out, Mrs. Lee. Custis is alive." She stared, and he touched her arm to make sure she understood. "He's a Union prisoner, but he's all right!"

Mary's head sank and she prayed thankfully. God had been kind. Clearing his throat, Mr. Caskie added, "The mayor's been helpless to stop the fire and the looting, and he went to the Federals under a flag of truce. Richmond has just been surrendered. The Union general's bringing order again."

From the Capitol a few blocks off a new banner flew above the haze of smoke. It was the flag of the United States. Mary looked at it for a long time, and buried her face in her hands.

Six days later, at Appomattox, Robert E. Lee stepped from a porch and walked toward his steed, Traveler. His words were low as he called out, "Orderly." Sighing, he mounted his horse; and Ulysses S. Grant, leaving the same building, halted and took off his hat. Instantly the other Federal officers did the same thing; Robert Lee lifted his in response, and rode quietly away.

A few days before he and his men might have cut their way out of the Federal trap. Yet what would have been the use? Only a short time could elapse before their opponents caught them again. They stood against a wall, beset by men in blue and also by the threat of hunger. For days scanty corn had been almost their only food, and little of that.

U. S. Grant was generous in victory. The men of the Army of Northern Virginia were paroled under a pledge not to take up arms against the United States. They would return to their homes; and meanwhile, at Lee's request, they were to receive their first full meal in a long time—Union Army rations. And when guns boomed and Federal troops began to celebrate, Grant ordered the demonstrations halted; he wanted no crowing, no boasting.

Robert E. Lee rode toward his soldiers, to give them his last orders. As they broke ranks and crowded forward, one or two cried to him:

"General, are we surrendered?"

"*Are* we surrendered?"

He told them then, and when he looked at the soldiers who had gone with him through years of travail, his eyes filled. His mouth moved, but after a moment he could say nothing more. "Good-by, my men . . ." Behind him they called:

"We'll still fight 'em!"

"Give the word, and we'll fight 'em yet!"

For another week Mary waited in uncertainty. Robert's men were going home now, to their spring plowing, she told herself; as her husband had said, they would take up where they stopped four years ago. She tried not to think of anything else. She must be here for Robert's return, to hear what he had to tell her—where they were to go, what they were to do. Most of all, however, she wanted to be with him. Often her eyes went to the outlines of burned buildings against the Richmond skies; no wait in her life had seemed so long.

Then finally Agnes came to tell her: "They say down the street that he's just crossed the river, and people are running over to Main to see him!" Before the words were out, Mary had called to her other daughters, and hurriedly they took her to the mirror, and then helped her down the stairs to the front hallway. There, clasping her hands to keep them from shaking, she told Mildred:

"Open the door, child."

A few squares off Robert Lee rode toward them, followed by several of his officers. Their animals, bony and tired, moved without spirit. A short distance behind this group of officers came several wagons with their belongings; on one a tattered quilt, replacing the customary canvas, flapped up and down.

At the growing sounds around him Robert glanced to right and left; he had not expected a crowd and he did not welcome it. Then he realized what was happening. A bent man pulled off his cap; a young woman held up her baby to see him, and she herself started to cry. Three Union soldiers, standing near the corner, removed their hats. Several girls waved, and a cheering broke out, steadily louder.

"General!"

"Bless you, God bless you!"

He had reached the house on East Franklin Street. When he left his saddle Mary bent forward in her chair, hands extended unconsciously to him. The people outside pressed around her husband, and their voices were louder than ever. She searched his face; he was so white, and so tired, so depleted . . .

As Mary Lee watched, cheers began again, and before her eyes a cluster of Federal soldiers moved toward Robert to join in the cries of the Richmonders. She could look no more; her sorrow and her joy were too strong.

Past the gate, up the front stairs he came toward her. He held out his hands, and the door closed upon them.

PART IV

"Misfortune nobly borne is good fortune."

MARCUS AURELIUS

Chapter 17

"It's so quiet here in the country, Robert; we can count the acorns as they drop."

With a tentative smile Mary let her glance fall from the branches of the oak tree, sweeping low past their shoulders, and turned toward her husband as he sat with troubled eyes on the far-off fields. In the four months since his return to her in Richmond his look had never changed for long; and he had remained in much the same spot, since their arrival a few weeks earlier at this cottage on the James River.

Hearing her words, Robert shifted in his chair and he smiled for a moment. "Count acorns . . . For a while, anyway, Mim, it sounds like a pleasant occupation. After that, you know what I'd like most? A farm of our own, no matter how small, and a chance to work it with the girls around us. And no more interruptions."

His voice fell away, and Robert let his head fall back. Anxiously Mary sought for something to take him from his meditation. "Did you see this?" She passed over a newspaper that carried a lively memoir of war experiences by a pair of Tennessee officers. With a dutiful nod he picked it up. "Interesting." Almost at once his hand moved again, and he set the journal aside.

Mary sighed to herself. It seemed impossible to interest him in anything; even the war seemed a closed issue. She herself did not feel altogether well; as she moved about in her wheel chair her arms and legs quivered with pain. But her main concern was for Robert.

It was good for all of them to be away, at least for the present, from the tensions and pressures of Richmond. In the first days after he came back to the city she had heard him walk nightly up and down the rear gallery of the East Franklin Street house. So much had happened in a short time: Abraham Lincoln murdered by the madman Booth, and Jefferson Davis arrested . . . Mary made a bitter grimace; it was the same fort to which she and Robert had gone after their marriage, the one to which Rooney had been taken.

On Robert's return from the war furtive, angry Southern men had knocked at their door in Richmond, and Mary heard whispers: Didn't General Lee think they should keep on in their struggle, with the last remnants of the armies or as guerrillas in remote sections? Older ones, less fiery yet no less bitter, also wanted his advice: Should they go to Mexico or Latin America to start over again? For every case Robert had almost the same answer: "Every man has to judge for himself, but I think Virginia needs us, and so do the other states. And the United States, too."

He mentioned the United States with deep emotion, for as Mary knew he believed that the division between North and South was a thing of the past. Some of his callers left with fixed lips, muttering to themselves and probably cursing Robert. More often, she hoped, his counsel had its effect.

"What Mr. Lee says he'll do *we'll* do," a stranger assured her on the street. For a moment she wondered: It was curious that so many said that kind of thing about Robert, whereas, while they had strong sympathy for Jefferson Davis in his imprisonment, few spoke the same way about Mr. Davis himself.

Some of the men they had known, lawyers and other professionals, were working now at a dollar a day, scraping mortar from bricks in the burned-over section of Richmond. Others had knocked at their door in sick uncertainty: a man about to start a five-hundred-mile journey on foot, back to his family in Alabama; a one-armed youth, preparing to plow his acres with his wife's help; a widow in homespun, with her four children.

Mary shook her head as she recalled that last case. The woman's house had been destroyed; her brother and brother-in-law and then her son had died in the war, and there were no other men

246

in the family. From the next room Mary had heard her story, and Robert's sympathetic advice.

She had been glad of what he did for the woman, as for others; yet for the Lees, too, the future had clouded, and she had gone to him, to take his hands in hers. "Robert, you can't possibly carry everybody's burden." When he looked silently at her, she read the concern and sorrow that were seldom far from him.

As to their own immediate future she had kept her thoughts to herself for a long time. Now she asked suddenly, "Won't you run for office? You could be the Governor of Virginia, you know."

Mary's conviction was shared by thousands of Virginians, but Robert looked at her with a pained expression.

"No, Mim. That isn't the kind of thing I could do. And don't you see—that for most people I'd be a reminder of the war and the Army? We've got to put the fighting behind us, and work to bury the past with its bitter hatred."

His answer irritated her. She had an impulse to point out that he would be far better in office than most of the miserable clowns and scoundrels who were now running the state. But she held her peace; this was Robert's decision, not hers.

She noticed that he had turned again to President Johnson's amnesty proclamation, under which Confederate leaders must make special application for pardon.

"Mim," he told her suddenly. "I think I should ask for the pardon."

Mary had secretly hoped that he would ignore the proclamation because she knew full well the danger of accepting it. This might be the worst mistake of his entire life. But she would not try to argue him out of it. She knew her husband too well to think that he would choose the easy course.

"I know how some people will hate me for it, Mim, but to me that's not important if by doing this I can help bring the two sections of this country together."

Nevertheless protests broke out at once, with grumblings on the corners. "I just can't understand," Mary heard. "He's practically said he was wrong in the war. That doesn't sound like the general."

For days after Robert signed the petition there were angry protests, many of which reached Mary's ears. Afterward, however, women began to stop beside her carriage and say, "My husband's taking the oath, the way the general did!" "He's set an example, and we can thank him for it." There was a surprising reaction from the North when General Grant and Henry Ward Beecher, the abolitionist, complimented General Lee on what he had done.

Robert thought it best for them to leave Richmond, for their income would not maintain them there in any case. It was Mary who decided their immediate destination. Robert had hoped to find that small farm of which he had spoken—not too expensive, not too isolated—and he had made one or two trips to check prospects. Meanwhile a note arrived from Mrs. Elizabeth Randolph Cocke, who lived sixty miles from Richmond.

Mrs. Cocke had a fully furnished overseer's cottage, and it was not in use. Wouldn't the Lees occupy it, if only for a while? Though Mrs. Cocke was a distant family connection, they had hesitated until Mrs. Cocke herself called on Mary. "All I want is to pay back something of what we all owe the general," their visitor offered in appeal. Mary's heart went out to the kindly woman, and they accepted. After they had been there several weeks she was glad they had made the choice.

Two of their boys had followed Robert's advice to get back as quickly as possible to work. Rooney went to the wrecked White House, taking over soon after the invaders left. Mary frowned when she heard of the leaky box of a cabin in which he lived, and of his struggle to find enough laborers to run the place. It was hard, she knew, for the boy to make a new start with Charlotte and their two children gone; there were many tragic memories, many sights to reproach him. Nevertheless his letters told of his determination and his gradual progress.

She and Robert had hoped that Rob would resume his schooling, but their youngest son shook his head. "I've no time for school." Instead he rode off to their Romancoke farm. Under Mr. Custis' will it was to be his, and he was ready to start working it. Robert helped with a few supplies from money he managed to scrape together. When Mary thought of the two boys she told herself she had faith in both of them. Rooney and Rob had proved themselves during the war years. It was Custis who worried her.

He was with them now at the overseer's cottage, and as she looked across the yard she saw that Custis was busy repairing the back steps. For this eldest boy there was no immediate solution. His heritage would have been Arlington. Though none of them mentioned their old home, the tragic memory of it still hung over them. And Custis, of course, had been trained at West Point; the Army had always been his life. How was he to use that training now?

As Custis moved away Mary's gaze followed him. More clearly than any of the others, perhaps, Custis had foreseen the disaster that was coming. The war had injured his prospects more than it had those of either of his brothers, and had left him more silent than ever, and gloomier.

As for Robert . . . Her mood changed; like most of them he was marking time. Earlier that week young Mary had summed up the situation as she worked beside her sisters in the kitchen. With her usual exactness the girl had said the thing that had been in all their minds: "People are ready to give Father everything, except what he wants most—a chance to earn his own living."

From where she sat, under the trees, Mary heard the sound of a carriage, and then her daughter Mildred came running across the lawn. "Mother, a gentleman's here to see Father, Judge Brockenbrough of Washington College. He wants to talk to him about something, and he certainly looks serious." Mary turned away. In these days so many Southerners had something to talk about, and something that made them look serious.

"Give him tea and biscuits," she whispered to the girl, and then reflected: If their guest did not eat too much, she might have enough for the family tonight. Then with a smile she wondered if it had ever occurred to her years ago that someday she would appraise how much a caller would consume.

So the visitor came from Washington College. Mary remembered that it was an old Virginia school, in the western part of the state. George Washington had had something to do with the founding of it and it had been named for him. What could this caller want of Robert? Suddenly she sensed that this visit would be important to both of them. She could hardly wait until Robert came rapidly across the lawn. The minute she saw his face she realized she had been right and that something had touched him deeply.

"The trustees want me to be president. I don't know what to say, Mim." He was staring at the distant trees, as if he saw nothing that lay before him. "It's a good school. It suffered badly in the war, but they're hoping to start rebuilding it this fall." Taking a seat beside her, he talked on with an excitement in his voice she had not heard for months.

"It might be a chance to do some of the things I've been telling others to do. From now on the South will certainly need education—for the young boys growing up and for the older ones who were in the Army."

"How much would it pay?"

"Fifteen hundred dollars a year."

Mary started to protest; for years he had earned much more than that, and it was far from adequate pay for the president of a college. Robert had anticipated her reaction: "A great many of us in the South will have to get along with less than we've had."

Again she objected: "It isn't one of the big schools."

"That isn't the question. It's what the college stands for and —well, what I could do there." He clasped his hands, and Mary realized that a doubt had crossed his own mind. "Still, am I qualified for the position? And if I took it"—he sat silent for more than a minute—"I might automatically turn people away and injure the school. A lot of them call me a traitor, you know." The last sentence hurt her, and she tried desperately to reassure him.

For days Robert debated the matter with himself; he paid a visit to a minister friend, and discussed the matter again and again with Mary and the children. In the end she went to him herself and put her arms around him. "Robert, stop worrying yourself sick over this decision. I want you to take it."

Afterward she had a sense of overwhelming relief; their course had been settled. She was sure now that Providence was pointing the way for them.

Robert rode away in September to get their house ready in Lexington. Soon his letters arrived, saying that he had begun a heavy schedule of work, coping with poor finances, lack of supplies, lack of nearly everything else. From the start, however, he found Washington College a place of great beauty. In moments of leisure he explored the mountainous surroundings—the waterfalls, the deep gorges, the heavily wooded hills. He loved, too, the rolling fields carpeted with blue grass.

While he was generally cheerful, it was obvious from his letters how much he missed them all. "I wish you were all with me. I feel very solitary and miss you all dreadfully . . . Life is indeed gliding away, and I have nothing of good to show for mine that is past."

Thoughtfully Mary put the last letter aside. She should be with him, to keep him from falling into such moods. Complications developed, and the house was not ready for them, but meanwhile the family received another piece of good news. The widely respected Virginia Military Institute, also at Lexington, had reopened its doors, and Custis was made a professor of civil engineering. Thus the son about whom she was concerned would be able to live with them. She knew that it would mean a great deal to Robert to have the company of the boy who had always been his favorite.

Custis preceded them to Lexington, and this time Robert wrote playfully to Mildred, urging her to join him at once. "You know I am a poor hand and can do nothing without your advice. Your brother, too, is wild for the want of admonitions." Mary smiled; when Robert joked again, it was a good sign.

On a chill December morning, after many arrangements had been made, a canalboat took her and the girls first to Bremo, on the James, and then to Lexington. When it touched the bank she found her husband waiting with Traveler on shore, bareheaded in spite of the cold. Stepping aboard, he carried her tenderly to the carriage. She talked only a little. It was enough to be in his care again.

They drove through Lexington. Mary saw for the first time a town of attractive frame and brick houses and behind them the blue-gray mountains. She would like it here. When the carriage stopped, she saw the two-storied brick house with its four white columns and shadowed gallery. It lacked the proportions of Arlington, perhaps, but it looked solid and comfortable. She was quick to say, "Robert, it's handsome. Very handsome."

Lifting her again, he carried her over the threshold, where her wheel chair awaited her. With the girls around her she moved curiously from the living room to the library and the study. "Are things all right?" Robert asked with marked apprehension, and in a moment she learned why. Few of the chambers were entirely furnished, and many of the new pieces were of an unconventional design, while others were in excellent taste. In the living room there was nothing except a grand piano, conspicuously in the center. This house plainly needed, above anything else, a woman's hand.

As she was wheeled from room to room she looked at the windows and the floors. Suddenly she recognized the pattern in curtain and rug; she cried out as she placed a number of old and familiar patterns and when she realized that these furnishings had come from Arlington, rescued by Aunt Maria and other relatives, and sent on ahead. There was an odd thickness at the edges of the rugs, and she immediately guessed why. Designed for much larger rooms, they had to be folded under. How much of this new life would have to be fitted to narrower limits? In spite of herself she remembered what was not here—the wall ornaments, pictures, the Washington punch bowl, so much of it . . .

Realizing what was going through her mind, Robert pushed her wheel chair quickly to the storeroom and pointed to jars and jars of food. "Our Lexington friends didn't want you to starve while you're getting settled." Before Mary could voice her gratitude he turned her toward the dining room. "Your first breakfast is ready; the ladies prepared it for us." From the kitchen and dining room drifted the aroma of coffee and hot bread, eggs, and spiced sausage. The genuineness of this welcome, the kindness of people she had never met made her eyes shine. The way from Arlington to Lexington had been long and arduous, but their wanderings had ended.

"Let us give thanks," she whispered.

At first there appeared to be only a few students in the college, but steadily the number grew. They arrived from all over the

South, from tidewater and hill land, from meager farms and long-established plantations. Because of their youth or perhaps because of a certain look in their eyes, Mary soon came to recognize those who had been in the war. Sometimes Robert pointed them out to her. "He served for nearly a year with me" . . . "I knew the tall one at Gettysburg." Once, after nodding to a thickset boy, Robert looked suddenly grave. "He lay on the field for hours at the Wilderness; I never expected to see him alive."

Now she could understand more clearly what went on in her husband's mind: The Wilderness, Chancellorsville, Petersburg, Fredericksburg—they were with him always. The faces of these boys brought back his years under fire. At night she heard him groan to himself and whisper the names of men and places, and she felt him turn beside her beneath the burden of his memories.

Little by little she began to see how the war had drained the South, leaving behind it desperate poverty. "Yesterday a woman brought her son," Robert told her. "She had saved everything from this year's crop, and she still lacked part of the tuition." Again he described a youth who had walked more than two hundred miles, with his entrance fee tied in his belt, and another who arrived from an Alabama town with all the funds his father and uncles could raise, and a gold watch to be sold to make up the rest.

"And today," Robert added, "we had a boy who was the youngest of six sons. All the others joined the Army, and he had to leave school to help care for the women. After that his time came to enlist at seventeen, and he did. Mary, he hadn't seen a book in years. When boys like that want to go to college, think what it means for us. All of us." Robert was close to tears.

"Can't you make concessions for them?"

"Yes." He nodded. "We're not turning them away. In this case a friend of the college is giving the boy lodgings outside of town. He'll walk three miles each way, and pay for his quarters by hiring himself out as a field laborer in the summer."

So much sacrifice, so much determination . . . Mary felt inadequate; there must be something more that she could do. Quickly she made up her mind. "At West Point the boys used to come to our home, didn't they? We don't have as much space here, or as much to offer. But ask them to call in the evenings, and I'll do what I can."

Thereafter the students arrived on certain nights, and Mary invited faculty members and their wives and encouraged Lexington girls to attend. Her daughters, Agnes and Mary, entertained the students as they once had entertained them at West Point, Mildred helped too. With practice Mary was learning to manage with scanty supplies—a few cakes, weak punch, apples when someone sent them. Like others around them, the Lees "made do."

By now Mary had organized her household. She had, of course, done that often enough in the past—St. Louis, Brooklyn, Baltimore, and Arlington. This time she had the challenge (and sometimes, she admitted, the exasperation) of trying to succeed with less than ever before. Plain fruit for dessert, or no dessert at all; stews with less meat and more dumplings than she would have thought feasible, and a budget that would once have been completely impossible. . . . She was becoming more of a mathematician as well as a homemaker.

One of the first additions to the household had been a yellow cat, of the kind her father had admired so much; now they had three and, she was sure, there would be many more.

Sitting with the young students, Mary realized occasionally that their eyes were on her sewing basket, where she worked over Robert's shirts and socks and undergarments. She shrugged; why shouldn't she darn them as long as they held together? And she smiled because a faculty wife gaped when Mary pointed to Robert's shaggy hair. "It's time for me to cut it again. Oh yes, I've become a pretty fair barber."

When one of their visitors, an old friend from Baltimore, went to bed, he put his shoes outside the door, presuming that a servant would black them. In the morning their guest found the shoes neatly polished; Robert, seeing them there, had done the work himself.

By now these necessary economies and menial tasks seemed the most normal of ways. They could be handled far more easily than the flare-ups of bitter sectionalisms which reached them even in remote Lexington.

One night a member of the faculty rang their bell, and Mary

overheard part of his conversation with Robert: "General, I hadn't supposed I'd tell you about this, but it's been on my mind. You know those young fellows that arrived from New Jersey. One or two Virginia boys have been making it hard for them, telling them they're 'not welcome' in a Southern school."

Robert returned to her, his face a violent red, the veins standing out near his temples. He said nothing of the matter, and, though the words had upset her, she didn't ask any questions. For the remainder of the evening he was preoccupied, and he left early in the morning.

Mary forgot all about the incident until later in the week she was told that several young Virginians were missing from the campus. She asked about them, and Robert answered simply, "They've left us, my dear." The matter had been settled.

Toward the end of that week Mary watched from her windows one of the campus parades. The college students were dressed in five or six different kinds of costumes, quite unlike the trim uniforms of the nearby Virginia Military Institute. Robert walked beside the institute's superintendent just ahead of the institute cadets. For the first time she noticed that Robert was taking care not to keep step with the marching feet behind him. During most of his life he had marched; now she realized that he purposely avoided marching.

When he came home she wheeled herself out to meet him. She spoke of the parade, and he nodded gravely. "Mim, the more I learn about civilian ways, the better I like them." And then he told her something she had never expected to hear. "I believe I made a mistake when I went into the Army in the first place. Mary, I've wasted the best of my life."

Chapter 18

As Mary looked at Robert across their lamplighted table in their living room, she realized that this was their second anniversary in Lexington. The last two years had been happy ones.

"I think we're going to have another good term, Mim. Good enough, anyway."

As always he spoke conservatively. Actually they were doing better than well, Mary assured herself. Washington College had grown steadily, and its influence was spreading all over the South.

She looked at the pile of recent letters from various educators in Europe, from a Midwestern leader of Congress, from a New England woman who had spent most of her life fighting against slavery and poverty. In the past few weeks all of them had written to tell Robert how much they thought of him and his work.

Mary was particularly impressed by the fact that one Northerner after another had begun to contribute funds to this college though it was under the direction of their recent enemy, Robert E. Lee.

"We can certainly use any money that comes in. You haven't had to turn anybody away yet, have you?"

He shook his head. "No, but we've had some narrow escapes from financial trouble." She knew it well—times when the budget could not be balanced, when faculty members had to wait for their salaries, when she and Robert had to forgo the purchase of a chair or a table for their sparsely furnished home because the money was needed for something else.

They had both worked hard—Robert for the college, Mary, for

the community. When the church needed money and she lacked any other way to contribute, she had painted dozens of small pictures, landscapes, likenesses of Robert and also of George Washington, to sell for the fund. Her wartime habit of working constantly with her bent hands had proved invaluable now.

She saw Robert was staring at a letter he had just opened. "Another insurance company?" she guessed.

He smiled, and started to fold it up. Of late he had received a dozen offers, from great organizations, including several which promised to pay handsomely. An Eastern company wished Robert to manage its Southern division; another corporation hoped he would manage a railroad. Each time he declined politely. He had been less polite when one brash gentleman offered him a sizable annual payment, "simply for the use of your name, sir." That caller had left in haste.

Robert silently handed her the letter he had just read. She scanned it quickly and learned that one of the most famous of Southern colleges wanted him to become its president. If he accepted this offer she would be closer to her old friends, and to the life she had always enjoyed. Then she realized that he was shaking his head. "I've cast my lot here, Mim, and here I stay."

She smiled. He was right, of course, and in any case another move would be hard for both of them, physically as well as emotionally. Of late Robert's health had disturbed her. There was little that appeared definite—a slightly lagging walk, a breathlessness, vague pains in the chest and shoulders. "Just rheumatism, left over from the war," he had explained.

It occurred to her tonight that he had not seen a doctor in some time. She reminded him of that and suggested that he go, simply as a precautionary measure.

He gave her an indulgent glance. "If it's worrying you, I'll see the doctor this week. Well, tomorrow, then."

The next day something came up which deferred Robert's visit to the doctor; but before the week's end he paid the call and returned with a half-humorous report. "Bad news," he joked. "I'll survive. He told me something I knew already—I shouldn't work so hard." Mary stared. This was somewhat reassuring; or was it?

In the next few weeks she was bothered less by personal worries than by developments in the outside world. In Washington City extremists pushed through brutally severe Reconstruction bills, overruling Andrew Johnson's moderate program. Mary saw Robert's lips contract as he read the words of the violent Thaddeus Stevens and the harsh results of military rule in the South.

"They don't want reunion," she cried to him. "What they're trying to do is crush us into the earth!"

"You may be right." Robert shook his head. "In the long run, though, the people themselves won't let it happen."

Mary twisted her hands in her lap. In the long run . . . It might be a mighty long one! For weeks she had been hearing rumors of violent arguments in the town, and tales of clashes between students and newcomers with Union sentiments. One day Robert came in with a face so set that she questioned him until he told her: A young student had approached a Negro meeting with a gun, had gotten into an argument and beaten one of the Negroes.

"There was more to it," he added sadly. "The boy admitted what had happened, and I expelled him. After all we try to teach, all our attempts to show them the need for peace and good will . . ."

Yet all the trouble did not come from "hotheaded Southerners." A veteran of the Federal Army came to Lexington and became so difficult that he was chased by a crowd of civilians and students. He got his revenge by writing a series of raging letters of accusation to the newspapers.

Washington College, said he and others as well, was a hotbed of rebels and preachers of disunion, a place in which Northerners were regularly insulted. The letters not only had a harmful effect on a fund-raising drive for Washington College, sponsored in the North by such people as Henry Ward Beecher and Horace Greeley, they also set off a series of reactions elsewhere.

"Look at this, Robert!" Mary's eyes burned when she handed him the latest journal from Baltimore. A newspaper offered what it called an interview with one of their former slaves, who said that Robert had been a harsh and unfeeling master. Another journal declared that Robert Lee's last act in Washington City at the outbreak of the War had been to call on General Scott, from whom he took detailed maps and drawings of the capital city's defenses, before deserting to the rebel side, and carrying them under his arm!

Trembling, Mary took the journal back from Robert and threw it into the fireplace. The last traces of calm had left her. Good will—it was a vanishing commodity in these years of hate. Who could guess what would happen next? "Reconstruction . . ." The word grated. Reconstruction by men without honor, without honesty.

If only she had Robert's forbearance . . . But she hadn't. Suddenly she wanted to be away from this place, from anything that reminded her of the spreading hostilities. She was thinking again of her youth in the stately house beside the Potomac, yearning for the people and places she had known in those earlier days. Her neighbors in Lexington had been more than kind, but still these blue mountains shut her off from the world she really loved and which she believed still existed.

As her unhappiness and desperation increased, she began again to feel sharp pains up and down her legs. She tried shifting her position, but it did not help. The look of agony on her face brought Robert hurrying to her side.

"Mim, Mim!"

As he held her she regained some of her self-control. After a while he said with determination, "Both of us need a rest at the springs. Yes, we *can* afford it." He argued until he had convinced her, and within the week they started out for North Carolina, with Custis and the girls.

In the green richness of Greenbrier White Sulphur Springs Mary found a welcome respite. For days, as her husband wheeled her about, she was content to doze under the trees. Hour by hour she swam in the warm waters, and at times she could tell herself she was back in those calmer years. Her improved condition showed in her face. She was often laughing now at something Robert or the children said.

She agreed with Robert as he nodded approvingly at the

changes in the resort and surroundings of the springs. "These people are building back. Most of them are avoiding oratory and are going to work." It was, of course, his own prescription for the South.

Toward the end of their stay he pushed her wheel chair into the main parlor for an evening's entertainment, and Mary's eyes rested on a group noticeably apart from the rest—a middle-aged man, his severe wife, and their two children.

"Yankees," a girl beside her said. "If they think anybody's going to talk to them, they'll wait till they take root here."

In the barbed stillness that followed Robert got to his feet. "We're not showing good manners. They're guests here, guests of all of us." He turned to a crowd of several young people standing near. "Who'll introduce me?" When he received no reply, Robert stood suddenly very erect and his voice was low. "Very well, I'll present myself. But won't some of you come along?"

Reluctantly a dark-haired girl joined him. "I'll go, General, under your orders."

"Not under my orders." The words were curt but the tone was kindly. "Still, I'd be grateful if you'd help me," he added.

When Robert and the girl approached the other group, silence settled over the big room. Across from them, Mary, watching intently, saw her husband bow and take his place beside the strangers. By degrees their resistance melted; they began to smile. And now she saw that Robert was bringing them over to her.

At the prospect Mary had an illogical urge to escape, to have Custis take her away. By this time every eye in the room was centered on her; and she knew she couldn't talk with those granite-faced people, who were somehow responsible for all those harsh accusations against her husband and the South.

Then she told herself: But if Robert could do it, why shouldn't she? She remembered her Northern acquaintances of other years, her father's friends from Massachusetts and Connecticut. With a fixed smile she looked up to receive the people from the North.

Back at Lexington, they settled down to a calmer period of busy days and evenings with student callers and faculty members with their wives. One night, with a puzzled frown, Robert handed her a note from an Illinois friend, who had seen their George Washington relics in the "captured" display at the Department of the Interior. With great interest she read on: The friend had been talking with officials who thought President Johnson would be willing to restore them to Mary as their owner.

"I'm not quite sure what we should do," Robert began.

"I am," Mary snapped. "They're mine, and I want to ask for them."

Robert agreed, and within a few weeks, while she waited with increasing hope, the arrangements were at last made. She would get back what was hers, the punch bowl, the famous tent valued by her father, four or five pictures, and several other pieces. They were not all she had lost, or even a small portion, but something.

Meanwhile in Washington City the extremists had heard of the pending transfer and were crying out against it. Those things had belonged to Robert Lee, the arch traitor who by his acts had forfeited claim to them.

The violent, untrue words were hard for Mary to take in silence, but she knew that there was no way for her to strike back. The matter went before Congress, and their enemies put through a resolution declaring that the Washington relics had become the property of the United States; to hand them over to the rebel Lee would be to insult loyal Americans.

"An 'insult,' to return your property!" Robert's face set in hard lines. "Let's hope that by keeping them they'll at least remember what George Washington stood for." Then slowly his anger went.

"We've got justice on our side," she told him.

"Yes." He was sadder. "These things are yours, and so is Arlington, by right; I'm the one who keeps it from you. If you hadn't married me . . ." He turned away, and Mary saw a stoop, a sinking of the fine shoulders.

The next day his stoop was even more pronounced and the slight cold which had bothered him for some time was worse. When he started toward his horse Traveler for an afternoon ride, he moved like a man who was forcing himself. When he came back he was wheezing. "Traveler isn't as easy to ride as he used to be." Then, as if this might be a reflection on his beloved steed, he added, "It's my fault."

The next morning, in spite of Robert's objections, Mary called a doctor, who summoned a second for an extended consultation. Afterward they brought Mary their joint report:

"An inflammation of the heart sac, perhaps, and a rheumatic condition—also, there is a certain physical exhaustion. He can get up again soon, but both of us think the general should take a long trip. Away from any routine, and in a warmer climate."

The words stunned her, but Mary made up her mind. No matter what stood in the way, Robert had to take the trip. By the time he got out of bed a few days later his colleagues had sent a message that they were ready to divide his duties among them if he would follow the doctor's recommendations. His eyes revealed how much he appreciated their concern, and he smiled. "I suppose I have no choice." Mary arranged to have Agnes go with him, and slowly his interest in the trip grew.

He hoped to visit Annie's grave in North Carolina. "During the war I couldn't get there, you know," he told her with a sad look. After that he would go on to several other towns on the coast, and also visit his sons on their farms. As she waved to him from the door Mary whispered a profound prayer: God grant that this trip do him good.

Intently she follow his itinerary: Warrenton, Raleigh, Charlotte, Wilmington, Norfolk, Portsmouth, Richmond. "I wish you could travel with Papa," Agnes wrote, "to see the affection and feeling shown toward him everywhere." The South was coming out to greet Robert Lee and to honor him for the part he played in the war and in the years since then.

With warming interest Mary read Agnes' successive letters. Along the way, learning that he was approaching, railroad telegraphers sent messages ahead. In town after town men and women gathered to call out to him or, in the case of his old soldiers, to stand and salute and perhaps to cry at the sight of him.

As she read Agnes' letters Mary also cried. She realized what this reception must mean to him. She remembered, too, that many of the places he was seeing once evoked grim and tragic memories. She had heard him talk of the smashing of homes, the killing and maiming of people, and she had wondered if within himself he had dreaded seeing the places where these things happened. Now he was returning to them after the battlefields had grown green again and the wreckage of the war had cleared away. His letters and Agnes' confirmed her hope that some of Robert's burdens were being lifted.

The journey came to its end and, late on a May afternoon of 1870 she waited in her chair under a grove of trees. As she opened her arms to embrace him, she saw that he looked heavier; his skin was pale and she wondered if the trip with all its exertions had been altogether good for him. For a time he did not talk much. "I'd just like to sit beside you, Mim. That's all."

When she asked him about the events of the trip he had almost nothing to say: "They were kind to an old rebel, very kind." He smiled and was silent; she was content to remain beside him in the fading sunlight, the only sounds the faint movements of small animals and insects in the leaves around them.

As dusk approached he began to talk again and with great earnestness. She knew at once that he had been thinking for a long time about what he wanted to say. "Mim, I don't regret what I did. I couldn't have done anything else." His voice fell. "Still, the South is better off for the ending of slavery. I think I'd gladly have gone through everything and lost what I did, to have that happen. . . . Sometimes what looks like failure can turn out to be a blessing."

Their eyes met, and then he spoke again.

"I won't be with you much longer, Mim. No, don't deny it. I'm sixty-three, and I've exposed myself a great deal." His face was very serious. "It's simply that I've been wondering . . . I've prayed, but I wish I could be sure of His acceptance."

Through her pain she told him: "Robert, if you're not sure of acceptance, I don't know who can be."

On a chill, dripping afternoon in late September, Robert dozed before the fire and, waking with a start, got to his feet. "An important vestry meeting," he told Mary. "I really should be there."

When he left, she frowned to herself, thinking that he should not have gone immediately out into the cold after staying so long beside the grate. As seven o'clock approached and passed she went into the dining room with the family. Robert was occasionally late for dinner and he always wanted them to start before him.

As they were about to sit down they heard his step in the hall. He came in at once and took his place at the head of the table. When he lowered his head to say grace, his lips formed a few words, but they heard no sound. Startled, Mary saw that he had slumped into his chair.

For a second time Robert made an effort to speak, and she could not understand his blurred words. Most of all it was the strangely submissive look on his face that told Mary how serious this was.

"Send for the doctor, Custis!" she cried.

The next hour was a blur of fear and hesitation. Not wishing him moved, the doctors had a bed brought down, after which they gave him some medicine and finally got him to sleep. The doctors answered her repeated questions with round and meaningless phrases: "It's not a stroke . . . a venous congestion." Whatever words they used, she understood that something was very wrong, and terror rose within her.

For hours of that night and the next day she stayed near Robert's side, studying the well-loved face in repose, the firm nose, and the whitened hair as it fell from his forehead.

Of course, she told herself, he would get better. But again she remembered the expression that had come over his face when he first tried to speak at the table—that air of acceptance. And, she cried to herself, he must not accept. The next day he dozed for hours, and finally woke. "Mim." He said it softly; and later he let her know he recognized her with a pressure of the fingers.

Several days went by, and their neighbors and the teachers and townspeople of Lexington called and left. Once Mary heard Traveler whinny, and one of the doctors told him: "You hear that? Hurry and get well. Traveler's been standing out there a long time."

While Mary watched, her husband shook his head. In the hall-way there came a heavy crash, and Custis tiptoed to her, his look a stricken one. "His picture fell off the wall."

"Put it right back," she whispered. She realized what the su-perstitious would say; she must not think of that. Nevertheless she did, and her eyes returned to the pale face, rested now and—she found the word—prepared. Mary's panic rose: She too must be prepared to go on as he would have done.

The bad weather grew steadily worse, mounting into a storm more violent than any of the people of the mountain area could remember. Late the next evening, seated with the doctors, Mary heard a shutter slam with a reverberation that went through the house. Against the windows rain pounded so heavily that she thought it would crack the panes. Thunder rolled across the skies, and yet the disturbances reached her only as distant echoes. With Robert's weak hand in hers, she watched steadily in the lamp-light.

Mildred came in to whisper, "There's terrible damage outside, houses blown over and bridges washed away . . . Lexington's cut off from the world." Tonight, however, Robert was Mary Lee's only concern. While the doctors hovered about showing increas-ing anxiety, he moved restlessly on the bed. And then his voice rang through the quiet room: "Tell Hill he must come up!"

Mary stared up at her son, Custis, and his eyes reflected her suffering. So Robert was reliving the war, the Virginia campaigns about which he had so long been silent. Mary heard a few more words, barely distinguishable—questions to his men, orders for battle formations. The rumbling thunder and a gust of rain would drown out his voice; and after a time there was only quiet.

Mary sat with head lowered over her hands, waiting for any word, listening to the feeble breath. With dawn he lay there, his chest barely moving. Eight o'clock, nine; the children stood around Mary, hearing the ticking of the clock. In the morning light she saw faculty and students walking about the grounds with subdued steps. A bell rang, and she realized that they had gone to prayers for Robert.

His voice came once again, and softly: "Strike the tent."

Outside the skies had brightened to a clear blue; the clouds had vanished. Glancing at the window, Mary realized that the October day would be a magnificent one. When she looked back at Robert, she knew that she was now alone.

Epilogue

"Turn here, driver."

In the June air along the Potomac the woman rode alone in the carriage. With gnarled hands Mary Lee drew her light coat closer; during these two and a half years since Robert's death it seemed to her that the world was growing steadily colder.

She still lived in Lexington, for Custis had succeeded her husband as president of the college. There she moved daily from room to room, seeing the places where Robert had stood, touching the table he used, and remembering. Was there a morning that she did not think of him on waking, and then again through the day and much of the night?

Mary had not planned this ride to Arlington. She had arrived a few days ago on a visit to Aunt Maria and the Fitzhughs. At the first sight of her aunt, still erect but clearly in her declining years, Mary had felt a little sad, remembering the older woman's extraordinary energy and the great good sense with which she had helped so many people. Aunt Maria, however, smiled brightly and talked as much about the present as the past. Repeatedly their conversations turned to Arlington.

Slowly her yearning to look at her old house returned. For years Mary had put the hope behind her. Now she realized that she would not be able to rest until she had made the trip; it would, of course, be the last time she would see her home.

The carriage swerved into a road that Mary could have found in her sleep, and with the warm smell of roses, the pale blossoms almost brushing the carriage window, she went back to another time.

She was remembering a day when she rode along this green passageway with the silver of the Potomac below her, and heard her father speak of his new play about George Washington; and then the day she and Robert drove anxiously home on their return from St. Louis, awaiting their reunion with their first daughter. And after that she thought of the time she came back from West Point, trembling, in the hope of finding her mother still alive.

The road swung to the side, and Arlington stood in the sun, with the thrust of its cornice against the clouds, the strength of the great columns and the balustrades protecting its doorway. Recognition was like a blow, nonetheless harsh because she expected it.

Yet Arlington had been changed—doors altered, a wing replaced; through its windows she saw only emptiness, the gray-white expanse of a public building. Although she had known that the furniture, the draperies, and paintings would be gone, she had not sensed how empty that would leave her house.

"Oh, ma'am! Ma'am!"

A dark woman came down the stairs, and behind her hobbled an old Negro with a cane.

She cried, "Salina . . . Daniel . . ."

Salina's hands were working on her apron as she advanced to the carriage. Mary saw that her eyes were yellowed and the lines of age had made deep carvings across the brown face. Otherwise Salina seemed almost the same as the day Mary had left.

"It's so good, Miss Mary. So good." They were crying together. Daniel approached and Mary took his hand; when he opened the door, however, she shook her head. Even had she been able to walk, she would have hesitated to enter those bare halls. Wiping her cheeks, she looked from one servant to the other. "You're well?"

"We all right." Salina's deep voice wavered. "Still, ma'am, it ain' the same, you know."

Daniel gave her a slow smile. "I can remember those Chris'mas parties, and your wedding party 'specially. And the time Gen'l Lee got back from Mexico and picked up the wrong lil' fellow."

Mary closed her eyes; she also recalled a great deal today, too much.

Turning in the seat, she caught for the first time the gleam of white crosses among the trees. Though she tried to prepare herself for the sight, she had not thought they would be so close to the house. And there were so many of them, stretching into the distance. . . . The dead had taken this place; and she realized finally that Arlington could never belong again to the Lees or their children.

When she looked in the other direction, she saw the edge of her mother's old garden, now in a neglected condition, and thought of the days she had spent there, sometimes with Claudia McBride. Curiously enough, she remembered that Claudia had once accused her of leading too sheltered a life to understand anything of the world. Perhaps Claudia had been right then; but in the end she had met life on its own terms, hadn't she? And she had not flinched because it became hard and violent.

Mary took Salina's hand, and Daniel's, then signaled to the driver and rode slowly down the hill. Behind her the portico of Arlington still challenged the skies, with the Potomac shining below and Washington City waiting in the distance.

Acknowledgements

During the past four years many persons in many places assisted me with letters of Mary Custis Lee and Robert E. Lee, letters of others of their families, documents relating to their lives, photographs, and other data. The Lees and the Custises carried on long correspondence with relatives, friends, and connections, and this unpublished material has been of primary value in giving insight into their characters, interests, and experiences.

I am grateful above all to Mrs. Hunter DeButts, Upperville, Virginia, and Mrs. Hanson Ely, Richmond, granddaughters of Robert E. Lee, for permission granted me to make a detailed study of the many hundreds of Lee family letters and related data in the Library of Congress. A number of quotations from this source, used in these pages, have never appeared before. Mrs. DeButts and Mrs. Ely also answered, to the best of their abilities, many of my questions.

David C. Mearns, chief of the manuscripts division of the Library of Congress, was unfailingly helpful during my visits to check into the Lee and other collections in that magnificently stocked unit.

Murray H. Nelligan of the National Park Service has made intensive and perceptive inquiry into the Lee-Custis story as it centers about the Arlington scene. Mr. Nelligan provided swift and authoritative responses, made his office facilities and data available to me on numerous occasions, and assisted in final checking of parts of the manuscript.

Mrs. Rose MacDonald Skoggs, the first biographer of Mrs. Lee, received me with hospitality at her home in Berryville, Virginia, helped in assembling scattered letters and data, and in answering numerous inquiries.

No one can write of matters touching Robert E. Lee without paying tribute to his distinguished biographer, the late Dr. Douglas Southall Freeman, of Richmond. Dr. Freeman helped guide my way through thousands of Lee documents, and made available to me his own collection of letters from R. E. Lee to Andrew Talcott.

Clifford Dowdey, Virginia's perceptive novelist, and Frances Dowdey aided with advice and time during many phases of my work. Virginius Dabney, editor of the Richmond *Times-Dispatch*, pointed out several paths on the way. Mrs. Ferguson Cary, Alexandria, Virginia, provided valuable clues to manuscripts and information. Mrs. U. R. Davis of Washington permitted me to inspect copies of letters relating to the Marshall branch of the Lee family. Orville Spreen of St. Louis gave particular help in assembling data on St. Louis phases.

Miss India Thomas, house regent of the Confederate Museum in Richmond, and her assistant, Miss Eleanor Brockenbrough, provided accurate copies of the Brigadier General R. H. Chilton papers and of other documents in the museum.

Miss Mattie Russell, assistant curator of manuscripts in the Duke University Library, arranged for the microfilming of several hundred items in the major Lee collections at that university.

At Washington and Lee University, of which Robert E. Lee was president, generous aid was given by Dr. Frances Pendleton Gaines, president; Dr. Allen W. Moger, professor of history; Henry E. Coleman, Jr., librarian; Marshall W. Fishwick, American Studies, who took time from a summer schedule to direct me to Lee material in his field; Francis L. Berkeley, Jr., University of Virginia.

Charles W. Porter III, chief of the preservation branch, National Park Service, assisted in my inquiries into Wickham and related family matters.

Randolph W. Church, state librarian of the Virginia State Library; William J. Van Schreeven, state archivist, and Milton C. Russell, head of the reference-circulating section, provided access to large collections of manuscripts relating directly or indirectly to the Lees.

The late Clayton Torrence, director and corresponding secretary of the Virginia Historical Library, housed in the wartime Lee House on East Franklin Street in Richmond, was speedy and courteous in his help on numerous occasions.

Mrs. Clelia Elliott Carleton of New York and Mrs. Sidney C. Lockwood permitted me to study the extensive collection of letters from Robert E. Lee to his classmate, John McKay, and other items.

Captain Johnson G. Cooper, Headquarters, Fort Hamilton, Brooklyn, guided me in efforts to develop facts about the Lees' period of residence in Brooklyn and Robert E. Lee's work in New York Harbor.

Mrs. Ralph Catterall of the Valentine Museum, Richmond, made it possible to track down many Richmond facts.

Allan Nevins, professor of history at Columbia University, gave me the benefit of his long experience in research and his advice in discovering source materials of the period.

James Ambler Johnston; Hatley Norton Mason, Jr., and Dr. and Mrs. Marsden Smith, all of Richmond, made available separate collections or copies of important documents and letters in their possession. Among others to whom I am especially grateful are:

Charles Van Ravenswaay, director of the Missouri Historical Society; Norma Cuthbert, department of manuscripts, Henry E. Huntington Library; V. L. Bedsole, head of the department of archives, Louisiana State University; the late Mrs. Ruth Campbell of the Louisiana Room, Louisiana State University; Louise W. Turpin, chief of the historical division, Brooklyn Public Library; Russell A. Scully, administrative assistant, and Richard G. Hensley, chief librarian, division of reference and research services, Boston Public Library.

Jesse Cunningham, librarian of the Cossitt Library, Memphis; Margaret Jemison, librarian, Emory University, Georgia; Richard Harwell, assistant librarian; Mrs. Vivien M. Lawson, reference librarian, University of Alabama, University, Alabama; Jack Dalton, librarian, Alderman Library, University of Virginia, Charlottesville; Marie Bankhead Owen, department of archives and history, Montgomery, Alabama; Fred Shelley, librarian, Maryland Historical Society, Baltimore.

Mildred Boatman, chief of the reference department, St. Louis Public Library; Joseph C. Wolf, head of the division of historical genealogy, Newberry Library, Chicago; Lucille T. Dickerson, librarian of the Jones Memorial Library, Lynchburg, Virginia; Mrs. J. L. Henderson, Carnegie Library, Rome, Georgia; and Lloyd Griffith, reference librarian, Peabody Institute, Baltimore; Paul North Rice, reference librarian, New York Public Library; and Sylvester Vigilante of the American History Room, and his assistant, F. I. Avellino.

Ruth Blair, executive secretary of the Atlanta Historical Society, and Miss Bessie Duke Small; Mrs. Lilla M. Hawes, director of the Georgia Historical society; Ida Padelford, Sondley Reference Library, Asheville, North Carolina; Dan M. Robison, state librarian and archivist, Nashville, Tennessee; Mary N. Barton, head of general reference, and Elizabeth C. Litsinger, head of the Maryland Department, Enock Pratt Free Library, Baltimore.

Ralph Newman of the Abraham Lincoln Bookshop, Chicago, and Mrs. Fidelia Anding of the Anding Bookstore, New Orleans.

Mrs. J. J. Overbey, librarian of the Pittsylvania County Public Library, Chatham, Virginia; David J. Harkness, division of university extension, University of Tennessee, Knoxville, Tennessee; Ella May Thornton, state librarian, Georgia State Library, Atlanta.

Mrs. Merrill Parrish Hudson, Memphis, Tennessee; Mrs. Isabel McLennan McMeeken, Louisville, Kentucky; J. Winston Coleman, Jr., Lexington, Kentucky; Mrs. Corinne Bailey, Jackson, Mississippi.

Mrs. Ferdinand C. Latrobe, Baltimore; Mrs. Edna Howard Fowler, Los Angeles; Miss Caroline Tunstall and Miss Edmonia Lee Whittle, Norfolk, Virginia; Mrs. Livingston Vann; Sidney Smith Lee, Miss Agnes Peter, Mrs. Oswalk McNeese, Mrs. Cazenove Lee, Mrs. Marjorie D. Synder, and Mr. Hudson Grunewald of the Washington *Star*, all of Washington, D.C.

Ruth Wallgren, Philadelphia; Dr. Henry Lee Smith and Mrs. Alexander Gordon, Baltimore; Colonel and Mrs. James M. Thomson, Gaylord, Virginia; the late Walter McElreath of Atlanta; Ludwell Lee Montague, historian, and Mrs. Robert M. Templeman, secretary, Society of the Lees of Virginia.

Mrs. Hugh Antrim, Mary F. Goodwin, Maude Henderson, Mrs. Alexander G. Brown, Jr., Stuart Cooke and Philip St. George Cooke, Mrs. Littleton Fitzgerald, Mrs. Susan Haskell, and Ann Mason Lee, all of Richmond.

Dr. John N. Ware, Shorter College, Rome, Georgia; Mrs. James Ball, Cardwell, Virginia; Frank A. Nelson, Chattanooga, Tennessee; Stanley Horn and Dr. Alfred Leland Crabb, Nashville, Tennessee; Mrs. William LeBaron Sands, New York; Dr. Robert D. Meade, Lynchburg, Virginia; Mrs. Mollie Banks Gray, Plain Dealing, Louisiana; Mrs. Otto Murphy, Springfield, Tennessee.

Mrs. Yvonne le Mercier Duquesnay and Miss Louise Koppel, New Orleans; Robert Meyer, New York; Mrs. George L. Upshur and Mrs. Alfred P. Upshur, New York; E. E. P. Tompkins, Lexington, Virginia.

Miss Louise Guyol, Judge Richard T. McBride, I. V. Shannon, Mrs. William Dinwiddie, Mrs. Maud O'Bryan Ronstrom, William Scheyd, Mrs. Camilla Mays, Matt Green, and Gerald Capers of New Orleans.

Mrs. Paula Coad, Frank Screven, and Alexander A. Lawrence of Savannah, Georgia.

Lindsey House, Pensacola, Florida; Cameron Plummer, Mobile, Alabama; Mrs. Rena Lee, Brownwood, Texas; Charles C. Wall, resident superintendent, Mt. Vernon, Virginia; Miss Ellen Hart Smith, Owensburg, Kentucky.

George Foster, New Orleans; Virginia Lewis Fort, Memphis, Tennessee; Dr. J. H. Slaughter, Bogalusa, Louisiana; Robert E. Eagon, Dallas, Texas; Mrs. Grover Sheppard, New Orleans; E. Y. Chapin, Chattanooga, Tennessee; Rudolph Vorbusch, New Orleans; Annabel Power, Jackson, Mississippi.

Jean Selby, Vicksburg, Mississippi; Mrs. Caroline S. Coleman, Fountain Inn, South Carolina; Mrs. Charles A. O'Neal, Jackson, Mississippi; Mrs. Roy W. McKinney, Paducah, Kentucky; Mrs. Martha Rivers Adams, Lynchburg, Virginia.

Dr. William McCain, director of the Mississippi Department of Archives and History at Jackson, and Charlotte Capers, acting director; Ben Mathews, director of the Louisiana State Museum; Mrs. Rosa Oliver, librarian, and Mrs. Frances Bryson Moore of the museum staff.

Dr. Garland Taylor, librarian of the Howard-Tilton Memorial Library of Tulane University, New Orleans; Marguerite Renshaw, formerly reference librarian, Mrs. Evangeline Thurber, Mrs. Beatricia Ford, and Miss Martha Ann Peters, Robert Greenwood, and Mrs. Ethel Usher.

John Hall Jacobs, librarian of the New Orleans Public Library; George King Logan, assistant librarian; Marguerite Ruckert, Ruth Renaud, Gladys Peyronnin and others of the staff.

Mrs. Florence Kane Reynolds and Anna Kane of New Orleans.

LeBaron Barker, Mavis McIntosh, and Barbara Zimmerman, who helped from beginning to end.

The late General Allison Owen, who first interested me in the subject, about twenty years ago, when he told me of Robert E. Lee and Jefferson Davis and his own impressions of them.

And the late Dr. George Bolling Lee of New York, son of "Rooney" Lee, with whom I held several conferences on matters relating to Robert E. Lee and the Davises.

Bibliography

Adam, G. M.   *The Life of General Robert E. Lee*. New York, 1905.

Adams, Charles Francis.   *Lee at Appomattox, and other papers*. Boston, 1902.

———.   *Lee's Centennial*. Boston, 1907.

Alexander, E. P.   "Lee at Appomattox," *Century Magazine*, Vol. 63, April 1901.

Alexander, F. W.   *Stratford Hall and the Lees Connected with Its History* . . . Oak Grove, Va., 1912.

Andrews, Marietta M.   *Scraps of Paper*. New York, 1929.

Andrews, Matthew Page.   *The Women of the South in War Times* . . . Baltimore, 1920.

Anson, A. R. H.   "General Lee as I Knew Him," *Harper's Magazine*, Vol. 122, February 1911.

Anson, C. H.   *General Robert E. Lee*. Milwaukee, 1890.

Armes, Ethel M.   *Stratford Hall, the Great House of the Lees*. Richmond, 1936.

———.   *Stratford on the Potomac*. Greenwich, Conn., 1928.

Babcock, B. S.   *Lighthorse Harry's Boy; the Boyhood of Robert E. Lee*. Philadelphia and London, 1931.

Benét, Stephen Vincent.   *John Brown's Body*. New York, 1927.

Bernard, George S. (ed.).   *War Talks of Confederate Veterans*. Petersburg, Virginia, 1892.

Beymer, William G.   *On Hazardous Service; Scouts and Spies of the North and South*. New York and London, 1912.

Blackford, Susan Leigh. (comp.).   *Memoirs of Life in and out of the Army in Virginia During the War between the States*. 2 vols. Lynchburg, Va., 1894–96.

Bond, Christiana. *Memories of General Robert E. Lee.* Baltimore, 1926.

Boyd, T. A. *Light-Horse Harry Lee.* New York, London, 1931.

Bradford, Gamaliel. *Confederate Portraits.* Boston, New York, 1914.

——. *Lee the American.* Boston, New York, 1912.

Brock, R. A. *Gen. Robert Edward Lee . . .* Richmond, 1897.

Brock, Sally. *Richmond During the War.* New York, 1867.

Brooks, William E. *Lee of Virginia . . .* Indianapolis, 1932.

Bruce, Philip A. "The National Spirit of General Lee," *South Atlantic Quarterly,* Vol. 10, January 1907.

——. *Robert E. Lee.* Philadelphia, 1907.

Buchanan, James. *Mr. Buchanan's Administration on the Eve of Rebellion.* New York, 1866.

Bullitt, T. W. "Lee and Scott," *Southern Historical Society Papers,* Vol. 11, December 1893.

Butler, Benjamin F. *Autobiography and Personal Reminiscences of Major-General Benj. F. Butler; Butler's Book.* Boston, 1892.

Cabell, D. S. G. "Lee as an Educator," *Southern Historical Society Papers,* Vol. 17, January–December 1889.

Cabell, J. B. "Letter to General Lee," *Atlantic Monthly,* Vol. 177, March 1946.

Capen, O. B. *Country Homes of Famous Americans.* New York, 1905.

Carter, W. H. "General Robert E. Lee," *Virginia Magazine of History and Biography,* Vol. 33, October 1925.

Catton, Bruce. *Mr. Lincoln's Army.* New York, 1951.

Chase, Enoch A. *The History of Arlington . . .* Washington, D.C., 1929.

Chesnut, Mary Boykin. *A Diary from Dixie . . .* New York, 1929.

Childe, Edward Lee. *The Life and Campaigns of General Lee.* London, 1875.

Clay, Mrs. Clement C. *A Belle of the Fifties.* New York, 1905.

Confederate, A. *The Grayjackets . . .* Richmond, 1867.

Conway, Moncure D. *Barons of the Potomack and the Rappahannock.* New York, 1892.

Cooke, J. E. *A Life of Gen. Robert E. Lee.* New York, 1871.

——. *. . . Robert E. Lee.* New York, 1899.

Cox, F. H. "Virginia and the Union." *Sewanee Review,* Vol. 9, July 1901.

Craven, Avery (ed.). *"To Markie." The Letters of Robert E. Lee to Martha Custis Williams* . . . Cambridge, 1933.

Curtis, George Ticknor. *Life of James Buchanan, Fifteenth President of the United States.* New York, 1883.

Custis, George Washington Parke. *Recollections and Private Memoirs of Washington.* New York, 1860.

Cuthbert, Norma B. "To Molly: Five Early Letters from Robert E. Lee to His Wife," *Huntington Library Quarterly,* Vol. 15, May 1952.

Daniel, John M. *The Richmond Examiner During the War* . . . New York, 1868.

Davis, Jefferson. *The Rise and Fall of the Confederate Government.* New York, 1881.

——. "Robert E. Lee," *North American Review,* Vol. 150, January 1890.

Davis, Varina Howell. *Jefferson Davis, Ex-president of the Confederate States of America, a Memoir by His Wife.* 2 vols. New York, 1890.

Decker, Karl, and McSween, Angua. *Historic Arlington* . . . Washington, 1892.

Deering, John R. *Lee and His Cause* . . . New York, Washington, 1907.

DeLeon, T. C. *Belles, Beaux and Brains of the 60's.* New York, 1909.

——. *Four Years in Rebel Capitals* . . . Mobile, 1890.

Dodd, William E. *Jefferson Davis.* Philadelphia, 1907.

——. "Lee and Reconstruction," *South Atlantic Quarterly,* Vol. 4, January 1905.

——. *Lincoln or Lee* . . . New York, London, 1928.

——. *Statesmen of the Old South* . . . New York, 1911.

Donald, David, and others. *Divided We Fought. A Pictorial History of the War, 1861–65.* New York, 1952.

Dowdey, Clifford. *Bugles Blow No More.* Boston, 1937.

——. *Experiment in Rebellion.* New York, 1946.

——. *The Proud Retreat.* New York, 1952.

Drumm, Stella. "Robert E. Lee and the Improvement of the Mississippi River," *Missouri Historical Society Collections,* Vol. 6, February 1929.

Ecker, Grace Dunlop. *A Portrait of Old George Town*. Richmond, 1933.

Elliott, Charles W. *Winfield Scott, the Soldier and the Man*. New York, 1937.

Ellis, E. S. *The Campfires of General Lee*. Philadelphia, 1886.

Ellis, Robert R. "The Lees at Fortress Monroe," *The Military Engineer*, Vol. 1-42, January–February 1950.

Fishwick, Marshall W. *A Critical Bibliography of Lee Material in the Washington and Lee University Library*. Lexington, Va., 1950.

———. "Virginians on Olympus: II, Robert E. Lee," *Virginia Magazine of History and Biography*. April, 1950.

———. and Hollis, W. M. *A Preliminary Checklist of Writings about Robert E. Lee*. Charlottesville, 1951.

Fiske, John. *The Mississippi Valley in the Civil War*. Boston, New York, 1900.

Flint, S. M. "I Saw Lee Surrender," *Saturday Evening Post*, Vol. 212, April 6, 1940.

Fox, E. D. *The American Colonization Society, 1817–1840*. Johns Hopkins Studies in History and Political Science. Baltimore, 1919.

Freeman, Douglas Southall. "Lee and the Ladies," *Scribner's Magazine*, Vol. 78, October and November 1925.

———. *Lee's Lieutenants*. 3 vols. New York, 1942–44.

———. *R. E. Lee, a Biography*. 4 vols. New York, 1937.

Fulgham, Matthew T. "Historic Fort Monroe." *The Iron Worker*, Vol. 15. Spring 1952.

Fuller, J. F. C. *Grant and Lee . . .* New York, 1933.

Garland, Hamlin. *Ulysses S. Grant; His Life and Character*. New York, 1920.

"Glimpses of the Past. Letters of Robert E. Lee to Henry Kayser, 1838–46," *Missouri Historical Society*, Vol. 3, January–February 1936.

Gordon, John B. *Reminiscences of the Civil War*. New York, 1903.

Graves, C. M. "Recollections of General Robert E. Lee," *Harper's Weekly*, Vol. 51, February 12, 1907.

Hall, G D. *Lee's Invasion of Northwest Virginia in 1861*. Chicago, 1911.

Harrison, Mrs. Burton. *Recollections—Grave and Gay*. New York, 1912.

Hendrick, B. J. *The Lees of Virginia*. Boston, 1935.

Henry, R. S. *The Story of the Confederacy*. Indianapolis, 1931.

Hoar, G. F. *A Boy Sixty Years Ago*. Boston, 1916.

Hopley, Catherine. *Life in the South During the War*. London, 1863.

Horn, Stanley. *The Robert E. Lee Reader*. Indianapolis, 1949.

Hoskins, W. W. "General Lee's Last Camp." *Southern Historical Society Papers*, January–December 1909.

Howard, O. O. "General Robert E. Lee," *Frank Leslie's Popular Monthly*, Vol. 42, December 1896.

Hoyt, W. D., Jr. "Some Personal Letters of Robert E. Lee, 1850–58," *Journal of Southern History*, Vol. 12, November 1946.

James, Marquis. *The Raven; A Biography of Sam Houston*. Indianapolis, 1929.

Johnson, Bradley T. *A Memoir of the Life and Public Service of Joseph E. Johnston . . .* Baltimore, 1891.

Johnson, R. J., and Buel, C. C. (eds.). *Battles and Leaders of the Civil War*. 4 vols. New York, 1887–88.

Johnston, Joseph E. *Narrative of Military Operations . . .* New York, 1874.

Johnstone, W. J. *Robert E. Lee the Christian at the Confederate States Capital*. New York, 1935.

Jones, J. William. *Life and Letters of Robert Edward Lee, Soldier and Man*. Washington, 1906.

———. *Personal Reminiscences, Anecdotes, and Letters of Gen. Robert E. Lee*. New York, 1874.

Jones, John B. *A Rebel War Clerk's Diary*. Philadelphia, 1866.

Joynes, E. S. "General Lee as College President," *Southern Historical Society Papers*, Vol. 28, January–December 1900.

Lea, J. H. "Lee of Virginia," *New England Historical and Genealogical Register*, Vol. 44, January 1890; Vol. 46, April 1892.

Lee, C. F. "Correspondence of General Robert E. Lee," *Southern Historical Society Papers*, Vol. 6, January–December 1878

Lee, Edmund Jennings. *Lee of Virginia. 1642–1892 . . .* Philadelphia, 1895.

Lee, F. G.   *Genealogy of the Family of Lee* . . . London, 1884.

Lee, Fitzhugh.   *General Lee.* New York, 1894.

Lee, George T.   "Reminiscences of Robert E. Lee, 1865–68," *South Atlantic Quarterly,* Vol. 26, July 1927.

Lee, Robert E. (ed.).   *Henry Lee's Memoirs of the War in the Southern Department of the United States.* New York, 1869.

Lee, Robert E., Jr.   *Recollections and Letters of General Lee.* New York, 1905.

——.   "Recollections of General Lee," *Frank Leslie's Popular Monthly,* Vol. 50, August–December 1900.

——.   "With My Father on the Battlefield," *Ladies' Home Journal,* Vol. 21, October 1904.

Lee, S. L.   "War Times in Alexandria, Virginia." *South Atlantic Quarterly,* Vol. 4, July, 1905.

Lee, W. B.   "Lee Family of Virginia," *New England Historical and Genealogical Register,* Vol. 47. January 1893.

Lee Miscellany, A.   *Virginia Magazine of History and Biography,* Vol. 33, October 1925.

Leech, Margaret.   *Reveille in Washington, 1860–1865.* New York, 1941.

Leech, Samuel V.   *The Raid of John Brown at Harper's Ferry as I Saw It.* New York, 1909.

Little, John P.   *History of Richmond.* Richmond, 1933.

Long, A. L.   *Memoirs of Robert E. Lee* . . . New York, 1886.

Lossing, Benson J.   *Pictorial History of the Civil War in the United States of America.* 3 vols. Philadelphia, 1866–68.

MacDonald, Rose Mortimer.   *Mrs. Robert E. Lee,* Boston, 1939.

——.   *Nelly Custis, Daughter of Mount Vernon.* Boston, 1937.

Mackenzie, George Norbury.   *Colonial Families of the United States of America.* . . New York, 1907.

Macrae, David.   *The Americans at Home* . . . 2 vols. Edinburgh, 1870.

McCabe, James D., Jr.   *Life and Campaigns of General Robert E. Lee.* New York, 1867.

McClellan, G. B.   *McClellan's Own Story* . . . New York, 1887.

McDonald, Cornelia.   *A Diary with Reminiscences of the War and Refugee Life in the Shenandoah Valley, 1860–1865.* Nashville, 1935.

McDonald, Hunter.   "General Lee After Appomattox," *Tennessee Historical Magazine,* Vol. 9, January 1926.

McElroy, Robert. *Jefferson Davis, the Unreal and the Real.* 2 vols. New York, 1937.

McGuire, Judith W. *Diary of a Southern Refugee* . . . Richmond, 1889.

McKim, Randolph H. *The Soul of Lee* . . . New York, 1918.

McMeekin, Isabel. *Robert E. Lee: Knight of the South.* New York, 1950.

Marshall, Charles. *An Aide-de-camp of Lee* . . . Boston, 1927.

Mason, Emily V. *Popular Life of Gen. Robert Edward Lee.* Baltimore, 1872.

Maurice, Major General Sir Frederick. *Robert E. Lee, the Soldier.* Boston, 1925.

———. *Statesmen and Soldiers of the Civil War* . . . Boston, 1926.

Mead, Edward C. *Genealogical History of the Lee Family* . . . New York, 1871.

Meade, Robert D. *Judah P. Benjamin.* Oxford, 1943.

Meredith, Roy. *The Face of Robert E. Lee in Life and Legend.* New York, 1947.

Merrett, W. "Note on the Surrender of Robert E. Lee," *Century Magazine,* Vol. 63, April 1904.

Mims, E. "Five Years of Robert E. Lee's Life," *Outlook,* Vol. 78, November 1904.

———. "General Lee's Place in History," *Outlook,* Vol. 84, December 1910.

Montague, M. P. "What did Marse Robert Think?" *Atlantic Monthly,* Vol. 121, June 1918.

Moore, Charles. *The Family Life of George Washington.* Boston, 1926.

Moore, Gay Montague. *Seaport in Virginia—George Washington's Alexandria.* Richmond, 1949.

Moore, M. V. "A Staff Officer's Recollections of General Lee," *Frank Leslie's Popular Monthly,* Vol. 42, September 1896.

Mosby, J. S. "Personal Recollections of General Lee," *Munsey's Magazine,* Vol. 45, April 1911.

Nelligan, Murray H. "American Nationalism on the Stage: The Plays of George Washington Parke Custis," *Virginia Magazine of History and Biography,* Vol. 58, July 1950.

———. *Lee Mansion, National Memorial.* Washington, 1950.

Nevins, Allan. *Ordeal of the Union.* 2 vols. New York, 1947.

Nickerson, H. "Grant and Lee," *American Redbook*, Vol. 4, November 1934.

Nicolay, Helen. *Our Capital on the Potomac*. New York, 1924.

O'Connor, Richard. "Robert E. Lee," *American Mercury*, Vol. 68, May 1949.

Packard, Joseph. *Recollections of a Long Life*. Washington, 1902.

Page, Thomas Nelson. *Robert E. Lee, Man and Soldier*. New York, 1911.

——. *Robert E. Lee, The Southerner*. New York, 1908.

Parks, L. "What a Boy Saw of the Civil War, with Glimpses of General Lee," *Century Magazine*, Vol. 70, June 1905.

Phillips, U. B. *Life and Labor in the Old South*. Boston, 1929.

Pollard, Edward A. *The Early Life, Campaigns and Public Services of Robert E. Lee* . . . New York, 1870.

——. *The Lost Cause* . . . New York, 1866.

Potts, Frank. *The Death of the Confederacy* . . . Richmond, 1928.

Preston, E. R. *Lee at Lexington*. Charlotte, Va., 1923.

Preston, Mrs. Margaret J. "Lee After the War," *Century*, Vol. 16, June 1889.

Pryor, Mrs. Roger A. *Reminiscences of Peace and War*. New York, 1905.

Putnam, Mrs. S. A. *Richmond During the War*. New York, 1867.

Ranson, A. R. H. "General Lee as I Knew Him," *Harper's Weekly*, Vol. 122, February 1911.

——. "New Stories of Lee and Jackson," *South Atlantic Quarterly*. Vol. 12, October 1913.

Rhodes, Charles Dudley. *Robert E. Lee, the West Pointer*. Richmond, 1932.

Rhodes, James F. *A History of the Civil War, 1861–1865*. New York, 1917.

Ridley, B. L. *Battles and Sketches of the Army of Tennessee*. Mexico, Mo., 1906.

Riley, Franklin R. *General Robert E. Lee After Appomattox*. New York, 1922.

Rister, Carl C. *Robert E. Lee in Texas*. Norman, Oklahoma, 1946.

Robbins, S. N. "General Robert E. Lee," *Frank Leslie's Popular Monthly*, Vol. 42, November 1896.

"Robert E. Lee: To Year 1859." *Frank Leslie's Popular Monthly*, Vol. 42, April 1896.

Ross, Fitzgerald. *A Visit to the Cities and Camps of the Confederate States*. Edinburgh, 1865.

Russell, William H. *My Diary North and South*. New York, 1863.

Sale, Edith T. *Manors of Virginia in Colonial Times*. Philadelphia, 1909.

Sandburg, Carl. *Abraham Lincoln. The War Years* 4 vols. New York, 1939.

Scott, Mary W. *Houses of Old Richmond*. Richmond, 1941.

Scott, W. W. "Some Personal Memories of General Robert E. Lee," *William and Mary College Quarterly*, Vol. 2, October 1926.

Shepherd, Henry E. *Life of Robert Edward Lee*. New York, 1906.

Smith, C. F. "Robert E. Lee Once More," *South Atlantic Quarterly*, Vol. 7, October 1908.

Smith, Edward C. *The Borderland in the Civil War*. New York, 1927.

Smith, H. L. *Lee the Educator*. Lexington, Va., 1929.

Smith, William Ernest. *The Francis Preston Blair Family in Politics*. 2 vols. New York, 1933.

Snow, William P. *Lee and His Generals*. New York, 1867.

Sorrell, G. M. *Recollections of a Confederate Staff Officer*. South Carolina, University of. *Robert E. Lee, Centennial Celebration of His Birth*. Columbia, 1907.

Stiles, Robert. *Four Years Under Marse Robert*. New York, 1903.

Sturgis, H. H. "General Lee's Status," *Harper's Weekly*, Vol. 53, November 13, 1909.

Swift, Eben. "The Military Education of Robert E. Lee," *Virginia Magazine of History and Biography*, Vol. 35, April 1927.

Taylor, Walter H. *General Lee, his Campaigns in Virginia, 1861–1865* . . . Norfolk, Va., 1906.

Torrence, Clayton (ed.). "Arlington and Mount Vernon, 1856, as Described in a Letter of Augusta Blanch Berard," *Virginia Magazine of History and Biography*, April 1952.

Waterman, Thomas T. *The Mansions of Virginia 1706–1776*. Chapel Hill, N. C., 1945.

Wayland, John W.   *Robert E. Lee and His Family*. Staunton, Va., 1951.

Wesley, C. H.   *The Collapse of the Confederacy*. Washington, 1937.

White, Henry A.   *Robert E. Lee and the Southern Confederacy, 1807–1870*. New York, 1897.

Wickham, H. T.   *Lee Family*. Ashland, Va., 1941.

Wiley, B. I.   *The Life of Johnny Reb*. New York, 1943.

Wilmer, Rt. Rev. Joseph P.   *General Robert E. Lee*. Nashville, 1872.

Wilson, Woodrow.   *Robert E. Lee, an Interpretation*. Chapel Hill, N. C., 1924.

Wilstach, Paul.   *Potomac Landings*. Indianapolis, 1932.

Winston, R. W.   *High Stakes and Hair Trigger; The Life of Jefferson Davis*. New York, 1930.

Wolseley, Frances Garnet.   "A Month's Visit to the Confederate Headquarters," *Blackwood's Edinburgh Magazine*, Vol. 93, January 1863.

Young, Robert.   *Marse Robert*. New York, 1929.